The 2016 Scythe Prize

Stories and Essays

RUSTY SCYTHE PUBLISHING

9805 Ellison Avenue Omaha, NE 68134

Cover design: Shutterstock image, standard license

Artwork by Jami Hubbard

Rusty Scythe Publishing trade paperback first edition: November 2016

Library of Congress Cataloging-in-Publication Data

Forrest, Eric 1983-

The 2016 Scythe Prize/ Eric Forrest – Rusty Scythe

ISBN 978-0-9969852-2-2

PRINTED IN THE UNITED STATES OF AMERICA

**For Mitch Hansen, whose impact was
and will probably never be known.**

The Scythe Prize would not be but for
the help of supporters and partners.

Thanks to the prize jury of Bob Darcy, Ozzie Nogg,
and Timothy Schaffert.

Thanks to my second and third pair of editing eyes,
Gloria Kaslow and Lynn Bolay.

Contents

Essays

Introduction

I've heard it a hundred times if once: "I think I could write a good novel/book for kids/screenplay/sitcom."

I don't believe writing is like taking a cake decorating class...one and done. It's a bit melodramatic, I know, and probably something of a cliché by now, but writing is something you have to do because you have no choice, not because you think it would be cool to do once, like parasailing. To that end, here is some theory I try to impart on my writing students that readers of this volume may find useful in locating platforms for their work.

Ultimately, like dieting advice, the solidest writing advice is not particularly magical. In fact, no one wants to hear it. You can try gimmicks, but what losing weight comes down to is committing to diet and exercise. No one likes that. We want a pill, a serum, a potion that somehow tricks our body into changing. And while I've been more successful and happy as a writer than I have as a dieter, I believe the commitment is comparable.

First of all, writers need time. They need to commit to their craft in every way they can, and there are no short cuts. For example, commitment means close reading of others' works to see how they craft characters and plot, how they turn a phrase, how they manage the exposition in their non-fiction. Also, to stand out from the million other writers out there who want to be published, you will have to do your homework. Whether you do this first or after you have written an entire manuscript depends on your own writing process. I tend to write something first, while the inspiration is still hot, then go back and see if I am operating within the boundaries of reality. Research has many definitions beyond the academic application. Research can be as simple as observing. You may be on a city bus and irritated that it's so crowded and hot and noisy. But since you're a writer, you get passed that without even knowing you have, because you find yourself observing and memorizing images. There are so many characters on board waiting for you to shape them: the college boy who's miser-

able that he has to be up so early and can't find a seat, and has no idea
that even scowling he is at the male peak of attractiveness; the woman
in her schmatta whose age you can't predict, who maybe hasn't eaten
in eleven years; the overdressed old man who has clearly given up
caring about social niceties like taking only one seat. The bus is not
an inconvenience for a writer, it's a place for gathering information,
images, sensations, feelings. The young writer does not call attention
to himself on public transportation by talking loudly with his friends
and laughing aggressively at any provocation. The young writer is
busy collecting information with his senses, and pretending at the
same time not to be.

Commitment ultimately means revision. If you want to showcase
your work in a collection like this, you're going to have to accept—
like I have, grudgingly—the realities of revision. I'll start with what
revision is not. It's not making sure the apostrophes are in the right
places and the homophones have all been checked for proper usage.
That's proofreading, which is important too, before you submit to a
publication. Proofreading is making sure your reader is not distracted
by surface errors. While a reader may quickly figure out what you
had intended, they should be gliding along on your prose instead of
doing double-takes. So by all means proofread—out loud if you can
stand it—but don't assume it's interchangeable with revision.

Revision means change, fundamental change. (That might even
mean, as I keep having to learn, scrapping the whole rough draft and
starting over.) This is easy advice to give, but I don't think the enor-
mity of the concept is evident to new writers. It's tempting to change
a line here and there, add something, move a paragraph to the beginning from where it sat awkwardly near the end, and call the piece
revised. But revision is as dreary and labor-intensive as those pesky
concepts of diet and exercise.

You may be able to revise on your own inspiration, but I always
have to ask others to read my work. Almost always they have heavy
news for me, ranging from some needed
major changes to the suggestion of a complete overhaul. When a
friend tells me they can't follow a presumption I've made in plotting

a story, or when some logic I've been working in an essay just isn't unfolding for them, I start to see the major
renovations I need to do on the foundation. I know I shouldn't be hurt that they didn't respond with how intensely they loved my work and then suggested anything bigger than correcting a hanging modifier or two. I remember once sending a manuscript of a YA novel I was writing (which eventually got published) to a friend of mine, who said that most systems in it were go, the secondary character was realistic, the plot was authentic and reasonable, the prose adequately poetic. The problem? The female protagonist didn't sound like a girl at all. In some places, the conversation between her and her best male friend sounded like the boy was talking to himself in the mirror. At first I was tempted to pretend she was only saying that because she was having a bad day or financial problems or had gained some weight. Then the better me settled in and realized she had verbalized what I probably already knew and was trying to get away with. And I could have sent the manuscript off to my agent, who may very well have had the same criticisms and dismissed the project, ending it entirely. Instead, I had some important feedback — discouraging, but specific — that opened my eyes to the need to distinguish between those two voices. I did the work, and was — belatedly — grateful for the critique. Then on my next novel, she told me the characters were great and well drawn, but that nothing happened…

This all leads to the rather prosaic advice to trust the process. No one wants to hear it, but at some point we have to accept that in art (and probably all disciplines), we need to embrace evolution over expedition. What you are reading now in this introduction may resemble what I started with, but that draft was a big rectangle of clay that I have tried to chisel into some kind of shape in at least a dozen revision sessions. That kind of experience is hard to translate in the writing classroom. Students have — much to my annoyance — other classes that compete for their attention, and jobs and families. I rarely come across a piece that has been worked to the wall, has been turned inside out and was submitted only when it was truly the best work the writer could produce at that point in their life's timeline. Mostly students write because they have to. That's the reality of academic writing courses. But if you want to write because you want to create,

if you want to get into volumes like this, then you will have to accept
that the process of getting things done is slow and often tedious, but
also exciting at times, and always an exercise in evolution.

-Peter Marino, State College of New York Adirondack

STORIES

Chad Broughman
Spalding University
"A Bicycle for Madeline"
- Winner of the 2016 Scythe Prize for Story

It's 3:15, time for the ice cream truck. Madeline springs from the sofa, the taut plastic cover shifts and crinkles. She levels out the creases with both hands, first one way, then the other. After taking a step back to inspect for hints of hidden folds, she bites at her thumbnail and moves in for another tug – here, there. Then she starts over. "Pa rum pum," she says, tapping the arm of the couch three times with her pointer finger. After the final credits rolls, she clicks off her soap opera and beelines for the big picture-frame window.

Amidst the comfort of central-air, she imagines the humidity outside, how it would feel against her skin, in her hair. She ponders its tastelessness, and its density on her tongue, like sticky cotton. To her, the city streets look wet, draped with the heavy June air. The heart of the urban center seems hardly moving, its blood beating thick as syrup. Softening the wail of sirens and low droning traffic is the faint laughter of children playing in the courtyard below. The young-sters' joy ignites a familiar, unwelcome ache in Madeline's womb – a longing for the little ones she'll never have. In her mind's eye, there's a boy and a girl, running to her, through a vast field of ripe, nutty grain. Their arms are spanned wide, reaching out. And she's reaching too. Then, she watches as they slam into her windowpane, their necks jolting and their bodies bouncing backward. Her arms still extended. The faceless children look past her, into the loneliness of her apartment; their faces wrench as if they've bitten lemons. They turn to one another, to her, their eyes slippery and bewildered. As they saunter away, the sky opens up. And warm, gray rain issues forth, with round, full drops, as if poured from a watering can. The chil-dren gambol in the cloudburst, holding on to one another, and never looking back.

"Change your thoughts, Madeline," she says aloud, shuddering some. And when she peels back the curtain, a vertical beam of light cuts through the parlor like a slice of cake. It's thin at first, then wider. "It's Tuesday," she says, "*Music Box Dancer* day." At first, the chimes of the white and yellow striped truck sound like a sparrow's warble, and Madeline smiles fully, humming the notes, wondering what a music box has to do with ice cream. But as the bright swirled cones painted on the truck's side come into view and the sound draws near, Madeline's mouth tightens, forming into a straight line across her jaw line. The trilling chimes hollow out into a mechanical echo. She pulls at a black tuft of hair dangling over her temple. "Oh, God." She pushes her ear against the pane until it flattens. "That's *Turkey in the Straw*. Oh no. No, no, no, no, no. It's Tuesday. Fuck. It's *Music Box Dancer* day."

Panic wells, and the acid crawls up her throat. Spinning on her heel, she trips over a neatly angled pile of sheet music. But the tune grows louder before she can get to the bedroom. "No, no, no!" she cries out, jerking wisps of hair from her sloe-black, patchy mane. The urge to leap from her body swells as the full-bellied snake reappears, slinking over her feet and up her legs, its scales oily and damp. It slides farther up, flicking its clammy tongue, but her feet are moored. Her vocal cords severed. "Think of other things," she says, over and over, then slaps her hands over her ears.

"The bike!" Look at your bike, she thinks; that'll balance things. She steps to the bedroom window and lifts the middle two blinds with her eyes pressed shut. When she pops open her eyes, an exhale escapes through pursed lips, for in the slender iron bars of an otherwise empty rack leans a mossy green bicycle. "Just one more day," she whispers. Through the faux wood slats, she studies her bike a long while. The loopy drop bars like a ram, head down, readying to butt and batter. Its worn wheels and perpendicular storage rack– the chrome flaking away like chapped skin. "My beautiful bicycle," she says, sucking in quickly, then breathing out, "And my nemesis." She reviews the plan in her head once more. Thirty-six steps – medium pace – to the exit. Twenty-one from the door to the tenement gardens, then four more to the bike rack. In exhausting detail, she envisions the path, from the beige bead-board in the corridor to the dank stairwell to the possible sounds– yipping dogs, car horns, and the wind through the Sugarberry trees that line the banks of a nearby brook, shrouded by the urban sprawl – or so she imagines - to the mix of city smells; garbage, distant hydrangeas, dog shit. As she anticipates, her nerves began to fire, low voltage. "Control your breathing. In through the nose, out through the mouth. Just like the doctor says." In, out. Still, her brain whirs. And she rushes to the foyer, for her cello. Atop the instrument is a post-it note, blue and crisp, it reads, Change Your Thoughts. Madeline pulls it from the instrument and taps its bridge three times, "Pa rum pum."

Madeline grips her cello like a hammer with one hand. With the other, she strokes the glassy wood, fingers the F-holes. She positions the end in the space between her legs, then closes her eyes, tilts back her head. The bow is no longer a tool, but a captive. And on this night, the eve before her re-acquaintance with the world, Madeline makes love. Her slender fingers caress and fondle the strings. And as she performs, she weeps, from the depths of her belly. She plays for fear. She plays for regret, at having vowed to leave her apartment. She thinks of her bicycle, calls it forlorn, then plays for that too. Her fist is clinched, knuckles white as eggs shells, and she skids across the four strands. The horse-hair is hot to the touch, sounding her lament– raw, deep and rich. "How did you come to this?" she says, "A covenant… with a damn bike?" Then she strums more wildly, for her step-father with his lazy eye and buttery smile. And she plucks away, for the too small tent and his special camping trips.

Madeline plays with abandon, till her fingers are stiff, her back wet– an inkblot test forming on her terry cloth shirt. "Just nine flights, Madeline," she says, "sixty-one stairs." She sits in silence, watching herself mount the three-speed Huffy. Her panting planes off. The urge to pray sneaks in. She hasn't petitioned God in years, not since the boys from 6B chose her to terrorize and mock. For a moment, she recalls the horrors– masturbation noises through her door, each night, snorting like feral animals, calling out her name; smeared shit on her knob, in the grooves of her gold-plated numbers, and cigarette smoke blown beneath her door. Not sure I should be talking to you, God, she muses. You don't seem particularly interested in my grief. But she laces her fingers together, pushes them against her forehead. "Give me strength tomorrow, God, let me get past this threshold. Let me sit on my bike. Please. You owe me that." She makes the sign of the cross, slow and clumsy, slumping down next to the cello.

Her mind drifts to a lighter time. To the first time she asked the black-eyed delivery boy to count his strides, coming and going, from the elevator. He twisted up his face, palmed his downy hair. "Describe the hallway to me, too," she had asked. "And take the stairs instead of the elevator some time, Saul. Tell me how they smell. How they feel."

"Pardon, ma'am?"

"You heard me, this door is thin. And why not? You could use the exercise. Or maybe the peephole adds some pounds." She remembers his laugh, low and hearty, and his grimace, crooked – handsomely so – and honest. The college-bound lad warmed up to Madeline, and she held that close. He handed back the sarcasm, two-fold. "Miss your Agoraphobics meeting again?" he'd ask. Or, "You know there's a cure, you mole, it's called weed." Madeline tried to keep her distance; he's moving away, she told herself,
over and over. But she knew that, to Saul, she was more than the crazy lady in 10B.

"How many steps today?" she'd ask.

"The same."

Then she'd slide the envelope under the doorframe and think, please don't leave me, Saul, "Pa rum pum," and tap the door. Through the tiny round hole, Madeline always watched Saul walk away. And after he'd gone, she'd look both ways, once, twice, three times, then pull in the groceries, quick like a scampering squirrel. Her heart broke every time as she trudged to the calendar and marked it off in red. Seven days till he returns.

Before leaving for college, on Saul's last delivery, Madeline double-checked the chain locks the night before and the morning of. Scared of missing his approach, she stood for an hour, pushed against the door, her body, her face, her hands. When he finally materialized, her heart raced, but she managed to sliver the door open and poke an envelope through. "It won't fit under the door," she spat. "Believe me, I've tried." She grabbed her trembling wrist with her free hand. "It's a little something extra, you know, for college."

"Ma'am, I can't – "

She cut him off, flapping it about. "Take it, you pain in the ass. Hurry up. You know how nutty I can get."

Saul culls the money from her hand, and Madeline watches herself close the door, heavily, then rest against it. She hears his guttural voice again. "Pa rum pum," he whispered. Then gave her three soft taps from the other side.

Amidst the summoning, Madeline avoided tomorrow's risky pilgrimage, for a moment. But now, she looks through the crystal clear pane and peers out at her bike, its reflectors glinting in the yellowy autumn sun. Pelted by the wet seasons and having baked beneath the red rage of many Indian summers, the Huffy is still beautiful to Madeline. Her innards churn for its aloneness. "I'll be strong, for you," she says, letting go of the string at the window's edge. Fatigued by the day's broken routines, Madeline's gait is slow, her head and heart are weighty. "It's Tuesday," she mutters, "*Music Box Dancer* day."

Madeline hears the mourning doves calling out their names. Her chest constricts. Now or never, she thinks. And after dressing in the clothes she chose months before – dark blue skirt, just above the knee, a light gray, long sleeve, nylon t-shirt, white sneakers, and finally, a Detroit Tigers baseball cap, pulled down over her brow – she makes her way. I don't feel real. Just don't stop, she tells herself, and stay in autopilot, so you can't turn back. Unlocking all of the latches and bolts, she forces herself to think about the ice cream truck, then whips open the door. She gasps at a swoosh of warm air, tepid and thick, like chicken soup. As planned, she sticks her foot between the frame and hardwood, keeping the door ajar, then mimes her way into the hall. With her hands and legs splayed out, she keeps her face to the wall, inching like a caterpillar. Half a step, then another. And another.

Stop.

In all the preparation for this day, Madeline never thought about a cable-man – or any man or woman for that matter – showing up as she flounders in the hall amidst her own shadow. Yet here he comes, striding closer, then closer. She stands still, a part of the wall, like broken sheetrock. With her cheek pressed to the wall, she can only see him with one eye. A broad-chested fellow, bearded and ungainly. Even with his cell phone cocked between his shoulder and ear and scribbling madly on a crumpled piece of paper resting in his palm, he takes notice of her. Madeline's face flushes hot, and there's a pang in her bladder. She twitches at the sharpness. The burly man with the bright white nametag passes by, peering at her from his periphery. Then he looks forward again and continues talking, pretending not to see.

The acid travels up her throat, burning her lips and gums. She pounds her fists against the drywall. And the snake begins to slither up her fine blue skirt.

****

As the sun goes down, Madeline stays crouched in the hallway, three feet from her apartment, legs tucked beneath her, aching from the hours of stillness. Another bout of urine spills onto the carpet, darkening the wide circle around her. Her plucked-out hair is strewn about the floor, some strands still caught in her fingers, others fixed in the stale piss, forked out like frayed crochet.

****

After the policeman maneuvers her back inside, and the doctor on call from the Skyland Psychiatry Clinic has gone, Madeline sits like stone upon the plastic slipcover. When the bicycle cries out to her, she snatches up her cello. Even amidst her angry concerto, she can still hear it wailing.

"You lied!"

She plays more frantically.

"You're a coward!"

Madeline draws the curtains across the window, in one fell swoop, and strides to the calendar. Without pause, she takes it down off the wall. "Pa rum pum," she says, tapping the barren and discolored space. Her hue is silvery, full-blooded. And she hunkers down on the floor again, next to her cello. "Thank you God. For the certainty, I mean." With her sleeve, she buffs out a fingerprint on the glossy cello then stands the bow upright. Then, she carefully positions the calendar under the instrument's endpin, like a towel. "No blood on the carpet, Madeline." As she drags her slight wrists down the coarse strings, she exhales, breathy, tired and composed.

Alec Greenfield
Algonquin College (Canada)
"Hullabaloo"

"Sir, are you calling me a liar?"

"I am, sir!"

The harsh words stung like a teeth-rattling slap.

"Very well. We will meet with pistols at dawn!"

But they weren't real pistols. It wasn't even a serious threat. Those who went to school with the two young lads in question would recognize this exchange as part of the ongoing farce.

Sure enough, seven-thirty came and the sun illuminated the dewy grass of Tristan's backyard. Tristan Mills -- twelve years old, blond-haired and ruggedly handsome in an immature fashion -- brandished a transparent, blue-colored water pistol. He stood at attention and back-to-back with his rival.

Jeffrey Vernon -- eleven and a-half, dark-haired, shorter and lankier -- held an oversized water weapon. The barrel of his gun pointed up into the air as he held it with his bent arm. Indeed, both boys assumed the classic stance of duelists.

This particular confrontation had started with a false accusation -- and Jeffrey knew it to be false. But he couldn't help it. He was the jealous type.

In Jeffrey's mind, he was the final authority on, well, everything. Therefore, a large part of his pride depended on being the smartest, best-informed, highest-achieving, and simply the best-at-everything student in his class at the public school.

That had been the case for the first five years of his scholastic career -- Jeffrey was always placed at the top the honor roll. But the situation had changed last year with the arrival of a strapping new boy from the west named Tristan Springthorpe Mills.

It wasn't really fair to Jeffrey. The new arrival was smart, athletic, and handsome. Most of the girls in the class had crushes on him and viewed him as the "eligible" type. And when Tristan supplanted him at the top of the honor roll that year -- well, that was the proverbial last straw as far as Jeffrey was concerned. They were in seventh grade now, and that disgrace would not be repeated.

The first science test of the fall term had come and gone. Predictably, Tristan had scored the top mark. As the teacher enunciated a public ranking of the top ten scores in front of the class -- Jeffrey had finished second -- an impulsive thought blazed through his agitated mind: *This is entirely too much! It may be time to send him a message.*

In this case, the message was a *J'accuse*-style letter, signed and promptly delivered into Tristan's desk two days later. The contents of the letter accused Tristan of being a cheat, a liar, and an all-round reprobate. The end of the matter could have been predicted by anyone who knew the two boys -- especially the classmates who kept their ears to the ground for such controversies. Gauntlet thrown down. Challenge accepted.

We shall turn and fire after five paces, right?" Tristan asked.

"Agreed!" was Jeffrey's answer.

One, two, three, four, five -- squirt!

Two minutes later, as Jeffrey wrung the bottom edge of his t-shirt, he had a consoling notion: *I only missed him by a couple of inches. My sidearm wasn't sighted properly. Yes, that must be the reason I missed him!*

But that theory was a comfort of the cold variety.

The two duelists parted, and Jeffrey rode home on his dirt bike with the malfunctioning water weapon in his backpack. *Thank goodness there's no one around at this time of morning,* he thought glumly.

Divine intervention often arrives in signs and portents. In Jeffrey's case, it presented itself in the form of a praying mantis.

Hullabaloo appeared on a Saturday. More accurately, the praying mantis who would be named Hullabaloo had crawled into Jeffrey's bedroom through the open window in the early morning hours of that day. The creature was resting in the center of the bedroom wall when Jeffrey awakened, groggy and squinting.

"Hello! What's this?" Jeffrey asked when he saw the wall opposite from his bed. The image appeared to be (in the subdued, early-morning light) something like a green corn husk. Upon closer examination, he saw that it was a mantis.

Like most boys his age, he had a fascination for living things belonging to the insect family. In addition to this, he had found himself with a diminishing circle of schoolyard chums -- owing to his recent display of temper. He quickly decided to adopt this impressive specimen as a pet.

Sensing the creature to be benign, in spite of the formidable front claws, Jeffrey placed it in an abandoned shoe box until a more permanent dwelling could be arranged.

Where did the name "Hullabaloo" come from? Jeffrey remembered hearing the word in a Disney animated film that had featured characters speaking with English accents. He had liked the sound of it. He would conduct a search for the vacant fish tank, stored somewhere in the attic of the house. *Hullabaloo, it shall be.*

The first oddity occurred that night.

The afternoon had been uneventful. He had cleaned the disused fish tank and had converted it into a suitable terrarium for Hullabaloo: a bit of gravel, a handful of dirt, a dish of water, and a tree branch. Hullabaloo was undemanding in his requests for furniture. Five o'clock. Feeding time. His new friend's first meal was a captured moth. *Gonna get you lots of crickets, boy,* Jeffrey thought.

Hullabaloo seemed to nod in agreement, clasping his large claws together as if in supplication. The tiny, smooth eyes shined in approval. *Yes, sir. Lots of cricket dinners for you!*

It had been a full day for Jeffrey, even though the only human being he had interacted with was his mother. After reading a couple of issues of *Iron Man*, Jeffrey yawned, noted the lateness of the hour, and then put on his pajama bottoms. Lights out.

Jeffrey vacillated between being a tosser-and-turner, or a narco-leptic. That night, he was the latter. He was half-way to the Land of Nod, and he took one more look, cobwebbed-eyed, at his new tenant. Hullabaloo hung upside down from the branch in the terrarium.

Out of the shadows, Jeffrey sensed music. Not too loud. Rather faint. It was a sad melody. He wondered, *Am I dreaming? Why am I dreaming of a harpsichord? Odd that. Very odd.*

Then he was down for the count.

By the following afternoon, the nocturnal melody had faded from his memory. Jeffrey attended to his new friend, Hullabaloo. Fresh water? Check. Fresh soil? Check. Live crickets bought at the local pet shop? Check.

Jeffrey picked up his lodger very carefully in the palm of his hand. Did it seem as if Hullabaloo made a bow to the young lad? Jeffrey seemed to think so. Indeed, the mantis almost seemed to be *purring*.

After a few minutes of playing, he returned the creature to his home. He had to prepare for the next round of battle with his archrival, Tristan. Tomorrow would be Monday, and that was the day for the monthly spelling bee in Jeffrey's class.

Stern discipline was required for the contest. Jeffrey had taken it upon himself to memorize his pocket dictionary from cover to cover as part of his preparations. Thus far, he had gotten about midway through the chunky little book. It was an ambitious training regimen, but he felt it was necessary for tomorrow's competition.

However, two hours of such drudgery had made an impact. Jeffrey yawned and glanced at his clock. Six-thirty. His eyelids drooped. *Please,* he thought in a haze. *Please let this be enough. If only*

I could beat him once, then the dam would break. I will get the respect I deserve. I'm certain of it.

He fell asleep, in spite of himself.

Mr. Poe once wrote: *Is all that we see or seem but a dream within a dream?* In Jeffrey's subconscious, Hullabaloo had attained the power of speech.

I know you better than you realize, Hullabaloo told Jeffrey in a tinny voice. *I know your greatest desire.*

How is that possible? the boy asked.

You told me your desire with your mind, and now I understand you. I have a talent for doing that. Mind reading. You believe me, don't you?

I believe, Jeffrey replied.

Good boy!

I can't beat him tomorrow. I just can't. He's better than me.

Let me attend to that. But I have a request to make of you.

Yes?

If I do this favor for you, fixing the spelling bee, then I can live here in your room forever.

What are you talking about? Do you have magic powers?

Oh, sure! Magic!

Explain the supernatural physics to me in a language I can understand, please. I'm only a boy.

Have a little faith in me, young man. Do you really want to beat him tomorrow?

Yes, Hullabaloo. More than anything in the whole wide world -- a victory above all else!

I love you, buddy!

The spelling bee on that Monday proved to be rather anticlimactic. Jeffrey, being a well-trained verbal athlete, had easily advanced to the final round. But his opponent would be Simon, a known under-achiever in the class.

Tristan was missing from the final showdown. Citing an acute case of brain fatigue, he had withdrawn from the proceedings in the early going.

As he stood at the head of the class, Jeffrey had to admit to himself a feeling of mild disappointment. *What a pity,* he thought. *I was looking forward to giving Tristan a thrashing, even if it is only a spelling bee. Now I'm up against a non-entity. Oh, well. Such is life.*

Jeffrey had won in a romp over Simon, and he received many hearty congratulations from his peers. He enjoyed the admiration. It had been a long drought, after all.

The triumph that day was complete. He had just one, small element of doubt.

Being perceptive, Jeffrey had noticed an unusually high number of religious terms that had been used during the elimination rounds of the spelling bee: benediction, heresy, apostate, dualism.

What was that about? This is not a seminary! Odd that. Very odd.

The bottom dropped out of Jeffrey's world in the late afternoon.

He came home, high on himself, and went to his room in order to share his good news with Hullabaloo.

A happy result, I see, Hullabaloo remarked while standing on the end of the branch.

"Yes, Hullabaloo -- we did it!" Jeffrey said, and smiled. "Unfortu-nately, Tristan didn't make it to the end."

No one ever does, my boy, the insect said. *Brain fatigue is only the start for Mr. Mills.*

"Well, it would have been nice to beat him honestly. Anyway, what are you getting at, Hullabaloo?"

His two antennae quivered slightly.

I meant, no one lasts. Brain fatigue is only the start of one's gradual decline.

"Huh?"

Oh, I have a few ideas for Tristan's end. It will be either a car crash or carbon monoxide poisoning -- I haven't quite decided yet. But someday soon he will earn the denouement he deserves!

"Hullabaloo! You don't mean --"

Death, my lad.

Jeffrey felt a chill that seemed to emanate from the core of his soul.

We're best friends now, Jeffrey, the insect told him with a generous dose of malice. *And friends don't keep secrets, do they? I want to tell you my secret...*

The boy felt a flicker of recognition. Nevertheless, he asked: "Who are you, really?"

Hullabaloo, of course.

"No -- what was your name before I gave you that one?" Jeffrey demanded.

Clever boy! Let me see -- so many names, so many forms. I have been called Abaddon, Belial, Beelzebub, and Mephistopheles. But you may call me Lucifer, and I will stay with you forever!

Sam Annis
University of Wisconsin
"All She Wants to Do is Dance"

The way Dad tells the story, he was almost a victim. George becomes a laughable, pitiful, embarrassment, and Dad is the man who George tried to dupe.

But Dad is no dope.

The way he tells the story, the conversation came from nowhere, a complete blindside. That was after George bungled his way through small talk, and said what he'd called to say.

In my dad's office, there is unorthodox mixture of objects: a large leather sofa and a grandfather clock from his early ventures into Craigslist; large wooden carvings of tropical fish purchased in Belize; a paint-by-numbers work my brother did of two wolves howling at the moon; a large oak bookshelf with glass doors taking up an entire wall and filled with decades of paperwork; area rugs lying on top of the wall-to-wall carpeting; a bronze cast of a man riding a bronco done in the style of Remington; a painting by Thomas Kinkade; a massive L-shaped desk, behind which my dad sits like an emperor, talking ceaselessly into the phone.

When I call him, the first thing I often hear is my dad finishing up his conversation with someone else on another line. He'll answer my call, but he doesn't say anything to me except maybe, "Hold on," before returning to the other conversation. For that time, I am connected to a stranger through my dad, each of us held in one of his hands, his voice moving through both of us.

Even when I didn't call, when I would casually drop in, he was always behind his desk, on his phone. Sometimes his cellphone, but usually the manila colored desk phone with a banana-shaped tongue on the back to make the job of cradling it against his shoulder easier. I don't know if he still owns that system. It's one of the types of technologies that never were improved upon. It moved from an almost spontaneous generation to antiquity in a matter of decades. There are no ancestors to the banana-shaped shoulder cradle.

When George called, my dad was already on the phone. The owner of an old fertilizer plant was looking to sell the property and attached buildings, but before he could do that he needed to completely clean up the land which had suffered from years of toxic spillage. There was a pond nearby that shone neon blue in the sun. It needed to be cleaned up or buried.

While George waited on hold, my dad discussed the various steps necessary to make the land sellable. The client wanted to move on the project as quickly as possible, but my dad told him that the soil samples coming back from the lab indicated that the ground and pond were far more polluted than previously assumed, that this was basically a superfund site, and that the probable cost of cleaning it up lay in the millions.

Teresa, my dad's secretary for many years, brought in a note saying that a George Paterson was on the line. It took my dad a few moments before he remembered who George Paterson was.

They met at MIT in the late 70s, both of them 18, both of them from rural backgrounds. They hadn't gone to prestigious high schools, they hadn't gotten particularly good grades, but they'd scored very well on the math portion of the SATs, and their entrance exams indicated a level of intelligence much higher than average.

My dad moved to Boston from Warren, New Jersey.

George moved to Boston from Bangor, Maine.

They shared some classes. In one of them, the professor had an explosion of white hair that looked like an action model of an atom. It was the "Einstein" style so many eccentric science/mathematics professors favored in those days. A coifed stamp of genius.

During one class, the professor brought in a hotel pan full of hotdogs. It was a lecture hall where the students sat in an ascending fan around the professor, like in a Greek theater. On a wooden table in the center of the room was a tub. White steam rolled out and down the sides of the tub.

"These," said the professor, picking up a bright pink hotdog, "are the effects of dry ice."

He began dipping the hotdogs into the tub, one by one, and then flinging them into the assembled students where they shattered into hundreds of pieces amidst the ducking bodies and binders held up as shields.

My dad and George were there. Before the class, they'd eaten the caps off of two hallucinogenic mushrooms. It was when the professor began throwing the flash-frozen hotdogs into the audience that they both peaked.

"I got a 'C' that semester," my dad told me. I don't know if it had anything to do with the mushrooms.

My dad and George started a small business together. They bought deconstructed boxes in bulk from a cardboard manufacturer, assembled them, and sold them to other students who were moving. They also designed and screen printed shirts to sell at the Boston Marathon. There must have been a decent market for boxes and the shirts because after a year they'd saved up enough to buy a house outside of the city and move there with their girlfriends. Unfortunately, all the time spent making boxes and printing shirts meant they failed every class that spring. Instead of returning to the world of academia, Dad and George dropped out.

The house was small, but it sat on several acres of farmland. All around the yard was a field of wheat, golden brown and crackling in the wind. They raised chickens and geese, smoked pot, and played music in the evenings, George on saxophone and Dad on the guitar. The girls, Debbie and Charlotte, cooked for them, danced with them, got high with them, slept with them.

It didn't take long for my dad to end the relationship with Charlotte. One night, during a fight, she told him that when Tyler, his brother, had come to visit she'd fucked him. That was bad, but

Dad forgave Charlotte. The following weekend, my Dad drove back
to New Jersey and got his revenge by sleeping with Tyler's finance.
Charlotte did not forgive him.

In less than a week, both Dad and Uncle Tyler were single.

With Charlotte out of the house, my dad wanted a fresh start. He
let George and Debbie, who married over the summer, buy my dad's
half of the house. He moved to Plainfield, NJ and used George and
Debbie's money to put a down payment on an oil truck.

For the next few years, he lived in a studio apartment down the street
from the Texas Wiener stand. Occasionally, while I was growing
up, he would go back there for a Texas Wiener and take me along. I
couldn't stand them, their greasy taste, and the tied-off end of the
sausage casing made me feel weird, like I was biting into a belly-
button.

"The best wieners in town," my dad would say. To my knowledge, they were the only wieners in town.

The leather couch in Dad's office is also a futon. I didn't know
this at first, but then my mom told me my dad was sleeping at the
office because she'd kicked him out of the house. I imagined him
spending all day there. One by one the other office staff closed down
their computers and filed away all the important documents. The
parking lot slowly emptied off all the vehicles until it was just my
dad's Explorer pickup that remained. He turned off all the lights,
locked the doors, and sat in the office surrounded by only himself.

The Kinkade hanging on the wall opposite the couch is like all other
Kinkades anywhere: a waterfall, a lake, a forest, a perfect sunset, and
a cabin all cohabiting in the same valley. A small dock juts out into
the lake, and a canoe is turned upside down at the end of it. A braid
of grey smoke comes out of the stone chimney, and somebody turned
on every light inside of the house.

My parents became obsessed with Thomas Kinkade one year when
they wandered into the Thomas Kinkade gallery in the Bridgewater
Mall. The gallery was dark, with black carpet covering the walls, and

all the saleswomen were young, blond, and had gleaming white teeth.

For a period of time, we went to the gallery once a week, and by the end of a year five Kinkades hung in the house. My brother and I wandered through the gallery while my parents talked about pricing and the opportunity to have a Kinkade apprentice come and touch up certain elements of the paintings. He and I pointed out our personal favorites and looked for all the hidden symbols we'd heard Kinkade liked to put into his work.

I wanted to walk down the streets so evenly covered by white, fluffy snow, and I wanted to live in a thatch-roofed cottage beside a brook in the mountains. I never noticed how Kinkade's paintings depict a landscape only one weather pattern away from complete annihilation.

Once purchased, the girls wrapped the paintings up like mummies and we drove them home. One was placed on the wall above the living room couch. Another went above my mom's desk. My brother and I were always told we could have one when we moved out and got married.

George and Dad didn't stay in touch. After the move, Dad was busy trying to get his infant company off the ground. He put in ten, eleven, twelve hour days behind the wheel of the oil truck, driving back and forth across central New Jersey, building a clientele of customers. He lived frugally off of rice and Texas Wieners, and he quickly saved up enough money to begin looking at houses. This was a time when you could buy a decent sized chunk of land 45 minutes away from New York without being a doctor or one of the Yankees.

The house was a shithole. It was located on 15 acres of land, mostly swamp, and it bordered a horse farm. There was one bedroom, a small kitchen, a bathroom with crumbling tile, and not much else. At night, the swamp became an abyss ruled over by bullfrogs and screaming foxes.

George and Debbie lived in the house near Boston for a few years, and then they moved deeper into the country. Debbie was beginning to show, and George wanted to get his child as far as possible from the toxic air around the city. The few times he and my dad talked during this time, George said things about FBI listening stations peppering the Boston subway, about the signals he'd picked up on his shortwave.

Those were the first stories I was ever told about George.

The Kinkades hung in the house while I grew up. Their frames were massive, elaborate, and made of exotic wood. Sometimes, while sitting on the couch in the living room, I would reach up and touch the frame, tilting it back and forth on the wall. I tried to decide which I liked the best, which I would take when I moved away.

Maybe the one with the horses in the cottage's front yard, the grass so shockingly green, and the peach tree in obscene bloom.

Maybe the one with the cottage that used to be a church, or maybe the cottage that sat in winter by the still trickling stream.

So many cottages, and all of them so clearly home to the most charming families. I wondered if people driving by our house looked down the driveway at our lit up windows and imagined us as happy as I imagined the people in the Kinkade. It didn't matter that there weren't actually any people in Kinkade's work. The blazing bright lights in the windows and the smoke from the chimneys proved that families inhabited all the homes.

They must be so happy.

By the mid-80s, George and Debbie had two small children rolling around their floor, getting dirty in the woods outside, learning to walk and speak. George worked construction on and off, and Debbie taught kindergarten at a local school. They did not have much money.

My Dad's business had taken off, and now he wanted a wife to give him babies. He contacted a dating service, lied his way through the questionnaire, and was matched up with Helen, the woman who became his wife, my mom. Five months after they met, they became engaged. A year after that, they married. A year after that, my brother was born.

Ignoring the past, Dad asked Tyler, who was trying to start his own carpentry business, to design a new house on the property in the swamp. The idea was to retain the old building and construct rooms around it, so the original kitchen and bedroom would be like a coin held tightly in a fist.

For the next few years, my parents lived in a perpetual state of construction. I was born during this time, but I don't remember anything of the milky plastic walls, the piles of shingles and roofing nails, the workers with thick boots stomping up and down the stairs.

My uncle never finished the house and my parents hired someone else, a skinny man with a mustache and threadbare blue jeans. His name was Peter Parlor Piano.

Over the holidays, George and my dad might send a card to one another. Occasionally, a phone call took place. One summer, Dad took my brother and me up to New Hampshire, where George and Debbie live. We drive down a gravel road for what seems like hours before their house appears, almost swallowed by shrubs and over-grown Poplars. In the yard are broken Tonka trucks and a rusting swing set. George stands on the sinking front porch, a stained child in his arms, smiling. He lifts one of the child's chubby arms and waves it limply at us.

The front door of the house is wide open, as are all the windows. It is over 90 degrees, humid, and I start to sweat as soon as Dad cut the engine to the car.

During the next several hours, my brother and I try to play with George's two children while Dad tries to talk to George and Debbie.

I can't understand the kids when they speak. They scream like barbarians, and they run around with berries smeared around their mouths. My dad sits on a couch without legs, his knees close to his chest, and drinks a cup of water while George tells him about the recordings the government makes of every phone conversation.

Finally, we leave. I don't look back to watch George and Debbie waving goodbye to our car.

The drive back to New Jersey is long, and my brother and I fall asleep looking out the window at New England.

When we get home, Mom comes out of the house and helps Dad carry us inside. I am mostly asleep, but I hear him tell her that George is a mess.

"We used to be so similar," he says. "Now the man's a lunatic."

The Kinkades became oppressive. They didn't make any sense. What sort of light was so bright that filled up the entire window, obscuring the inside of the house, and why were such bright lights on in the middle of the day? The trees are all green and blooming: it's the height of summer, so why is smoke pouring from the chimneys? The paintings attempt to contain everything that we want to see, all the memories we want to have, but either they don't recognize the phys- ical limitations that prevent these idealized scenes from happening, or the scenes aren't idylls at all.

The orange and yellow lights in the windows are flames. The smoke coming from the chimney isn't a banner of domesticity, but a terrible transformation. The interior of these wooden cottages has combusted, and the whole structure will go up soon as well, but for now, just the inhabitants are being cooked and shuttled up the flue in the form of grey soot and ash.

All those smiling faces we never got to see are being burned alive.

Dad finally finishes his conversation. He places the phone on the cradle and looks at the blinking red light telling him someone is waiting on line five. He looks at Teresa's note. Cupping the phone between his jaw and his shoulder again, he pushes the blinking button.

"Hello? George?"

George was so happy to hear Dad's voice. He told him he'd

been thinking about calling him for months, but today he finally made it happen.

"It's good to hear you too, George," said Dad.

They caught up. My dad told George that his business was doing extremely well.

"I never in a million years thought I'd be this successful," Dad said. "I've got a beautiful wife, two wonderful and smart sons, and a thriving company."

Dad told George he's bought a lake house, and he mentioned the art he's begun collecting.

George laughed high and girlish, happy that my dad is so happy.

"It's so exciting," he said, "that we've both come so far, that our lives are where we always wanted them to be."

Dad said that he's glad to hear George sounding so healthy, that the last time they'd seen one another, during that muggy summer, George had seemed melancholic.

"You're right, and things have turned around completely," said George.

"You and Debbie finally moved out of the shack, huh?"

"Actually, Debbie and I are divorced."

Dad said he was really sorry to hear about that. He thought about George and Debbie's children, about the divided home they'd grow up in, and he shook his head.

"We talked about it," said George, "and we're still friends, but we decided this was the best situation."

"But your kids--"

"Henry," said George, "I've got something I want to tell you."

"Okay," said Dad.

"Henry," said George, "the reason Debbie and I got divorced is because I realized that I wasn't who we thought I was. All this time, as long as I can remember, I've been defined as one thing when in reality I was something, I am something, different."

"Okay," said Dad.

"I've changed my name."

Dad didn't say anything.

"I'm Martha."

Dad looked across his desk at the painting.

"I go out now, I meet people. I go on dates, and I play music again, and I am happy, like we used to be when we all lived in that small house, remember? The girls would dance for us, and I always wanted to be just like them, dancing. I go dancing all the time now. Do you remember that house, Henry? Do you ever go dancing? I would love to go dancing with you. Do you ever go dancing?"

"George," Dad said, "there's an emergency call coming in on another line. I'll call you back tomorrow."

That night, over a dinner Mom made, Dad told us the story and we laughed at George/Martha.

"And he asked me if I wanted to go *dancing*," Dad said, and we laughed so hard. We laughed and laughed and laughed.

Five years later, during a Christmas party, my Dad touched my seven-year-old cousin in the basement of our house. She told my aunt while they were driving back home, and my aunt called my mom. Mom said it's not possible, and hangs up the phone. Five months later, Dad's bail was posted at $100,000. His picture was on the evening news.

I'm living in Washington with the woman who will become my wife.

Our walls are empty.

It took a few years, but my Dad accepted a plea bargain, went to prison, and came back out. He had an affair with a woman ten years older, and Mom divorced him. He lived in the office and the wooden fish kept him company at night.

Sometimes, I can't help but think that he's an asshole.

All Martha wanted to do was dance.

Sarah Bazar
Murray State University
"Closeted"

*Marshmallow fluff. Cumulus clouds. Billowing white scarves in
the wind.*

Charlotte thought of these things with a vague distaste as she
stared at the mound of Cool Whip resting atop the trifle. On a normal
day, she would find quiet delight in globs of marshmallow fluff and
thick clouds scattered across the horizon; but today was not a normal
day, a very abnormal day indeed, and she didn't have time for billowy
Cool Whip. What she needed was efficient, pristine—professional. Yes,
that was the word.

Lightly lifting a metal tablespoon from her cutlery drawer—
second insert from the left, always, the spoons—she pressed the
back of the curve into the outward edge of the whipped topping and
made the spoon glide sideways, concave meeting convex to somehow
produce this smooth, rounded surface that was much more appropriate for her boss's promotion party, much more presentable by the
time she was through: one icy mound of snow, a drift of cream.

It was 5:45 p.m. precisely, and the Jell-O in the trifle had set at the
exact moment she had expected it to, as she knew it would. The trifle,
the whole creation, sat mute as a masterpiece on the spotless granite
countertop. The swath of topping shivered above layers of red
berries, cubes of sponge cake soaked in strawberry gelatin, and
another container's worth of Cool Whip, piled in dense thicknesses
between each section. As a girl, Charlotte always fondly associated
her mother's specialty dessert with Christmas, due to the colors—a
thought her mother met - had met - with a dismissive frown. Now it
looked to her like the earth cut open, layers of crust and lava pressing
against her best crystal bowl.

She slid the trifle back into the gleaming refrigerator with care,
trying to avoid jostling the layers too much. The bottle of Grand

Cellier caught her eye, and she had to press her fingers against the polished wide surface to ensure that it was chilled. She rearranged and corrected the positioning and separation of the fruit and cheese platter she had designed—for Heaven's sake, the dip bowls should be in the *corners*, not the middle, it needs balance—and fluffed the Caesar salad she had prepared because the chicken was too middle-heavy in the bowl. She ducked her head low, tilted it right and left and up to make sure everything seemed perfect before she closed the door to the fridge.

After freeing the quicksilver surface of her oily fingerprints, she pulled a neatly folded sheet of paper and a pen from the front pocket of her apron, made a few quick strikes on the sheet, and then reviewed it, double-checking, before folding it back up and dropping the pen and paper both into her pocket. She beamed at the clock on the stove—a successful 5:50 p.m.

Charlotte slipped off her apron and hung it carefully inside the laundry nook on her way to her bedroom, shutting the door behind her. A full-length gilded mirror sat on a stand by the closet door. The mirror was darkly tarnished in the grooves and weighty in its age, but the gold had a soft sheen to it that can only be gotten from years of loving touches. Charlotte's dress was immaculate, such a dark navy blue that it was almost black, frilling out a little at the bottom hem. She would stand out in this dress: everyone else would be in lackluster business attire that was clearly Friday-wear, but Charlotte had left work early to prepare for the party.

Everyone was surprised when 'Chardonnay Charlotte' (as she knew they called her, intending to imply that she was expensive and thought herself superior to them) suggested that they throw McNeely a promotion celebration and offered to host it herself, at her own place. Charlotte herself was a bit surprised, too, because in doing so, she was making a minor addition to (she was trying not to think of it as a 'deviation from') her plan, which mentioned nothing about throwing a party. However, the idea bubbled from her mouth the week before when McNeely announced to the office that the following Friday would be his last day there. Charlotte's excitement had bypassed her mental filter, and once the words were out, she realized that, though she knew she was already in good standing with the committee deciding who would take the spot as Head of Public Relations, it would be an opportunity to finally make an impression on McNeely and encourage him to put in a good word for her to his higher-ups. Besides, she reasoned, not everything had to be by the plan. She was tired of the plan.

Charlotte looked into her wide brown eyes in the mirror, tucked a stray curl behind her ear and ruffled her dress. She couldn't help but smile. How many times as a young girl had she pictured herself at this point in life, prepared to accept a position that would pay her enough and support her enough to satisfy both herself and her mother? It would be an outstanding job, really, one that would sound good and look good to everyone.

Charlotte's mother had always been very insistent that appearance—what you seemed like to others and what others thought of you—could influence your whole destiny. You always had to be aware—when you were planning your life on the front porch in August with a pencil and notepad (*'Oh, how darling—but you must always use a pen, dear, so they know you're firm and committed'*); when you were eating ice cream in Lawrence Park under the shade of the old Piccalo tree (*'Don't stick your tongue out that far, Charlotte—you don't want people saying you enjoy doing such lewd things, do you'*); when you went walking about your neighborhood in muddy jeans and a tank top with Paul, the neighborhood stray with only three legs and a stump of a tail (*'He looks so mangy, dear, and you don't want people thinking you keep bad company—and your clothes are practically unwearable'*)—of what you looked like to others, of what you seemed, because if they saw you again you would want them to remember you, and remember you well, not as if you're an undignified tramp who only has half a brain.

"You must always be in control of yourself, always confident and strong and sure," her mother would say, "because the men can see it in you, sense it in you if you're not. And if you're not, they'll tear you right to bits and spit you into someone else's mouth. If you are—and you should be, don't let them think they control you—then you've got

to be pretty, too, Charlotte, or they'll not even bother. And you've got
to let them know all of that, right there and then when they see you,
and all of that comes into your appearance. It must be perfect. Everything must be perfect. Appearance," she would finish, with a grave
expression and severe frown, "is identity. It is power."

Charlotte pulled her bedroom door tightly shut behind her.

At 6:16 p.m., Fred Stueffa showed up with a ten-dollar bottle of
brandy under one meaty arm and a roll of ribbon under the other. It
was dubious that his suit cost much more than the brandy, the red and
brown plaid pattern going faint in the threads, and his already rotund
face was so red it was almost purple, giving him the appearance of a
large, sun-faded radish. Charlotte ushered him inside, not looking at
the little dirt crumbs left by his worn loafers, and offered him a glass
of champagne. She herself had just downed one in two swallows to
calm her nerves.

"I'll have a water first, please and thanks. So sorry, Charlotte,
showing up like this. You must think I'm a mess. The air is out in my
car—oh, ice, please, if you have it, thanks—this heat is absolutely
atrocious, could burn the panties right off Greta, I daresay—"

"It's quite fine, Fred. Here, have this glass of water. Do you want
me to take your jacket for you? Is it cool enough in here?" She dug her
teeth into her tongue to keep from continuing as she turned to hang
up the man's jacket. It only smelled a little like stale body heat.

After fetching scissors for Fred to curl and secure a strand of
ribbon onto the bottle, Charlotte settled on the arm of the white
leather couch and watched him. He had sinewy arms like a squirrel,
not good at all, and his large face was innocent of much intelligence.
Thin grey hair was thinning even more on the sides of his head, the
part in the middle a shiny flesh-sea of sadness, Charlotte imagined.
He couldn't have been more than 44, he was just…weathered. Yes,
weathered.

He looked at her from the corners of his eyes as he finished, an unsteady hand tucking the roll of thin blue ribbon into a pocket in his shirt. "Baby ribbon," he said, his voice winking in and out like a bobber at sea. He cleared his throat. "I'd forgotten to get something and all I could find at Costco was baby shower ribbon."

"I'm sure he won't notice," Charlotte said.

Fred smiled, and a silence fell between them. The metal tray with precisely poured champagne straddled the corner of her coffee table, etched horses prancing around the lip of it. She admired the tension of their muscles under blankets of skin, the way in which their legs reached out to strike at the ground, the tight, rebellious curve of their necks.

She thought of Raymond Shektor and how he was so unlike the disheveled Fred sitting in the room with her. Her mother had introduced him to her when she was seventeen during lunch at the country club: he was all bright green eyes and short brown hair with an easy smile. Ray worked at the club part-time while he saved up to attend the University of Louisiana the next fall, which was ultimately the reason for his and Charlotte's breakup. Charlotte knew her mother had pushed him on her for his more desirable qualities like his looks and ambition, but she herself liked him because he was not the shallow and manipulative creature she had come to believe men were, the way her mother had painted them to be. He wanted to become a sexual psychologist for a living—something her mother definitely did not know—because he had seen how taboo and oppressed sexuality was in his hometown. He was the first to show her how to open up, how to truly be herself without so much focus on what others would think (*'It's just us here, Charlotte, don't think on it'*), and she thought of his rough weight on top of her body, softened by the fake fur of his fur suit against her skin before she got her own, the way his calf muscles strained against the material and the hair of his mane would shiver against her back—

"It's a pretty tray," Fred said after clearing his throat. "Do you like horses?"

Charlotte started, then blinked at him a few times. "Yes. Yes, I suppose you could say that." Fred's face furrowed and he opened his mouth, but Charlotte said, "I should go check on the trifle, excuse me," and left the room.

From the kitchen, she could partially see him, still seated on the couch and looking at his lap. She had probably upset him, she knew, but she did not know how to fix her mistake. Sweat had beaded on her forehead and she was debating on calling the whole thing off when the doorbell rang. It was 6:24.

Within fifteen minutes, three-quarters of the people expected—including Fred—had arrived, much to Charlotte's relief. She danced between them all with the tray of champagne, light on her feet and quick to smile as she monitored their glasses, flitting in and out of conversations without paying more than a modicum of attention. When she had gone to refill the champagne tray for the second time and McNeely was still not there, Charlotte tipped back a glass of the fizzy wine herself.

She wandered back into the living room and stared silently at the people amassed in her house. Someone had taken her iPod off of the speakers and plugged their phone in, replacing her background jazz with deep bass and pop hits. Greta Vetter, Records Director, actually seemed to be trying to smile at poor Donovan Chansey, who was blotting fruit dip from his white button-up shirt with a bit of toilet paper he must have brought with him.

No one had heard from McNeely.

A man named Brutus Overbe was talking with Fred Stueffa about some figures from last quarter, who nodded along to everything Brutus said.

"Bullshit! He's blowing the right cock and that's how he got that promotion," Mathilda Cranch said over the music. She was dressed in grey business slacks and a men's white shirt. Tufts of her black hair stuck up like vulture feathers from the humidity of the summer, but she wore a smile. Charlotte began moving towards her, and Laura Ingleton, a new intern, shifted away from Mathilda.

"Whatever you heard," Charlotte interrupted, stepping into the conversation and noting the drop in volume around her, "you can keep to yourself. McNeely got that promotion through his hard work and dedication, two things which one could say you are lacking in. We're here to celebrate McNeely's work and his achievements, and I will not have him walking into a roast party when he gets here."

Mathilda's eyes were lazy and dark. "And when is he getting here, exactly?"

Charlotte straightened her posture, held her chin high, looked down at Mathilda's unkempt hair and smug eyes, and though she made herself smile, she could feel her eyes narrow. "Any minute now."

Another trip to the kitchen and Charlotte opened another bottle of champagne. She went around the living room, refilling drinks more briskly and laughing less often. Her mother's voice was a constant in her mind. *Don't stay in one spot too long. Always make eye contact. Always appear too busy to talk to but too gracious to refuse. Appearance is everything. Everything must be perfect.*

Charlotte took her mother's mantras and ran with them, beginning at the age of nine to plan her academic career, and by ten, she had moved on to her professional career. "My little planner," her mother would say, patting her on the head before going inside. Charlotte would sit on the front step of their house, tiny notepad and a pen in her fingers, eyes scrunched together as her brain worked with the minimal information it had about jobs. Something small, she knew, starting out as almost nothing but, over time, through her charm and wit, she knew also there would be promotions to follow. If she found the right company, she could easily get a comfortable job by the age of 40.

As soon as Charlotte read the piece in the Sun called "Knox Knocks Feminism," she knew Knox Enterprises was that company. A small marketing firm ran out of Elk Grove, CA, they were floundering in bad publicity over an especially inconvenient typo made by an intern in a front-page headline, but they had no idea what to do with it. Starns, head of the Public Relations Department, when Charlotte had met with him eight years ago, had that jolty appearance of someone about to go mad. She had laughed quietly at his ignorance, which baffled him, and she proceeded to further that emotion by speaking fluently the language of media and relations and the importance of appearances. She was hired within the week at entry level, and she now sat as Assistant PR Supervisor. Her plan was vague enough to allow for a wide range of foreseeable mishaps, and so had gone quite smoothly up to this night, so unexpected and unplanned in comparison to the rest of her life. She worried now. McNeely's lateness was foreboding—if he didn't show, it wouldn't look good for her to the others there, people who she would be in charge of, if she did land the promotion. And if he didn't show up, what did that bode for her if he influenced the committee's decision? Charlotte took a gulp of champagne from the closest glass to her.

After another half-bottle of champagne had been dispersed, Charlotte's house phone rang. She answered in the kitchen, still smiling at Fred's impression of Donald Trump—not because it was particularly good, but because she couldn't stop picturing him with the hairpiece. "Hello?"

"Hey, Charlotte?" Pause. "It's Mike, Mike McNeely."

"Oh, Mr. McNeely, hi." Charlotte instantly tensed, waiting for bad news. The slight buzz from the champagne disappeared and left her with a sense of emptiness in her stomach. "Is everything okay?

"Yes, everything's fine. Look, I just wanted to call and apologize for being late—there was a wreck on I-80, and I was stuck in traffic for thirty minutes. Just started moving again and got to a cell spot. I'll be there in about five minutes, give or take two. Is that okay?"

"Yes! That's perfect. We'll be here." Charlotte hung up and spun around on her heels, striding into the living room. Working around people and champagne glasses, she changed the music on the phone to less intrusive background instrumentals and disposed of the garbage littering the table. She freshened the salad and cheese tray and rearranged the gifts her coworkers had gotten their soon-to-be-ex-boss on a small end table by the TV. The others, catching on to her sudden change, began to tidy themselves, too, but only half-heartedly.

Fred even opted to take his tie completely off.

Charlotte examined the room again, dubbing it a worthy scene for McNeely. She herself needed to freshen up and slipped into her bedroom. Standing before the long mirror again, she calmed the spokes of hair curling away from her face and brushed lint and the odd crumb off of her dress. Her face was pale and drawn in the reflection, her arms limp by her sides.

The door to her closet was somewhat open and she could see the soft hooves of her own equine fur suit peeking out from a row of her dresses in the back. Its fur was still soft on her fingers. She had owned it for about ten years now, though she didn't use it often. Occasionally, she would find a listing on craigslist for anonymous 'parties' where people from the area would show up fully costumed and ready to go. There was no pressure, no judgment, no disgust, and no normalcy or standard at those meetings. Charlotte would crawl and buck and nuzzle to her heart's content, feel herself begin to shift into that mentality, becoming the being that didn't have a plan, would have eaten the plan for breakfast. It was a freedom that she only allowed herself to indulge if things got dire and she needed an escape.

Charlotte pulled the costume from its hanger and sat on the bed with it on her lap in a bundle. This new job would take up more of her time, put her under more scrutiny, and alienate her more from those she worked with. And after she got it, what came then? Retirement and death? The fur tickled her nose as she buried her face in it and closed her eyes, trying to get a whiff of that feeling again.

She was about to stand to put it up when there was a sharp knock on her door and a drunk Mathilda Cranch walked in. "Mike, I found her, she's in here—hey, what is that?" Mathilda blinked once, twice, and then her jaw dropped.

Oh no.

"Did you say she was in here?" Mike. *McNeely.*

Oh, god, no.

Charlotte commanded her legs to walk, but they did not respond. Mathilda stared at her with an incredulous expression on her face.

McNeely rounded the door and paused, his eyes two blue marbles swirling from person to person in an attempt to understand the situation he had just walked into. "What the devil?"

Charlotte said nothing. She felt in her chest as though a rift were tearing open, and great bursts of wind were howling through her body, though she sat rigid and blank on the mattress. Brutus and Greta wandered up to the door, and there was a dense beat of silence between them all, the people and the horse costume that was Charlotte's only temptation, only deviant indulgence; her secret now out in the open. For what else could it be? She was sure they could see the tail and its obvious application. There would be no doubt.

Fred Stueffa shuffled quietly up to the door, and in the crook of his arm was Charlotte's trifle. He held a large spoon that she assumed he was going to use to serve the dessert. Without saying a word, Charlotte rose from the bed, letting the costume fall to the floor, and walked past McNeely and Mathilda without meeting their eyes. In her peripheral vision, Charlotte saw Fred gaping at her. As she passed him, she slid her hand under the bowl of trifle and then flipped it upside down and out of Fred's hands.

The crystal shattered on the floor, flinging cream and berries and sponge cake and pudding over them all. No one tried to stop Charlotte from leaving.

James Westman
Laurentian University (Canada)
"Twenty Fifty-Two"

Feng Cabot trudged over scorched earth through the rows of corn under a blistering sun to resume his labor. He would perform the same task as the day before, and the day before that, and tomorrow – harvest for the New East Empire. The temperature was thirty-six degrees centigrade. He could already feel the areas of his pink skin that had peeled yesterday, burning again. It was early November in the former province of Saskatchewan. The harvest season in the former U.S.P.A.C. (United States and Provinces of America and Canada) prairies had moved forward a month, and the start of the growing season back to March since the turn of the century. For a time, this was a fortunate development. Now, it simply meant that Feng toiled two months longer in the dust swept fields each passing year – each passing year the growing season increasing by a few days – that rate itself increasing – while the rest of the world starved, or killed for crumbs and starved.

Faster! A voice shouted in Mandarin. Feng barely understood Mandarin, but he knew the words of his work orders and could otherwise surmise from the barking tone. He shuffled his feet faster until he found himself where he had finished yesterday.

"Zao!" It was Shunyuan.

"Zao," Feng muttered.

"I said, good morning!" Feng turned, pressed his finger to his lips, and let out a harsh: shhhh!

"Whatever! Zao, good morning, means the same thing. As long as I rip the rotten corn off this pathetic stalk and toss it in this here rickety ol' basket, everybody's happy."

"You want the shit kicked out of you again? Don't speak English," Feng hissed through his teeth. "If you don't know Mandarin, don't

talk." Feng began to fill his baskets. Chinese soldiers were walking up
and down the rows; he could see them in the rows ahead and behind
him, through the browning, wilting stalks. Every now and then a
soldier would crack a peeler in the arm with the butt of their rifle,
causing the basket to drop and empty its contents, or smash the peeler
in the back, instantly dropping them to the ground. Sometimes this
was because they were working too slowly; sometimes they were
looking the wrong way; sometimes they were humming a tune; sometimes it was just to relieve boredom. More often than not, a peeler had
let slip a word of English. Or one was rambling on in the old language,
practically begging for a broken rib. Feng hated working near Shunyuan
for this reason.

"I remember when East Manchuria was just Alaska. Hell, I
remember when East Manchuria was just the eastern part of
Manchuria…all the way back in China. Those were the days. Gooks
in gook-land, Patriots in the United States of Patriotic Americans and
Canadians. I still don't get how we lost the war. Well, of course, it
was the EMP…two hundred and fifty miles above Kansas; course, we
didn't see that coming. We were too busy fighting ourselves."

"Shut, up, Shunyuan," Feng muttered, and moved a couple stalks
over to distance himself from the foreign syllables.

"I know you remember it, too, Feng! Now the Constitutionalists,
I understand why they lost Alaska – if they even fought. I think they
just stood on the shore and waved: c'mon over, there's room here for
the nine hundred million of you left! Fucking Constitutionalists. Yes,
we went a bit crazy with the round ups and the camps. I never agreed
with that aspect of the Patriot party. But hell if we couldn't protect our
own damn continent from the chinks" – a rotten cob of corn smacked
Shunyuan in the cheek.

"It's bad enough you're speaking English – but using that word –
you want to get yourself shot in the fucking head?" Feng hissed. All
he could ever do was hiss.

"Chink, chink, chink! Everywhere a chink!" Shunyuan lowered
his voice at least; he was not fully committed to suicide. "Chinks and

peelers. Never knew why we called them chinks, but I know why they call us peelers" – he grabbed the bottom of a cob with one hand and ripped off half the skin from the top with the other. "Well that, and this." Shunyuan pinched a piece of dead skin on his forearm and pulled for as long as he could, loosening a translucent piece and holding it up to the sun, trying to look through it. Despite himself, Feng laughed.

"Oh well…" Shunyuan bent over and gingerly dropped it in the basket. Before he could stand up straight, the butt of a rifle flew between the stalks, caught him in the jawbone, and sent a spatter of blood and fragment of tooth onto the corn.

The soldier was screaming in Mandarin. Feng could not understand a word, the speech was too rapid. Shunyuan lay curled on the ground, holding his face, blood gushing between his fingers. The soldier kept yelling; he was ordering Shunyuan to do something. A black boot collided with his gut. The peeler howled. The boot returned and Shunyuan spat reflexively; red-iron splashed the basket beside his head. Feng was in a panic – they were going to kill him. A second soldier appeared from the stalks and grabbed the first before he could punt again. They started arguing in Mandarin, with the first soldier pointing, arm shaking in fury, at Shunyuan, intermittently screaming only one word in English: peeler. Miraculously, Feng caught a Mandarin term he knew.

"Pledge!" He cried out both in realization and as a lifeline to Shunyuan. The end of the rifle drove into his chest. Feng fell. The pain immense, winded, he put one hand in the dirt to push himself up and began in Mandarin: *"Highest Emperor, I pledge myself to you and the New East Empire. I pledge myself to the health and prosperity of East Manchuria."* Shunyuan dragged himself to his knees and joined in – *"I humbly beg you forgiveness of my transgression, Highest Emperor."* These were the only three proper phrases Feng knew.

The soldiers had stopped shouting. The first spat on Shunyuan's bowed head, and both departed to find some other delinquent peelers. Shunyuan's face was a scarlet mess; his ribs had been spared, but his jaw was broken. Feng wanted to tell him he was lucky to be alive, but he did not know the words and dared not speak the old language.

Feng trudged home – if no floor, three and a half walls and a roof or corrugated steel could be called a home. He supported Shunyuan's weight for the four mile journey. It was five p.m., and still hot outside. The day had been hotter, especially for Shunyuan. There were drinking barrels of filthy water at the end of the corn rows; the contamination of peelers did not matter to the Empire; they were a wholly expendable workforce; there were hundreds of millions of East Manchurian citizens to replace them. Feng had no way to bring hydration to the wounded peeler. He tried to keep his fingers sealed as he cupped his hands to keep the water in, but it was always gone well before he got to the middle of the row.

With Shunyuan heavy on his shoulder, Feng passed through the main gate that would close in an hour, into the bustling shanty town. Peeler Town. The air was foul: filled with smoke of roasting rotten corn the Chinese discarded to feed their workers – shit, piss, and puke (always puke from contaminated water) – and disease. Always the sickening stench of illness; of death. As they lurched through the labyrinth of steel shacks, all became a blur of black, grey, brown and red. Dirt covered in ashes in front of the shacks; brown, sometimes charcoal piles of feces; grey vomit; bright red burned skin from over-exposure; dried blood and rusted steel walls, the colors often indistinguishable.

Feng stopped in front of a shack. Two small girls ran out, excited, but drew back in horror at their father's mangled face. Shunyuan's wife emerged from the door and took him in from Feng, wordlessly. Her face showed shock at the damage, but it was not enough to cry out over. Feng left them without saying goodbye; he had done enough. The sun was getting low and soon it would be dark but for the moon, stars, fires, and soldier's flashlights. It was best not to be wandering during such hours.

After the long day of heat and violence, Feng at least had one thing to which he could look forward. Home was close to the fences by the forest. All the fields they worked had been woodland until the East Manchurian army knocked it down. Crops grew better further north than the traditional prairies to the south, which were halfway to being desert; further south, the old American mid-West was fully desert. The silhouette of the evergreens loomed above. Feng was home.

Qiu raced into his arms as he walked through the door. Glad as he was to see her, he was sore and let out a groan he had planned on suppressing.

"Oh, what's wrong? What happened?" She whispered – always a whisper. The patrols rarely caught the hushed voices of peelers, even with the two wide glassless windows on each side of the door of every shack. But those openings ensured no one had loud conversations in the old tongue. There was no way to police whispers. Unofficially, they were acceptable. Blatant displays of the old culture were what was most offensive.

"I'm fine," Feng hushed. "Shunyuan, not so much."

"He was running his mouth again?" Feng nodded. "Lie down, you need rest." The peeler took his place on the dirty blankets amassed on the ground that made up their bed. Qiu lay down beside him. "I have a surprise for us, John." Feng's arm around Qiu stiffened.

"Don't call me that. You know that's not my name."

"Of course it is, *John*" – she intoned loudly, within the parameters of whisper. "You're John and I'm Mattea."

"No. I'm Feng and you are Qiu. Those are our names, because if" – he lowered his voice further – "John and Mattea use their names, Mattea and John can end up bodies thrown in a pile and set on fire to make steam to give power to the New East Empire." Feng stared into Qiu's eyes attempting to convey the graveness of his concern. Qiu stared back at him...

"...Oh, you're no fun, John. I should have shacked up with a different peeler." Feng rolled his eyes at her and felt, despite himself, more at ease. "I have to show you the surprise!"

"Okay, okay, what's the surprise? A ripe yellow cob?"

"Almost as good." Qiu reached under the blankets and pulled out an object Feng had not seen in a decade, maybe two.

"Where did you get that?" He asked amazed…and then grave: "*How* did you get that?"

"Nicked it from one of the houses today."

"Jesus, Qiu, what were you thinking – if you were to get caught."

"They were fourth rank, won't make a fuss. Our place is almost as nice, except for no power." Feng rolled his eyes again. He took the dull, dented object from her hand and turned it over: *Designed in California. Made in China.*

"How about that…" A 16 GB, 2015 silver iPod Nano. "Well we can never listen to it anyway."

"Sure we can. This model had a built-in speaker. I had one as a kid." Feng's face lit up. "I've been waiting for you to get home to listen to it." The dissident began to scroll through the artists. Indignant and joyous –

"This is *our* music! Why is this even on here? You found this…?"

"In a little girl's room."

"Imagine that. It's all English: American, Canadian, British," he said, moving his thumb over the click-wheel. "This is all illegal. Why is she listening to this?"

"Because she can, I'm sure, Feng," drawing out the last syllable. "Now pick a song, already."

"Oh, I already have!" Qiu beamed.

"What is it?" Feng turned the crack screen toward her. "I don't know that one!"

"Of course you know it, everybody knows it – trust me, you'll recognize it. Fifty years before my time but I know it. Ready?"

"One second." Qiu squeezed herself closer to Feng. "Ready." They pressed play together.

AH-AH-AHHHHH-AH!

"Too loud!"

AH-AH-AHHHHH-AH!

"Turn it down!"

WE COME FROM THE LAND OF THE ICE AND SNOW FROM THE MIDNIGHT SUN WHERE THE HOT SPRINGS FLOW

"I'm trying!"

THE HAMMER OF THE GODS

"It's not working!"

WILL DRIVE OUR SHIPS TO NEW LANDS

A beam of cold light blasted through the window.

TO FIGHT THE HORDES, SINGING AND CRYING

"It's frozen, it won't turn off!"

VALHALLA, I AM COMING!

Two more beams joined the first, swooping, circling, on the back wall.

ON WE SWEEP WITH – "Hurry!" – *THRESHING OAR*

Mandarin shouts moved in their direction.

OUR ONLY GOAL WILL BE THE WESTERN SHORE

Two more beams.

AH-AH-AHHHHH-AH!

Qiu stuffed the iPod deep under the blankets and threw her weight on top, muffling the sound.

AH-AH-AHHHHH-AH!

Too late. They came in as a storm: their Mandarin roars, thunder;

the blow to Feng's head, lightning. He watched from the floor as one soldier grabbed Qiu by her hair and dragged her out the door, the others following: no longer shouting – laughing at their spoil. The image of her face contorted in pain, much more than physically – displaying the knowledge of where she was being taken – was the last thing Feng saw before darkness. The last soldier out fired his boot into Feng's ribs, rolling him over and stopping his heart.

****

He awoke to the usual sounds. Crackling fires. Hushed voices. Chatting Mandarin. How long had it been? That did not matter. Feng pried open his eyes. The walls were blurry. His eyes were moist – running. He touched his fingers to their sides and the put them in front. A blur of ruby. That did not matter. A white hot rage seared, shook his bones. He would kill them. All of them.

Feng pulled himself to his feet unsteadily. He felt drunk; he could hardly stand. There were no white beams swooping in the lane outside. He stepped out the door, turned left into a perpendicular alley, and charged for the evergreens. Several times he tripped and went flying forward into the dirt and the shit outside the shacks, but he had begun the process of rising to his feet before his face hit the ground.

The fence was in front of him: twelve feet tall, barbed wire top. He raced along it in the dark, running his hands over the steel wiring. Could not be far. His fingers clasped air. An opening. The soldiers were in a hurry. Did not want to rile up all of Peeler Town. Feng slipped through quickly but quietly, and bolted headlong into the trees.

He stopped. Listened. Nothing. He kept sprinting, tripped on a root, got back up again, ran. He stopped. Listened…voices. They were coming from the north – Mandarin – celebratory. Feng used all his mental faculty to slow his body down and approach quietly. There was a sliver of moon, and coupled with the stars, it was enough to see into the clearing. The shapes were blurry but he could make out a wall of bodies, encircling. There was a rock tighter in his hand than he had ever held anything. The rock was his plan. He did not even remember picking it up.

Then a sound in the still of the forest – the soldiers were no longer shouting or laughing, merely steadfast in intention – that rang out like a gunshot to Feng. The creak of a well-worn zipper descending. Mental faculties were abandoned from the spot at which Feng's body departed, surging toward the circle as if an animal jumped out of his skin. Before he could reach them – two more sounds, one followed instantaneously by the other. A whish – a whistle – traveling through the air at supernatural speed – then gasping and gurgling.

Mandarin screams echoed through the clearing, and the soldiers scattered in multiple directions. One passed right by Feng, heading south to where they had come from. Both were too shocked to act on their proximity. Feng heard light footsteps.

"Qiu," he cried and dove to the ground to cover her. Thank God, Feng exalted. She was still clothed. "I'm here, I'm here, I'm here, I'm here," he repeated and held her trembling body. The footsteps grew closer and the gurgling persisted; the gasping had stopped. "Who are you?" Feng demanded, voice quavering. The figure stopped, looming above him. Through the blur in his eyes and by the light of the moon sliver and stars, John saw a face. A ghost.

Her features were uncanny. So strange, yet so familiar. He had not seen a face like hers since he was a teenager. "You're Indian!" The ghost snorted in derision, bent forward and pulled an arrow out of the soldier's neck. The gurgling ceased.

"That's right, I charted the last plane out of New Delhi before the bombs landed."

"I mean – I mean, Native! That's what you were called, right? But I thought – I thought there were none of you left."

"You thought the Patriots killed us all. You thought you killed us all."

"No, I was never a Patriot. Well, I was, technically, living in the Patriot states. But I hated the Patriots. I supported the Constitutionalists."

"What did you do to support them?"

"Well, I was only a teenager" –

"Old enough to pick sides. Old enough to try to stop it."

"I did! I mean, I wanted to, but they would have killed me and my whole family. Anyone who was a Constitutionalist..."

"Believe me, I know what it's like to have your whole family killed in front of you. I was in the camps." John fell silent. "You weren't in the camps, were you?"

"No – I – I..."

"So you weren't a Constitutionalist."

"If I hadn't sworn allegiance to the Patriots."

"If all people like you had refused to swear allegiance to the Patriots, we would not be here right now. I would not be in these woods, with the blood of a dead East Manchurian soldier on my arrow, and I would not be looking here for any lost survivors of my kind. For my people – Patriot or Constitutionalist - it did not matter, we were thrown in the camps. And it wasn't so wonderful for us before that either, not in U.S.P.A.C., not even in Canada." The ghost turned to leave.

"Wait! You saved our lives. Please, take us with you."

"No."

"Please! You can train us. To live your way."

"Train you? To live like us? You think we can all fire a bow and arrow and hit our mark in the woods at night? Some of us haven't lived our way for over a century. We need to teach our own again to live our way." John paused, grasping for a response.

"I know how to shoot, right Mattea?"

"John, let's just go! There's no time. We need to get out of here. We can go anywhere. Anywhere but here!" John ignored her.

"I fought in the war. I can teach you how to defend yourself – all of yourselves. Against the East Manchurians. Against the remaining

Patriots. We'll find guns. You'll be safer – stronger. We can teach you our way." The ghost's face looked at John, eyes ablaze.

"You already did."

And she slipped away into the black trees.

A hurricane of voices drew near.

Mandarin.

A.C. Monks
Endicott College
"Ink Inherent"

It started the day some genius idiot invented hereditary tattoos.

The celebrities were, of course, the first to indulge. At ten years old, Jennabelle Marqette remembered seeing little hearts and stars and skulls plastering her sidebar news feeds in vibrant color, accompanied by words like "Vivianna Shee says, 'The heart is so my future kid knows I love her—always.'" But "hereditary tattoo" was a hassle to pronounce, especially drunk, which was when a number of people considered getting one. The inventors called it legacy ink.

Nine months after legacy ink darkened the first scrap of famous skin, the mothers who'd gotten pregnant as fast as possible (for their prime grab at publicity) started popping out little darlings with a new kind of birthmark. Jennabelle's mother wrinkled her nose at the dinner table—a cedar circle made for three, but which only held two and a faux-flower centerpiece.

"Why is it," the older woman sighed, her breath burdened, "that we get hereditary tattoos before we get something useful? Like teleportation."

"I think the legacy ink is cool," remarked Jennabelle, who was now eleven and starting to consider silly things like individualism and teenage rebellion. Her shoulder itched for a blue crescent moon for the second she turned eighteen. Literally. There was a 24/7 tattoo parlor in the next city over, though she heard you had to reserve midnight appointments a year in advance. Her plan wasn't original. Most of Jennabelle's plans weren't.

"In fourth grade, you thought pink camouflage was cool," said her mother. "Trust me, Jensie, those kids are going to hate them."

Jennabelle plowed her fork through store-brand diet spaghetti and low-cal tomato sauce, forcing the stiff strands into a frowny face.

"But it's like a birthmark. Besides, *you* have a tattoo." The fork was jabbed in her mother's direction. It wasn't a polite gesture, but it was plenty pointed.

"I chose my tattoo," her mother defended. One protective hand flew to cover the white dove at the back of her neck. "Tattoos are supposed to be something to define yourself with, not something your parents pick for you."

"Yeah?" Jennabelle argued. "Well, I didn't get to pick my hair color either, but you won't let me dye it. At least legacy ink *says* something about where you come from."

The words echoed. Not in the room, but in a choir of voices as they became legacy ink's strongest defense. When older generations launched campaigns against the fad, the media and its youthful followers tried to soothe them by saying, "Being born with legacy ink is like a way of honoring your heritage."

Jennabelle held firmly to this belief. She smiled at babies in supermarkets bearing bracelets of roses. One child of two legacy ink-bearing parents possessed a jagged pattern overlaid with the outline of a butterfly — a design Jennabelle critiqued as *distinctive.* Seeing a marked parent holding a clean-slate child became strange. They were *blank*, somehow. They were like the new building at her school had been before the Phantom Painters Graffiti Gang got to it. Now it was a mural. Koi fish commenced a Piscean ballet with slick-scaled dragons across galaxies of stars: newborn, dying, and stars that were not stars but snowflakes. The students called it the Wall of Inspiration. The faculty, minus her eccentric psychology teacher, called it an act of delinquency. Jennabelle loved it. A body-wide zing sparked through her whenever her hands raked across the painted grit, or whenever she secretly kissed it like her own personal Blarney Stone (minus the hanging upside down part). She wished she could join its creators, but they weren't called the Phantom Painters because they were easy to find. None of them had ever been caught. Also, Jennabelle sucked at art. Making faces out her spaghetti had been her best talent.

In her head, though, she liked to entertain this fantasy of stumbling in on the middle of a night-dipped project — of meeting a tall figure in a black, paint-splotched hoodie, who would swear her to secrecy under the light of a single street lamp. He'd have to keep an eye on her, of course, and then love would take them, as inevitable as the tide taking the beach. She imagined if he got legacy ink, it would be something exotic and beautiful. Her blue crescent moon would fit flawlessly into it and their child would be a true work of art. This little daydream usually played out during various science classes, sometimes history.

In high school, she both marveled and pouted from the under-eighteen corner as her friends were marked, one by one. Everyone except for Joshy, her lab partner, who often said the same things Jennabelle's mother said. He was a nice guy, but he was too conscientious of the rules and always scowled at the latest trends, dubbing them "superficial" and "sociological oppression of individual expression." He wasn't what Jennabelle would call young at heart. As she counted down the days on the calendar until her birthday, he leaned over and asked, "What's the thirty-seven for?"

"Nosy," she chided, clutching the tablet to her chest. God forbid he glimpse the slew of misshapen doodles — definitely *not* up to spaghetti-face par. Joshy's hands shot skywards in surrender. He couldn't have looked any less criminal. Jennabelle was pondering a retort she hoped was witty when her friend Franklyn rolled her chair clear across the room, playing one-way bumper-cars with Joshy.

"It's how many days until she's old enough to get legacy ink," Franklyn sang, flashing her own legacy inked ankle — the Chinese symbol for *dream*. She'd been debating between that and the symbol for *bad*. As in, *bad-to-the-bone*. Franklyn was all leather, coffee, and dark lipstick; the terrible influence everyone secretly wanted in their lives.

Excluding Joshy, it would seem. He looked so downcast about Jennabelle's legacy ink idealism that she might as well have insulted him and all his ancestors for the last three-thousand years. She told him as much. It had been the kind of witty comment she was looking for earlier, and she was pleased when it got a snort from Franklyn. Joshy, if anything, became more serious. "Why don't you just get a normal tattoo? You know, and *not* voluntarily mutate your DNA skin-cell by skin-cell?"

"Because getting legacy ink is like…passing down a piece of your soul to your kid," Jennabelle said, quite possibly plagiarizing a forum somewhere.

"Yeah," Franklyn agreed. She threw her arms behind her choppy-haired head, an act of such nonchalance that it challenged Joshy's very existence. "Have you ever seen those orphans and they're like, 'This is all I have left of my mom-slash-dad?' Why wouldn't you want to? Even I got one, and chances are I won't be pumping out kids, but, you know, just in case. It's sweet."

"Sweet?" Joshy's eyebrows and vocal pitch climbed too high to be natural. "Tell that to my four-year-old cousin, who's a boy with a daisy chain on his ankle. He's going to be mocked for life—or have to always wear high socks."

Franklyn kicked Joshy's chair. Always with the kicking. "Sexist. No one's going to care about that."

"What about six generations from now? People will be covered head-to-toe in these things and they'll all be so different that it will look like some tattoo artist was high when he picked up the needle."

It was his only point that Jennabelle hesitated at, seizing a moment so small that it was like catching a firefly, and she pictured herself with bracelets on every limb and a miscellany of images up and down her back. Skulls next to song lyrics, dragons wearing daffodils, crosses battling zigzags. But wasn't that exactly what the Phantom Painters had depicted in their crowning mural? A dozen souls mingling into a single picture? A miniature universe? Maybe that was the kind of world people were meant to live in. The moment blinked out, suffocated by Franklyn's speech, as the girl said, "It will be a family tree. But visible. You'll see—no pun intended. It'll be cool."

Three years after that conversation, straight-backed Joshy was outed as part of the Phantom Painters Graffiti Gang. They'd been hitting an underpass, transforming it into a medley of Van Gogh's works with their own spin, when *wee-ooh-wee-ooh-wee-ooh- drop the spray paints, kids.* Three were caught, and it was unknown how many dark shapes had darted into the shadows, drops of ink disappearing into an inkwell. The dashboard cam's video went viral. Jennabelle's high school friends spammed her social media walls with it.

What struck her most was how *innocent* Joshy had looked as the cop slammed him against the front of the car, ripping off his hood and black mask. His face was a freeze frame of a boy falling off a bike for the first time, gravel imminent. It didn't fit- *arrested* and *vandal.* That image made it into every single petition to reduce the Painters' punishments. Meanwhile, the unfinished work began attracting the attention of local photographers, then national photographers, then news teams and arts activists, until the Painters were not only released with a slap on the wrist, but were begrudgingly given permission to finish the piece. The power of PR. All hail.

The whole ordeal left Jennabelle's mouth twisted and soured. Her fantasies were fraudulent. All those daydreams of meeting a Phantom Painter, falling in love, having legacy inked children, watching art inherited across generations until people became murals? Joshy had condemned every single one. So had his Painter friends. Examining the blue crescent moon on her shoulder, Jennabelle decided it was time to reconstruct her fantasies. They began to include the boy from her college Counterculture Literature seminar.

Jennabelle's son screamed at the harsh fluorescent lights of the maternity ward eleven years later, eight months after her wedding and two months after her divorce, with a crescent moon on his left shoulder and a metal chain around his bicep. She thought about the adoption paperwork she'd half-filled out after her ex stopped answering her calls. She could finish it. She could sign her name, get skin-tightening surgery on her stomach, pack up the surprise baby shower gifts, and it would be like none of this had ever happened. She'd seen what single motherhood had done to her own mother, sitting not two feet away from her: eye bags, grocery bags, tight lips, tight budget, thin skin thinly veiled with too much make-up, and a smile that lacked shine. Then Jennabelle looked at her son's shoulder, and she looked at her shoulder, and she knew she would make that trade. Tracing the empty space between the moon and the chain on his arm, she whispered, "How about Shamus?"

The painkillers helped her ignore the part of her brain that told her the first syllable of that was "shame."

She also ignored (or tried to ignore) the protestors on the screens and in the rumors—teenage extremists pushing laws for skin-graft tattoo removal surgery at an earlier age and with partial insurance coverage. Anna Luke, the figurehead of the movement, was the twenty-year-old daughter of Mary Luke-Hayes, one of the first stars to get legacy ink. This young woman's fake strawberry blonde hair and heart-shaped face gained weekly coverage, and she would end every press event with her arms held stiffly open, as if to hug the audience. The gesture was not as friendly as that. It showcased the scars on her wrists, most striking through a tangle of lines—two legacy inks that hadn't agreed, gnawing at each other. "The only reason I don't get this mess removed," she said, "is so you all can all *see*. Although, sadly, for most, the damage has already been done. Your choice has become our disease."

More and more rules were placed on legacy ink procedures until it became all but illegal. Jennabelle watched the restrictions fly through the courthouses: only unisex legacy inks allowed; only the designs listed below allowed; only *this* size; only *this* many; only with *these* taxes; only with these *higher* taxes; only after psychological evaluation; only-only-only.

In a world of only, Shamus turned thirteen.

"Why did you do this to me?!" he screeched, yanking up his T-shirt sleeve as far as it would go. A blue crescent moon and a chain, forever separate. Shamus had always been an easy crier, though he refused to now, because being grown up meant a red-stained, but dry face. His hair, perpetually spiky like his father's, crept in on *bird's nest* territory, and she knew he'd been pulling at it hard like she'd told him not to. *Do you want to go bald early?* The skin around the legacy ink was scratched raw. All of the online forums, blogs, and news articles that Jennabelle had sifted through told her that wasn't unusual, that it could have been worse. *Girl burns shoulder in attempt to remove legacy ink. Illegal skin-graft ring discovered. Drug-use rates rising: Connection to second-generation legacy ink-bearers?* Facts and figures filed through her head as, again, he yelled, "Why?"

"You should be proud," Jennabelle said. Her fingernails dug into her hips with her feet spread and her chin jutting upward, almost looking down her nose, the way her mother had always done. Yet her sleeves were carefully arranged to conceal the mark. They had been for a while. "It's a piece of your heritage."

"No, it's something you and my dead-beat dad thought was cool when you were eighteen. Now, it's a stupid decision I have to live with."

Jennabelle wanted to tell him that the world was much more stupid than that; that in a few years, he'd see it in all its messy, screwed-up glory. If she didn't have to be the adult here, she would scream, then whisper, then tell him about the Phantom Painters, including Joshy, and her ironic high-school daydreams.

But she did have to be the adult here, and she couldn't tell him what she wanted to, so she forced herself to remember that the problem here was Shamus' disrespect, not her own muddled past. She tried to look more imposing. "You are *not* talking to me like that," Jennabelle seethed. "Keep it up and I'm going to block access to your gaming sites."

"Go ahead!" Shamus' face grew red and, with all of these violently exaggerated gestures, it was a wonder he hadn't run himself out of breath yet. It looked like running a marathon, Jennabelle might have said. Shamus would have compared it instead to running into a brick wall. Repeatedly. With the aim to get amnesia.

"Consider yourself grounded."

Shamus rolled his eyes and stomped down the hall. His hand stopped dead on the doorknob to his room. Without turning, he said, "Just so you know, I asked Maygan out. She said, 'No.' Because she's clean. And I'm not. And that's your fault."

There is no love like that of a child or hate like that of an adult. Staring at Shamus, Jennabelle saw more adult than child. A half-hearted, default speech about melodrama began building in her throat. He must have sensed it coming. The door slammed shut, almost on her toes, loudly enough to make her eardrums ring. In contrast, her subsequent escape through the front door was nothing but a sigh.

Jennabelle was going grocery shopping. She needed ingredients for a tried-and-true heartbreak helper: absurd quantities of coffee, chocolate, ice cream, and diet pills. Of course, like in any proper bad day, as soon as she pulled into the parking lot, it started raining. Cold, wet condemnation. With a huff, she grabbed a cart and began what was meant to be a silent storm down the aisles. The cart wheels squeaked when she turned. By the time she reached the deli, where a televised newsfeed perched on the counter to entertain people while they waited, she was ready to hit something. And break it.

Anna Luke the Revolutionary was the last person she wanted to see blinking onto the screen. The legacy ink's main protestor spread her arms in her signature rebar embrace. The subtitles glared, "As of last week, Anna Luke is officially the adoptive mother of an unfortunate legacy inked baby." Up popped a picture of a baby with black scribbles like Anna Luke's, but ingrained from his face down to his shoulder. "According to a recent study, legacy inked babies are five times less likely to be adopted as clean babies."

Jennabelle's mother had often told her of a time when the news was occasionally printed on paper. She wished this news was on paper. Then she could have torn it to shreds. Goodbye, Anna Luke.

Behind Jennabelle, a small family slipped into line. The mother was bouncing her child on her hip, hoping to calm him. Jennabelle stared—which probably weirded them out, but she knew they must have gotten it all the time. The father bore ink lines on all visible parts of his skin, minus his face. The mother was almost as blanketed. Their child, though, had skin like snow before footprints were smashed into it. Blank, white, *clean*.

When was the last time Jennabelle had seen a child with inked parents and not thought how strange it was that the markings weren't passed down alongside oversized ears and short stature? Jennebelle thought about being eighteen again, sitting on the chair at the tattoo parlor, signing papers that said she understood the implications of getting legacy ink -- as much as an eighteen-year-old understood anything. There had been a spark of doubt across her synapses. In classic cartoon style, she'd felt an angel and a devil weighing on her shoulders, though neither of them had worn costumes to say which was which. (In the end, who wore the wings and who wore the horns was always unstably subjective.) She'd imagined her shoulder-guides to be Joshy and Franklyn. One, the liar, with a secret life as a "vandal" and a passion for art, had told her that this was a decision she wasn't making for just herself. The other, a vibrant girl who never even *planned* to have kids, had told her it was cool. She'd swiped Joshy off her shoulder, and put a blue crescent moon in his place.

Jennabelle glanced from the supermarket television to the couple; Anna Luke to the clean baby. She cleared her throat, though that didn't remove all of the gruffness. "He looks like a sweetheart. What's his name?"

"Shamus," the couple said in tandem. Recited.

Jennabelle forced a faint upward twitch of the lips. She hoped it looked like a smile. "Funny. That's my son's name, too."

"It's a good name," the mother said. "Number 286 on the list of popular names, so it's not too popular, but not too weird."

"Is he adopted?"

The mother's head shook like a dog in the rain — hard and enthusiastic. "We have normal tattoos. I have to tell you, though, it was so strange when he came out clean. I guess I just kind of expected that he wouldn't. All this legacy ink stuff."

"Are you glad? That you didn't get one?"

There's something to be said for asking questions you don't want the answers to. That something was probably a four letter word not allowed on broadcast television, even after ten at night.

"Every day."

Numbly, Jennabelle finished her shopping and sat in her car. The keys rested in the ignition, unturned. If she didn't drive back soon, the ice cream in the trunk was going to melt. She reached for the key, only for her hand to fall back into her lap. Ten seconds passed. Twenty. She had to battle the deadness inside just to grab her phone.

"Mom?"

"Jennabelle?" her mother answered. "What's wrong? You usually don't call me unless something's wrong. And why are you blocking the video feed?"

You usually don't call me unless something's wrong. Jennabelle pursed her lips and tried to ignore the nausea in her stomach. "Oh, you know, bad hair day," she lied with a pitiful laugh. Not that that could trick Hayley Marquette. The woman knew *bad hair day* was more-or-less code for *I'm so upset my mascara is smearing.* "I was wondering if you could take Shamus for the weekend."

"Need some down time, huh?"

"We both do." An invisible hand seemed to clench around her throat. Another one held a fire poker to the crescent moon on her shoulder. She decided it was because she hadn't had enough coffee, chocolate, ice cream, or diet pills yet, since they were still sitting in the trunk. "We had another fight. It wasn't even the worst one, but… Shamus hates me. He thinks the legacy ink ruined his life and it doesn't matter that I like it, because he *hates* it, Mom. He hates it so much. And I know you told me so, so you don't have to say it."

Her mother sighed, the phone screen capturing every inch that her shoulders dropped. "Jensie, all kids hate their parents for something. Sometimes, they're things we can control. Others, they're not. You

used to get mad at me for your hair color. *'I want to be blonde, like Dad.'*
On and on you'd go, until you came back from a slumber party at
fifteen with the blondest blonde hair possible. You were all set to start
screaming about free will as soon as you walked through the door."

Jennabelle remembered. The lingering smell of bleach, the jitter
of fresh guilt, the prepared anger. "I was so sure I was going to be
grounded." Plans on how to spend a weekend in her room. "But
you said—"

"Honey blonde would have looked better." Her mother reeked of
wryness and amusement, snorting at that memory. "Oh, God, the look
on your face."

The look of someone who needed the Heimlich because she was
choking on shouts that had nowhere to go. "I'm sure it was hilarious,"
Jennabelle muttered. "From your perspective." She put her hand on
her temple, recalling how she'd tested out color after color, seeing
which one would piss her mom off the most. Pink had come the
closest. "But seriously, Mom, can you take Shamus this weekend?"

"I could," said Hayley Marquette, "but I'm not going to."

"What? Why?!"

"It won't solve the problem."

"Mom—"

"Eh, sorry, you're—*crrrrr*—breaking up." Her mother made pitiful
attempts to sound like static. Apparently, she hadn't gotten the fake
static app yet. She blacked out the camera with her thumb. "Talk to
you—*crrrrr*—soon. Love you, bye."

Beep. Jennabelle gawked open-mouthed at the phone. Did she
really just…? Yes, yes she did. Jennabelle half-laughed at the situation,
and half-sobbed into her palms, face against the steering wheel, ice
cream continuing to melt in the trunk.

Twenty minutes later, she stood at her son's door, pressing apologies
through the wood. "I'm sorry, Shamus."

"No, you're not. Leave me alone."

Her rain-chilled fingers brushed over her mark. "What do you want me to say? It seemed like a good idea at the time? I still like it and, back then, I thought you would appreciate it, too." She thought about the day he was born—how seeing that tiny moon had dissuaded her from finishing the adoption paperwork. "In my defense, you weren't exactly there to weigh in on the matter."

There was a creek, the small earthquake of a teenage boy walking, and then the door cracked open. Shamus stood there with his arms crossed and his eyes boring holes in the floor, still more adult than child. "Grandma told you not to."

"If I'd done everything Grandma told me to do, I'd be damn boring." She smirked; the rare swearing had caught Shamus off guard. In her mind, she knew he'd heard worse on the bus. "I also would have had nicer hair in my high school senior picture, but that's beyond the point. What I mean is: sure, I made mistakes, but that's part of growing up, or so all those cheesy movies tell me. You'll screw up plenty before you're my age. So I'm not sorry I got the ink, but I'm sorry it hurt you."

Shamus lifted his head to meet her eyes. It felt like some sort of victory—not exactly a white flag of surrender; more like living to see another sunrise on the battlefield. The war wasn't over, but this was another night you hadn't died.

"…Why a crescent moon?" he asked at last. "Why, really?"

She opened her mouth, made a sound that was more like a frog's croak than a human word, then closed her mouth. Of course she knew. Deep down, she knew, even if she'd always answered, "Because it's cool" or "mysterious" or "symbolizes change." Those were easier to say. But this was *necessary* to say. Her hand lifted from her moon-graced shoulder, uncovering it. "Did I ever tell you your Grandpa was an amateur astronomer?" She knew she hadn't. Her memory wasn't that bad yet. "He could name the craters on the moon, the lunatic. The only one I remember is Grimaldi, because he told me it looked like the man in the moon had a mole." She gazed at Shamus as if through new eyes. There were her father's dorky ears and his high eyebrows; and wasn't that the expression she'd seen in a photo of him on his birthday, when they'd replaced the normal candles with trick candles that didn't go out no matter how hard you blew? Jennabelle laughed despite the severity of the situation. "So, I guess I thought it was appropriate. The legacy ink was my piece of him that I could pass down to you."

Shamus looked away.

Her son did not forgive her on the spot. Actually, he didn't forgive her at all, but he did stop shouting about it as much. By the time he hit eighteen, skin therapy became evolved and accessible enough to remove his legacy ink permanently. He looked freer that summer, dashing about with clean skin, a grin as wide as it ever had been. He hugged her more. He talked about Someone Special.

Then two summers later, the blue crescent moon returned, chain-less though stark, and Jennabelle was ready to cry. She thought, *The therapy stopped working* and *Shamus will go back to hating me*. Her son halted her mid-panic-attack. "Mom, calm down," he said, smiling with all the softness of a summer cloud. "It's just a regular tattoo."

Somewhere during her contest-winning fish impression, Jenna-belle remembered how to pronounce the word "Why?"

Shamus shrugged. "Feels right this time. Like it means something because I chose it."

She snapped a picture of him with it and went through the trouble to get it printed on gloss-paper and framed for her work desk. This was also the picture she made into her phone's background for the first high school reunion she bothered going to, which Franklyn did not attend, but Joshy did. Since graduation, he'd been living a decent life as a freelance graphic designer, spurred on by that run of Phantom Painters publicity, like crime was the greatest asset to his résumé. She didn't get much of a chance to talk to him, what with his popularity. However, their brief conversation mostly revolved around pretending to fathom why they'd lost touch. Then the night ended, communications returned to radio silence, and they didn't meet up at any subsequent reunions.

Over the race of years approaching and passing, like signs on a highway without a map, Jennabelle soon realized she was lucky: her shoulder ink had aged well, unlike a few of her friends, who now had legacy inks and tattoos that sagged with their skin. Those unfortunate few would often go into the winter with the mark and come out of it with a clear complexion.

Jennabelle kept her own, under the impression she'd be dishonoring *Shamus* now if she had it taken off. His wife thought his was cute. His daughter adopted it onto her ankle.

Maybe there could be different kinds of hereditary.

Joseph Pardoe
University of Bradford (England)
"Live Without Limits"

Welcome, ladies and gentlemen. I am Reverend Maguire. A title which ought to be entirely inconsequential to you this evening. I exist only as your conduit to a new life.

A murmur of affirmation resounded through the conference hall. Taylor's voice, lost among thousands.

I want you all to close your eyes.

Taylor did as she was told after glancing around to make sure everyone else was playing ball. She'd always been that kind of person; unerringly cautious until she saw that others were willing to place their trust first.

We're going to embark upon a journey together tonight. But remember, in order to coexist, one must first annihilate the self. I say again, we're in this *together*!

When Maguire said - actually, shouted - that last bit, something ignited in Taylor's chest. She became uncontrollably excited. It was as though she teetered at the summit of a rollercoaster: Maguire's voice, the tick-tick-tick tease of the last few feet of track before…

Excellent. I see a lot of smiling faces. Ardent. Expectant. My next instruction is the most important, so please listen very carefully and do exactly as I say.

Taylor held her breath. The anticipation was intense. It had been a fortnight since she'd picked up the flyer at her local community center: "Live Without Limits", the typeface had baited. Well, here she was at last, ready and willing to do whatever it took in the name of freeing herself.

Castor sugar. Reappear. Constellation. Bronchial.

Maguire began stringing together a series of random words. It reminded Taylor of when she'd installed voice recognition software on her laptop; the program had had to get used to her voice before it could operate properly. She opened her eyes a tiny peep: Those around her kept theirs closed, obediently. Some nodded as Maguire went on, as though they understood something Taylor could not.

Consternation. Dominican. Homestead. Steadfast.

Maguire paused. People shifted in their seats.

If any of you still have your eyes open, please close them tightly. And keep them closed.

Taylor obeyed.

Hope. Keepsake. Longevity. Forester.

The silence that followed seemed to last for a long time.

You are each within me now. And I, within you.

Taylor was overwhelmed by an enormous sense of anticlimax. Something was definitely supposed to have happened. There ought to have been some "Internal Realignment"; that's what the flyer had promised. All you had to do was sit there and listen.

Here, the chains of fear lie broken. The burdens of confusion and hopelessness are offloaded forevermore. In me, you invest your trust wholeheartedly and I shall reward your faith handsomely. Tonight, we bear witness to the advent of a brave new world.

Tears began to dampen Taylor's cheeks. Still, she felt nothing.

But first, sweethearts, you each have a duty to fulfill. You were handed a tool when you arrived, yes?

Taylor gripped the handle of her cleaver tightly. Upon entering the building that evening, she'd watched those ahead of her in the queue receive a 'tool' of their own from the doormen; knives, hammers, screwdrivers, bundles of barbed wire. Everyone had accepted theirs as par for the course, so it seemed, so Taylor had followed suit.

I'm going to count down from three. When I reach zero, we will root out any unbelievers that may be corrupting the sanctity of this hall. Then, we shall take to the streets. If we do not purge this city, our home, of impure souls, then we can never advance to the next step. And if we shirk our responsibility here, we will never...

You could hear a pin drop.

Live without limits.

Taylor nodded vigorously. She didn't understand what was going on, but the promise of freedom cut through loud and clear. Since dropping out of university, she'd worked a succession of menial labour jobs to make ends meet. Limits, in other words. Her life consisted of little else.

Three. Two. Ready, sweethearts? One... Zero.

A sudden, piercingly loud scraping sound echoed through the conference hall. It sounded like a gigantic guillotine being dropped from a rusted frame. After seconds of fighting the urge, Taylor opened her eyes. Every member of the three thousand-strong audience had turned their chairs towards her at precisely the same moment. Their eyes were wide and staring, filled with ecstatic hatred. Jaws hung open. Drool trickled from chins. They held their 'tools' above their heads; scorpions with poisonous stingers, poised to strike.

Ladies and gentlemen, we have our unbeliever.

Rebecca Kaplan
University of Michigan Law School
"The Way Home"

The forest that surrounded Hawley College was mostly unknown, though many had marked trails through it. Many also claimed that they knew the forest like the back of their hand. However, when asked to guide others to a certain cabin or river, those who boasted this were often puzzled to find that the path they *knew* would lead to certain cabin or river in fact did not. Still these claimants knew more about the forest than most, so they were deemed "experts." Subsequently, they taught lectures on the forest, wrote books on it and even gave guided tours on the parts of the forest which they had explored most thoroughly.

The experts created many rules for exploring the forest. Usually these rules were followed because the experts had experienced more of the forest than anyone else, and therefore, more readily understood its dangers and what needed protection within. Some of these rules were necessary ("You shall not chase anyone through the forest with an axe") and some were arbitrary ("You shall not pluck daisies along the beaten path"). However, the experts generally agreed to one overarching rule: "Unless there is a preexisting rule, you can do as you please."

Naturally, critics claimed that this rule was irrelevant because there were so many preexisting rules that one could never truly do as they pleased, but even these critics accepted that in the abstract this principle made sense because it allowed forest-explorers freedom in discovering new aspects of the forest which could benefit society overall.

The biggest proponent of the experts' overarching rule was Randolph Burger. The thirty-year-old Randolph had a forehead wider than his chin—as was common among keen thinkers—a beaklike nose, little ears and a scrutinizing gaze. The other experts delighted in conversing with Randolph, so quick and so bright, proficient at hiding his despair at never knowing the full depths of the forest. Even unsure undergraduates and weary travelers felt quicker and brighter after speaking with him. Indeed, he attracted a massive following of those who sought to feel intelligent as his challenges to others' ideas and his discourse concerning the rules of the forest made each listener feel expert.

When spring had flowered every dogwood tree and blossomed every iris, Randolph Burger hosted a small get-together at his chalet. He sent on compostable paper an invitation to every renowned expert and one no one had heard of: Viola Clark. He read in the campus newspaper about her research concerning the recent rise of phosphorous in the forest's southernmost ponds. Randolph, who fancied that which was "ahead of the curve" and found her reasoning valid and her topic of interest, felt that she would make an excellent addition to his guest list. *Perhaps*, he thought, *she will earn the respect of enough experts at the party to become mainstream.*

The first guest at Randolph's party was the soft-spoken Francis Mae, darling of the Biology department. Randolph had just finished researching the migration of crows from the west of the forest to the east. He mentioned his research to Francis as she entered. He called the migration as all fashionable experts called it: "The exodus."

"How intriguing," said Francis, impressed by Randolph's handling of a topic as complex as crow migration. She wore a pink cardigan and gray knit skirt, socks with a koala print, and a faint smile. She greeted Randolph with a light hug, which seemed to display both her entire strength and the quietude of her enthusiasm. She spoke with the tranquility of a parent soothing a temperamental child as she helped herself to brie and Stilton. "I must know how you stumbled upon this subject."

"I found it the way that any expert finds anything," said Randolph. "Through exploration of the forest, I noticed that the crows that woke me each morning had suddenly vanished, and so I looked everywhere until I found them on the eastern side."

"What about your survey on the minerals of the northern rocks? I thought researching them was your primary goal."

"It was preempted. I know I have a propensity for unoriginal subject matter."

"A truly honorable expert would rescind his work so you could research what you pleased."

"You're charming," said Randolph. The words fell flat—caught between delight by her patronage and disgust at her conclusion. "Tell me, do you know anything about Viola Clark?"

"She's quite new," said Francis. She shut in like a daylily at the touch of night. "Why? Has she spoken about me?"

"I only know her from the campus newspaper. They published an article on her research."

"It might be wise to take the opposite view of whatever she's arguing."

"Dear Francis, I'm not sure that she's one I want to fight."

"I'm just saying that she seems like the type to favor entirely original ideas over the refinement of theories, so even counterarguments to her work would be generally original."

Yes, thought Randolph. *That seems fair.*

"Additionally," said Francis, "in creating her article, she would've conducted most of the research for you."

Randolph nodded vigorously. "You make an excellent point!"

Randolph moved actively as though animated by the concepts and ideas he sought to explore, while Francis tread cautiously. She brought to Randolph's mind a ballerina dancing on glass: Pretty, perfect and isolated, careful not to misstep, and aware of an audience that she must not disappoint. Even when hurt, she thought highly of her station and kept a downward glance at the world, which compelled her to refuse help when offered.

Still, Randolph felt obliged to try.

"I'm sure she says kind things about you," said Randolph.

"Please," said Francis. "She doesn't even know me."

Within hours, guests filled the chalet. Only the finest experts gathered there. They remarked on the delicacy of the china, the rustic lamps hanging from the wall, the wildflowers, which Randolph had picked from the forest that morning, decked throughout the rooms. Even the first expert attended the party. She brought Australasian wine brewed from elderberries and rose.

Randolph greeted each guest with a hug and assembled their food and drink on the increasingly cluttered banquet table. Randolph handled the situation tactically, setting the least enjoyable food and drink ("gluten-free quinoa mash" and "kale beer") at the edges, while setting the more popular meals in the middle. The food and drink at the edges required a firm touch to ensure their steadiness. The guests laughed to mask their worry that the food and drink that they brought would fall, and secretly the guests severed any attachment to whatever they brought to enjoy the evening more freely.

The last arrival was a tall woman with a strong jawline, long dark hair, a leather jacket, a pearl-colored blouse, slacks and heels. This was, without a doubt, Viola Clark. Randolph drank a healthy dose of wine. Though he was one of the most cited experts, his hands shook as he approached her. He could only attribute this nervousness to the certainty and pride with which she stood, and her stern, acute gaze.

"Welcome to my little get-together," said Randolph. He hugged her, and she awkwardly reciprocated. "Allow me to take your food or drink."

"I apologize," she said. "I didn't bring any."

Randolph, afraid that his assumption embarrassed her, attempted to save the situation: "Well then, permit me to get you some."

"If you wish."

He collected a plate of food for her as he spoke: "I found your research on the ponds extremely interesting. It caught my eye in the campus newspaper."

"If I had known that other experts read it, then I wouldn't have accepted the interview."

"Well, only proper experts read the newspaper, but I'm afraid I don't follow, why would you have refused the interview?"

"I'm somewhat protective of my work in the researching phase," said Viola. Randolph attempted to make eye contact, but she kept her gaze on the table. "Someone could extrapolate from what the newspaper published and write my article before I do."

"No honorable expert would do that."

"I want to believe you, but I question whether the competitiveness in our field deters us from having honor." She smiled — a crack in the veneer. "In any case, I'm pleased that someone noticed my work. I worry that ultimately it will have no impact."

"Why, my dear," said Randolph as he poured her a full glass of wine. "Your work is of the utmost importance."

Randolph and Viola sat between two experts debating the veracity of the first expert's claims, and another pair speaking quite softly about the mechanics of fungi. Randolph considered learning about Viola's research in a more professional sense. He would not steal it from her, but he would heed Francis's advice and write the opposition. First, though, he had to convince Viola that he was not attacking her by writing such a thing.

"Care now," he said as he handed the food and drink to her. "The wine is quite acidic."

She drank and drew back from the taste. She coughed somewhat and took another sip. This amused him, and he reclined against the sofa as he helped himself to one of the cheeses on her plate. Viola's gaze softened as she took a piece of the mimolette for herself.

"Inviting me here was very kind of you," she said. "Make no mistake, I'm pleased that you care about my work."

"I would like to see it someday."

She tapped the glass in a moment of pensiveness. "You could see it now."

Randolph nearly choked. He had not expected her to be so open with him, and so soon. What would the guests think if he left with her at this hour? Not only would he forsake his duties as a host, but possibly his departure from the party with Viola—a beautiful, new expert—would incite rumors that would injure both their reputations. However, Viola had put herself out there, which meant that she trusted him. She looked at him expectantly. This new and tenuous trust would be easily shattered if he refused her. It was evident that if he wanted to engage with her professionally at all, then he would have to accept her offer now.

"Of course," he said. "I would be delighted."

She adopted a true and genuine smile that broke the harshness of her confidence and seriously enchanted Randolph. In that instant, she was approachable.

****

The forest was entirely dark save for the beams of Viola and Randolph's flashlights. The sounds of the party grew fainter as Viola led Randolph farther and farther off the path. Randolph realized several truths throughout this excursion: (1) The forest was unnervingly quiet at night; (2) The farther he wandered from the path, the more he questioned his certainty of the forest's layout; (3) Just because he could not hear the animals of the forest or see the forest because of the incredible darkness did not mean he was not within the forest. He wondered, in fact, whether the forest extended beyond the trees he associated with it, whether he had ever really left the forest and even whether the forest ended at all.

"I don't like it," he said.

"What?" asked Viola, sounding perfectly aware.

"Being here."

She laughed in a manner both pleasant and cruel.

"Then you shouldn't have become an expert in it," she said.

"I couldn't help it, you know. This was the only thing I was good at. It suits my logic, and I can use my research to help people."

"I think we should endeavor to pursue that in which we believe rather than that which suits us and happens to benefit people."

"In what way can you believe in a forest?"

"There are many ways." She helped him over a log. She dug her feet into the dirt to steady herself. Her grasp felt strong and sure. As they walked she lifted branches for him, and when she sensed him trailing behind, she slowed her pace. "You can believe in its ability to help people by producing resources, or in its role as a natural landmark, or even in the significance of its eternal growth—how it develops according to its inhabitants and surroundings."

They reached the ponds. Their ripples caught the light of Viola and Randolph's flashlights, and the ponds embodied general characteristics of the forest—its serenity, quietness and vast arrangement of wildlife. However, where the forest seemed eternally massive and macroscopically ever-changing, the ponds were limited to the stretch of their water and their biggest changes were too small for the human eye. The reeds, grasses and flowers surrounding the ponds seemed infinitesimal beside the oaks, and the water captured only a fraction of the canopy's blackness.

"How long will this be?" asked Randolph, tucking his hands into his armpits as though it would shield him from discomfort.

"Just a few minutes."

"I expect my guests would like me back."

His shakiness could have either been attributed to his slight fear of the forest's darkness and silence, or to his concern that his guests would think poorly of him for leaving.

Viola showed him her samples and explained how they related to her research. She reasoned that the factories just beyond the forest likely contributed to the rising phosphorous levels of the lake by dumping toxins into the river upstream. She concluded, therefore, to reduce the phosphorous levels of the ponds to normal and thereby, preserve their natural state of wildlife, regulations against the corporations should be enacted and enforced. Her research was valid and relevant, and it convinced Randolph that he should engage with it.

"Viola," he said. "What you have is incredible. Is there any way I could reference it?"

"Certainly," she said. "You're the only expert who's taken a true interest in my work. I would be happy to receive your reference."

"What if I combat it?"

"I don't see why you would. My research and conclusions are correct."

"My work would simply be more original if I wrote the opposing view."

Viola spoke reluctantly, the budding regret of showing Randolph her work apparent: "But it would be wrong."

"I don't know if there is right and wrong. Our conclusions are all subjective, and besides, an adversarial system makes for great progress. We could uncover something truly remarkable through our disagreement that we never would've discovered on our own."

"I'm very thorough."

"And of course," he added, "the rule of the forest is that if there's no preexisting rule, you can do as you please. I'm fairly certain there's no rule specifically barring the factories from dumping toxins upstream. Therefore, their conduct is perfectly permissible."

"Even if no rule exists that bars their conduct, it's still not right."

"So even if I promised to recommend you in my article, you would reject my reference to your work?"

Viola looked at the water in a way that could only suggest defeat.

"No," she said. "You may write what you wish."

****

With Viola resigned, Randolph attempted to lead them back to the party, but this walk lasted far longer than the walk to the ponds. It became evident that Viola and Randolph were lost when they approached a river they had not encountered before. The river's smoothness and flatness contrasted to the coarse, furrowed appearance of the trees. The rivers were thought to exist before the forest, and were, in fact, hypothesized to have caused the forest's growth. Thus, the river was especially important to experts and served as a major source of study.

"This is not right," said Viola.

"I'm aware," said Randolph. He shifted as he spotted something odd about the water. He moved closer to it.

"If you're truly lost then I could lead."

"I still think I can get us back. They say any path will lead us home as long as it's not forbidden. I'm pretty sure we can wander until we reach my house."

There was something familiar about the figures in the water.

"No," said Viola. "I think there's a right way. Shall I lead us?"

"Well," he said quietly. "I suppose it couldn't hurt to let you try."

She turned around as Randolph finally discovered what made him so uncomfortable. The figures were fish, and the fish were strong and young, but they floated on the river lifelessly. Their eyes were locked in place and their mouths fell slightly open. Their look, if anything, was their last cry for help. The water pushed them gently along, and some of the fish kept their gaze on Randolph as they drifted away, but the current eventually turned those around, hiding their expressions from his view. And there, just beyond the trees, on the other side of the river, he saw spots of dark liquid in the grass.

****

As she led Randolph through the forest, Viola examined the branches and logs and the position of the moon where she could spot it. The walk was uncomfortably quiet. Randolph knew Viola likely distrusted him, or at least believed that he did not respect her research, and he was overcome with dismay at the thought that she would never engage him again.

"Viola," said Randolph. "I think you were right about the phosphorous levels in the lake. I think someone is dumping chemicals in there, and it's hurting the environment, and even if it would benefit me, it's not right for me to oppose your argument for the sake of self-interest."

Viola moved silently, but slower now. She kept her gaze ahead. Randolph briefly wondered if she cared about his confession.

"I will write an article endorsing you and your work, even if it's not terribly original," said Randolph. "I'm sorry that I've offended you by making you think that I only wanted your company so I could capitalize on your research. The trust you've shown me is generous and your competency is superb. I was wrong."

Viola stopped. She was hurting, and Randolph could tell that she wanted to say something.

"Is there any way I can make this up to you?" asked Randolph.

Forgiveness was as much a resource as it was a weakness, and Viola understood that if she forgave everyone who betrayed her, then she would become a doormat. Yet, Randolph had not entirely betrayed her, and his influence would raise her credibility as an expert. Furthermore, she sensed a tenderness between them that she wanted to encourage because it made her feel vulnerability without fear, and intrigue without superficiality. He was, in fact, her equal, though they did not know it.

"You could return to the party with me," she said, and she pulled back the branches to reveal his chalet sitting atop a hill.

Randolph, genuinely shocked, asked: "How did you know what to do?"

"I paid attention. I focused. I followed my gut."

In that moment, astounded by the simplicity of her reasoning, Randolph forgot his position as an expert. He stepped with her through the backdoor into the kitchen, where the party was very much alive. Viola returned to her cheese plate. Francis entered the kitchen and handed him a beer. She expressed her shock at witnessing the first expert's cribbage skills and the unfashionableness of her culottes. The experts on the sofa talked their talk of fungi and their research and the paths of the forest. Everyone was so consumed with proving their expertise that no one had noticed he had left.

David Smithson
St. Charles Community College
"Poor Lorne"

Ewan McGregor is a manager at Faber's Market, a corporation that doesn't give a damn about Ewan, but he - the famous Scottish actor - thinks the world of his workplace. He has a framed picture at his apartment hanging on the wall with him shaking hands with Mr. Faber the year he won the Employee of The Month Award. He's worked there longer than he can remember. Ewan McGregor is a giant boob, an adorable but supple breast.

Two things that need to be made clear.

Firstly: Ewan McGregor is Lorne.

Secondly: Lorne is the giant boob.

Lorne lives by a mantra. A philosophical portrayal of the world as he knows it: *You can't help some people. Some people can't stand to be helped. Others think they're too smart for the world, while others live in a world, but their own and the real one can't penetrate their sad little lives.*

In other words, Lorne finds people hopelessly stupid. He sees them on the highway putting on their tie or mascara. They don't notice the coffee stain on their shirt since Tuesday and its Thursday, and they're staring him in the face like they don't have a clue. He pities these people, and pity is something he finds tedious and boring for any extended amount of time.

Lorne watches them bounce off the walls, go in another direction, and call it life. Doe-eyed little creatures that'll die of something unre-markable. Choking on the toothpick in their tuna sandwich.

When Lorne's shift is over at Faber's he heads home to cuddle up with a T.V. dinner while he watches Letterman. Boy, does Lorne love the stars. He daydreams a hundred times a day about being Ewan McGregor. He thinks he even looks a little like Ewan, as he brushes his teeth at night and studies his reflection in the mirror, massaging a slight dimple into his chin. Lorne actually resembles a nearsighted pineapple who decided to grow its hair out for the winter.

He is in the midst of one of his daydreams at work, a recurring dream where Lorne pictures himself to in fact be Ewan McGregor. He doesn't find this intrinsically homoerotic, but guesses that if he told anyone else about his little daydreams that they might. His wire glasses slipping down his perspiring nose as he death grips a plum he is supposed to be stacking, his eyes unfocused and listing slowly to the right, his knuckles turning white, Lorne slipping deeper into the dream.

The fluorescent lights in the store bounce off the blue and gray linoleum. Signs read "Fresh," "Half-Off," and "Deals! Deals! Deals!"

Lorne - or rather Ewan - is basking in the sun on a remote island sipping out of a coconut. Ewan stands up as a lovely lady in white comes bouncing down the beautiful coast line, wind in her hair, blue skies at her back, white sand kicking up from her elegant strides. The gorgeous woman is Liv Tyler. She jaunts up to Ewan, kissing him hard on the lips and sinking low and fast, kissing his chest then his abdomen and then beginning to -

"Lorne?"

Surprised and torn away from his daydreaming, Ewan - or rather Lorne - grips the plum in his hand so hard it explodes.

"I - uh - sorry. How can I help you?" Plum juice drips all over Lorne as he stammers back to reality.

"Oh jeez. No. I'm sorry. What a mess! But I thought that was you Lorne. Jesus, what's it been, eh? Fifteen? Twenty years?" A beefy man stands a pace away looking at Lorne with a large, toothy smile.

"I'm sorry. Who are you?" Then Lorne recognizes the man. He feels like he has to piss; his penis feels shrunken, almost like it has gone back inside him.

Tim Albeni used to beat the living crap out of Lorne. Tim used to pin him down to the ground and dangle ropes of spit in Lorne's face; used to corner him in the bathroom and pee on his shoes; used to put tampons full of ketchup on his lunch tray. He'd torture Lorne, and now here he was, Tim Albeni, the same bully from so long ago looking Lorne in the face and smiling.

Lorne, out of pure instinct, picks up the pipe wrench from the bottom of his cart, the wrench he used when that stupid women's restroom toilet went on the fritz, and splits Tim's smiling face in two.

Well, Ewan McGregor uses the pipe wrench to cleave the bully's head open. As Lorne stands there unable to speak or think how he wants. His brain slipping into default mode.

"Oh yeah. Tim. Hey there, how are you buddy?" Lorne felt sick at his phony pleasantries as he made failing attempts to clean up some of the plum juice and bits of the fruit from off and around himself. The plum really did explode, but only in Lorne's direction. Tim and his vicinity were perfectly spotless.

"You know, I've been good," said Tim like a person who's used to being pandered to, and people pretending to care about how he has been doing. "Kids been great. Wife seems happy. Heck, you know, I even started my own practice last week now that you mention it."

Tim smiles a huge toothy smile attached to his huge block of a head, covered in a mop of dirty blonde hair.

"Oh you missed a spot there," Tim said, pointing to a chunk of plum hanging from Lorne's shirt collar. Instead of letting Lorne struggle to find the bit, Tim plucks it from his collar.

"There ya go," said Tim with a grin, looking around for some place to dispose of the bit of fruit, finding nothing. Tim pulls out a Kleenex from his pocket and deposits it there, then stuffing the tissue back where he found it, continuing to smile at Lorne.

Kids? Wife? Lorne couldn't believe it. *Since I mentioned it?! I didn't mention anything!*

"How you been?" asked Tim.

Lorne couldn't be sure. Lorne was still half in the throes of a murderous pipe-wrench-daydream.

"Oh. Yeah. Great. Work and you know. Life. It's pretty great."

Ewan mercilessly wailed on the twitching body, blood galloping off from the curve of the pipe-wrench and flying up into the air.

"It is, isn't it!?" Tim laughed, unaware of the mega-movie star bashing in his brains.

Lorne searched for something to say. Anything that sounded casual and normal.

"Oh hey." Lorne noticed the items in Tim's cart. "Having a barbeque are we?"

"Yeah, sure are. Should be a good time," said Tim. "Well hey, you know, it's been nice seeing you but I'm kind of in a hurry," Tim pauses, perhaps to think better of what he was about to say, taking a glance at his wrist watch, but shakes his head and continues anyway. "Me and the wife are having the barbeque this Sunday after church. You could stop by if you like. Nothing fancy really." Tim dug in his pleated khakis. "Here's my card. Call me. Especially if you have a tooth ache." He winked. "Take care!"

Ewan McGregor stood straddling his kill, soaked in blood and guts, heaving great gasping breaths of victory.

Lorne watched Tim waltz away, his hips sashaying ever so slightly. *He's having a great day,* thought Lorne.

Lorne turned back wide eyed at the heap of plums, then at the empty space where more plums were supposed to be, and then back at his cart that was also void of any more plums. He was going to have to order more before he left for the day.

****

Ewan McGregor sat in the back of Lorne's green Volkswagen Bug, smoking a Parliament cigarette with a calmness that bordered on laziness. His long and elegant fingers moved slowly to the arch of the rolled down window to flick his ash, half of it escaping out into the world while the rest came back shooting upwards and everywhere, scattering about Lorne's upholstery. Ewan rubbed the smoke from his eyes.

"It doesn't matter," said Lorne under his breath. He had been muttering this phrase to himself ever since he had run into Tim Albeni. He couldn't shake the bubbling acid feeling in the pit of his stomach surging up to his esophagus anytime his mind wandered back to the days of helplessness and the only real terror he had ever known.

Ewan stoked up a query, whispering in Lorne's ear, "Do you think Tim even remembers?"

Lorne thought he was going to vomit on Friday, when unbeknownst to himself he had picked up the receiver and dialed Tim Albeni's house number on the card Tim had given him. The card was crumpled on all sides, and a bit faded, from Lorne's excessive deliberation over it.

"Hello, Albeni residence," said a woman in a practiced tone.

"Yes. Hello. Is Tim there?" asked Lorne, the receiver wet in his palm.

"Just a moment," singed-songed the woman. "Tim, the phone." The voice trailed off in the distance.

Lorne had the quick impulse to hang up the phone with a bang. He wondered why on Earth he hadn't done that already, and why he still stood there looking at the middle distance of his apartment waiting to speak with a man he surely hated.

"Hello?"

Lorne gave a start, "Hello. Hi. Tim?"

"Yes. Hello. How may I help you?"

"It's Lorne."

"Lorne?" said Tim, "Oh, Lorne. Yeah, Lorne! Hey there, got a tooth ache pal?" Tim smiled into the receiver.

"I was – no - calling to say hey and that I'd like to come, so yeah." Lorne smiled back into the receiver, painfully.

"Come?" asked Tim.

"To come – yeah – your barbeque?" Lorne's stomach tipped over.

"Oh, yeah the barbeque. Okay. Yeah. Sure. Come on by man!"

"Let me just find, a, uh writing utensil."

****

Lorne looked at himself in the rearview mirror of his car.

"It doesn't matter," he whispered as he exited the highway into the middle of suburbia on a beautiful Sunday afternoon. Lorne and Ewan's eyes met in the rearview mirror. Ewan winked big and smiled.

"You know this might even be fun," mused Ewan as he fingered a cigarette burn in the seat next to him. Lorne was sweating, even with all the windows of his little Bug rolled down. It was a warm day, and he was wearing a button up shirt, tie, and an expensive leather jacket he had picked up the day after the exploding plum incident. He couldn't imagine who he was trying to impress. *Certainly not Tim,* Lorne thought.

As Lorne drew closer to Tim's residence, his GPS whistling directions every few minutes, Lorne started developing a plan. He wasn't going to this barbeque to make friends. He couldn't, and wouldn't, do that. His honor was at stake. Lorne smiled, brushing his auburn hair from his green eyes. Ewan did the same to his auburn hair, still smiling and smoking underneath big designer sunglasses.

"It doesn't matter," Lorne said again, the sides of his mouth sucking hard against his teeth with a pain that felt right and justified.

Pulling up to the house, Lorne felt a stab of embarrassment for his little car. In the driveway and all around the cul-de-sac of Tim's house were brilliantly elegant luxury cars, with ironic vanity license plates, shiny paint jobs, and gleaming chromed wheels. Lorne shook it off, the embarrassment almost breaking his resolve. He put his chin a bit higher.

He was going to show Tim, and all Tim's friends, that he wasn't the type of guy you could push around or intimidate. Lorne had grown up to be just like every other man's man, assertive, demanding respect, good under pressure, and above all else Lorne was going to show them that he, Lorne, was cool, even if he did drive a lime green Volkswagen Beetle Bug.

Lorne got out of his car, carrying the mustard potato salad he had made from his mother's recipe, with conviction and an air of confidence that he had never known. Ewan McGregor followed up from the rear, wearing a leather jacket, a toothpick poking from out the corner of his mouth. Ewan slapped Lorne's ass.

"Hey there!" called a good looking woman in a summer dress that coiled around her body, the slight breeze hugging it to every curve.

"Hey yourself," said Lorne, smiling out of the side of his mouth.

"I'm Debbie Albeni." She laughed. "And welcome to our humble abode. I know it isn't much, but we try." Debbie winked, and splayed her arm around at her very nice house with a perfectly manicured lawn and garden.

"Who might you be?" she asked of Lorne.

"Name's Lorne. How do you do?" Lorne stuck out his hand, shaking Debbie's, making his hand as firm as possible, but without a hint of squeezing. He'd let her do that. She did.

"Lorne? Oh my, yes of course! Lorne. Tim will be so happy to hear that you made it. He has just been talking up a storm about you." Debbie poked Lorne in the chest playfully, taking the potato salad from him. "Follow me." She absolutely beamed, spinning around, letting her dress catch the air. "All the boys are in the back. I like your jacket, by the way."

Debbie swung open the white plastic gate to her backyard, revealing a large patio surrounded by bright fescue grass. A Chinese Maple stood near the rear of the gated yard, elegant with its orange and pink blossoms. A kid's playhouse, which looked handmade, sat in the middle of the yard. Little boys and girls swung from all sides of the playhouse, their dads sipping lite beer on the patio, their moms chatting over mimosas in the kitchen.

Coolers lined the fence, with informational posters attached so as to help anyone with their choice of beverage. Twelve men stood or sat around the patio, talking and drinking. Their different colored polos stood out stark against the fence and trees.

"Hey everybody, Tim - look who's here." Debbie looked at Lorne and tilted her head with a slight curve into his ear. "It's L-o-r-n-e?" Debbie drug out the phonetics of his name in hopes of pronouncing it right. Lorne nodded. "It's Lorne!" the dentist's wife said to the crowd.

"Hey, Lorne, buddy. How's it going?" said Tim, who was easily the tallest out of all the men. He wasted no time jogging over to Lorne in greeting, taking Lorne's hand and wringing it.

"Man, glad you made it! Here, come on, grab a beer." Tim took a few steps to the cooler with the sign that read "Beer," plunging his hand into the ice and pulling out a can of lite beer, popping the top.

"Something to wet your whistle," said Tim, smiling boyishly as he pushed the can into Lorne's hand. "And here are the guys."

Tim straddled Lorne's shoulders with his large arm and guided him towards the group of men. Lorne met each of the men with a stiff and firm handshake, shaking each hand forcefully up and down no more than twice, and almost throwing the other man's hand back towards their pocket. Lorne joked at a few of the men's last names, and careers.

"Mike Litoris? Litoris, eh? I bet your wife gets off on that!"

"A gynecologist, really? I guess we do what we love right?"

Lorne mingled and meshed with the guys. He listened to them talk about their wives and kids, and he imagined evoking envy from all these married men about wild tales of his singledom.

****

Lorne continued to snag beer from the cooler for over two hours. The sun was beginning to paint the sky in magenta and orange as the smoke from the barbeque sweetened the air with cooking meats. Great billowing clouds listed slowly about the sky. Lorne could just make out the pale waxing moon in the distance.

"So what is that you do?" asked one of the wives.

"I own a grocery store. Faber's Market."

"You own Faber's?" asked Tim with an air of what Lorne thought verged on respect.

"Sure do," said Lorne. "Bought it off of old man Faber, clean. Well, with a sizable loan from the bank of course, am I right?" He laughed with the woman and Tim, all raising their drinks as if to say "Of course," and taking a drink.

Lorne felt on top of the world. He raised his beer to Ewan McGregor, who was standing at the grill just behind Tim, taking long and exaggerated whiffs of the searing meats. Ewan raised his beer back at Lorne and nodded.

"Yup, I'm a mover and a shaker, that's for certain," said Lorne as he plopped down into a chair and put his arm around one of the men. Lorne was oozing machismo.

"Tim here, he don't know it yet," Lorne winked at Tim in his "Kiss The Cook Apron" as Tim continued to smile and mind the grill. "Tim knew me when I hadn't been me. You know, before you turn into the real you? The you that doesn't give a damn, and takes the world by storm." Lorne put his nose in the air taking great wafts of the summer air, and closed his eyes in the sunshine.

"Hey, watch it," said Lorne.

A man named Greg had just trotted on his foot.

"Watch what?" laughed the man.

"Never mind," said Lorne.

Ewan sniffed the fat man.

"Smells like cabbage. A soggy poofter wrapped in bacon," Ewan slipped into Lorne's ear, his breath tickling Lorne's cartilage. "You know he isn't fond of you. He shops at Faber's. You've seen him. Talked to him. He never remembers where anything is. A waste of space he is. A regular blow hard. He doesn't respect you. He knows you don't own Faber's. He'll expose you."

"So what is it you do? Lorne, was it?" asked Greg.

The acid began to boil in the pit of Lorne's stomach. Ewan McGregor sat up from a crimson lawn chair from the middle of the yard, pushing his designer sunglasses up into his hair, giving him that dashing devil may care look.

"My foot. You just stepped on it," said Lorne raising his voice over the chatter.

The pastel polo shirts and sundresses paused from sipping mimosas, hearing the spit escape Lorne's mouth in a hiss.

Tim Albeni looked up from his meats sizzling on the grill, his eyes watering from the smoke.

"Sorry pal," laughed Greg, who was a big man in height and girth, with a large hard stomach from years of cook outs and lite beer. He was jovial, but had a stern look about him as well. Greg turned back to the conversation he was having with one of his friends.

"Pal?" said Lorne, with indignation. "Pal? I'm not your pal, buddy."

He pushed on Greg's shoulder.

The polo shirts and sundresses shifted nervously.

"Okay. You're not my pal," said Greg.

Lorne was focused on Greg's pudding eating face. The red and engorged jowls that swaggered from Greg's portly face taunted him. They swung like a pendulum. Lorne was transported back into the fray of the packed hallways and pimpled faced teenagers. He recalled all the smirks and jeers at his misery. His lack of ability to fit in amongst his peers was under constant scrutiny behind every corner. Greg's beady and sunken eyes mimicked the eyes of the people who refused to accept him. The teenage Lorne wanted to shout and throw a fit. Wanted to wring the little bodies out of their pretentious social order, and into his shoes. Lorne intended to swap, to see how it felt. How it could feel to make someone hurt.

"Hey, fatty, where do you think you're going?" said Lorne, his voice ringing in the treetops and across the yard.

A palpable silence eased amongst the group, the worried whispers ceasing, everyone sharing surreptitious and worried glances.

"What's your malfunction?" Greg said, smiling and taking a drink of his margarita, keeping his voice calm and collected. "If I stepped on your toesies, I'm sorry. We're trying to have a nice time. Have a sausage." Greg fingered a sausage from the grill and held it in front of Lorne's face.

Lorne smacked it to the ground where it rolled to Ewan's feet. Ewan bit into the smoking flesh; the juices running into his dimpled chin.

"Hey, hey, guys, break it up why don't you?" laughed Tim, getting in between the them.

Lorne ducked Tim's outstretched arm and shoved him out of his way. A woman gasped.

The cauldron in Lorne's belly was raging and pouring over the sides into every nook and cranny of his body, filling him completely with rage and contempt. Lorne looked Tim up and down with complete and utter disgust plastered on his face before turning back to Greg.

"I'm sorry," started Lorne. "I didn't notice you were having a nice time. See, my version of a nice time, comes with a bit more vinegar."

Ewan was in Lorne's ear whispering.

"I thought this was a party? Is this not a party, Tim?" Lorne recited from Ewan's whispering. "Is this not a party? Or is it just where you feed your cattle?" Lorne waved his arm up and down at Greg.

Lorne turned from Tim to survey the crowd, his eyes meeting darting glances, perplexed stares, wrinkled noses, abhorrent scowls.

"Am I right or what? Look at him!" said Lorne.

"I think it's about that time for you to skedaddle," said Greg with a condescending smile. Putting his beefy hand on Lorne's shoulder, Greg raised his other arm to point towards the gate, wiggling his fat fingers.

Ewan roared at Lorne, "Doesn't he know who we are?"

Lorne punched Greg's fat gut. Greg doubled over, spilling his margarita, all the air in his lungs escaping.

"Lorne!" yelled Tim, stepping up into Lorne's face, "What the hell? What are you doing?" Lorne pushed into Tim's body, trying to get at Greg on his hands and knees, dry heaving great gulps, unable to catch his breath.

"You need to stop this!" said Tim grabbing Lorne by the shoulders.

Lorne lurched out of Tim's grasp.

"Make me," said Lorne. "Make me like you used to make me do your homework. Make me like you used to make me eat whatever you could find on the bottom of your shoe." Ewan was bouncing on his heels, wringing and punching his fists. Lorne spit at Tim's feet.

Ewan unzipped his pants and started to pee on Tim's loafers, the stream of yellow urine steaming off the polished leather.

"I'm going to call the police if you don't leave. Now, please, just leave," said Tim.

A look Lorne knew all too well slipped over Tim's face. The look that Lorne had all but forgotten until that day in Faber's Market.

Lorne blinked and Ewan burst into a thousand iridescent little pieces. He could just make out a faint scream of terror from the movie star that faded as quickly as it had come. His shoulders slouched. The weight of his world came rushing back, setting itself directly on top of his head like one of those large mason jars women from Africa would carry on the National Geographic channel, gathering water for their families.

The reality of Lorne's life, his dead-end job, his lonely apartment, his constantly-in-need-of-repair green Volkswagen Bug came all at once back to the forefront of his mind as his face dwindled from determination to defeat under Tim's familiar glare.

Lorne turned around and the crowd of parents parted to let him go, all of them whispering to each other behind their hands. Lorne shuffled his feet across the lawn towards the gate. The beer he was holding slipped from his hand, his leather jacket catching the low angled rays of sunshine.

"Fuck this loser up, Tim" Greg said, his wife helping his great mass of a body up from the ground.

Lorne wilted, the last vestiges of defense falling from him. The pieces of himself tumbling down some ancient hill in a place long forgotten, crumbled and morose. The hill that witnessed every fall of man now saw Lorne beaten and broken at its base. He was no longer himself. No longer a man. A shell of an existence. A vehicle for inhabitation by anyone willing to drive. The stars - or rather a single star - would guide this dauntless creature for now on.

Ewan McGregor cracked back into existence. Lorne stopped

walking and turned back to face Tim and Greg. The movie star stared from beneath his eyebrows with a wicked grin, the toothpick protruding from the corner of his mouth. Lorne slipped into Ewan, their leather jackets merging as one. Green eyes and auburn hair, fusing together.

Lorne's muscles bristled with a power he never felt. He was something more than a manager at Faber's Market.

Police sirens emerged from the distance, growing louder every second.

Ewan rushed the two men, his teeth bared, his knuckles stark white. He wanted to gobble up the manicured fescue lawn and rip into the polo shirts and eat their fake smiles. He wailed on Tim and he beat Greg.

A few women screamed, summer dresses somersaulting around their legs as they scooped up the gaping faces of their children in their arms and covered their eyes from what men can do. Tim and Greg's friends stood with their arms made of iron, hanging perpendicular to the ground, lifeless. Their legs were rooted to the ground for some reason that later they wouldn't be able to explain to the bruised and battered faces of their friends. They looked on helplessly as Lorne ripped into his victims with a frenzy.

All the years of Ewan McGregor being passed over by his favorite directors, just to see Brad Pitt, Heath Ledger, and Ryan Gosling, those pretty boy types that didn't have half the talent that he does, take the roles he desperately wanted, rushed by in a nauseating blur. Ewan's stomach ached with every blow he landed on Tim Albeni's face, the acid in his gut rising up to sear the walls of his esophagus. His belly squirmed every time his fist connected with Greg's fat body. But he stayed through the pain, replacing their faces with all the faces of the producers that said he didn't "fit the role," only to cast Jude Law, Johnny Depp, Leonardo DiCaprio, or mother-Matthew-fucking-McConaughey.

The police burst through the gate, following the screams and yells. Lorne wailing away on the polo shirts and khaki shorts.

Eighty-thousand volts of electricity surged through Lorne's body. Eleven ounces of pepper spray seared every millimeter of his eyes and the inside of his nose. Lorne was tackled to the ground and punched in the groin. His face was mashed into the patio by a black leathered hand. Lorne was handcuffed and dragged to a police car. He was read his rights and shoved into the back seat, the door snapping shut.

Lorne looked at the group of people, all shaking their heads in unison. He met Tim's eyes, or at least one of them as Tim was holding a pack of Green Giant frozen peas to the left side of his face. Tim lingered for only a second on Lorne's confused, bloody, puffed up face before putting his arm around his wife, shaking his head, and turning back to talk to a police officer.

Lorne stared at the middle distance out of the police car's windshield for a good while before the police officer got into the vehicle and drove off without a word.

Ewan slapped Lorne's knee hard but playfully. They looked at each other, green eyes meeting green eyes. Both their auburn hair disheveled from the fight.

"Well I can't imagine that going any better," said Ewan.

Lorne didn't say anything. He turned away to look out at the last vestiges of sunlight peeking over the horizon, a brilliant purple crescent hue bordering the world. He thought of the plum that exploded in his hand when Tim came strolling back into his life, and it hit him. His stomach slipped into the car seat below.

"I forgot -" said Lorne.

"Shut it," said the officer.

"I forgot to order more plums," sighed Lorne.

Jessye Scott
Florida State University
"True Love"

It was the last day of the Greek Pottery Exhibit's stint in the Boston Museum of Fine Arts. Mimi had thought about cancelling their trip — she considered creating some emergency at work — but Oliver bought their tickets two months in advance as a late birthday present to himself. Mimi took solace in knowing that, even under the guise of a professional obligation, he would have seen right through the transparent excuse.

As she stared at one of the vases, Mimi could feel her wine-stained lips cracking under the dry lipstick. She might have reached into her purse in search of lip balm, but she couldn't risk drawing attention to her buzzing phone. She turned her attention back to the vase in front of them. On it, a figure sat playing a musical instrument as a man and woman looked on. The plate in front read *Orpheus playing lyre for Thracian man, neglects women of Thrace.*

"It's incredible," Oliver said behind her. She prayed that the buzzing would stay muffled. "You know the story of Orpheus? He was the one who went to hell to bring his wife back from the dead, but turned around on their way back and lost her forever. According to one myth, he was so devastated after losing her that he retreated into his music, making the women of Thrace feel neglected. Eventually, they felt so rejected that they grouped together and killed him." He placed his hands softly on her hips. She could feel him breathing in the remnants of *True Love*, a perfume he had gifted her that smelled of freshly picked cranberries. "It sounds like an article from one of those tabloids you like, right? Maybe men haven't changed that much."

"But women have," Mimi said as she broke away from his embrace. The buzzing stopped in her purse but her shoulders remained tense. The Aoba Japan International School had called on time, as they promised, to inform her if she would be offered a position to teach. Oliver did not know she had applied.

She turned and walked down the corridor, lined with hand-crafted vases on each side. Oliver followed behind, keeping with the pace of her sharp footsteps. Mimi glanced at each vase that she passed. She saw depictions of men running with spears in their hands, the Minotaur tearing apart young virgins with his hands, a newlywed couple departing in their wedding chariot. She offered slight glances to most of the pieces, only lingering when a depiction triggered a spark within her memory.

"Are you coming home after this?" Mimi said without looking back. She had pulled her frizzy hair into a tight ponytail on the commute to work and could feel a migraine stirring up. She pushed the thought of work out of her mind as quickly as it had appeared. She saw no potential in being a data entry clerk for a transition resources corporation, having only accepted the position because it was the first offer she received in Boston. She dreamed of the aspirin in the medicine cabinet that Oliver kept fully stocked in case of emergencies.

"Probably not," he said. She could imagine his grey eyes darkening with concern behind the boxy frames that were constantly sliding down his nose. "I have to stop by the library. I'll try my best, though, and I'll call you when I'm there."

They had moved into their one bedroom, one bathroom apartment in Allston seven months ago. Oliver had been short on time from the moment they left Logan International Airport, leaving Mimi to unpack the few boxes they'd had shipped. While he was off completing his thesis on Greek cooking utensils, Mimi would fill her time alone with the weekly recipes her mother would email her. She'd sit down to her dinner of roasted garlic shepherd's pie or panko-crusted tuna steaks and scroll through her phone, pausing on pictures of her goddaughter's third birthday party, and invitations to participate in a marathon along the Charles River. Some nights, when the only shows on TV were re-runs she knew by heart, she would rearrange the furniture according to an article on *feng shui* she had accidentally clicked on, or reorganize the stacks of magazines and catalogues that were lying on the coffee table.

It was during one of these nights that she had accidentally clicked on an advertisement that read, "Dream of Teaching English Abroad? Move to Japan Today!" As she scrolled through lists of advantages to living in Asia and application fees, she remembered how those drunken plans to study abroad were never realized. Her mother constantly reminded her of how she had asked for a globe for her thirteenth birthday, only to color in all of South America with her pink and blue Crayola markers. Her plans to travel, she decided, must have dissipated around the time she met Oliver. When they were discussing their summer plans a few weeks after they met, Mimi mentioned that she was looking into backpacking around Europe.

"Why spend all that money?" he asked her. It was around midterms, and they had been sitting in a coffee shop that was only a few minutes from the library. "Stay here with me and I'll plan something for us."

What would it be like, she imagined, to be free to walk through an empty museum with nothing but her own knowledge to guide her? She had learned most of her facts relating to art history from their gallery visits; although Oliver's specialty was classical Greece, he had been the one to introduce her to the destruction of the *Rokeby Venus* and had entertained her with an hour-long diatribe against the many faults of Picasso's *Blue Period*. They had spent their second date wandering the halls of a local gallery with their fingers intertwined, admiring the visiting paints of Georges Seurat, and after he had finished explaining how Seurat had been instrumental in the development of pointillism, he kissed her for the first time; they had been standing in front of *A Sunday Afternoon on the Island of La Grande Jatte*, his fingers threaded through her recently bobbed hair.

Now, as she looked through the alternating red-figure and black-figure pottery, Mimi could recognize some of the names from the books Oliver liked to read to her when she had trouble sleeping: Aphrodite, Sparta, the Muses, the Trojan Horse. She had never shown much interest in history or mythology as a child; it wasn't until someone else instilled a reason to learn that she began to pay attention.

"Isn't this incredible? I can't even imagine the amount of time that had to go into each vase," Oliver said.

"It doesn't even compare to the Monet exhibit we saw last January. Greek art isn't as relevant to modern art as, say, Renoir or Degas."

"In what way is Greek history not relevant nowadays? Greek ideas are the backbone to modern society. They've given us democracy! Debates! Olive oil! Can you even begin to imagine life without olive oil? Greek art is a cornerstone in one of the most influent periods of all time. The impressionist movement isn't even on the same plane."

Mimi looked back at Oliver as he continued to explain the extended influence of Greek culture on modern society. His eyes were focused on the vase, his hands moving at a rapid pace in an attempt to keep up with his voice. Since he had begun teaching an undergraduate course on rhetoric of Greek debates, he had begun to adopt that same style of lecturing used in a classroom into his everyday vernacular.

"You don't even like Greek food," she reminded him.

Oliver continued to follow her down the corridor. The exhibit was empty enough for her to hear his keys jingling in his pocket, just as they had been when he had met her in the parking lot half an hour ago. It wasn't until his cherry red Mercedes pulled up next to her white Honda that she realized their cars hadn't been parked next to each other outside their driveway in months.

When they first met in Tallahassee — he was a history under-graduate in pursuit of an honors thesis, she was an English major who loved romance novels and couldn't decide on a minor — they had both been driving around in used cars gifted down from their parents. They had met through a group of mutual friends at a party and, by the third beer, Mimi was instantly and inexplicably on his hook. He was ambitious and intellectual, a welcome change from the hometown stoner boys she had grown up around. She slept with him the night of their first date, and he made her a copy of his key by their fourth month together. Mimi was suddenly caught up in her very own retelling of the romance novels she loved so much, and she treasured every second together.

Three years into their relationship, two people could fill the space between them. The separation had crept in slowly, an inch here and there when they were among mixed company. She had been eerily aware of the emptiness when it first appeared within their relationship; she would remind herself to place her hand on his lower back at birthday parties and readjust herself when accidentally leaning in the opposite direction during a movie. Now, the distance was so familiar they rarely acknowledged it. She would reflexively step away if someone tried to walk between them. They ate their meals at the times that best suited their individual schedules. His phone's password was no longer his father's birth year. She refused to rearrange her last-minute plans to accommodate his needs.

"What about this one?" Oliver asked. They had paused in front of a vase with a plaque that read *Aphrodite seduces Adonis*. Adonis, the seated figure, had his torso turned to face the goddess standing behind him.

"It looks like a woman trying to pursue a man who isn't worth her time."

"You take everything at face value," Oliver said. "Aphrodite loved Adonis more than any other man. When he died, she grew sea anemones everywhere his blood was spilt. That's something beautiful, isn't it? An entire ocean floor was filled with color in memory of a single person."

Mimi crossed her arms over her chest. "That wouldn't happen in real life."

"Well, obviously it's a myth. But the sentiment is universal. I'd do the same if you died, or something similar. I don't know how I would move on from that. It would be like losing a part of me, you know?

I would find some way to memorialize you like that."

Mimi looked at her feet. "I wouldn't want you to." She remembered her phone, buried at the bottom of her purse, holding onto a piece of news that could decimate the union she had grown to define herself by. She might not even have the courage to go through with moving away, she thought. She might receive an offer to teach and realize that everything she ever wanted was already sleeping next to her, if she had the strength to look past his flaws. She might be able to stop looking in the bathroom mirror before bed and reminding herself, "You love him. He's the one for you."

They continued to walk throughout the exhibit. The farther they walked into the exhibit, the sharper Mimi's heels clacked against the tile floor. She hadn't even wanted to come today; it had originally been Oliver's idea, recommended by one of his professors. Yet here they were, in a chilled exhibit, walking through the halls at different paces.

Two months ago, they had attended a benefit to raise money for the classics department at Oliver's university. After reading an article titled "Take Back Your Man: Ten Must-Do's for True Love," Mimi resolved to improve their relationship. The seventh must-do had ordered her to remain unpredictable, so she drove to a local consignment store and bought a slinky black dress with tiny silver beads embedded in the bodice. One of her coworkers offered to curl her hair and apply makeup in a style she called, "Vixen of the Night." Mimi arrived half an hour early to the event and waited inside her car for Oliver.

He showed up an hour late. He called her when he was walking inside, and she picked up her purse and ran after him. She found him after ten minutes of searching the banquet hall. He was standing next to one of his professors, dressed in a navy suit she didn't recognize.

"You are beautiful," he said when he saw her. "All this time together, and I'm still wowed every time you walk into a room."

Mimi smiled and thanked him; the fourth must-do instructed her to show appreciation as often as possible. When Oliver walked off in search of free champagne, one of his classmates pulled Mimi aside and confided her worry over Oliver's seemingly apathetic disposition.

"I'm worried about him," she said. She took a cursory look at the woman's frizzy curls and thick horn-rimmed glasses and dismissed her as a threat. "He hasn't been himself lately. How is he at home? Depressed?"

"He's fine," Mimi promised. She rambled on for a few minutes about how Oliver was going through a busy time, having just lost his father to lung cancer and moving to a new city; he simply had a lot going on. No, they were both doing well. No, they were happy. No, she didn't want to elaborate.

Oliver reappeared, and his classmate melted away into the crowd. She watched as the woman left and thought about how strange the encounter had been, though she chose not to mention it. Oliver handed her a glass of champagne, and she smiled approvingly in his direction. The tenth must-do, after all, had warned her to never let her imagination run away with any temporary doubts.

The museum had its air conditioning running on full blast, and Mimi crossed her arms to stop herself from shivering. She pulled her phone out of her purse and saw that there was one new voicemail message waiting. She would not be able to listen to it until she was safely sitting in her car, doors locked, and Oliver was pulling out of the parking lot.

"Are you cold?" he said.

"No." She pushed her arms closer to her body and tried to regain control of her shivering body.

"Here," he said. "Take my jacket."

"I'm fine."

"Come on," he said. She could hear a zipper opening. "Just take it."

Mimi looked back at him for the first time since they had entered the museum. The lighting was dim and she could barely make out his eyes. He stood there, patiently waiting for her to continue, his arms at his side. She thought for a moment that maybe here, alone in the quiet hall, was the perfect time to build their ending.

"I'm not cold," she said.

Oliver slid his hands into his jacket's pockets. Mimi looked over at the vase between them. Two women stood on either side of the vase, with a man caught in the middle. The plaque read *Hera follows Zeus to Alcmene's birth.*

Oliver cleared his throat, and she glanced over at him. "You know, Alcmene was the mother of Heracles. Not Hercules, as most people call him. The Disney movie was completely off base, no matter how much you like the songs. Hades never tried to kill Hercules as a baby, it was Hera. Zeus got this thought to trick her into nursing Hercules, but when she discovered the truth she ripped him from her breast. The milk sprayed across the heavens and created the Milky Way."

"How would—"

"He disguised Heracles as one of Hera's children. She wasn't very happy that her husband had conceived a child with a mortal woman, of course. She even got revenge with some of his affairs."

Mimi stared at Hera, who was indefinitely frozen while looking at her husband and his lover. She saw so much of the last few months in the vase: the unexplainable late night errands, sudden long periods of silence throughout the day, a sudden commitment to wearing condoms. Then, one morning when he ran outside to grab the mail, she heard his phone ringing on the bathroom counter. In a moment she was not proud of, she answered it.

She had been sitting on the perfectly made bed when he returned, staring at a picture of them from an old vacation to Disney World. As Oliver promised in the beginnings months of their relationship, he surprised her with two tickets to the Orlando theme park during the first week of their summer break. The picture had been taken in front of Cinderella's castle, and they were wearing matching Mickey and Minnie mouse ears. Mimi did not take her eyes away from the picture, not even when he asked what was wrong.

When she found the will to speak, nothing but a whimper came out. After a few minutes, that whimper evolved into a question. Once Oliver realized what was going on, the question escalated into a yell. Soon enough, Mimi was standing on their bed as she screamed into Oliver's ears. Oliver, in return, began to cry.

In between hours of fighting, they began to question whether they should abandon what remained of their relationship. They approached topics that had previously been gathering dust under their many rugs. Did they still want to get married the summer after Oliver completed his master's degree? Would Mimi trust him to father the two children they had planned on? Would Oliver finally take Mimi on the Alaskan cruise he had once promised? Did either of them feel completely satisfied when they woke up in the morning and looked over at the other?

Mimi packed a handful of dresses in an old camping backpack and left the apartment. She booked a room in a motel half an hour away, one that offered a free continental breakfast. She sat on the queen sized bed in the second story room with the blinds pulled open, completely naked except for a pair of fuzzy pink socks. She stretched her arms out and bared her breasts to the street lamps and flashing billboards.

In the morning, she sat down to a breakfast of crunchy toast and runny eggs. A man was sitting at the table adjacent to hers; he was wearing a tailored grey suit and a gold watch that Oliver would dismiss as excessive. He looked at her over his copy of *The Economist* and smiled her way. Mimi waved back, almost instantly cringing once she realized what she had done. How long had it been since she had last flirted with a stranger? She looked back down at her unwanted breakfast and decided that she was not going to eat it. As she folded up her napkin and set it on her plate, she decided that she wanted a nice, properly cooked English breakfast. She would invite the man in the suit to join her, as well. They would go somewhere with laminated menus and he would offer to pay. When she looked back up towards him, his newspaper was on the table and he was nowhere in sight.

Mimi went for a jog that afternoon. She did not buy into the belief that exercise is necessary for a happy life, but she figured adding it to her current situation couldn't do much harm. She drove to Walmart to buy a pair of sneakers and a six-pack of women's briefs and then continued on towards the Charles River. She parked her car and jogged along the water's edge, smiling at a woman pushing a stroller in the opposite direction. Mimi panted as she admired the surrounding trees and wondered how the sun could feel so hot in the winter months. The run did not continue for much longer; when she approached a nearby ice cream stand, Mimi slowed to a brisk walk and stood in line for a ladybug-shaped ice pop. She sat on a bench overlooking the water, licking a rapidly melting ice pop, and thought about the romance novels she had discovered on her mother's nightstands as a child. In those novels, the women never ended up unhappy. The brief period of hopelessness would always be followed by a resolution.

Following several weeks of deliberation, Mimi decided to forgive Oliver. It hadn't been an easy choice, but something inside of her still wanted to believe that he was her true love. As her mother had coached her over the phone, nobody is perfect. He admitted his mistake, which is more than most men do. And they had invested three years in their relationship, which shouldn't be put to waste. Mimi took him back on the condition that their relationship would improve over time, and she could see that Oliver seemed to be making a real effort. He talked to fill their silences and asked questions when he was unsure of what she was thinking. When he couldn't come home on time, he'd call and text and offer to Skype to verify his location. He told her he loved her twice a day. Everything should have been fine between them now.

Mimi stared at the tiny bronze vase in front of them. "Of course, the scorned wife is cast as the villain. It's always the woman. It's not like Zeus destroyed their relationship. All she did was love him, yet he still chose to cheat on her. How could she stay with him?"

"Not everything needs to be turned into a new wave-feminist argument."

"I'm voicing my own interpretation of the piece."

Oliver sighed. "Hera loved Zeus, so she forgave his transgressions"

"She wasn't any happier for it." The woman's name was Maribelle. That's as much as Oliver would reveal about her, and even with that small admission he looked as though he was trying not to throw up. Mimi had spent hours searching her name on social media, looking for mentions of her online, desperately trying to locate an image of her, to no avail. She looked back over at Oliver and wondered if he had made Maribelle cry when he ended the affair. She hoped there had been endless tears.

"Everyone makes mistakes, Mimi. If the gods aren't perfect, how can anyone be?"

Mimi sighed, allowing the wait between exhaling and inhaling to fill the room. "Sure, they might have had their good times. But wasn't she miserable by this point? Wouldn't they have been happier apart?" She paused, remembering the first night after she discovered the betrayal. She had lain crying in their bed, no friends or close coworkers in this unfamiliar city, and searched the internet for makeup tutorials to cover up a crying face. "Why didn't she give up on him?"

Mimi looked over at Oliver, who continued to stare appraisingly at the ancient vase. She kept her lips tightly pressed and her arms folded against her chest. His eyes eventually shifted towards her direction, maybe hoping Mimi would move on to a different vase or point out another flaw with the artwork, but she remained silent and still. He opened his mouth, then closed it. She saw him scan her face, possibly searching for some vulnerability or lack of certainty. When he found none, his mouth dropped and let out the faintest, "Oh. I don't know."

Now they both stood inside an empty museum, maintaining the

same degree of silence. Neither broke the other's gaze. The exhibit wouldn't close for another hour, and it didn't seem to be getting any busier. Against the silence, Oliver's lips pressed tightly together, an expression Mimi hadn't seen since he told his mother he wouldn't be able to spend Christmas with her because he was going to visit Mimi's family instead.

"What do you want?" he said. "Do you want pizza? We don't have to stay here. How about that new gyro shop downtown? I've heard great things; my friend was telling me that he goes there at least once a week. Are you hungry? We'll go wherever you want this time."

Mimi hung her head in silence. She thought of herself in this museum, herself in Tokyo, Oliver sitting alone in an empty apartment. She knew that, if she were to announce that she was moving abroad, he would have nothing but encouraging things to say to her. He would recommend different foods, mention historical facts, and offer to drop her off at the airport. He would not ask her to stay, or offer to move, or even try to saddle her with the guilt of leaving him behind. No, she knew that he would not wait quietly for her as she had for him.

"We should go home," she said.

From behind, Oliver took a step forward — pausing for just a brief moment — then took another step, and another. She could smell a hint of his cologne; she never thought he would wear *True Love for Men* when she surprised him with it on Valentine's Day, a subtle shift that had arisen when she realized that Oliver had already bought himself the cashmere sweater she had been saving for. The familiar counterpart to her own perfume greeted her, softening her shoulders for when he slid his arms around them, and she tried not to think about what would come next.

Valeria Overbeck
Kirkwood Community College
"Expectations"

"Here, here's a picture of what I painted last time," he said as he showed me a beautiful demonic dragon bursting out of her chest, wings spread from shoulder to shoulder. It had rotten looking teeth and long twisty horns. All of these features had been applied with water-based Wolfe brand face paint, some of the highest quality make-up you can find. One of the dragon's paws rested on the right side of her chest while the other grasped what was supposed to be her heart. Blood dripped from the heart, and an exit wound could be seen around the abdomen of the beast. "She wanted the dragon to be entering through her backside, too," he mentioned as he offered another photo. This one was the dragon's hind legs, complete with yellowed talons and a spiny tail that slithered up and around her back before plummeting downward again, as if the dragon was shooing a fly. The wound on her back was more detailed than the one on the front, and I found myself inspecting it, making sure it was indeed artwork and not an actual injury.

"I don't know if I can pull this off, dude," I told him, shaking my head. We had worked side by side at a haunted corn maze for three years now, and frequently complimented each other's face art, modestly arguing over whose work was better. "Your work always kicks ass!" he reminded me. I knew he was right, too. I always felt I was in over my head whenever an actor showed up with a particularly ambitious reference photo, but I always managed to surprise myself at how well I pulled it off after about thirty-five minutes of painstaking brushstrokes. Jeff could produce wonderfully detailed works in no time at all which to me was the mark of a great artist. This job, however, would prove to be much different than any painting I'd ever done. It was to be done in the privacy of Jeff's mother's home, rather than the laid-back group setting I had grown accustomed to at the haunted attraction.

"Plus, my mom's paying $50 and will have pizza there for us.

She's not picky, she just wants to have fun with it," he continued.
I nodded. I'm a fairly easy going person, so I quickly accepted. We
scheduled the job for a week later, and I spent that time looking at all
kinds of dragons online. Paintings, computer generated dragons from
movies, tattoos, and even amateur face paint jobs. The more I looked at
these mythical creatures, the more anxious I became. What a daunting
task, recreating her son's winged serpent from the week before. How
ridiculous of me to think she'd like my work even half as much as her
own son's. Furthermore, how dare Jeff invite me to fail like this! I was
sure there was no way I could make her happy with this piece. But
hey, fifty bucks is fifty bucks, and I've never turned down pizza in my
life. We worked out the logistics and solidified our plans.

About a week later, we caravanned to his mom's simple ranch-
style house in a small town about thirty minutes away. Upon arrival,
Jeff and I were each served up two slices of the strangest pizza
toppings. The flavor of the juicy pineapple clashed with the salti-
ness of the black olives, but I ate it anyway in an effort to be polite.
Honestly, I didn't taste one bite. Aside from my nerves, there were
plenty of environmental distractions. I quickly noticed the walls and
shelves were busy with beautiful knickknacks, family photos, and
framed puzzles. The awkwardness was slowly overshadowed by
conversation about Jeff's personal life. His mother questioned his love
life and asked how his daughter was doing. Occasionally, she'd turn
to me to include me in their exchange. "How about you? Do you have
any children?"

It was hard to focus, however. She had spiky red hair that pointed
in every direction, similar to characters in the Hunger Games movies.
She also had a gigantic mole on her upper lip which seemed to flap
with every word she spoke. Don't stare...Don't stare...Don't stare.
I struggled to ignore this feature, and I could feel my own cheeks
beginning to redden.

When I wasn't answering get-to-know-you questions, my attention
was on their 110 pound golden retriever, Bosley. As the hour of catching
up passed, the tumbleweed of dog hair at my feet grew and grew until
Jeff's father gently chased poor Bosley out of the room with the vacuum.

Jeff checked his watch and said he had to leave to meet his date. He made his exit rather abruptly. As soon as the headlights of his jalopy disappeared from the window, Brenda handed me a beer and said "All right, I didn't want to say this in front of Jeff, but he didn't paint anything near what I wanted last week!" She was referring to the photos Jeff showed me, the very ones I had spent so much time studying and committing to memory. She began to describe an elaborate dragon erupting through her abdomen. She traced her fingers along her torso right where she wanted everything: a long neck slithering up her chest with wings covering her right breast and the creature's head over her left breast. As I listened, I could imagine what she wanted. How strange it was to have a sixty year old woman motioning to her breasts with the expectation that I paint them.

Every so often, she would look at her husband for his approval. He quietly nodded at each cue, and the real reason I was there became more and more apparent. They had obviously discussed this in private many times before and had collaborated on the idea. I never asked what activities they would engage in after I left, and I'm not sure I wanted to know. All I could gather in this moment was they were trying to spice things up in the bedroom after years of being committed to one another. They wanted me to deliver some piece of art they could both could enjoy sexually.

I had to remember to keep a poker face. I didn't want them to feel judged; after all, we all want new and exciting things with our lovers. My initial response was void of any real emotion or thought. This realization of why I was there, and what I was actually providing for this couple, didn't faze me in the slightest. I didn't dwell on this new information at all, and made a conscious effort to look as unsurprised and accepting as I could.

Once I clarified the specifics of the painting, we began. She slipped her robe down her shoulders and tried to sit still on a stool while holding bunches of fabric against her chest in an effort to remain decently covered. Her efforts were futile though; there were more nip slips than Miami Beach during spring break. I could see she was getting nervous, so I told her not to worry because I wasn't shy. She immediately took that as a sign to go topless.

She removed the robe and tossed it aside. All that remained was her Betty Boop pajama pants and some brown moccasins. Suddenly, I didn't notice her mole anymore.

You know that old saying about how if you're nervous, just picture your audience naked? I'm here to tell you, it works. My stress and anxiety melted away as I became a fixture in the room while a 60-year-old topless woman became the focal point. I became focused on my work and no longer saw Brenda as a person. She was now the canvas, a beautifully-aged and proud woman with nothing to lose by exposing herself to me.

At this point, I was glad I had accepted the erotic nature of the visit. If I hadn't picked up on the sexual tension between Brenda and her husband during her consultation just moments before, I think I might have fainted at the sight of her nipples. I immediately admired her bravery. As a twenty-eight year old woman, I always felt like the time for public nudity was when I was 18 and at the peak of my physical form. Brenda swiftly challenged that thought, and made me contemplate the aging process. Do we become less inhibited the older we get?

I started mixing three shades of green together on the paper plate that was my palette. I decided to start with the head, which I thought would be the most detailed and difficult part. I painted the general shape of the snout and cranium, then used yellow and black to show depth. I referenced the horns from Jeff's original paint job, much to her delight. I even threw a heart in the beast's mouth complete with realistic blood drips. I used a pale blue for the dragon's eyes.

As soon as the face was done, I immediately regretted choosing blue for the eyes. I had made my demonic creature look like a sad puppy with those two small dots! I didn't dwell on it though. Once the paint dried, I could easily cover it with red or orange or gold.

I then traced its neck down to just above her abdomen and added simple brush strokes to give the basic idea of scales. Next, I created the wound, something I am well-versed in doing as a horror makeup artist. Last on her front side were the wings. They took almost no time at all to apply to her exposed breast, but the very moment I touched the brush to her chest her husband began taking pictures. I looked up at him, startled to see the flash. With giddy excitement, he asked if I was okay with him "documenting the process." I nodded politely and said, "Sure! I can get out of the way if you'd like." He shook his head quickly and said he'd prefer the artist to be captured in the candid moments. A bit unprepared to be part of this sexual journey that I now found myself in the middle of, I took a quick peek in the mirror to make sure I looked presentable. I might as well play the role well, right? After licking my fingers and taming some of my flyaway hairs, I again pulled out the black and yellow to add dimension. I caught Brenda smiling at her husband who was trying in vain to not look so amused.

I felt a bit like a frog in hot water. Brenda and her husband were incrementally turning up the sexual heat. The more time I spent in that living room, the more I felt as if this were a ménage a trois. It occurred to me that this might have been their plan the whole time, to feel me out and see just how far they could go before I became uncomfortable and made my exit. Lucky for them, I have a high tolerance for awkwardness. In fact, some of life's best lessons can be found lurking in the middle of a strange happening, such as conversing with a topless senior citizen.

To see a human without the burden of clothing is to see them at the very basic level of humanity. Once nude, they have nothing left to hide and become almost infallible when expressing their passions and regrets. We spoke candidly about an array of topics until we landed on one that stuck. Art.

She and I both felt creative, but that we lacked talent. She described all kinds of art supplies she purchased but never opened or used because she was afraid her final project wouldn't pan out as she had imagined. I told her I could relate, often hoarding supplies and waiting endlessly for the perfect project to make itself known.

I started painting her backside as she recounted all the years she spent buying art kits: Mosaic projects, scrapbooking supplies, bead sets, hemp cord, and expensive canvases that had never seen the light of day. She said over and over she was just so nervous she'd waste time and material only to be left with a mess of garbage and feelings of regret. I smiled knowingly and went over my own list of half started projects and half-baked ideas. She laughed and told me the universe must have brought us together. She had a recent brush with death, too, and was saved by a bystander who performed CPR. She didn't reveal too many details about her story, but shared she made a promise to herself to throw expectation to the wind and simply enjoy her time doing things she loves.

It was at that moment I decided she could be right about the seemingly cosmic connection between us. She had opened up to me in the most intimate of settings. She suddenly became a reflection of my future self. Would I ever find the peace that she has found? With thoughts of my own past and uncertain future, I sighed a deep sigh and finished the spikes and talons on her backside. I realized how truly free Brenda must feel, shooting the breeze with someone who was a stranger just sixty minutes prior.

The time came for her to inspect the final product. As she stood at the mirror, I also looked at the piece in its entirety for the first time. I wasn't pleased. The lines were wonky, the edges were sloppy and the color blending was off. Worse yet, I realized I forgot to change the eye color. I felt a bit disappointed, but before I could offer a change, she said "Blue eyes! Love it! It makes the scary beast lovable. It's perfect!" She smiled proudly at her body in the mirror, as if she physically looked the way she had always seen herself in her mind's eye.

I was relieved at her response. At least one of us was impressed. Upon closer inspection, I was able to find aspects of the piece I thought came out well, but I definitely knew there were things I'd change if I was given another chance. Brenda didn't notice my reaction, nor did I tell her. It wasn't my place. In her mind, she finally had the body art she'd always wanted.

As I exited their home and drove the 20 minutes back to my apartment, I realized my presence was their foreplay. How courageous of this couple to allow someone into their proverbial bedroom with them. Instead of feeling uncomfortable, I smiled to myself and felt I was part of something absolutely beautiful. Although my dragon wasn't a perfect piece of art, worthy of framing and keeping forever, the act of painting it was. And that, I think, is something to be proud of.

Jake Hills
Rutgers University
"I Can Feel You"

When I was ten, my mother used to tell me a story before I went to bed. It was the same little tale every time, and it went something like this: "The sky is as vast and blue as the world's oceans, bigger than you or I and everything that lies in between. Trees the size of skyscrapers seem to brush against the sky, while blades of grass like the strands of your hair stay hushed to the ground beneath your feet. Critters of all shapes and sizes, some as big as you…" – here she would gently trace her finger along the length of my body – "crawl, walk, jump, flutter, fly…just as you move about on two legs. And if you push far enough in either direction…" –she demonstrated this by placing a fingertip atop my head and another on the sole of my foot, and then slowly lifting them away – "you'll disappear from this world entirely."

My mother would often lean in close to me at this point in the story, and I'd reach out with my tiny little hands to feel the outline of her lips as she spoke. "There are depths in the oceans that no one has ever seen, and there are galaxies in the deepest of space that will stay hidden until the end of time."

"Not even you have been there?" I asked her, even though I knew the answer.

"Not even me," she'd whisper, kissing the tips of my fingers and placing them over the top of her eyelids. I could feel her eyes moving underneath the skin, as if they were searching for the world of light which had been shut out.

"Alright, my angel", she'd say. It was her way of letting me know that I had free reign, that for a few precious moments each night I could begin to commit the features of my mother's face to memory. I learned to know her spatially: where her thin fuzzy eyebrows ended and the warm flush of her cheekbones began, or the spot on her forehead where her hair dangled. It was the closest I would ever get to knowing her the way other people did. Father always said her eyes were the color of emeralds and her hair that of dark chestnut, but I only knew green as the color of grass and brown as mud.

When my few moments in heaven were up, my mother would lightly kiss my forehead and tuck me in to bed, flicking the light switch before the door to my room closed with a soft clink. Nothing had changed, but I knew it was dark.

****

"The Lord gives just as he taketh away, and it is important to remember that though we loved Anna Taylor, she was never ours to keep." The priest's final words echoed in my head as I exited the funeral parlor with my brother Brian. It was just beginning to rain, and I could sense the swift sounds of departure as muffled footsteps shuffled towards already idling engines.

I heard a click and the rain seemed to suddenly stop falling. "Here, hold this." Brian placed the familiar grip of the umbrella I used for rainy days at the bus stop into my hand. "Stay here," he said. "I'm going to check on Dad."

And just like that I was alone, reduced to that helpless little girl without her cane. I'm not even sure how I left the house without it, but we were already fifteen minutes down the road and turning back was out of the question. I mean, imagine if we were late to our own mother's funeral? How awfully insensitive we'd have looked, but only for a moment, I'm sure of it. They'd see whatever it is I am, and suddenly feel a lump in their throats, ashamed they forgot the burden the Taylor family still carried, and which was now all the more poignant due to Anna's absence. No, she would never have let that happen. Today she would remain invisible. Today was for her mother.

Someone called out: "Don't forget we have to pick up the kids on th-" A car door slammed somewhere nearby, wheels crunching over the gravel lot as another connection to Mrs. Taylor was severed forever.

Another voice, soft and wispy, came from nearby.

"Is that her?"

"Yes, yes, I'm sure of it."

I could hear the sound of footsteps approaching. I wanted to move away, to go back home and hide under the covers so that for once nobody could see me, and the world and I would stand on even ground. Where the hell was Brian?

"Ahem."

"Well, go ahead David; she's not deaf," whispered a womanly voice.

"Right, uh, hello there Annie. My name is Mr. Krenshaw. Ahem. I, uh, worked with your mother, and I just want you to know that if you ever need anything, well, I'm only a phone call away."

I remained silent; one of the perks of not being able to see is an exemption from social etiquette. Pity did have its place.

The man chuckled dryly. "Right, well, here's my card." His hand brushed against mine and left me grasping the familiar shape of a business card much like the one my mother handed out to her clients. "Just, uh, let your father hold on to that."

The rain began to pick up, and a sudden surge of wind sent it spattering across my face. "So sorry about your mother, Annie," the woman chimed in, and then more quietly, "Let's go David."

They left as quickly as they came; their departure sounded like everyone else. Crunch, crunch, and away they went.

Something clutched my shoulder and I nearly jumped out of my skin. "Sorry, Annie." It was Brian. He sighed. "Dad is going to stay behind for a little while."

I dropped my head against my chest and lowered the umbrella, letting the rain soak my clothes. "She's really gone, isn't she?"

I felt dead weight drape across my shoulders and Brian pulled me

in close, resting his chin on my head. My eyes twitched, and I shuddered under the weight of tears that didn't fall. "I can't even cry for
her," I said. "Brian, I can't even cry."

He pulled me closer, wrapping both of his arms around me and
rocking ever so slightly. "Shhh. Mom loved you more than anything
else in this world, kiddo. She would hate to see you cry."

We stood like this for a few moments, the rain continuing to fall
without measure, and I realized how quiet everything had become.
Everyone who had come to see my mother was leaving or already
gone, reassuming happy demeanors that were all the more robust after
their morning brush with death, while I would forever be missing a
part of me.

"C'mon," Brian said softly, releasing from our embrace and sliding
his arm under mine like he used to do when we were younger and I
was too scared to walk around the house without my cane. "Let's go
home."

He jingled the car keys and nudged me playfully. "Maybe I'll let
you drive."

****

Sometimes I have trouble locating myself. That sounds funny,
doesn't it? I can place a hand on my face and there I am, and my feet
firmly rooted to the ground do their best to fixate me in the world. But
I am not here, that is, where you are.

Once on a train ride with the whole family to New York City, a
little boy asked me what it is like to be blind. I was somewhat taken
aback by the bluntness of the question, for I had grown up used to
people who tried so hard to pretend that I *wasn't* blind, which was
always worse.

"Well," I said, "without turning your head, tell me what you see
behind you." There was a short pause, and I imagine the boy must
have been thinking hard about his answer.

"Hmmm, that's not fair," the boy mumbled, disappointed that I ruined his fun.

"No, it isn't," I said.

That train ride was one of the few times that I had felt sorry for myself, for my mother made certain that I viewed my condition not as a curse but a virtue.

Just one month before she died from a brain tumor, Dad, Brian and I threw a surprise birthday party for her in our backyard. We invited everyone we could think of; distant relatives and co-workers whom I had never met all came with gifts and a belly full of laughter. Before my mother opened her presents, everyone began calling for pictures with the birthday girl, and I sat quietly off to the side listening to the snaps of cameras that captured my mother's last days of happiness before she went into surgery.

In the midst of the clicks of cameras, I heard her say, "Just a moment," and then, "I want my Annie with me." She led me over to where she was and sat me down next to her, wrapping her arm around me and pressing her cheek against mine. I could feel her smiling, and I couldn't help but do the same.

Snap. "Aren't they precious?" Snap. "Oh my god, look at how adorable they are together." Snap. "We should have brought Isabelle instead of getting a babysitter."

When all was done my mother kissed my cheek and nudged her nose against mine. "All of these people can see me, but you know me better than anyone else, Annie," she whispered. She blew out the candles on the double fudge cake that I had specially picked out for her, a round of applause went up, and then everyone quieted down to a low murmur to eat dessert.

Three weeks later my mother checked in to Saint Peter's hospital. I never saw her again.

****

"And just where do you think you're going?" my father's voice rang from the kitchen over to where I sat at the bottom of the living room steps.

"Out," I said, sliding my other foot into the heavy steel-toed boot.

The faucet was running, and I could hear him furiously scrubbing some piece of silverware or dish. There was tension in his tone. "You're going to see that girl again, aren't you? The one with the freckles and red hair?"

"Her name is Melanie," I mumbled under my breath. I felt near the door for my cane, which I always left propped by the corner of the wall whenever I walked into the house. I knew my way around inside well enough without it.

"Watch it, Annie." He scoffed, or maybe it was a sigh. "I thought I told you I didn't want you hanging around her anymore." A sharp clanging came from the other room; he was probably loading the dishwasher.

"Mom never cared, so why should you?"

The water stopped running, and I waited a moment for him to say something, but he didn't. I felt the blood rush into my face, ashamed for speaking so freely. It had been two weeks since we buried mom, and nothing had been as it used to.

Dad scoured the house day and night: putting things in their place when they never used to have one, vacuuming rooms twice or three times over and shouting at Brian and me if we left our shoes on in the house, and washing dishes that he seemed to dirty purposely. Brian fortified himself in his room and didn't come out unless it was to use the bathroom or the kitchen, though that was probably for the best since dad was so volatile nowadays.

I knew they were hurting because I was too, but I couldn't stay in that house any longer. I grabbed my cane and opened the door, listening for just a bit longer to hear if the sink would turn back on. "Sorry daddy," I whispered, and closed the door behind me.

****

I moved my cane in an arc in front of me, tapping the ground when it reached the apex of each swing until the pavement of our driveway ended and I stood at the edge of Wicken Street, near the spot where the school bus stopped to pick me up. I listened for the sound of oncoming traffic, and felt for any vibrations on the road before crossing to the other side. A few clicks in front of me lay a bridge that crossed over the canal, and I followed it until I stood on the familiar dirt path that ran parallel to the water's edge and continued for miles in either direction. I veered to the left and made my way along the path, which I knew from countless walks with my mother stretched straight as an arrow, with only minor turns here and there. I wondered if Mel was already waiting at our spot.

After a few minutes my cane hit something hard, and I knew I had arrived. Ever since I started meeting Mel over here I decided to make a landmark on the edge of the dirt path out of rocks that she had fished out of the canal. It was much easier this way, since the bench we met at was situated off to the side on the edge of the waterfront. I touched tentatively with my cane, feeling for the change in slope, and stepped off the path.

My stomach clenched in worry as I moved forward. I had not seen Mel since my mother's funeral, and I was scared that the color of death would suddenly make her see me the way everyone else did.

Leaves crackled beneath my feet as the ground became flat again, and I knew that the bench lay directly in front of me.

Mel's voice broke into the air with a sweet ring. "Annie," she said. From somewhere in front of me she shuffled over and hugged me fiercely. I nearly collapsed into her arms, as if the weight of the world had hung on my shoulders and now someone else could help me carry it.

I felt her pull back ever so slightly. She pushed my hair back over my ear and gently stroked the outline of my jaw with her fingers. "I'm so sorry about your mum, Annie."

"Thanks," I said, suddenly short of breath. My eyes went through the motions as if I was going to cry, but nothing came out. "I want to cry Mel," I shuddered, "but my stupid eyes won't let me." My heart was beating fast and I tried to catch my breath.

"Oh, Annie," she said, slipping her hand into mine and rubbing her thumb along my fingers. "Come, let's sit."

For a few moments we sat in silence, our hands entwined, and I felt as though I could sit like this forever and just let the world pass us by.

"You look pretty," Mel said, "just like your mum." I wanted to say something, but my heart was pounding against my chest and I couldn't find the words. I thought about how I left dad, and suddenly I didn't know what I was doing here anymore.

"Talk to me Annie."

"I think I should go," I said quietly, though I made no motion to leave. "I –my dad, he's in so much pain. I shouldn't be here."

I felt her shift and her hand loosened from mine, but she didn't let go. "You know I love you more than anything, Annie. And I know that Brian and your father must be hurting, but so are you. You've been hurting since the day I met you." She sniffled, and her voice became uneven. "No one understands you the way I do. *Looks* at you the way I do. "Oh, Annie." She let go of my hand, sharply breathing in as she began to sob.

The sound of her crying was enough: I didn't need to see her for it to break my heart. I felt along the bench with my hand, searching for her, and rested my palm on her thigh, just above the kneecap. I pulled myself towards her, so that our legs touched, and turned my head in her direction.

Her crying had stopped, reduced back to small sniffles. We must have been looking at each other, for I could feel her breath on me, warm and smelling of peppermints. I reached out, like I did with my mother all those years ago, and traced my fingers over her thin lips, letting them slide over her cheek until I cupped her face in my hand. She didn't feel so different from mom. "I'm not going anywhere, Mel."

I felt her move, her lips meeting mine. She hovered there, waiting. "It's okay," I said. I kissed her back, my lips hungry against hers, drinking her in.

I wanted her. All of her. To feel her as intensely as she saw me. To know her like no else ever could.

I would love her until the day she died, and like my mother, I would always remember the way she felt.

Haleigh Williams
Tufts University
"Paper Tiger"

Kate thought her pills might help me sleep.

I thought Kate was full of shit, but I was desperate for sleep in that haughty, Cambridge-bred way. I didn't ask about side effects. I popped two with a swig of Fresca and then I saw Kate's half-siblings — twins, Alex and Jess, ten years my junior, twelve Kate's — and swallowed a third, dry. Elsewhere, my thesis begged to be coaxed into being.

Where was the kid with the color-coded notebooks? With flash-cards decked out with facts about each new school, the oft-advertised teacher-to-student ratio, the way the sun infused a stone ledge with permanent warmth and leaves whispered underfoot? Where was that smart kid, smart enough to write a bird into existence and humble enough not to cage it?

Now, I can say what no one bothered to tell me: Your first institutional foray *should* leave you stupid. And then, asleep. If you're lucky.

****

I remember thinking that Adams might have been — I don't know what I was thinking. When our hands were splayed out on the table between us, I could see only one ring: mine, the unblemished opal adornment my mother had handed down to me years ago in a show of defeat expedited by her weakened state and which I, drunk with groundless reverence, had proceeded to wear religiously.

Stitching my veins like colorful, flimsy, insubstantial spools of thread, methodically but without order.

When it came time to move on, I wondered: Where from? And at that ceremony, I spent all of the time during which the orators, McCray included, were giving their speeches staring up at Adams where he was seated on the stage. The day before, sitting in my car, I watched the workers mow the field. The steering wheel burned from neglect, and I wasted twenty minutes running the air conditioning before I could feel okay to drive. Down the road, an expert in my field suggests I move to Tucson for work, if I can get it in my contract that I'll get a parking space in a covered lot. He says, "It's a good move if you can handle the heat." A moment passes. "And the snakes." The air too heavy, my skin too clammy and pink and sensate, breath forced from sponge. As the workers walked to their cars, the only ones left in the lot besides mine, they looked at me sideways, inquiring. I watched them drive away, and then I counted to thirty before running for the trashcan.

I remember thinking of that June day from the previous year. Who can say which moment leads to any other? I offer only that the antecedent sultry daybreak *saw* the opportunity to stop our dominoes in their tracks; paused; sat idly by, up on its pedestal, unassailable, beaming; did nothing in the name of prevention.

We were standing together near the doorway of his office, a cramped, dreary affair further suffocated by the impatience of youth and an intimidating book collection — deep cuts, the lot of them, the kind of books you might hate if they could be trotted out and lined up on any old shelves. Two such tomes lay open on his desk, a standard-issue steel monstrosity which flirted dangerously with an increasingly scuffed wall and was responsible for the abrasions on his hipbones, which catalogued the times when he had tried, naively, to force himself between the two in an attempt to gain access to the room's sole window.

Now, I am glad I fail to recall the color of the walls. He had been speaking quietly before abruptly falling silent. Beige? *Eggshell*? I wanted to contribute and I suspected that he had something more to say — that the idea and perhaps even the words for its expression were there, and he lacked only the courage or the impropriety to mouth them for me. He was on the verge of speaking, it seemed, when he suddenly closed up, as though he had seen an ominous specter through the window of the door behind me. But my own eyes happened upon no ghost and no cause for concern, only a door across the hall falling unobtrusively shut.

Later, during the postmortem, my mother speaks to me in her old voice, the one that first lulled me to sleep—you are here because your mother can no longer lull you to sleep—and says that not being there is the accident, but *being* there, well, that's sanctification, if you ask me. She has hair like cotton candy, soft and fine and ethereal. When the Bakers showed up to tour our house, they took one look at my mother and knew that they were getting the better end of the deal. But I hope they forgot to clean the vents.

How ingenuous I was, thinking that it must have been an idea that came to him suddenly or a flashback of some sort that had given him pause. A delayed-release passage from one of the two exposed novels; an urge to pry open the semi-operational window even if the task consumed the whole of his strength and life force. But it's not enough.

So I push onward in our colloquy, feeling like fire, and he lets me, though it is clear from that point forward that something distinct has been taken from him by whatever anonymous force willed him to bite his tongue. He stares at the doorway for a minute and then at the place where my imitation bluebird rests on his desk. Fleetingly, I wonder if it flew to him of its own accord.

And, there it is: not enough to push him to interfere with my own strong will and my need to make him see what I see; barely enough to do what it actually does in that dark, seasonally abandoned building. Perhaps its most noteworthy effect is leaving me with the anxious, youthful question of what will happen when the reminder of that weight is removed. That the weight itself will still be there does not strike me until post-bereavement.

Wildly, stupidly, I smashed my fist into the mirror before me. A second time. A third time. Blood trickled down the embankments of my knuckles. My whole hand like fire, again, no order. A fourth time. The already-splintered glass broke completely. I held my hand up in

front of me and saw red. Exhaling heavily, I washed the wound in
the sink before, feeling like an idiot, I wrapped it in a stretch of gauze
Kate had purchased the first time she sprained her ankle.

Am I moving forward or backward? Away from the acid waterfall?

****

I pried my laptop open again, only to be met with my manifestly
incomplete exposition, and I stared. I prayed dumbly (knowing it
was dumb and meaning it still, forcefully, with a futile, stunted confidence) that I might be absorbed into the computer, lost in a miasma
of zeros and ones and ciphers for whomever to untangle and so effect
my liberation.

****

Kate is not stupid, not by any stretch of the imagination. She is
a second-year law student at a prestigious school with a sky-high
post-graduate employment rate; academically, she does what she does
quite well. She can, without question, hold her own in intellectual
conversations revolving around any number of subjects. She correctly
pronounces words like "mischievous" and "hierarchy" and she never
says "good" when "well" would better suit her purpose.

But I am the product of my environment, of my upbringing, and,
though my thoughts are usually not so black and white, I, if the truth,
detached and callous though it may be, be told, did not feel that she
could measure up.

****

McCray doesn't laugh the way he used to. The first time he said
hello to me, then a stranger, in an emptying lunchroom, I caught his
eye as I turned around, compelled to look back as I left by the sheer
potency of his good cheer.

"Weltschmerz," he mutters reflexively. I can't unhear it.

I fold my sonnets into origami animals to bring him back to life, and it works in the stretches between one lesson and another, a resuscitation contingent upon the channeling of both our powers of observation. Much later, I use the phrase in a neurobiology lab report and some Philistine of a TA writes "This isn't Hogwarts," and I think, "You're fucking lucky it's not."

McCray tells me he's going to call his autobiography "A Recovery," and I beam at the indefinite article. Quite some time ago, I lost that power — in the menagerie over which I no longer claim ownership — both of them dreaming up new ways to bring me back to life.

****

"Are you visiting someone?"

I spun around hastily. The innocent woman sitting across the aisle smiled.

"No… I'm going home."

Outside my window, darkened storefronts blurred together.

"Well, you should have stayed! It's supposed to snow tomorrow. Can you believe it? This time of year?"

I could. Thai food. Dry-cleaning. Nail salon. I pressed my fingertips against the lifeless, frozen glass of the windowpane and painted a rainbow of smudges.

At South Station, I hailed a cab to take me back to my apartment, where Kate slept soundly in her room and I, soon, would sleep peacefully in mine for the first time in too long.

****

Adams: donning a lengthy black robe lined with electric blue and magenta (the closest they could get to the officially sanctioned maroon, I'm told), clear-eyed and worry-free, glowing healthfully. Perspiring mildly. Is he happy? I don't know. (Two weeks beforehand, he pulls me aside to share the flattering but functionally profitless news that the organizers have overestimated his height by a full two inches.)

Regardless, they can always pick out the hottest day of the year months in advance. The air is thick, sultry, heavy with allergens, tamping my lungs. When you can barely breathe, you feel it deep in the pit of your stomach, like nausea.

Adams *was* a moment. Smiling. Nothing, nothing, such a far cry from a few months earlier, when, good God, he seemed to have taken up permanent residence on the proverbial ledge. (It is only after the epoch in question passes that I realize just how little it takes to push a good man off: just one distinct moment of impulsiveness, which is a comelier word for lucidity.) I had never dealt forthrightly with that particular stage. Each and every time I endeavored to force myself to meet the challenge, my resolve turned to nothing, eclipsed by my pseudo-pragmatic indifference, a vestigial defense mechanism I had developed of perceived necessity in my still younger years.

I am buoyant. I am cool. I cannot fold myself into silence.

Nothing seems preordained in the moment, but retrospection pushes everything into this neat little column of memorials, all of which seem to fit together flawlessly, naturally, like the broken, melted-down fragments from a million shattered vessels, uniting even where they should not. Years later, an avuncular lecturer tells me that there is only one odorant receptor in the entire human olfactory system that responds to just one scent — that of freshly cut grass — and I believe him.

As I shake the executor's hand, I look out into the crowd and feel overpoweringly motherless.

****

When I wake up and tell Kate her love has ruined me, I condense the l-word so you can't even grasp the vowels, and she presses her lips together like she's stopping them from inventing *A-E-I-O-U* on my behalf.

"Not nearly as literary as despair," I offer — but my voice sounds reedy and insubstantial to my own ears.

It's been said before. Your father's *lv* ruined your mother *twice* and Alex and Jess will ruin him and someone else whose name I never even learned so fuck it and I leave her out.

It wasn't his love and besides my mother isn't ruined; she's just centering herself around painting right now. (Pictures. Because there are no words.)

I want to slam a nail into my thesis.

Kate wants to see a movie in the square.

****

Two weeks into April, we see the sun again, and I surrender two collated, stapled, properly labeled copies of my thesis to a maternal administrative assistant with the thick, full-body cough and yellowing fingernails of a woman on the brink. In another biosphere…

Adams.

It was his masterpiece, really, which my own mechanical exertion had charmed into existence without ever really touching it. (A flicker of Kate reminds me that this is helpful for plausible deniability.)

When I close my eyes and see his face, it takes a full four minutes before I remember he's dead now and I finally get to call myself *haunted*.

In the eye of my bewitched mind, he tries to tell me that an undertaking like mine, conducted by someone like me, is supposed to be an exercise in collaboration anyway. But, of course — of *course*, stupid me, I didn't know — there is no such thing.

****

I lied. I had known instinctively that I'd lost him, buried beneath the weight of our merging indecision. It seems ridiculous, but it's true: nothing ever brought me closer to the brink of internal war than that—that hopelessly dissected vision of the two of us gallivanting around a new town where we *could* gallivant or else crumbling simultaneously. But I had lived for years inside of my own head, and that had broken something irreparable. If we had ever had a chance to make a change, God knows I didn't see it.

I wondered briefly if any of it had really happened outside of me, wondered if at any point I could have shaken myself awake and walked away from that tie, the anchor that latched onto me and never stopped dragging.

No closure, no advancement. Six days into my newest exploit, I had fainted with such matchless abandon that the resulting lesion continued to bleed even after fifteen minutes of continuous pressure, and then a clean-shaven young doctor gave me four stitches and told me to drink more water. I watched the fluorescent lights dance on his wedding ring as he sewed and I assured him that I would, but I didn't drink a drop of anything until much later that night.

The shadows of furniture turned themselves into fiends along the walls. I wondered what would happen on the following day. I felt terribly unprepared, untrained. I thought of the relatives and the gifts and the ceremony—I had successfully avoided all three for four years.

I dreamed that Kate got sick with E. coli and her mother lost her modishness to mad cow disease and her father fell prey to swine flu. I dreamed that McCray stood in the hallway, powerless to help, willing to help, made to help, trying tirelessly to help. I dreamed that I had nothing to do with it, and that was all that struck me as particularly surreal.

I wondered if I would ever get far enough away to be able to
look back.

****

McCray: two hundred and fifty miles outside of his comfort zone,
trying to help me relive and rewrite.

He is seated with my family in the crowd at commencement.
When we have a moment to ourselves, he looks at me forlornly, and I
wonder if he would have come all this way just for the ceremony.

"I will never blame you."

After reading a sonnet, he would fold it back along the creases
into the perfect form of the animal it had once been, and it would
be indistinguishable from the creature I had given to him—a talent I
remain in awe of to this day.

Kenneth West
Louisiana Tech University
"Straightening the Way"

I

I shut my Bible with reluctance, and I fingered the length of the spine. I picked it up to inhale the musky scent of the pages, before walking over to look out of the peephole of my door. The good book is the world's only wholesome woman.

The hall is empty, and the coast is clear.

They know who I am, and they will not let me out. My keeper is deaf to my pleas and blind to reality itself. She does not see the way the curtains turn to serpents poised as if to bite the bun (big and ugly) as a rat off her head. There are certain places that once we leave we can never hope to see again.

Take me for instance. I used to see time in a straight line, the way you, Mama, and Uncle Hosea used to see it, the way my keeper used to see it. But she is so stupid, that woman; the only reason I feel sorry for her is cause I'm a Christian. I am more Christian than you or anybody else, for that matter, but nobody sees that. Anyway, that stupid woman had it coming for her, Lord forgive me. Pull the unborn words from beneath my tongue and squeeze them to dust. Let my words be as pure as my thoughts and actions.

My life changed the day He entered my heart. I was ten years old when the Lord flew into my heart like a bird gliding into an open window, but God is a bird which one cannot and should not shoo away. I remember when Reverend Benjamin gripped me by the shoulder and plunged my face into the water. My head hit the bottom of the basin hard. I was down there for so long that I think I fell asleep.

But when I awoke, Reverend Benjamin's clean shaven face floated above me, smooth as the top of a polished table. I cast my eyes to the corner of the church, where I saw a figure, a man in a tunic pacing behind the back aisle. He turned and looked at me with eyes that danced like tiny flames. He made the sign of the cross and walked right through a shut window.

Water gushed out of my ears, and it took a long time for me to stop coughing. I looked around me and all of the men and women were humming the hymns which we all carry inside of us. Two deacons hoisted me by my armpits and dragged me out of the church, where my mother sat weeping, for a reason I could not discern. They were oblivious to what had happened. They were all sleeping with their eyes open.

My father came here not long after the Civil War. He was one of the first settlers, along with Judge Grey, The Mayor, and Joshua Sherman. Yes, he was one of those illustrious men whose names will one day be written in the books of history. My father was a God-fearing man of great principles, or so I have heard many say, but he died from the fever when I was four. I have seen his shade wander through our house though. He is always wearing a dark brown suit and the fob of his watch is always shining even though his eyes lack the luster of the living. He is silent, as all shades are, but his countenance is doleful. He paces around the room with his head bowed, and he always leaves through the very same wall which he entered.

Mama did not take father's death well. She held it deep within until I was fourteen. As far as I know, I am the only one who can remember. I remember the day when her chord snapped and I stood helpless as the blue figure broke free from her flesh. A great chasm opened up in the middle of our living room and I watched as her shade fell in, head first, and the chasm slammed clam shut behind her. She was never the same again. They took her away. And even now she is in a hospital in New York. She still walks, a body without its shade.

This is how at fourteen I came into the hands of my keeper. She was a relative, an aunt, or something of that nature and because of her for eight years, I burned.

"What are you doing?" she asked.

I did not hear her enter the kitchen, and the shock from being startled made me drop the jar. The glass hit the floor, and it screamed, not unlike the time I saw a woman tumble down Roan Hill. She was there in the darkest hours of the night, no doubt to do something sinful. Her screech was so loud that she woke up the entire town, and all of us were launched like catapults from our beds.

II

"Thank you, Mr. Mayor" I said.

The Mayor had just made a long-winded speech, as politicians are apt to do. He bloviated about his sovereign duty, the menace of crime, and his unwavering desire to protect our people. But we all know that by *our* people, he meant *his* people. The truth of this life is simple. Politicians talk, and people like me *do*.

The Mayor had just appointed me the town's first sheriff, but you couldn't tell from his speech, which consisted of him talking about himself and his values. It was an election year, but The Mayor had been elected three times without opposition. Nobody in this town, except The Mayor, gives a damn about politics. We never have, and we never will. We have more pressing concerns to worry about.

Jim Greevy had six watermelons stolen from his yard last week. The town's only school got set ablaze a month ago, and those Santorums are up to no good again. As the old men say, I can feel it deep in my bones.

I looked into the eyes of the people as they walked away from the town square. I saw Horace Freeman, balding, but still clinging to a few tufts of white hair; Jules Nelson, the barber, (staring at the back of Horace's head; Ulysses Johnson, standing hunched over from years spent at the plough; and Adam Davis looking down at his hands, dirty and big as baby pigs, and I felt a hand touch my shoulder. It was the Mayor.

"You're going to do a great job, son. You're one of the most upstanding men amongst us. I am proud of you, and I know you'll do a marvelous job. We all have faith in you."

"Thank you, sir. I'll do my best."

III

After my sister died, my nephew was never the same. He sometimes spoke of her as if she were alive, that is if I could get him to talk to me at all. It's not easy to lose both of your parents, especially at such a young age. It's such a tragedy to see such a bright and promising young man descend into madness. I just wish I could reach him. He reminds me so much of my own son, my sweet Gabriel; that is before he went to Harlem to join one of those heathen jazz bands.

That new music will be the death of our young people. But John wasn't like that. John wasn't a wayward prodigal child, like my Gabriel. No, John never drank, nor listened to the Devil's songs. He would sit in his room all day reading. Perhaps, it was the books that made him this way. Maybe Mr. Washington was right. Maybe it is not good to always be reading books.

I never was much of one for reading myself. I didn't even finish the second grade. We didn't need words and numbers back then. That was back before all these great changes, when this town was even more modest than it is now. Just a few small houses clustered around a one room courthouse.

I went up north as soon as I sprouted my stubby, little adult wings. I went to Chicago, where I heard that it was possible, even for us, to become millionaires. But my hopes crumbled more quickly than the cookies I took with me in my pocket. I wasn't the only small town girl with skyscraper dreams. When I got there, the only job I could find was the world's oldest one. But my daddy was a mean one. He would take all my money and pounded me with his fists whenever he felt like it.

I hate that my sister died. I mean it, I really do, but I am glad that it brought me back home away from the danger and the uncertainty. I still wonder why things are the way they are. I wonder where my poor Gabriel, angry, with the choler of wedlock's children, is in this wide world. I wonder why I was born with a heart already half broken. But looking after John would be a distraction from all of this, and perhaps I could even save him.

All of these things were on my mind that morning when I woke up and got out of bed. There were a lot of strange happenings in our town lately. Crime was on the rise, so it scared the shit out of me when I heard cabinets banging in the kitchen.

IV

My dinner was disrupted by a knock at the door so loud that my silverware shook, as if in trepidation of the news that was to follow. It was Maggie Sikes, and she grabbed me by my collar, sobbing.

"Sheriff, come quick! I found two bodies at Sutter's Place."

"Wait, Maggie. For Christ's sake. Calm down. Tell me exactly what happened."

"I was going to see Rachel, on account of a dress she'd paid me to make her… but I didn't expect this. I didn't…"

"That's enough, Maggie. Calm down, and get some rest. Hell, Maggie, get a drink. You look like you need it."

I grabbed my hat and my coat, and I rushed to my new Model T, leaving Maggie on the porch. I fired her up, and inside I cursed God. Why me? Why was I charged with keeping the people of this god awful town safe?

When I reached Sutter's place, it was twilight, and all of the windows were shut tight against the world, but the grass outside was still green. Maggie had left the door ajar, and when I entered the living room, the wood panels on the floor creaked when I walked across them. I found the first body. It was Rachel, seated at the piano, and her face was smashed against the keys. Thin lines of dried blood were etched along the corners of her mouth. And at her feet was a circle of her teeth, arranged, almost methodically. I counted them. Eight teeth.

Eight teeth, white as the shirt of the milkman whose body lay on the other side of the room. His body was swollen and blue from bruises. If I were not a man of reason, a man of logic, I would say that a demon had taken up residence inside of him. Whoever did this must have been a person of tremendous strength. My feet nearly turned to water in my boots. It was my responsibility to subdue this man and to put him in prison.

I walked into the kitchen, which was neat, and nearly everything seemed to be in its proper place, except for a broken jam jar, with all of its contents licked clean. Then, a thought struck me. The only reason Rachel had returned to town was to care for her nephew. He was a twenty-something man-child by the name of John. Nobody knew much about him, except that he was once a promising youth, but he had gone crazy from the loss of both of his parents. I wonder if what had gotten Rachel and the milkman had also gotten John. I searched throughout the house, but I couldn't find him in any of the rooms. Maybe John had done this. I had to find him. Where would I go if I were him? Where would a loose cannon launch the remnants of his mind?

V

The fish always fly in the right direction. They always fly home, so any wanderer who uses them as a lodestar will never be lost, but rather, he will always arrive in precisely the place he needs to be, as if he were ferried there on angels' righteous wings. If I told you the truth I would tell you I was scared. I am the arm of God. I always tell the truth, exactly the way it happened, no embellishments. I was indeed fearful, but when I remembered my duty, I disposed of such inappropriate feelings, and I took a deep draught from the fountain of faith, that great and blessed fountain which resides in each of us, and which never fails to sustain those of us who consistently solicit its salubrious waters.

Indeed, without faith I would be nothing. Because of faith, I escaped that wicked woman. The keeper sent by Satan himself to stop the work that I am destined to accomplish. Oh wait, forgive my prideful tongue, which sings the boasts of my conceited flesh. I mean the work that God will accomplish, using me as a conduit.
All of the glory is his alone.

I must remain humble. I must not give in to all of the pressures this world endeavors to offer me. People get lost in their perception of themselves, and they allow the bigger picture to become blurred in the process. But I am studious, and I learn from the transgressions of others.

I am imperfect, and my spirit is still fond of the flesh's foibles, but my master is perfect, and when he comes, he will make this world anew. He will bathe the world in fire, and all of the sinners will be branded with the mark of their evil.

It is my duty to prepare the world for my master's arrival. Like John the Baptist, I must ready the people for the coming of a new kingdom. I am charged with the work of a king greater than any this world has ever seen, a king greater than Caesar or Charlemagne or Louis XIV. This is why so many want me dead. This is why my keeper hated me. This is why she scalds me with her demon eyes. But no matter, I took care of her. She sleeps soundly now, as befits one of Lucifer's finest angels.

I hate to take life, but a man must do what he is compelled to do. A prophet must have a world that is willing to hear him. This must be achieved, regardless of the cost, and anyone who attempts to prevent the world from hearing my message must die. Thus sayeth the Lord. When Pharaoh and the Egyptians prevented the Israelites from departing Egypt, Moses took matters into his own hands, so it should come to you as no surprise, that I, a prophet with a destiny far greater than that of Moses should do likewise.

Yes, I killed the keeper, and I would do it a thousand times over, if I were only given the opportunity. I killed the milkman too, and I almost regret it, but then I remember that he was in that moment an accomplice of evil, albeit an unwilling one. Sometimes we convince ourselves into believing that some people are in the wrong place at the wrong time, but when we think these thoughts, it is we who are wrong. Everything happens, because *He* wills it to happen.

It was a messy task, but someone had to do it. In my younger and more naïve years, I would have vomited at my actions, but the spirit of the Lord hardens hearts, and it hardens hands. I did not wretch when my keeper's blood ran down my arms. I licked it, and savored its metallic taste. When I ran out of the house in the wee hours of the morning, my red-speckled arms were swinging.

VI

I hopped into my car and began to drive through town. There is a madman on the loose, and I had to find him, before he hurt anyone else. I banged my fist on the steering wheel. My first day on the job, my first fucking day, and this happened. I go my entire life with never seeing nothin' but petty drama, but as soon as they stick a rusty, bronze badge on my ass all of these crazy people's crazy shit happens. I mean they make sanitariums for a reason. I always thought those Sutters were a herd of wild jackasses. Goddamn Methodists.

Where would he be? I wonder if I walk around calling him, would he come to me? Probably not. Crazy and stupid are mutually exclusive. That boy might be crazy, but he isn't stupid. He knows that somebody is after him. He might be in New York, or somewhere on the other side of the earth.

Then an idea hit me hard, like someone threw a rock at my head. I should check the swamp. I cranked my Model T into high gear. I was going fifteen miles per hour, I almost slowed down until I realized I was the sheriff, and no one could give me a ticket. I cranked my speed up to twenty.

I zipped past the Santorums' compound of shacks on the outskirts of town, and I came to the end of the old dirt road. I parked my car in a cluster of bushes, and I prayed that those low down sons-of-bitches did not try to steal it.

My boots grew soggy from swiftly jogging over the wet ground. I knew that John had to be somewhere in here. I trudged into the shallow water of the bayou, and before I knew it, I was wiggling my soaking wet toes. If he came through here, then he probably crossed the water. He likely would think that someone would send the dogs after him.

In front of me was a large cypress tree that was large and weathered with age. It was so tall that when I looked above me, I could not see the top branches, even if I squinted. Its gnarled, gargantuan roots, extended to some place a foot above my face. The trunk had a lot of holes, huge holes in fact, and I found myself examining them, looking for a spot in which a man could hide himself.

But as I peeked into one of them, my vision grew black and fuzzy. I could feel something on top of me, sinking its nails into my face.

"Welcome, my dear friend!" It said.

I knew that it was John. He hurled me flat onto the ground, and I felt the agony of his fists slamming into my face, one after the other, with a rhythmic intensity, and my body became a set of drums. I don't know much of what happened, except that I passed out at least twice. Then something, be it grace, or some obscure force of physics, propelled him off of me.

I reached for my revolver, but my holster was empty. *Why the hell did I forget my gun, at precisely the moment I needed it most?* He was getting up, and I knew I could not take him down on my own without a gun, so I ran as fast as I could in the direction of my car.

I glanced over my shoulder, and I saw him running in pursuit of me, his back was bent low, and he ran with hands grazing the ground, as if he were a wild beast, a dinosaur, or some other un-christened fiend of hell.

My heart lurched with the sound of each snapping branch upon the ground, and the sucking noises that were made as John imbibed the air around him in tremendous gulps. He was gaining on me. I knew I could not turn to face him. He was too strong for me to stand alone against him with only my bare fists.

As the air whizzed around me I felt myself collapse. I hit the ground, and I could feel the skin on my arm slice open against a jagged rock. *God help me, I'm a good man. I'm too young to die. Save me, and I'll put more money in the offering basket on Sundays, and I'll only drink whiskey after sundown.*

My prayer ended with a booming thwack. I looked up and I saw John on the earth about two yards away from me.

"Sheriff, I reckon you owe me one."

Standing above me in a mangled shirt, and a scent that could make a man's knees wobble, was none other than Cletis Santorum with an ancient and dusty Fayetteville rifle held at his side. Cletis, at about seventeen, was Phil Santorum's youngest son. That god-awful clan of no good, poor white trash had been clogging up our tiny jail since the beginning of time. On the eighth day, after God had finished making the earth, the first Santorum had gotten into trouble with the Old Man for taking the first piss in the yet new and pristine ocean water.

At that moment, I did what by honor a man was bound to do. I grabbed his grimy hand, and shook it, while looking into his grey and empty eyes.

"You saved my life. I definitely owe you one."

I went to John, and I kicked him over, so that his ventral side was facing me. He had died with his eyes open. His pupils were dilated and his eyes bulged in their sockets. When I looked at them I felt like a snake was slithering up my spine. I felt as if his dead people eyes were staring not at me, but through me.

I looked away. I thought about how funny it would be to take John's head, put it on a platter, and serve it to the mayor at one of his weekly luncheons for the town's elite. I thought about all of those widows falling face first out of their chairs, but I rebuked myself.

I grabbed the corpse's hands and Cletis grabbed his feet. We lifted in unison, as if he and I were one man, and together, we threw the body into the car.

Ivana Leskanich
Colorado State University
"Reynardine"

Once upon a time, when the world was at war, there was a place that earth herself rejected. In this place, men made arrogant mountains from barbed wire and scrap metal that stretched to the wary gray sky. The sun was blocked out by dull, thudding objects that flew down for countless death sentences. In this gray world, humans were, paradoxically, either black or white. And black was the heart of Dietrich, a commander at *Wehrmacht* headquarters, a hidden military base tucked into the ravaged woods of Ukraine. Dietrich, despite his rotten core, was beautiful on the outside. His thick brown hair, piercing blue eyes, and stiff, ironed uniform gave the impression of a powerful and intelligent man. When he left home, his wife tearfully mourned the departure of her beautiful German husband, even as she looked into his hypnotizing eyes, which at times had the slightest cloudy film over them. Dietrich, though, knew no sorrow. He was a man who believed only in what he could see, and what he could see was his own godlike strength and the power of the just over the weak. In the darkest of nights he would reassure himself of the cause when his sweaty nightclothes would cling to his cold and clammy back.

But Dietrich's cause was built at the expense of another. The world of sharpened steel relied on the tender backs of innocent boys and old men. One such boy was Danyiko, stolen from the arms of his family and village. Danyiko's heart was not white, but golden, and it shone through his bright green eyes. Danyiko had been forced to facilitate the construction of *Wehrmacht's* underground tunnels, the observational platforms, the cinema, the tea house, and the swimming pool, all for *Herr Hitler*. He and a group of other Ukrainian and Polish boys had been snatched from their old lives to find their ends in this prison where their insides were slowly being choked to death.

Danyiko worked tirelessly at the construction of this kingdom, keeping his mind fixed off of the reality of it all, and instead, focused on warm memories of the past. But he did not think about the future, for the future was a precious gift that he dared not hope for, since by hoping, he would only make himself an easy target for fate. Although Danyiko believed fate was good, he knew that even she could fall into despair with mankind's destructive patterns. He was wise enough not to tempt her sometimes contrary nature. So he slaved away until the fat was worked off his warm body, turning his skin to yellowy ash and sending shivers through his failing limbs. Mud caked his once-shiny black hair, and he dreamed of food: his sister's delicious, sugary *pampusky* and the *guliash* that his mother made when he and his father had had a successful hunt in the nearby forest. He achingly remembered how the fragrant food would slide into his belly, and he'd sit still, listening to his parents' gentle conversation, while the dog would whine mournfully at his feet. He missed them so much he thought his heart might split.

But most of all, he missed *her*, the only girl that he had ever fallen in love with, the one to whom he made a promise. He replayed that moment when, bumping into her on the street the evening of the feast of Saint Michael, he had awkwardly confessed to her all that she meant to him. He offered her a *grotulja*, a necklace made of shelled walnuts, as a token of love, just as his grandparents and great-grandparents had done before him. He remembered how her lips had felt against his in that sudden movement when she took him by surprise. Never had he been happier than he was in that moment. Now not seeing her, not knowing where she was, or if the future existed, was worse than laboring all day for the sick overlords. He hacked into the dead rocky ground, shivering and murmuring something incomprehensible, solely comforted by the smell and feel of his memories.

One day, while making his rounds and scanning the workers, Dietrich noticed this black-haired boy. He observed his persistence with the pick-axe, as opposed to the other workers who gazed aimlessly, stopping work every so often when they thought no one was watching. But this one was different. His iron resolve was so marked that even the commander was impressed. On an unusual impulse, Dietrich stepped his newly-polished leather boots in the direction of the young man, ignoring the thunder and slicing rain that flooded the courtyard. The fur collar of his petrified winter coat rubbed against his cheeks as he formulated a decision.

He stood over the hunched boy and cleared his throat loudly. The boy looked up, faintly surprised and blinking as his eyes adjusted to the harsh paleness of the sky, while struggling to make out the features of the dark outline above him.

Boy, I have a proposition.

He waited.

I have noticed your strong work for our establishment. What I am about to ask you is, yes, unusual, but not unjustified.

A momentary pause.

I have made the decision to enlist you as a soldier for our army. This is a great honor. I will have a soldat make the arrangements for your promotion.

He turned away with a click of his tongue against his sharp, smooth teeth but stopped as he heard the young man's feeble laugh. Dietrich looked back to see him doubled over in hysterical laughter, shaking his head either in disbelief or in protest. The boy's laughter stopped suddenly and he gazed at the officer with a deadpan look.

No. Never.

The young man turned back and carried on tearing at the earth with a pick axe for a few moments. Then shots rang out. Danyiko landed face down in the rubble he had just plowed, rain running over his frail body, his back blooming with three red circles. Dietrich finally moved away with a small nod of his head and a *humph*. He felt momentarily embarrassed for ever having walked over to make such a preposterous arrangement. No matter, *problem behoben.*

Many years later, Dietrich was a settled man who often told others he had long forgotten about the war. He was portly now, with a round belly and an insatiable appetite. He had moved to Ukraine with his family after receiving many medals of honor from the Nazi army for his accomplishments there. On this particular day in late November, when the ground was icy from frost and the pine trees absorbed all sound, he was out hunting rabbits, his favorite animal to hunt. He admired their quickness which all the more highlighted his stealth when he managed to catch one. The best part was when he would string them up in his shed for his son to admire. Their filmy little black eyes sometimes seemed to stare at him when hanging from the ceiling, but Dietrich reminded himself that they were stone cold and lifeless now.

Rabbit rabbit rabbit

He whispered under his breath.

Nothing. He gave a sigh of disappointment after his unfruitful hunt. The day was starting to fade into night and the cold was quickly drawing in, nipping peskily at his ears. Just as he was about to give up and trudge back to his simple, silly wife, he heard a sound. It was the slightest of sounds, like a muffled moan, that a regular person would not hear, but Dietrich's ears had been trained to pick up on any irregularities while hunting. He smiled to himself, already tasting the pleasure of the kill on his salivating tongue.

He circled around in the freshly falling snow then heard the sound again. This time it was closer, sounding more like a gurgling wail, and Dietrich suddenly felt a shiver creep down his spine. He thought he saw a shadowy figure in the distance and felt relieved, certain that a fellow hunter was nearby. He called out expectantly, but only the wind greeted him. Dietrich had the sudden impulse to run despite his realization that he was being incredibly childish. Both ashamed and agitated, he took off, feet slamming against the uneven ground. Snow fell down in a blinding flurry and Dietrich's fat legs wobbled under him, until he smacked his head into a tree branch and hurtled to the earth. He gasped, winded, and then felt sharp claws lightly scrape his shoulder.

Hardly daring to breathe, he slowly rolled onto his back, and like a wounded animal, gazed up into the eyes of his capturer. She was the most horrifyingly beautiful thing he had ever seen. The thick white sheepskin that she wore was torn in several places, revealing slivers of olive skin underneath. Her eyes were of the deepest red, like the color of a maple leaf just before it falls. Her small hands, unreflective of her sheer strength, gripped his meaty throat and jolted him out of his trance. His stomach lurched while looking up at her, yet he had the pulsing urge to kiss her. Her lips, sleek as wet poppies, tormented him. In a daze, he flung his arms out to grab her dangling hair and forced his mouth onto hers. He pushed his slimy tongue down her throat. She swiftly pried him loose with a shudder, her eyes burning like red halos in the night. Full of rage, he spat in her face.

Filthy whore.

She cracked her heel against his forehead and everything returned to blackness.

He woke up, arms strapped to a concrete slab in the middle of a clearing. Somehow he felt as though he had been there before, although he had no idea how. Groggily, he pushed himself upwards, hoping to make an escape. Yet, just as he was about to pry himself loose, she reappeared, staring emotionless into his face.

Please. Have mercy.

He pleaded. The words were foreign to his mouth.

She turned her head for a minute then crept towards him. She leaned in close, so close that he could have clamped his teeth down on her. Instead, her smell assailed him, a strange mixture of earth, dampness, and something else that he recognized instantly with flood of horror. It was the foul, sulfurous odor of the chemicals that they had used in the gas chambers or in village raids. The stinging smell brought involuntary tears into his foggy blue eyes.

I don't have any company, since you took him away from me.

She whispered into his ear, brushing those taunting lips against his shivering face. She closed her eyes and wrenched a necklace from her throat, throwing it at his face. He was nothing now. She had destroyed him already. Knowing this, she sunk her sharp teeth and claws deep into his chest, three times over. Blood stained the fat German's coat and seeped down into the white, blank snow.

Matt Peel
Eastern Kentucky University
"Dances with Waylon Jennings"

The stage lights blazed overhead. One too many shots of whiskey colored his baited breath, but at least his nerves were calm.

Shake off the buzz.

His pale green button-down didn't fit quite right; thrift shop formalwear tends to feel that way. The coal black of his hair shined, though whether lustrous or greasy no one could tell. The dark braids stuffed up under his Stetson cowboy hat didn't help. Two little Indian braids, hiding from those prying eyes beaming up out of a sea of expectant white faces. The strap of his old guitar chafed his back and shoulders. Had chafed them for centuries.

"Good evening everyone." The words poured from his mouth. Some other man's words. Someone who belonged on this stage.

Awkward seconds passed; white children fidgeted in their cush-ioned seats. Urging himself into action, he strummed a chord. Felt the rhythm. A warrior never flinches, that's what his dad would have said. But his dad wasn't here, was he? His dad hadn't stood in line at the ticket counter for a chance to see this, to see a warrior take the stage. A warrior, he thought. Could've fooled me.

The rhythm of tradition carried him through the first song. Though he hadn't written it, he knew it by heart. The audience seemed mildly pleased, much to his chagrin. That had been his favorite one. Maybe they didn't like "The Song of the Badger Medi-cine." Perhaps they would prefer Hank Williams Jr. Yes, yes they did. This was a new sensation for him, feeling the thunder of applause reverberate through his mic stand. At first the echoing in his soul thrilled him. But as he looked into their faces, he couldn't help but feel they were clapping not for him, but for their own heroes, of which he could never be one. Nevertheless, he played on. George Strait received equal applause, as did Merle Haggard and Garth Brooks.

Now that he had warmed them up, he thought he'd pull out his best.

"My favorite version of this song is by one of my biggest inspirations, Willie Nelson." A few people whistled or cheered. "I used to think I liked Willie for his music, but now I've decided it's because he's the only white guy who can out-drink me *and* look good in braids!" No one laughed. That's really funny, he thought, quite offended. He recalled drunken Indians rolling on the floor after he told that joke from the stages of reservation bars. Just then he felt a knot begin tightening in his stomach. Your gut always has a way of knowing. Dad said that, too. Choosing to ignore it, however, he twanged through "Georgia on My Mind" with his eyes mostly closed. They clapped for Willie too, so he talked with his eyes still half open.

"I've never been to Georgia, but the way Willie talks it sure sounds like somewhere worth going." His mystic smile dropped suddenly as a large man in the second row burst out laughing. Looking down at the man, his expression turned to confusion.

"You don't like Georgia?" he asked bluntly, although he surmised that the man wasn't offended by a state. The man shook his head condescendingly, his own Stetson nearly sliding off of his bald head.

"I got nothin' against Georgia boy, I don't like *you*. Mr. Dances with Waylon Jennings over here gets off the chain for a few hours and suddenly he's gonna tour the nation. You sing pretty good boy, but don't get ahead of yourself. Circus monkeys don't get to drive the bus. So why don't you sing us some more Hank Jr. and remember your place." The vein in the man's temple throbbed, but his demeanor never changed. Some sitting around him glared up at the stage, a few seemed embarrassed. But no one spoke. Several thousand pairs of eyes waited in suspense for a response. Silent seconds passed as the lone guitarist stared back at his challenger. The beat of the war drum filled his ears, hot like wildfire. The warrior commanded him to attack, but his gut tightened ever more.

The first few notes seemed to whistle, like the thrush denouncing the late winter snow. But the ones that followed rose up, filled the hall with sound and magic. The warrior's eyes never left his target as he stepped back up to the mic. The drums grew louder now, drowning out everything but its own pounding in his ears. He plucked and picked his heritage all over the stage, strummed his own soul to the beat of every Indian he knew and some he didn't. He chanted the tongue of his mother and her mother before her. He even chanted the language of his father because blood runs thicker than whiskey. He played and sang and danced and played for what seemed like hours before his eyes landed once more upon General George Armstrong Custer in the second row. Crazy horse must be smiling down at him. Or up at him. Or maybe he's just a little more peaceful lying in his grave.

When the music stopped, the drums slowly subsided. Sweat dripped from his brow, splashed up from his guitar. He smiled a smile of victory until he opened his eyes. The drum beat resumed, but this time only the man in the second row clapped along. Less than a dozen people remained in the audience. Several more filed out as he looked out over the now-desolate auditorium. "I guess you showed me, son." The man in the second row smirked as he rose from his seat. "Maybe next time a white guy tries to help you out, you'll take his advice instead of making a fool of yourself." He laughed hysterically as he strutted down the main aisle and out of the auditorium.

Rage sprang up inside him once more, causing the room to swim before his eyes and the distant edges of the auditorium to fade into a blur. Wrenching the microphone from the stand, he hurled it across the auditorium in the direction that the white man had walked. Turning away from the mostly empty seats, he charged through the curtain behind him, snapping cords and overturning tables as he went. He bum-rushed the back-alley exit, emerged into the cool night air, and toppled over the handrail. The snapping of the guitar neck resounded cacophonously against the red brick and concrete. Louder still was the sound of his back smacking squarely on the pavement below. He thought he had died until he heard Willie Nelson's rough voice floating towards him. Then he was sure of it. "Willie has come to parade me into the Sand Hills, or Heaven, or a bar on Route 66. Maybe all three."

When he finally managed to open his eyes, he lay in the dark with his guitar still strapped to his chest. Instead of cold concrete or warm sand, however, his back touched soft cushion. His hands met the worn wood of the guitar and found it quite intact. A beer bottle lay upside down on his chest, its pungent odor filling his nostrils. Willie was crooning "Just an old sweet song keeps Georgia on my mind" from the dusty record player in the corner of the cramped bedroom. Struggling to raise himself from the prostrate recliner, he laughed to himself. Dances with Waylon Jennings. The unmade bed housed various empty alcohol containers. Lyric sheets and scratched records carpeted the floor, and there on a shelf, underneath a tattered Willie Nelson poster, rested the war drum.

James Blevins
College of Central Florida
"For All the Bending"

The bar wavered around Clay in bold, neon colors; it oscillated to the acoustic slush coming off a nearby stage. Long, perverse contrails of smoke curled about the cherry of his cigarette — rising to mask his tired, drunk face.

In front of him: a dirty, white picnic table was placed, littered with debris — dead glass-soldiers in reverie; smeared ash in the grain; a pack of cigarettes lonely, gasping in a puddle of condensation; a green lighter next to a notebook and pen, with three words written on top of a solitary page — *"possibly the truth"* — and nothing else.

Clay was sitting outside on a chilly patio behind an Irish pub, an awning was spread overhead, wooden trellises in the place of walls. A portly, bearded man was playing an acoustic guitar from a small stage set at the far back of the scene; sweat glistening on his ruddy cheeks, lit by several long strands of red and green Christmas lights strung over and behind the modest setup.

Over the slush, words began to stream in a private river within Clay's head; he began to write them down in the form of a poem, joining the three words already placed there.

It was then that a heavy hand came thundering down on Clay's left shoulder, forcing his right-hand — the one holding the pen and writing a fever — to shirk off the page, leaving a blue streak, like a cut, across the white paper. The hand was rough: a digger's hand. Its forearm was corded in muscle and ended past the elbow where a blue denim shirt began. Clay looked up into the eyes of heartbreak and saw his reflection nestled inside.

The man was deeply tanned, thick of neck and chest, with dirty jeans over dirty boots. His hair, a sun-stained blonde, was cut close to the skull.

A deep sadness welled abysmal in the core of this man, giving off heat.

The man quickly used his other muscled forearm, with a sudden, feral yelp of anguish, like a dog, to clear off Clay's table, smashing bottle after bottle onto the rocky patio floor.

The notepad went airborne, along with the cigarettes and lighter, careening off the small rocks on the ground; the notepad settled below a patron's hovering right heel. Clay stared at his words on the floor from a far; the pen still grasped in his right hand. A cigarette dangled from his pale, pink lips. His eyes raised from the distant notepad, found the man's rage, no more than three feet from his eyelashes.

Sweat poured from the man's jowls and down the open part of his denim shirt, causing his chest to glisten in the twinkling Christmas lights. He paced back and forth in front of Clay's now barren table.

Clay sat immobile, watching this theater play out — something about this man struck him as familiar.

"Her hands...my hands," the man started with wounded inflection. "Pressed into skin, as soft, like pillows are soft."

The words struck Clay like a slap. Of course, he recognized them. Screaming, the man continued to recite.

"Smearing fingerprints, like paint, on each other — with heat: that weeping hollow inside us — ; but I can fill it, if you let me."

A vacuum seemed to be set between them. Clay only heard the man's words, and light, delicate sounds between the lines, like microscopic punctuation points, from time to time.

"I can fill it, if you let me." He repeated.

Anger bled into the man's voice, laced with muscles bunching under denim-skin.

"With tangles of sweet intentions and fingers, lost in your hair, in your face, in your lips: where I long to be lost — that is where you'll find me, always, when you want me found."

The man's voice mingled with the substance of Clay's inner-thoughts…

****

Somewhere above the earth, a hearth warm enough for all beings hums along contentedly, cracking good-naturedly; it looks down, this fireplace, and smiles tenderly on all the poets, the heartbroken, and the weaker of the loved; those left dotted amongst the cracks on the surface of the planet. It smiles and nods its approval of their good work. It dips hands into a cup, insisting to all that what is cupped is pure for all to drink — a basin for all to be held within its embrace.

Free to all…

****

"Wet between what I've said and what I need: you hold me harder than I can perceive."

The man's voice -his words- pull Clay from a metaphysical reverie he can't explain. He stares earnestly into the man's fury. He knows what will come next from the man's clenched teeth.

But somehow, I feel you there.

"But somehow…

"I feel you there…at the nexus of me. Like the beat of a shared heart, hitched to all that is meaningful and true. Do say, sweet girl, of whom I love, is it just me, with my tempered eyes of bark, that feels what is braced between us?

"Our hearts placed to hearth is warmth. Our mouths pressed to together is love."

The pub began to give off a perceivable resonance to Clay's ears, as if two poets were speaking at once: one in whispers, the other in hurt shouts.

The man paced and stomped in rain dance circles, and recited Clay's poetry at him, like machine gun fire, relentless.

Cigarette smoke was there; the smell of broken, spilt beer bounced about in his nostrils. Spittle decorated his glasses. A mist of spit, poetry and glimpses into a not-too-distant past rained down—too painful to take all of its weight.

Something else added its weight to Clay's dream state—something remembered…

****

Somewhere, a man sits in a booth at a smoky, red bar—a very old man with a story to tell. Clay was there and he heard this old man have his say. The old man told a tale of the day he found his wife dead, at home, by a self-inflicted gunshot wound. Many decades ago, the old man was accustomed to storing guns in his house; he loved guns. Every kind of gun was poetry for this poor, weathered man. His wife, she had taken one of his .45s, early morning, Valentine's Day, and put a hollow-point round into her heart. She timed it perfectly; twenty minutes, as she knew, before her husband arrived home from his job. He found her, as if asleep, on the couch. Her blood was gray in the low-light of dawn.

The old man had suggested a toast to Clay, eagerly raising his glass.

"To the bending." The old man said.

"To the what?" Clay had asked.

"Always drink to the bending," the old man continued. "The bending we all endure, but never break.

"Always drink to the bending."

So they did. Glasses touched and a toast was made.

****

Clay murmured under his breath, coming back from his recollection, while staring at the angry denim man, whose sweat was now saturated into everything, as if anger was a new liquid only he could produce.

Clay looked at the jealous man. The man whose wife he had slept with, wrote a poem about, and distributed around town in a zine of his own making, called *For All the Bending*.

They locked eyes. Locked in what had come to be shared and disseminated between them. Carnal knowledge has that particular kind of residue to it, as both men knew. The angry man had made his point.

The earth seemed to take another turn before Clay came to realize he was sitting on the back patio of the pub all by himself. His cigarette a mere nub in his mouth, close enough to singe the skin of his lips.

He tossed the butt in the rocks, landing beside his now discarded notepad. The small cherry of the dying cigarette lit the lone page on display. Several more words now lay illuminated, beside a blue cut of ink:

"possibly the truth —

pitched wholly into the dark void of evening

now beer-stained and ashen within separate wet circles;

my words would be given time to breathe,

just out of sight, in the periphery, but close enough to count amongst the moisture of leaves."

****

Rising from the chair, Clay walked to the main bar housed off the back patio, took a seat on an empty stool and lit another cigarette. The bartender walked over to Clay, leaned across the bar top, taking his patron in as if for the first time.

"What the hell was that all about?" he asked.

Clay took a long deep drag from his cigarette, exhaled violently.

"I slept with his wife, and then wrote a poem about her."

"Wow, man."

The bartender went under the bar, retrieved some whiskey and two empty shot glasses. He poured an inch in both and handed one to Clay before titling the other back in a single motion down his yawning throat.

"Was it worth it?" The bartender asked after returning the empty shot glass to the bar top—inlaid with little shamrocks in see-through lucite.

Clay threw back his own shot, trembled for a second as the drink shook his foundation. Dragged his smoke again and looked at the bartender with dead-on eyes, after placing his drained glass precisely over a four-leaf clover.

"Of course."

The bartender stared Clay down, discerning something off about his given response.

"I was talking about the girl."

Never parting from the bartender's eyes, Clay smiled, looking both serious and playful at the same time—but honest—yes, very possibly honest.

"I was talking about the poem."

Samantha Buoye
University of Central Florida
"Hands"

Hands pull me into arms, soft and protective, a human security blanket during sleep, half-conscious, and I am reminded of other hands - yours.

Yours, broader, stronger hands, with callouses from boot camp, a scar on the left hand from the fight we had that one Thanksgiving, a humid, damp day where I couldn't do anything right—I'm sorry, I've never cooked a turkey before—and that left hand went through the wall, inches from my face, and I covered the hole with a picture of the dog that you loved more than me before your mom got there, and I had to smile all night; all night, hands that had once canvassed my body, learning things even I didn't know - that freckle on my thigh and the scar on my back that I thought had faded but when you press on it, it's still sore - hands that pulled my hair and told me it felt good, even after I cried- cried, when the hands no longer touched me, walked out the door and left me in nothing but a towel, water drops still sprinkled on my upper back, water drops falling down my cheeks onto the dog you loved more than me, she licked the salty wet off my face; my face, disfigured by a chipped right brow bone, the one that matched the deep purple bruises around my eye—I didn't know skin could be such a vibrant color— the whites of my eyes red, the burst capillaries making me look like a comic book villain, it made a child cry so I lived in sunglasses for a week, and my dad still doesn't believe that it was an accident, when you missed the wall, and hit me- me, the entity I lost when I was with you; you, who still wakes me up in the night, screams and dreams of those fucking hands- hands, the soft ones that pull me in, the ones that have no idea I still think about you.

Erin Ruffino
State University of New York at Fredonia
"The Forgotten Faults"

Never had Ryland thought fire was beautiful. It was always ugly in its blaze, wicked in its power, and sinister in the way it left charcoal scars upon the earth where it had reduced greatness to rubble. And as he looked down into the valley town below, Ryland couldn't help but think the inferno resembled an open flesh wound. The light reached up and cupped his chin, blowing soft kisses of red and orange onto his face. His eyes stung and watered, wetting and cooling his warm cheeks.

The fire called out to him, a voice like the splinter of wood and the slithering of smoke. *Ryland, Ryland, come down and play. We have something of yours, Darling.* Despite the heat, he felt a chill run up his spine. The fire had taken his town, and he felt it heading towards his home, his mother, his little sister.

He batted the light's embrace away, shucked off his rucksack of poetry books not pausing to see where it had landed, hanging by its thin straps in a bushel of roses—thorns licking their sharp teeth—and bolted down the dirt path that led to his house. He leapt over puddles and didn't slow. Even when his boots sank into mud, he simply flew out of them and ran barefoot, pebbles biting into his soles every step of the way. It didn't matter. None of the pain mattered. There was only his family to find, and he *would* find them, he thought, alive and well. Perfectly safe. Perfectly fine. There was no other way.

And when a mountain of fire loomed over him, smothering what used to be his home, his legs gave out and he fell hard to his knees. The flames festered and boiled off the roof and the siding, throwing pieces away the way a lover plucks the petals off a daisy- *He loves me, he loves me not.*

Something slammed into his side, knocking the wind from his already heaving lungs.

"Ryland!" it shouted. He turned and saw his friend with soot blackening her hair and a film of dust dulling her skin. Her small hands hooked into his shoulders and shook him, begging him to understand.

"Where are they?" he pleaded. Her eyes shrank away but he could see the tears now, cutting through the dirt, twinkling paths running down her cheeks. Now it was he who dug his fingers into her arms, the arch of his knuckles threatening to pop through the skin. "Charlie, *please*. Where are they?"

"I'm so sorry, Ryland," her wet eyes darted to his blazing house. Her mouth opened once more and with a voice like splintering glass, she whispered, "They're — They're still inside."

The yells of his friend were lost among the laughing of the flames. Ryland shouldered his way through the sizzling front door, pulling out the black bandanna he always kept in his pocket. Charlie had given it to him five years ago, for his 11th birthday. Together, they made a mischievous duo, even back then. Sprung out of boredom and some primal desire to rebel, Charlie had decided they should take up thievery. She complained often of undeserving people having nice things and decided that stealing from others who stole wasn't *exactly* stealing in itself. Ryland had disagreed, and then she argued, as she usually did, half-correctly citing some piece of philosophy she'd accidently stumbled upon called Divine Commandment Theory and said that God unfairly rearranged our possessions and that she was going to rearrange them back.

Eventually, Charlie wore him down, as she usually did, and excitedly told him all thieves need a proper disguise. And so the black bandanna became their trademark and they were infamous in the lower part of town for pick pocketing and lifting whatever they liked, whenever they liked. The greasy shopkeepers and slimy crooks even had a nickname for them—or well, for *one* of them. The townspeople never did figure out there were actually two thieves clearing their shelves, and that was part of the reason their set-up worked. *The*

Rook, they'd say, *The Rook lives in the shadows—no real name or identity. The Rook up and outs before you even know you've been robbed blind. Like* smoke, they'd say, *there one second and gone the next.*

Upon hearing their new nickname, Ryland had complained it was his least favorite chess piece, the castle-looking one. Charlie had laughed at him. "Rook" meant scammer, she'd explained, or deceiver. In the library the two of them frequented, she had showed him an ornithology field guide, flipped to the *Corvidae* section, and pointed to a bird that looked like a crow but had a mask of gray, featherless skin around its beak. It's funny, she'd said, because it wears a mask like us, in the same place as us, but really it's the exact opposite of us. It has no feathers where we wear ours. She'd smiled then like the Devil himself after he'd fallen from heaven, all sharp teeth and eyes so dark you could drown in them.

Ryland thought of all this in the brief moment when he tied the bandanna around his nose and chin, hoping to block out at least some of the smoke that clouded up the entire home. Immediately, his eyes streamed in pain but he did his best to ignore it all. He had to find his mother and sister. He wouldn't let them burn. A hurricane of smoke and ash and boiling heat licked his eyes. He felt every prick of burning dust bite into his skin, a thousand bursts of electric agony.

Half-blind, he stumbled his way through what was left of the foyer. There was only gray and the thundering of flames. He managed to find the staircase and after tripping over the first step, he pulled himself up using the rail to guide him higher and higher into the thick haze. His forgotten boots left far behind on the dirt path on the hill meant he now left a bloody trail of footprints as he went up the steps, soles torn from the sharp rocks. Now they were throbbing from the heat rising up through the floor. He knew he didn't have time to stop and try to bandage them; he'd take whatever torment the fire sent his way.

And then his vision was alight. The fire was feasting here at the top of the stairs and down the left hallway where his bedroom used to be. It ate up the red carpet, the walls, the pictures of his family. Glass from their frames shattered into a million tiny, blazing, shooting stars. Ryland tried to duck away, but the shards gravitated to him, slicing just above the bandana in three thick ugly scars. The blood welled and drenched the already sweat-soaked cloth. Ryland turned his back to the flames and headed down the other hallway towards his mother's room.

The golden knob scorched his skin raw, but he pushed inside anyway. A wind hotter than dragon's breath slammed into him, knocking him down. From the ground, he saw the room ablaze in every sick shade of auburn, umber, mahogany, and rust. The fire lunged at him, thankful for being released. He dragged himself away on hands and knees, further down the hall to try his sister's room. Maybe Mom already got away, he hoped weakly.

The smoke had started to take its toll, the walls of his mind crumbling. Every breath was crushed glass, every inch of movement a battle he fought to win. Ryland heard nothing but the demonic swell of fiery destruction ripping, tearing, chewing, and howling. His nose only smelled the tang of melting rubber and burnt flesh—his or someone else's he could not bear to guess.

He did not remember finding his way into his little sister's room, but now he stood there and for a second imagined he'd see her by the window, playing with her dolls. She was not there.

He felt his chest contract, lungs clawing for clean air. The blood from the cuts on his cheek had started to crust over. He felt himself stop. The sudden quietness and absence of smoke paralyzed him. Rae's room was exactly as he last left it the night before. No smoke, no fire. Ryland had tucked his sister into bed and sat on the edge of it, reading her a poem that compared angels to flowers. No trace of smoke lingered here, no lick of flame or breath of warmth. There was only the icy moonlight that filtered in through the window. There was no trace of the desolation that stalked just outside the room's threshold.

And amidst the quietness, he heard a whimper.

Ryland threw himself to the floor. There, *there,* under the bed, his hands brushed something soft. And then came a splintering screech, the kind only a throat made raw from crying could form. It tore through Ryland's mind, an axe through wood. He gripped little hands and pulled a small body into his arms. She was shaking, face gray, hair matted, eyes wide but unseeing.

Trying to speak through the dryness in his throat was like sawing through bone. Wheezing, Ryland said, "Rae? It's OK. I have you. It's going to be OK now." She made no response, no signal she even heard him. Her skin was glazed in sweat and was paling by the second.

Quicker than his head appreciated, Ryland stood with Rae draped awkwardly in his arms. Every muscle throbbing, he brought her up onto the bed, wrapped her in a thick blanket like some sort of cocoon, and carried her out into the maelstrom of fire.

The flames had spread to this wing. They burned along the ceiling, both walls of the hallway, and even the floor. They blocked his path to the stairs, taunting and teasing him, *We will have you now, boy.* Ryland gathered whatever courage or stupidity he had left and braced himself. He ran down the hall and leapt through the flames. They grabbed at his clothes and hair, but were not fast enough for him. The Rook. The thief who vanished into air. The Thief with No Name.

Ryland sailed through the ring of fire like he was playing a sick carnival game and collapsed on the other side. Rae fell from his arms, unmoving. Ryland cursed his own weakness. He wrapped her back into her nest and raised her, one arm under her head, the other under her legs. Though she was only six, her dead-weight made his arms shake in pain. The heat made the soles of his feet slit open and leak pus and blood onto the landing. He tried his best to ignore all of this, but would not admit he felt himself slipping, failing.

He put his foot down onto the top step, descending into the inferno. Then the second step. On the third, he brought his foot down on an iron nail. It tore through his heel, his skin in ribbons. Come on, he thought, come on! But his feet were now made of concrete, his arms pulled down by chains, his head heavy with a crown of guilt

and thorns. He was not the thief who vanished into air. He was not
The Thief with No Name. He never had been. He was just the fool
who would die by his own blade.

And then he was falling both in body and mind: down, down, *down*.

His vision came and went in patches of color and light. A kalei-
doscope of wildfire and smoke. He felt no pain now. His head clear,
his arms weightless, he felt safe. Peaceful even. He did not think of
Rae, who had slipped headfirst from his arms like a baby bird from its
nest, who could not yet fly and save herself.

He laid there on his back, mind weaving from vision to vision,
while the flames closed in on their prey. *You've played a good game,
Darling.* He felt hollow. His will shattered into ash, the kind his body
would soon become. If this was what death felt like, he no longer
wanted life. There was no suffering in this place. No trial or torment.
No misunderstanding. No one was innocent here, but no one was
guilty either. He let his heart slow, his lungs shuddered and squirmed.
That's it, my boy, just fall away. Darkness descended upon him.

A memory was brought to Ryland from the recesses of his mind:
once again, Charlie had plucked some piece of ancient philosophy
from a book and read it aloud as carefully and compassionately as if it
were own her own thoughts, her own ideas, her own insights. It was
a passage from Rene Descartes' *Meditations.* It's brilliant, she'd smiled.
This guy can prove you exist with only one sentence: "*I think, therefore
I am.*" It's that simple! Technically, "I am" is all you need to prove
your own existence. Can you believe that? she'd asked him. No, he'd
said. I don't think it's that simple. Nothing's that simple.

It was some time after—how long exactly, Ryland could not say,
for there was no time in the place between worlds. The shadows had

158

swallowed him whole when Ryland heard a faint cawing. There was a cool wind that flowed through his being and a brush of feathers against his skin. The darkness was a bird, enveloping him, flying upwards. The first color he saw was gray. The gray of featherless skin. Then the indigos and the emeralds and the sapphires burst from the bird's feathers. He saw the bone color of its beak open and move, and then the bird was speaking his name into the shadows, over and over, a hymn for returning from nothingness.

As they rose, the air began to warm. One by one, the bird's feathers ignited into curling golden flames. They fell as they burned, as does the morning star. In the bird's eyes, Ryland could see constellations. The stars were alight, blazing, collapsing. They burned themselves away until there was only a dark coal color left. Gray.

Ryland felt her name. *Charlie.* A church bell rattling his teeth, his blood, his bones. He reached upwards with his hand, ripping out feathers, peeling off skin. He reached and reached, up, up, *up.* He felt himself climbing onto the bird's snapping beak. He knew what he must do.

Fire tugged at his hand and mind, but he would not let it hold him. He leapt with every ounce of strength he had left. He leapt with every nerve and every atom of his being, all screaming out for life.

From above, her voice called out to him.

He let the dying, featherless Rook fall away.

He lifted his hands one last time, and felt the brush of her fingertips.

My morning star.

"Are you with me, Ryland?"

I am.

* * * *

When Ryland woke up seven days later, the first thing he saw
was gray. The storm clouds in Charlie's eyes rained down on him,
cooling off the burns in his lungs, the rawness of his mind. He had
once thought her eyes were cold—merciless even—and had bitterly
compared them to the Devil's own. But then, she looked fragile.
Something she'd never been, or at least had never let him see before.
It was because of her that he was brought back from the place
between worlds. It was because of her that he was alive.

But it was because of her that the fires were lit. It was because of her
that his mother and his sister burned up. It was because of her that
there were no bodies to bury, no house to go home to. There was only
cinder and ash.

For their entire wayward criminal career, she was the Rook.
He only distracted their targets. He only stood watch. *She* was the
thief who vanished into thin air. She was The Thief with No Real
Name. She was the one who stole from the wrong person. And that
person—not knowing who to blame—had taken his revenge out on
entire the town.

But her house didn't burn. Her parents didn't burn. She didn't burn.
Maybe she should've, Ryland had thought in the weeks after, when
the weight of his loss had come crashing down. In that time, he woke
from nightmares of hell and of the black bandanna wrapping tighter
and tighter around his throat. Charlie tried to reassure him that it
had fallen off and gotten left behind when she dragged him from his
burning home. Ryland's anger snuffed itself out, and instead guilt
clouded his mind.

Charlie had become his keeper, making sure he ate, waiting out
his mood swings, calming him down after his nightmares. Once she
found him in his room with a down pillow torn open on one end.
Feathers stuck out of his skin, bleeding where he had pushed them in.
He was using the blood as paint and on the walls he wrote line after
line: *The Thief with No Real Name.*

Charlie didn't try to stop him this time. She simply sat on the edge
of his bed, white feathers all around her, and read him a poem that

spoke of the beauty of angels and flowers. He had paused, rivers of red streaming down his arms.

Charlie set aside the book, stood, and began reciting the poem from memory. She held his hand and together their palms collected a pool of crimson that overflowed and then filled itself up again. She plucked the feathers from his skin and let them fall to his feet. It was then Ryland reached behind him and tore the white curtains down off the windows. They had been there since Ryland arrived, always blocking out the sun and keeping him in the dark. No longer.

Light poured in. Ryland ripped off a piece of the curtain's lace trim and turned to look at her, his wayward soul. She had hurt and been hurt, and it was time to repent.

"My morning star," he whispered.

He tied the white cloth loosely around her wrist.

"*I am*," she whispered back.

They collapsed together in a heap, crying. Charlie cried for the destruction she had caused, for the flames she never meant to be unleashed. Ryland cried for his family and for himself, for they were the ones burned by it. He cried for her damned soul, and hoped maybe his tears could wash it clean.

Zachary Scott Hamilton
Portland Community College
"Shaving Sister"

We piled on the lattice work until, near the black lake, we had it steady in the corners, matched up in places. The orange-gloves grow worn on the outside, slimy on the inside. The orange gloves we hang in trees each day, a golden ray of them, wheel barrels full of gloves that get wheeled to the dump site, and strategically hung with a thin-fishing line. I think it's 10 pound.

Davis grovels, attaining a long lattice piece from the pile, and standing it up edgewise so that it flaps over in the breeze, he stares at it and rummages through his jumpsuit. A roll of duct tape comes with receipt papers, and his lighter, which he sets down near a rock.

I tear down walls of the lattice, and throw it aggressively, getting deep inside of the cube (where more lattice –older lattice – stained from rot, is revealed beneath).

The sound of a woman, singing, whistles through the Oak woods. The voice echoes from a cabin I know of, down half a mile. I hide under the fur of my cap, tearing off lattice and throwing it.

Davis has built something out of it: a smiling female. She stands there, made of gloves and lattice. I nod. Good. Behind him, a naked blond with red-genital hair sings. She takes some orange gloves down and puts them on like shoes. Her vocal fold is visibly shaking and it annoys me. I bend down and pop open the red tool box, pulling out a Splitting maul. I tear off another layer of lattice from the cube and turn to the female – raise the maul over my head and smash the lattice woman through the middle. Davis screams, and the woman, singing, naked, grabs him and pulls him swiftly toward the river, where she salutes me and picks Davis up off of his feet. He screams, but I pull out a television remote control unit from the toolbox (RCU) and press mute.

The water rises high above the trees; all of the river in one, long, rising water fall grows. I turn back to the cube and tear through eight sheets of lattice, getting into what seems like a center. The water made of collaged pictures of a female begin opening their mouths, and Davis cuts out paper in the middle of the rising storm, laughing at me and pointing the scissors before the water starts to fall.

I get through, in the darkness, and the water crashes into the bank, releasing paper cut out naked women all over the shore. They all stand up and line dance to a country song one has playing on a radio, and the cube takes out its legs from the ground: the cube starts line dancing with a naked girl with red nipples, who licks the top wall away, and I see her. She has a horn and blows a song through it.

Sara Gregory
New College of Florida
"Flood Gate"

He pulled her through the night, like an angel, to the side of the pale blue house. Up close, her dark eyes were running and down her thighs thundered blood. His hands were shaking as his lips nipped at her with fish teeth. Flashing at the scales of his scalp, her fingers matted in his hair. Her mouth was cool like the tide and stony like salt. He felt her body, groped at her and pressed her downward, to earth and to weeds.

Her throat was drowning with a scream that would not crest. Ocean-wide with confusion, she is rushing against the side of the pale blue house. His breath was curling smoke against her eyes, tangled and burning with sea water. She is spinning and then on the ground, wet grass twisting in her hair. His hands are rough on her hips and with dread she feels the hard line of him.

With dread she knows he will insist.

Holding her with velvet hands, and she is now shaking: a girl, paper-thin and his, poised for shatter. A shard of smile cuts at his face and he presses through her harder, harder. Release splints his body smooth—relief bright, urgent against her gaze hanging like a mist.

A sigh scatters from his lips and roars in her ears. He strokes her hair, damp with silence dripping from temple, curling down the cut of her curving jaw, lapping at the fog of his fingertips.

He leaves, wading away from the girl on the ground.

Numb, she is left, glinting like ground bits of sea stone, battered against the side of the pale blue house. In solitude, her rolling mind wanders and runs red by drink and by sex. From the cracks of her river-bed mind, she waters the weeds and darkens the earth.

Not knowing she is already overflowing, he returns.

He brought her a glass of water.

"Oh, fuck."

She is pulled through the fallen night and into the pale blue house. She is shelved to white tiles and a porcelain toilet. He pulls off her green sweater and untangles her braided hair. He runs the shower and shakes his head, watching the steam throw ghosts around her dark eyes. She will scream the next morning, when, like a flood, she remembers.

Liam Strong
Northwestern Michigan College
"Yellow Kite"

The yellow kite, its viscera entangled in the rampart branches of the oak just outside of the fence, up there beyond the reach of our 20-foot ladder, made me hate the sky that much more, having to look at that little linen sun every time as if there were two, in passing, out of the corner of my eye, because I can't forget it and the wind that never ceases. If anything moves, the kite moves more than the rest of the abiotic world. You told me feeling the wind was the same as seeing it if we could. I'm still having trouble believing this but I felt that everything short of your view went right over my head, like the kite. I often look down and although my neck hurts from it some days, the habitual deprivation of my sight of the sky keeps me from losing more than I have, and it's funny too, when looking down I'll see your hair and fiddle with it between my thumb and index fingers, but think nothing of it. The single strand of long hair like a flow of energy from one point to the other, no split ends. Like the fucking kite tail when the wind tugs on it.

My father dropped a small box of apples by the other day and I knew I didn't deserve the ability to taste just yet, but the forced sour was hard to disbelieve. I ate one every day but the autumn felt like the greater doctoral influence now, and apples couldn't keep an entire season away, so I let the therapy come. Just last week, I saw the cement truck down the block and the men creating the foundation for which the sidewalk would be placed all along the road and cutting across the front of our lawn and, just like you said three months ago when the paper was talking about the commission and the millage to support the new sidewalks along the entire highway, they ripped out the mailbox and just left it there. You were right. When they finally came to our yard I didn't watch for long, but the cement patiently lying there where you used to wait excited for the mailman to deliver your magazines made me want to devour all the adhesive myself so I could be frozen stiff like you. Instead I would have the possibility of going on living like you wanted. Maybe it's just a cliché, but the men out there pouring the cement reminded me of eating paste in elementary school, even though I never did and never knew anyone that did. You told me one day that people have a "natural breath" in which they shouldn't ever exceed the words allotted for a single easy breath, the sentences intentionally short.

I asked if my thoughts count as an exception since they do not need to breathe?

You said you must have something on your mind all the time to be always thinking like that.

I think about the world a lot. And you. And the house. And the mortgage, with a sigh.

See, you speak in shots though. She smiled and breathed.

What do you think about?

Well, I don't think of the world much.

Why's that? I asked.

I haven't got the mind for it like you do. And you smiled.

You smile when you're thinking of something, I said.

You have this habit of smiling without smiling, you said. And I did just that and have never killed that habit even after you left. And the sky you loved could never see you anymore, but I'm sure you could still feel its air- the hot, the cold. You said once that God is in the skies and I said if He was up in the sky then that must be why we were meant to live above ground. Yes, you said. Continuing: I feel bad for the hagfish and the earthworms and everything else that can't see the sun or the sky everyday like us. Maybe it was just where they were meant to be, I said. I wondered if He meant the same for you, to be down in the earthy dark; if He meant for you to be down there. But I wanted to love you more than the dirt that divided us. I wanted to be your God and love you. And I wouldn't have let you die. But I suppose this was never meant to be, I realize.

I like the difference of us, you said. You thinking of the world and me thinking about life.

So do I, I said. We don't have to be the same.

And I never stand to watch your grave, silent and immovable in its earthen pedestal, the grass and flowers already grown back from when I excavated them from their roots. I wanted to be down there with you, if not instead of you. I wanted my roots to remain down there, in that captivity. But I watch the yellow kite like an uprooted plant with its dangling tail and unforgotten uses, because it still has so much to live through. And nothing will bring that down or you back up except something beyond this world, but I keep on hoping the earth can do it.

And I'm always wrong.

Abigail Sims
Houston Baptist University
"Blue Plum Jelly"

Mrs. Anna Schaap sank to the scarlet whorled rug on her living room floor. She did not cry.

The creature in the mirror before her was not human. Eyes, hair, and an ostentatious nose, all sat in the places those features ought to be. The eyes blinked. The nose drew in air. But the face did not live. It was a face, a little pale face, unremarkable against any other olive-cheeked, paste-eyed face.

Her hand clenched the threadbare carpeting. A little came away on her palm, crumbling like a receding hairline.

****

That morning, she had shuffled out of bed, a little stiffly, in the little tan bedroom she shared with Tom. The apartment hung in near silence. In the hour before dawn, the electric city smiled, and waited respectfully for someone else to begin the day's conversation.

Anna liked mornings. Once she set the water for Tom's coffee, and eggs on to boil, she coiled by the window to watch the sun rise, blinking and film-eyed like a dreamy lizard. Once last year, she took pictures of the fresh light through plum tree blossoms and hung them by clothespins in a line behind the curtains.

Tom snored sometimes, harsh and heavy as a station wagon rumble, but that was all right.

Later, dress on and ends tucked gingerly in, she marshalled wee blueberry scones and two glasses of orange juice in neat lines on the table. Tom stalked in, boots undone, undershirt tucked in, expensive suspenders well-mended, and sat down. He reached for the paper.

"Don't like these boots. They're half too long in the heel, feet are sliding around in them like fish in a paper basket. Going to stop by the Jeffery's tonight."

"Are you sure?" asked Anna, quietly, as Tom disappeared behind the paper. The boots were new.

"Think I know my own shoe size. Besides, you know they run big."

"All right."

Anna passed him the butter, quietly. Tom went on. "These are just like Jim's down at the yard. You know Jim? He's a big fellow, arms like a tank. But he's so dumb, God, he's just like an ox."

Tom paused to paw for the jelly. Anna slid it closer to his hand.

"Or like that one movie star, what's her name? Garbo? The vacant stare, like she's looking into a camera that goes on forever."

He lowered the paper enough for her to see his face, mouth open, eyes wide.

"Like that, see? She's like that. Like, oh, look at me, I'm a fat whore and I bathe in money so you can take my picture."

Anna nodded, smiling like the lip of a tin can. Tom laughed at his own joke, and retreated again behind the paper.

"You know, I don't like this Wagner fellow. He's going to do bad business for the city. As if there aren't enough communists in this godforsaken country..."

Tom went on, informing the room at large about the current political scene. The immigrants were coming for us, he said. They were coming to get us all.

Anna ate her egg and did not listen.

****

Tom had been a nice enough fellow when they met. A country boy by birth, his time in New York added a street-corner charm and smoothness to his rural speech and bearing. During their first courting, he'd taken her into the city to see movies, to skate, and drive on the long dark roads at night, the city spread for them like a carnival game. The car, she learned later, had not been his.

Conversation came easy with Tom. He didn't leave much room for cat-eyed silence at all. He talked easily and smiled often, pleasant to walk with or ride beside. He made her laugh, sometimes—and what more could you ask for in a man, really?

When Tom came to visit their pleasant home on Long Island, Anna's father had liked him too. Anxious to appear American and progressive, when his daughter's beau came knocking, Mr. Sasaki took Tom out for drinks at once. When they came back, it was settled. Anna Sasaki would become Mrs. Tom Schapp, and go to live with Mr. Schapp, the businessman, in his apartment in downtown Manhattan.

Anna had crushed her sketchbook into her lap and laughed out loud. The city! To a woman who ticked out her life in luscious checkerboard gardens and peeled orange living rooms, only allowed alone to the drugstore or the grocer's stand, the city seemed unreachable. Manhattan, in all its foreign glory, had dwindled to a side-show observed on the arms of men whose attention was her office.

And now she was to live there.

Anna's mother smiled and hugged her daughter. The wedding would be very soon, she said. Mr. Tom would make a fine husband, and have many fine children with her.

Tom had smiled at that. "I hope so, Mrs. Sassqi."

A month later, they were married on the golden June grass of Mr. Sasaki's lawn. Anna's little sisters threw flowers from the garden, giggling and blushing when anyone glanced too long in their direction. Anna brushed the petals off her husband's chartreuse jacket and clung to his arm as he waved. Many of his bandy-hat friends from work had come and lined up by the refreshments table, whisky tended in their hands and obligation in their grins.

Anna waved at them, but their applause was not for her, she thought. She turned to her mother, instead, with a toss of her petal skirt. Her mother smiled back, and threw her an eighteen-circled rose.

After the wedding, Tom drove her back to his apartment, streamers flying out behind the car. His friend's car. Anna held her purse in her lap and waited. He needed both hands to drive.

She did not see her mother again.

Years passed in the quiet apartment. Tom came and went to work. Sometimes he brought the groceries, sometimes Anna would go down to the grocer's herself. She learned to pick the good meat from the cuts that had sat out all day. No more movies, no more rides around the city. But a plum tree grew by the window, and one day it might give fruit.

Anna wondered if they had children, if this would change. Tom had wanted children, she knew. He told her this the first night in her new home, when she drifted off too soon for a wedding night, he said. She had to do her share, he said, and Anna had tried, night after night. Tom had not given up easily.

But no children came.

****

After the first night, Tom did not speak to her about babies again. He joked often about rescuing his friends from the pressures and perils of fatherhood, and providing a haven for men from their wife's shopping lists and nagging.

Anna smiled, dumped the ashtrays, and went to bed early.

He brought friends over often, and they drank in the front room facing the sky, feet up on the coffee table, cigars smoldering in their fingers. Every man of them had a wife and children at home.

Hours after she had fallen asleep, Tom would droop into bed, stinking and paunchy.

"No good, no good. Got a dud. 's not fair," he'd say, pawing her awake. "Wha's wrong with you, woman?"

He slapped her, hard.

The first time, she had screamed, thinking someone had broken in. Tom beat her then, leaving red-gold bruises blooming over her shoulders and waist for weeks. She did not scream again, but it made no difference.

Anna fastened her chemise a little tighter, old-fashioned, and wore another sweater, just in case. It would be canning season soon, and the trees in the apartment garden carried green fruit.

Tom never apologized in the mornings, but that was all right.

****

Tom came in one evening, grey suit jacket slung over his shoulder, followed by a blonde woman on the arm of a much younger man.

"Anna, this is my supervisor, Mr. McLellan."

The younger man laughed, hair pasted flat to his scalp, and waved the title away, as if it meant very little to a man at the head of a company. He shook her hand, and Anna thought he couldn't be a day over twenty. Jim, he said, his name was Jim.

"Jim, Mrs. Schapp. I think we've met before."

They hadn't.

The slight woman behind him shook hands too, and gave her a perfunctory little smile. Her dress hung on her like a little yellow mushroom, loose and comfortable. Her rounded belly preceded her, small and ostentatious and brimming with life.

"Mary. Pleased to meet you," she said, and sighed.

Anna took them all into the living room and served them fake-orange cheese. Jim splayed himself on the couch at once, a glass in one hand, banter ready in the other. His hair stuck to his head like a child's pasteboard concoction. Mary perched on the other end of the sofa, studying the carpet with a connoisseur's fixation. Tom looked at her, swallowed, and looked away.

Anna offered him the cheese plate. It took a moment for him to acknowledge her, to tear his eyes off Mary's obedient form. He blinked at Anna, scale-eyed, and his mouth sank into disgust. He waved the plate away.

Mary did not want cheese either, but when she shook her head, her collar shifted a little. The unmarked girlish skin dissolved into purple just below the collarbone.

The women met each other's eyes for the first time.

Mary flinched, and pulled her collar closer.

"No thanks, no dairy for me. The baby doesn't like it."

Jim had glared at Anna then and she returned the plate to the kitchen, hands shaking. A row of glass jars waited in prim lines on the counter.

Tom followed her, bristling. His breath ghosted harsh and damp across her cheek.

"Leave that poor woman alone," he said, grabbing her wrist. "Can't you see she's delicate?"

Anna tried to pull away from him. "Yes. I know."

Tom shoved her wrist behind her back.

"Then let her alone." He pulled her closer, grip tightening until she could not feel her hand.

Jim's laugh rang out from the living room, high and raucous.

"You are jealous," she said.

Tom hit her, close-fisted, across the cheekbone.

"Shut up, woman. You don't know! You don't know anything!"

Anna cupped her cheek with her free hand, curled in over herself, looking fixed at the cloth on the kitchen table.

"You don't understand," he said, pulling her in close. His sweaty lips brushed her ear. "I will get a son, you know. I will."

Red checks on a gold field. A small stain where the lamp had spilled. Anna struggled against his arms to look up, eyes blank and wide.

"What, did you think you were the only one?" He laughed. "She's mine. Jim has no idea."

It was funny, wasn't it?

Tom let her go. "Let's get the good stuff out now, shall we?"

Anna turned away quietly, opened the cabinet, and handed him a full bottle of gin.

A bowl of blue plums waited on the table.

****

That night, after Jim and Mary had gone, and after Tom had long since wandered out, singing an old Italian ballad far off-key, Anna settled to her cooking.

The peeled fruit, diced, all set off to one side, the mushy ones separated. Sugar measured out in white bowls on the table, little dunes spread out on a cambric sea. The water boiled.

A third bowl, off to the side, blue. Another pale dune, smaller than the other two.

Anna emptied the fruit and the two white bowls into the boiling water, beating her wooden spoon against the edges periodically, testing the jell, sticky with the sweetness of it.

The slight curve of her belly under her apron, nearly hidden.

The blue bowl, the off-white powder, emptied into the boiling fruit.

****

The next morning came like many other Tuesday mornings. Anna set the table quietly, and had breakfast ready when Tom came downstairs.

She wondered if it would be a boy or a girl.

"You know, I don't like this Wagner fellow," said Tom, buttering a scone. "He's going to do bad business for the city."

"Oh, really?" said Anna, cutting an egg white with her fork and not listening.

The glass bowl of sugared fruit glittered in the middle of the table, gold against the red tablecloth. Tom spooned several heavy scoops onto his plate.

She watched, lifting her fork to her mouth punctually, as Tom ate three scones with plum jelly.

"Excuse me, dear," she said, standing.

Tom coughed, scratching at his throat absently, and did not look up from his paper.

****

Mrs. Anna Schapp sank to the floor in the living room, fingers threading through the carpet.

The kitchen had been quiet for some time now.

The choking had long since stilled.

And that was all right.

Aditi Choudhary
Delhi Public School, Bhopal (India)
The Light

Deepak was what he was called, literally meaning a Diya. A small lamp which seemed to light up his tiny world including his parents and sisters.

"Ghar ka beta hai tu, Deepu. Hamara naam roshan karega."
(You are the son of the family, Deepu. Make us proud.)

The son in a family with two daughters, he had grown up listening to these words. At first, they felt good. He would get the extra toffee, the ice cream with more topping, the riper mango. He would smile and bask in the glory of being the son of the family, being the *Kul Deepak, the lamp of the clan.*

But as his smile started to show teeth instead of blank gaps, for the first time, a doubt rose in his mind. Is the definition of success the same for him and his family? The more his father pushed protractors and compasses in his hands, his fingers sought paint brushes and canvas.

Engineer banna hai tumhe, his dad would say.
You have to become an engineer when you grow up, okay?

He would smile and nod, but the moment the old man turned, the page meant for figures would turn into a scenery. His art was something which took breath away and captured the soul of its observer. True rays of light from this little lamp. His fingers always worked on their own accord; he couldn't help it.

As the time passed, those words no longer felt bright. They felt like a burden he constantly had to carry and couldn't get rid of. His father always frowned at his report card, commenting sharply at the Bs and Cs in Math and Science. Not once did his father notice the straight As in Art.

He'll see when I get admission in a good art college, he would console himself. And so, the days turned into months, months into years.

He remembered the day when his letter of acceptance finally arrived. He could feel the grin that spread on his face at the words *full scholarship*. He had shown he was a Kul Deepak. He would make them all proud.

The memories were all too clear in his mind as he swung himself absently in the cold morning breeze. He could hear himself shouting for his dad, waving the letter. The smile, the laughter which lit up his heart as his dad read the letter.

And that was where the dream broke.

His father's words were firm and precise, emotionless.

Art? Was he out of his mind? Why, just day before yesterday Sharma Ji's son got his engineering degree! That's what he was supposed to do as well. No wonder the grades were always B and C. But he still has time, even now. Study hard, and of course he'll get an admission! Why waste time in things as useless as *Art*? It doesn't bring money or fame- the things that matter. Now stop fooling around and get to work.

The world had come crashing down around him. But then deep in his heart, he had perhaps always known that the *Kul Deepak's* flame was too bright to last long.

He stood up on the swing, looping his mother's stole around the pole. Smiling, he pulled out a piece of paper and sent it on the ground before he closed his eyes, never to open them again.

They found him next morning, hanging limp with a sketch at his feet- a sketch of an extinguished lamp.

Anna Priore
St. Olaf College
"The Table"

Everything at the garage sale is marked down to a dollar or less. Lime green price stickers adorn bins of bedraggled Beanie Babies and chipped Burger King collector cups. Nick's hand is spongy in mine as we meander through the labyrinth of junk. It's hot and windy. The tattooed woman in the Teenage Mutant Ninja Turtles tank top behind the cash register fans herself with a pizza box lid.

Amidst a chaotic mess of plastic limbs and heads, I find a small action figure of Batman. He's missing a hand and a long-forgotten puppy has nibbled his vinyl cape, but his face still looks just the way I remember it. I set it on the table. It's a wooden table, old and splintered, and I see my name etched into the surface, my five-year-old handwriting, scratched with a spoon handle when mom wasn't looking.

The hot July wind gusts again, roaring back decades through the weathered rows of Norway pines that surrounded my old house like silent sentinels. On the kitchen counter is a bowl of limes, brown and hard as stones, and a dusty block of gleaming knives. There is the table in the back corner, stained from watercolors and crayons, scalded from gravy boats and heavy cast iron skillets, gashed from pumpkin carving contests.

Every night, the four of us sat around the table and prayed. There is a candle burning in the center and, sometimes, a vase of flowers. Before broadcasting went digital, we had a little Sony TV with rabbit ears that never worked.

After Dad had abandoned us for his leather armchair and *Batman*, Mom would lecture me about my flabby stomach; Caroline and I would tussle over who had to sweep the floor, and we would both tell mom she had to stand up to Dad screaming at her.

When I left for college, I would always think of the table. Caroline sitting where I used to be, Dad chewing loudly and never looking up, Mom staring straight ahead at the oily wallpaper. Mom finally told

Dad to stop screaming at her. Dad left three weeks later, and we sold our house. And the table.

"The table ain't for sale," says the woman in the tank top.

"I'll give you fifty dollars for it," I say, even though I haven't had that much money since my mother died.

"It's so busted up my son's gonna haul it away for firewood. It ain't even worth a dollar."

I look at Nick. We already have a kitchen table. But I would move this one into our bedroom and use it as an altar, the slab on which we make a new family, a new mistake, a new sacrifice that sits around in greasy white silence.

The woman has bloodshot eyes, like Caroline when she would come home from one of her drinking binges. I touch the table. "Burn it, then," I say. "For the love of God, burn it to hell."

Anne Whitehouse
Harvard College
"The Cyclist"

On my bike, I am leaving the park, down shuttered side streets, across the avenues' uneven intersections. I listen to the bump and whir of my wheels against the asphalt. I pass blunttopped towers between shafts of darkness.

My shirt flares behind me, and I am straddling the narrow seat, pedaling fast as the street inclines gently down. The buildings grow smaller, older; fire escapes crisscross their faces. Figures blur past me as if in a dream: a man on a grey concrete stoop drinks from a flask; a woman leans from a window; two boys jump towards an orange ball poised in a ring. Their shouts meet me like a hot wind, and I travel through them.

Past patterns of scaling walls, doorways that open to darkness, I lean, and the bike turns; the street reflects fisheyes in a pool at the base of an opened hydrant. A cloud shifts in that black liquid. Behind me, the sun is lowering; its warm streaks caress my back. Again the street has changed; its surface is a smooth black glass, obsidian. I see that I am approaching the shores of a river of sorrow. Every morning the sun flees from it. Down there a man plays an accordion and a dancing monkey is waving his cup. Rats sleep in the splintering wharves; the benches are bolted into place.

But all moves away from me. All disappears in the bicycle's receding wake. I turn away from the shadowy river. An elderly man points his cane at my spokes. "So the silver spiral unwinds," he says, "into its valley at last." And the street opens.

A street of single houses from a century ago, brown sea stone cut in blocks, black gates of wrought iron, and window boxes where the velvet petals of geraniums bloom in utter stillness. The hooks of questions prick me. I am slowed. I stop and walk the bicycle, a finger laid across the handlebars. At first it seems the only living thing on the block is the light that slides across the windows. It catches each fire, burns, and leaves a crystal. Depths open in the glass. I am looking into a room. A study, a library. Ever so slowly, I slide past in the windows, while the light from across the sky turns the brown stones pink. The heart of a rose smokes in them, a stain of ash on the sidewalk. The spokes of my wheels are dulled to the luster of old pewter.

Here, I am unknown; no one misses me in the glistening windows. A breath of mist on a table, wiped away. Does the street exist? I have stopped. I am sitting on a step, drinking water from a plastic bottle. My bicycle leans on an iron gate. Even when I close my eyes, I cannot hear the breeze lifting the hair from my neck. And when I open them, the light is deeper and the shadows of clipped hedges wave across the stones. In the room above me, a pen scrapes over paper and someone hums a lullaby from long ago.

And yet the song is not from the room after all. A little girl is singing it, and she is coming down the street towards me, balancing a large metal hoop with a stick. She beats it lightly to her rhythm--tap, tap, tap. Then gravity accelerates it, and she hurries. It slants an oval down the street; her thin legs make shadows like the bicycle's spokes. Her hair is dark silk, waving like a fringe, hiding her face as she looks only at her hoop. In the world, only her hoop exists, and the song she is humming. It passes me in snatches like thoughts said aloud. In spite of her running, she is a long time coming to me. Her feet clatter on the walk like rain on the roof of a country house. Her hoop is a swish of wind.

And when she reaches me, she looks up and her eyes meet mine. Blue-grey immeasurable distance. I gaze steadily back, not blinking. I am rooted to the stoop like the geranium to its box. She is so close to me that her features dissolve, and only her eyes, a child's clear eyes, fill my vision. Neither of us speak. I feel the air touching my eyes. I feel naked. I know without looking that the hoop is perfectly poised. With only the top of her stick touching it, it balances on an infinites-imal point like a world stilled.

Her eyes are like pearls washed by changing light, yet itself changeless. It is then, when I am almost lost in her look, that she speaks. Her voice catches as it surfaces; it is as ragged as the grass trampled in the park and as the torn streets I have travelled. "Do you know me?" she says, and waits, and her mouth crumples. I am afraid she will cry.

"No," I say, "I have never seen you," but she has not lingered. Mirrored in the windows of silent pink-brown houses, she runs with the whirling hoop down to the end of the street, towards the river, where it is already dark.

Jamie Samson
Saint Francis Xavier University (Canada)
"Beetles"

A minute clicking sound could be heard in the otherwise silent room. A boy sat on his parents' faded rug in front of an unlit fireplace; the oppressive summer heat lay thick and choking over everything, the air seeming to be replaced with boiling water. The boy could feel his starched cotton shirt sticking to him as he dug his hand through the small bucket of marbles he'd been given by his grandfather. His carefully gelled hair, lank and damp, kept falling over his forehead. The bucket had his name written on it in clumsy black letters: *Henry*, the "R" facing backwards like a lopsided balloon tied with two strings, to make extra sure it wouldn't fly away. He grabbed one marble, rolled it across the floor from one hand to the other, and then placed it at one corner of one square of the checkered pattern on the rug. Almost a quarter of the rug, white squares dimmed to gray over the years, now held little glowing blue-green spheres in perfect lines. The boy thought they looked like a troop of beetles marching through an absurdly easy maze. The clock ticked quietly from its perch on the mantelpiece.

The dimly lit hallway was silent; the paintings hanging straight: pictures of flowers, fields, seaside towns. Car keys had been thrown unceremoniously onto the scuffed little brown table that stood by the door. One room down from where the boy sat on the thick, worn carpet, all was silent in the kitchen. Three plates of limp cheese sandwiches had been placed carefully on the table. All three triangles faced the same way, like little white mountains surrounded by fields of filigree roses. None had been touched; the humidity molded the three layers together like mismatched portions of the earth's crust. One seat was occupied. The boy's father sat alone; the ceiling fan overhead gently stirring the few hairs on the top of his balding head. A small bead of sweat rolled down his sun-browned nose. The garden sitting in front of the squat brown house was impressive in its strict boundaries, lush blooms, and perfectly weed-free soil. The watering can sat half full next to the cracked concrete front steps where it was placed every morning after Henry's father carefully washed the soil with the gritty water taken from the hose.

The man sat at the kitchen table with the newspaper flicked out purposefully in front of him, the headlines ignored by his eyes. The only thing he could see was the picture he'd placed carefully against the table's edge so that its white rim made a blip in the middle of the solid line of mahogany. The subject of the picture, a young man in sepia tones, waved a wide-brimmed hat at the camera, leaning on the edge of a chipped wooden fence. The man who sat in the kitchen looked like his father, but on the back of the photo had been written, in hastily scribbled cursive, *Dad*. The man stared at the picture, the sweat on his nose mingling with the tears on his cheeks.

Up the muffled carpeted stairs, past the landing where an action figure lay with his arms pointing straight up in the air, a door was closed. Inside the small master bedroom, a woman sat on her bed; a simple wooden rosary wound lovingly around her fingers, more reverently than pearls on a lady's neck. The dark hair was loose on her shoulders, the hair clip sitting like a washed up seashell on the worn blue bedspread and prayers were whispered as softly as the kiss of foam on the beach. Henry's mother stared at a woman like her, the Virgin Mary's soft face looking down from the dresser, the nose worn from peach to white where it had been caressed by a worshipping thumb. She prayed for her husband, her son, and the soul of the man in the picture. She could still hear the phone ringing in her ears, its stilted, mournful ring like the cry of a lost bird. Henry did not know that Grandpa was gone. He placed the marbles at the corners in the rug, thinking how much they looked like insects, and wondering if perhaps his mother would mind if he left them that way.

Kira Martin
Chemeketa Community College
"Family Values"

Opening my laptop, I logged into the blue wash of social media, clicked onto her profile and scrolled down until I found the post. I stared at it for a long time, the words still stinging three weeks later.

Years ago, I had decided to keep an eye on my daughters. My sons didn't worry me, not as much as my three daughters did. It's always the girls that are preyed upon. As my concern grew with their age, I tried to keep tabs on them. They refused to friend me on Facebook, so I took matters into my own hands. A man's got to keep his daughters safe. I'd always been tech savvy; I had a long-standing blog with a few thousand followers as a testament to that. I had made myself a new profile, and I named myself "Monica Smith." I let it sit for a few months, friending teenagers who were too trusting and popping out the occasional post to make it seem convincing. Then I friended my youngest son. I knew he would accept; he's always been too trusting, no matter how many times I've warned him. Once I had one child, I knew I could get all four others. My youngest daughter Sadie's request pended for the longest time out of them all.

The kids had never found out, and that suited me just fine. After the divorce four years ago, I got the house, and my wife got the kids. She wedged a distance between us that was amplified as they grew up. I merely found an unconventional solution that worked to partially bridge the gap. Now they were all out of my wife's nest, one in college, the rest married or close to it. All except Sadie. She was still in high school. Just about to graduate if I remembered correctly.

I stared hard at the post, reading the words over and over as if they would sting less. Sadie had always been against the family and my beliefs, but the open betrayal hurt. The post wrote us off, labeled us as crazy where she thought I couldn't see, and further stratified her from the rest of the family. She had always been different, the odd one out. I read the post again, the words ghosting on my lips.

How does anybody believe this? A blurred photo was attached to the text. It was a photo I myself had taken during a rare sighting. It had been taken from my own blog out of a post that I published about six months ago. It had been a huge breakthrough for me, a revelation. An actual honest-to-god picture of a *Homo <u>Sasquatchis</u>*. A Sasquatch. It was closer that I had ever gotten before to proving to the world that the supernatural exists. The text read on. *These people are delusional. I'm so sick and tired of seeing grainy pictures of bears. It's insane. People need to pick up and move on with their lives instead of camping out in the forest with night vision goggles.*

I stared at her profile picture, a girl with dark wavy hair and a crooked smile that cracked her cherry colored lips. She looked like me, dark eyes, brown hair. Yet she had always been the complete opposite. She was like a stranger in my home; she had always been. The family trips to the woods, each of my towheaded children armed with a flash light and a camera. She was the one who always stood out like a sore thumb. It wasn't because she was the only one who didn't resemble her mother, it was that she always seemed skeptical despite everyone's disapproval, even her siblings. She wrote off each of my educated claims, even as a child, refuting that men didn't turn into wolves at full moon, that vampires belonged only in bad fiction, and that anything resembling a dragon was extinct.

At that point, my blog was in its early stages and I had dealt with enough skepticism. But she fought harder than my toughest critic. She was never cruel, not like that post now was. She was always patient and treated me like *she* was the grown up. Sadie believed in only what she could see. It was strange, irrational, and bizarre. I was sure I raised her better than that. She wouldn't wear the rose quartz pendant for protection and she never once as a child had come to me and her mother in the middle of the night with fears of what was under her bed. Not that we could have assured her much without the quartz.

Of course by now, my wife has remarried another man and has thrown away the beliefs that shaped her life only years ago when she shared it with me. Jack. He's an iron strong unbeliever. Sadie's friends with him on Facebook. She's not as picky as my other daughters, but then again, Sadie adores him. It didn't really bother me until that post, nothing about Sadie and her peculiarities did. Now, they couldn't stop gnawing at me. She said from the beginning that she didn't believe us. It had stung then. I didn't know the child I had raised, and I wasn't sure I much cared to at that point. Until she made the post. I wanted to know her better. What made her brain tick. How could I convince her? I had learned that fact, the hardest to get of all evidence, would be the only ticket to her belief.

But then a week ago, though, something miraculous happened. I had already spent two weeks stewing in my office, unable to find the strength to write a blog post about a kidnapping that pointed towards a fae changeling (the boy returned home suspiciously quiet after three days), until my hunting buddies pulled me out of my funk. I had found them about six years ago when my blog picked up speed and my marriage started to fall apart. As my children became busy with their lives and plans, unable to stay up those long nights with me, the hunting buddies took their place. We drank beers with a shot gun on our knees, waiting for creatures that had been sighted in the woods before, usually Sasquatch or extra-terrestrials. They had become a big part of my life over the last four years.

I know that I will never top last week's find, and despite the stinging of Sadie's words, I know she'll have to eat them when she sees what I've found. I know I'll finally have her. There's nothing more factual than physical evidence. We went out that night, Harriet, Murry, and Ed. And we found something. I haven't written a post about it yet. At this point, I don't think it would be wise. Once the government found it, they would surely break into my home and steal it away from me. Probably murder me to keep me quiet about it. A shiver curled up my spine. No wonder the sheep-like majority of the population believe their lies and cover ups. But despite the risk, I had to show her. Despite the vulnerable position it put me in, Sadie would be the one other soul, other than me and my buddies, who would ever see it. Sharing my beliefs would connect us.

The sound of the door unlocking down the hall pulled me back into the present: Sadie. The last of the kids at home, she had her own car. With it came the freedom to go between her mother's kitchen and mine, eating the best snacks. I only ever bought much for her. My laptop made a soft sound as I pushed it down, left my office, and met her at the door.

"Hey, dad." Her voice was clear and strong.

"Hi, Sadie." I smiled. She gave me a dry hug and then slipped off her backpack at the entry way and made a beeline for the fridge. She must have just gotten off from school. The day had gone by fast, like it always did on my days off from the clinic.

"I'm starving," she said, pulling open the fridge doors. She rooted around for a second, pulling a few pieces of ham from a bag.

"How's school?"

I already knew the answer to the question. Sadie shrugged, mouth full and brown locks catching light. Her answer was muffled. "Good."

She had a C in one of her classes, and there was a boy who kept kicking her seat in math. She had ranted about him on Facebook two days ago.

"So, what was it that you wanted to talk about?" Her voice held a note of wariness, hand absently on the fridge door as she faced me. I didn't sense that she wanted to settle in. No matter. Soon she would. I felt a smile growing on my lips.

"I want to show you something." I couldn't contain myself anymore. "But you have to promise not to tell *anyone*." Any leakage could prove detrimental to my life, but one thing Sadie would never do is lie. I knew if I made her promise, she wouldn't tell.

Her chest moved almost indecipherably with a sigh and she said, "Okay, dad."

"Good. Okay, open the freezer." I pressed my hands together to stop them from shaking. This was it. The moment I had been waiting for. I couldn't keep a grin off my face. Maybe I would take her out to dinner after, if she didn't have too much homework. I'd have to check on her Facebook to see if she's complained about any.

She pushed the top doors closed, and leaned down to pull open the freezer. She looked uncertainly at me, and then pulled at my eager nod. She stared in the open door for a second in shock before coughing in a way that seemed more like a gag.

"Oh god, Dad! That's disgusting! I'm eating," she moaned and threw what was left of the slabs of ham on the counter. I made a mental note to collect those and not let them collect mold like leftover food so often did. The kitchen was generally a mess, but I'd managed to keep it clean for the last three days after a big clean up and I intended to keep it that way.

Icy smoke rose from the creature's skin and I peered in, delighted. How many times over the last week had I looked at it? Too many. The freezer door had to be overworked. But there it sat in a zip-lock bag, body no more than a foot long, swimming in loose, wrinkled, graying skin, its face like a collapsed cave.

"It's an extra-terrestrial. An alien. A gray," I said triumphantly, inspecting her face letting it all sink in.

We had been lucky to find it in such good condition. Its ship must have left only hours before, leaving one of its own for dead. It had hardly decomposed, but from the looks of it, a wild animal had been at it. We hadn't realized that they would be so small. We had heard before how small they were, but it was always assumed that the gray aliens were around three feet, whereas the shape shifting reptilians were around six feet. Murry had suggested that it was a young that had been lost in childbirth perhaps, and I was inclined to believe him with the evidence given. If it wouldn't risk our lives, this information would prove fruitless to the efforts of studying the grays. Maybe I would publish the findings in thirty years from now when I'm 79 and decrepit and don't care about dying.

Sadie closed her eyes for a moment, then looked at me like I was crazy. Hand over her nose, she peered into the freezer again.

"Dad." Her voice was surprisingly disappointed. "There's a tail."

I felt my eyebrows drop. Sadie leaned in closer, hovering a few inches above it, pointing, but not quite touching the plastic.

"I think that's a whisker." She straightened herself. "You've never said anything about grays having whiskers."

"We saw those things." I brushed her concerns off. "We're not stupid. We think that those are antennae for their ship's tracker. It's built similar to an animal's because nature truly does have the perfect universal design." It made sense, and sense was always what Sadie could see best.

She ran a hand through her hair, the long wisps unsettled in a few places. "Dad… It's just an animal. It looks like something was wrong with its head, like it was deformed or something."

My jaw tightened. I honest to god could not believe what I was hearing. Here I have actual, physical, undeniable proof, and she was still doing this? Still?

"Sadie," I said, keeping my tone smooth. "Then why would it have no fur?"

She sighed deeply. "I don't know, Dad. It looks like a possum that's all kinds of messed up."

"Sadie! It's an *alien* life form. It's a little different than we expected, yes, but it's the find of a century. This is something not of earth." After all these years and all of her asking for proof and I finally have it. Proof that people would kill for and that no one else in existence could ever hope to find. And here my eighteen-year-old daughter was refuting it.

Her eyebrows raised. "Dad, it's pretty creepy, but it's definitely earthly."

"Why, Sadie? *Why?* Why do you have to do this? You know the facts. These things can't be made up. I have proof, you have none." I rubbed my temple, trying to erase the headache that was setting in.

Sadie leveled a long look at me, her eyes no longer a cautious warm brown. She slammed the freezer shut. I started to regret all of it. Why had I tried to get close to her, to prove myself? My face started to flush. I should have known better.

"Dad, all you have to do is go to a vet, they run a test, do whatever they do, and they'll confirm if it's a possum… or an alien."

"No!" I hadn't meant to raise my voice, but she jumped regardless. I quieted. "I can't do that. You know what will happen when the vet figures it out. Their boss finds out. It goes up the rung. Next thing I know the FBI's after me. You know how it works. They can so easily make people disappear. You know what happened to SupernaturalSue, the woman who ran a blog like mine years ago? You know what I'm risking to get the truth to people?"

"Dad, she just stopped posting!" There was an angry pause. I had never expected this. Ever. It hadn't even crossed my mind. My whole body was filled with disbelief. I tried to shake it away, but it clung to me still. I sighed, trying to hide the slight watering of my eyes.

"Look, it doesn't matter. But you need to keep your promise. I can't be looking behind my shoulder for men in suits every day."

She stared at me for almost a minute before answering. "But listen, Dad, I'll make you a deal. If you go to a vet and they say it's an alien, I'll believe you. On everything. The chupacabras, the fae, the alien. Everything. But if they say it's a possum, you need to admit that you were wrong. Not even about everything. Just this." Her eyes were wide and earnest, her eyebrows arched up.

Temptation rippled through my brain. It would be so easy. I would risk my life for her, but not for something she should already believe. I shook my head. "No, that's not how it works. I'm not making a deal with you. Promise me you won't tell anyone."

She shook her head, not meeting my eyes. "You don't need to make me promise."

"Good." I relaxed slightly, the tightness I didn't know I was carrying disappearing slightly. "I just… I just honestly can't believe that after everything, you honestly don't believe any of it. Even after I told you how I was awakened one night when I was seventeen and couldn't move. There was an extra-terrestrial on my chest, Sadie! It had me in its beam. You know that's why I always go off in metal detectors. You know that it put an implant in me." She pushed past me into the entry way with a sound of disgust. What an ingrate. After all I've done to protect her? Would she realize what was true if I took away her shield to the world?

"I'm going."

"What? No, you're not. Come back, we're not done talking."

Slinging her backpack on her shoulders, keys in her hand, she said, "Dad, I've heard you tell that story a thousand times over. It was a night terror. That's what they do to you. You hallucinate and you have a weight on your chest. Your brain fills in the details."

She pulled a card from her backpack pocket. She fumbled it in her hands for a moment, then looked up, chin strong. "I'm never going to believe what you believe." She pushed the card into my hand before I could react.

"It's an invitation to my graduation."

I flipped it over to see her smiling face on paper next to a date and time. I looked up to see her face stony and so starkly different. Her mouth twisted. She started her sentence once, then mustered the courage it seemed to finish her thought.

"Mom doesn't want you to come."

I blinked, startled away from our conversation. "What?"

"She said she doesn't want you arguing with Jack like you did at my last soccer match."

Rage built up in me. Jack wasn't going to stop me from watching my daughter graduate high school.

"I hardly—"

"Dad, I don't care. I just don't. Good bye." Her voice was harsh, the last word cut off by the finality of the closing door.

I stood in stunned silence for a time. I'd let her take the kids, I hadn't come to her wedding, I wore a tie to the parent-teacher conferences. But now? I was always a pleasant sort of fellow, if maybe a bit energetic. Now she was trying to stop me from seeing my daughter? Now, when I was trying to be closer to Sadie? Shaking with anger, I retreated into my office, dropped myself into my desk chair, and slammed out an angry post onto Facebook.

The content was almost entirely made up. It described a fight between me and my non-existent female teen friend. I had gotten into a bad habit of venting through "Monica." The mask it provided and the sympathy from the few youngsters I'd connected with felt strangely good. It also provided a few instances for me to talk to my children. Without ever even meeting "Monica," we became acquaintances. All I had to do was post on their walls once every month or so.

I switched back to my blog, and checked through my messages. I vented more by raging at a few skeptics who kept leaving nasty comments on my posts. This one, SkeptismNotSheep, had been following me for years, leaving thoughtful and annoying posts. Even his username was a jab at a post I had made years ago. I didn't have the heart to block him. He amped up the traffic on the site. A couple hours later, I made myself a dry ham sandwich. There wasn't much else, it had been a while since I last shopped. I stopped myself from calling my wife. I knew that at this point my rage had not subsided enough. Murry called before I went to bed and had been almost as disappointed as I was at how Sadie had taken the news. I woke up the next morning and took a shower before I headed into work. It made me feel better, clean.

Plopping into my computer chair for a quick five minutes before I headed out, I saw that someone commented on my Facebook post. There were a few words of sympathy, and I rewarded them with a like. I then went to Monica's newsfeed and scrolled down. I had hidden everyone else's feeds except for my children's, so I saw Sadie's new post right away.

I wish I had a dad that I could actually rely on. I can't even believe him. I wish that I actually wanted him at my graduation...

What the hell? A feeling like a stone falling through water filled my body. I clicked onto the comments, seeing that three people had already replied. Her mother's was first.

Honey, you know he's like this. He's still your father.

Sadie replied below.

Mom, he has a fucking possum in his freezer. He thinks it's an alien life form —

Darkness leaked into my vision, blacking out all other words but "alien." All of a sudden I could hear blood pumping through my veins as if I had run a mile, beating loudly in my ears like a tribal drum.

Without thinking, I punched out, *I told you not to tell anyone, Sadie. You betrayed me.*

I pressed enter, my hand shaking with adrenaline. My neck felt itchy and I couldn't help but look over my shoulder.

The reply was almost instantaneous.

What are you talking about?

Her response made me realize that I was not who she thought I was, that I was not "Dad" now, I was Monica. Perhaps that was the only reason her reply wasn't so cutting. I was too far gone now. I replied.

You promised me that you wouldn't tell anyone.

Oh my god. Dad? I can't —

I slammed shut the computer and jumped up. Cold grew against my skin; I had already sweated through my work clothes.

Work! I jerked to look at the clock. Late. Running for my car, I ripped out of the driveway, anger giving me speed.

She didn't want me at her graduation. She told the world about my secret. She lied. Did she really want me murdered? What had I done to so badly wrong her? These questions revolved around my head for the entirety of the double shift I worked, checking vitals and examining patients. I'd seen my fair share of supernatural injuries here.

Twelve hours later, I returned home. My house was a stranger. It was almost nine o'clock and night took over. I tread lightly, locking the door behind me, and made my way directly to the freezer. Pulling it open, anxious to find relief but finding none. It was gone. They had been here. Fear pricked through me, and suddenly I sensed footsteps. I whirled around, ready to attack.

There was a cry of alarm. I knew the voice and paused. Sadie stood there, eyes rimmed in red and determined. In her hand she held a watery gray zip-lock bag.

"What are you doing with that? How long has it been out? You'll ruin it!"

I snatched it from her and inspected it. A strip of flesh had been peeled from a shoulder.

"How long were you pretending to be her?" Her voice was full of tearful anger.

I glared at her.

"What did you do? Why is there skin missing?"

She let out a shaky sigh and shook her head, not looking at me but rather the countertops.

"I had it tested."

My heart dropped. If they didn't know about it before, they did now.

"Don't bother freaking out. It's a possum. The government's not out to get you." Papers appeared that I hadn't seen before at her side. "It's all right here. It was young. It had several issues. Apparently, it had an infection in its brain that caused its death, as well as some skin issues likely stemming from an allergy and a few deformities. It's not an alien. It's a dead possum."

I shook my head. "No, it's an alien. It's a gray." I would never touch those papers, much less look at them.

"Dad… no. It's no more an alien than you are Monica Smith," she said quietly. Anger tinged through me.

She set the papers on the counter, tears streaking down her face before she shifted into darkness. This was not the face of victory.

"Do you honestly think that if there was a chance the FBI would come after you, that I would turn you in? Dad… think about it." She collected herself and then she was gone.

The way she left was so final. Not a teary glance was thrown in my direction. She honestly, with all her soul, would never believe any of it, would she? Sadie was rooted in as strongly as I was, maybe more. A strange emotion flooded through me, erasing my anger and leaving a dry feeling in my body.

I stepped towards the papers uncertainly.

Caleb Adebayo
Nigerian Law School, Lagos Campus
"Bits and Pieces"

He was seated on the boulder under the guava tree in our school compound when I first saw him. It was in an area of the sprawling yard that was almost always deserted. The guavas were just beginning to ripen then. It was against school policy to stone the guavas. They had to fall before we ate them. One had just fallen, and I was going to pick it, euphoric at my good fortune, when I saw him. He was crying, so I thought the guava must have hit him when it fell. I told him sorry and picked the guava. There would be no begging today. Njideka and Oreva were not with me. I was heading for the tap to wash the fruit, but he was still crying so I stopped and looked at him. He was small. I figured he should be in primary one, two classes below me. He had fine hair that arranged itself in neat curls. I could not see his face. It was wedged between his knees.

I went over to him and attempted to raise his face. He shook my hand off. I asked him what was the matter. Who beat you? Why are you crying? Did you lose your snack money? It couldn't be the guava that hit him that made him cry. Nobody cried that long from a guava hitting his head.

He didn't respond. He just kept crying.

There was something about the way he cried. It could have been because his whole body was crying. I studied him. He had golden skin and tiny legs, and rabbit ears that branched off from his head like the letter 'Y'. Hearing him cry, I felt pained. I pitied him. It was sad that anything should make a boy so young to cry so much and refuse to stop. Didn't he even have any friends?

"What is your name?" I asked.

He didn't stop crying. I ached to console him. His crying was sincere. It was the way one cried when he lost someone. My mother had cried that way when her junior brother died. When my brother,

Uzo, had the accident, I had cried that way.

I felt like crying too as I listened to him cry. It was a strange feeling. My heart was feeling heavy. Like a stone had been dropped on my chest.

"Stop crying, please." I pleaded, patting his back.

"Tell me what it is. I can be your friend. Please stop crying. Let's share my guava."

"Are you hungry? We can share my snacks money. I have not spent it yet."

I said everything I thought would help, then I stooped to get a peek at his face. That was when he raised his head and began to sing.

He had a voice like nothing I had ever heard. Like there was a piano with a skilled player in his throat. Not even the choir mistress at our church sang that beautifully. The melody was too perfect for a person so young. I could see his face now; tender like that of a baby. He had a birthmark on his forehead above full brows and eyes that looked gloomy. Looking at his face now, his ears fit into place.

He kept singing, staring ahead like I wasn't there. He was not singing in English. It was Yoruba, I knew. But coming from him, they sounded like tongues. Those things my mother spoke when she prayed.

The sound that came out of his mouth was smooth. Just how Blue Band slithered out of the sachet when you pressed it. But it was not a happy song, I could tell, because as he sang, his eyes were glum and he cried. Yet his voice did not shift.

I felt myself cave in, crumple like folded paper under this melancholic influence. I did not understand the language in which he sang, yet I felt the hands of the song. Strong hands that pulled me inside it till I was helpless. I dropped the guava and began to cry. I sat by him on the boulder, my back resting on the tree. He was still singing when he took my hands. I felt something course through me like an electric shock, only milder and for longer. I was trembling all over and bawling.

He was dancing now, as he sat, moving his body to the rhythm he had given the song, tapping his feet. Then abruptly, he stopped singing.

He stopped crying too, not as abruptly, yet I was still crying, finding it difficult to stop. The grief in him had engulfed me. He started another tune, quietly at first, then slowly his voice rose. He was singing in English this time. About someone who had died. He called the person Ayo. He asked another person, Olorun, why he had taken Ayo away. I wanted to see who this Olorun was that had taken his friend and made him cry.

I cried as he sang in English.

"What is your name?" He said, after he had stopped singing. His talking voice was shy, almost a whisper; nothing like his singing voice.

"Vera." I wiped my eyes and snuffled.

"Veronica?"

"No, Vera."

"But what is the full name?"

"It's Veronica, but I like Vera. That's what everybody calls me."

"Okay. Vera. Tunde is my own name."

"You're Yoruba?"

"Yes."

"I'm Igbo. Who is Olorun?"

"God. That is God in Yoruba."

"I thought God was Eledumare in Yoruba. That's what Mrs. Uduaghan taught us."

"Yes. That also."

"Do you speak Yoruba?"

"Yes."

"Why were you crying? Is it because your friend died?"

"No."

Silence. I picked the guava and played with it.

"Then why?"

"I like crying."

"You like crying?"

"Yes. My mother says it cleanses."

"What does that mean?"

He made his first move since he stopped singing. He stood up and I saw that he was really small. And short.

"The song I sang is called a dirge."

"The Yoruba own or the English own?"

"Both."

"What is a dirge?"

"A mourning song."

"So you were mourning Ayo?"

"Yes."

"Was he your friend?"

"No."

"Your brother then?"

"No."

"Who then?"

"Someone who is no longer in our house."

"He used to stay with you?"

"Yes."

"Why did he leave?"

"My father sent him away."

"Why?"

"When he slept with my sister and beat my mother?"

"Ayo?"

"No. My father. My father slept with my sister."

I covered my mouth with my hand. I was nonplussed.

"Ayo means joy in Yoruba. That was when joy left our house." He continued as though he hadn't noticed my reaction.

I now understood.

"Since when?"

"Two years. My sister ran away to my aunt. She doesn't want to come home."

"And your mother?"

"My father still beats her. He likes drinking too much. When he drinks he will beat her."

"But what did your mother do to him?"

"Your father does not beat your mother?" He looked at me oddly.

I shook my head no. He didn't respond.

"You have a fine voice. Where did you learn the song you were singing?" I continued.

"I formed it. My mother taught me how to sing dirges. She was a traditional mourner in her village."

"Is that why you like crying?"

"Yes. It helps me to forget all the bad things. My mother says so. Are you the only child?"

"No," I replied. "But I am the only girl. I have two younger brothers."

"That was how it was in our family too before my sister ran away."

"Sorry."

"Don't tell me that." His retort was brusque. "My mother said that people should never tell me sorry. She said I should never cry for people to tell me sorry, but for cleansing."

"Okay. Sorry I will not tell you." I realized I had said it again.

He carried on. "My mother tells me mourning and crying are not the same thing. That is why she teaches me to sing dirges."

"So that you can mourn?"

"Mm mm." He shook his head sideways as he gave the hummed reply, "So that I can only cry when I want to."

"Do you always sing about Ayo?"

"No. I sing about different things."

"Did you sing about your sister?"

"Yes."

Njideka and Oreva were scuttling to meet me. I could see them in the distance.

"My friends are coming. Break will soon be over. Let's go back to the class. Which class are you?"

"Primary one."

"How old are you?"

"Seven."

"Don't you have any friends?"

"Just one."

"Why? Where is he?"

"She," he said, looking at me. Apparently, I was his only friend.

"Me?"

"You told me you wanted to be my friend."

I recalled I had said so.

"Yes. Are you a Christian?"

My mother did well to ensure all my friends were Christians. There was a verse she usually quoted when she said it. Something from the New Testament. She was very churchy.

"No."

I was chagrined. My mother wouldn't like it. And I wanted to be Tunde's friend.

"Muslim?"

"No."

Now I was stunned.

"Then what are you?"

"We worship Ogun. My mother and I."

"Traditional religion?"

"Yes."

I was now alarmed. He was just not a Christian, he worshipped Ogun. I thought it was only in the olden days people worshipped such things.

"My father is the one who is Christian," he added.

"Two different religions?"

"Mmm," he went again. I expected him to say more, to defend how a family could have two different religions, but he said nothing.

"So you and your mother don't go to church?"

"We go sometimes."

I was now baffled, puzzling myself about how one could serve Ogun and go to church, how a father could sleep with his daughter. It wasn't supposed to be that way. He was her father. Fathers slept with mothers, not daughters. Our teacher taught us that it was bad. Incest, she said.

Njideka and Oreva were now a few feet away. They had stopped. They were tittering and pointing. I knew what they were saying. I would have done the same for either of them if I saw them sitting with a boy. Talking with a boy.

"Let's start going to class. Your friends are already here."

"Yes." We both stood up.

"We can still see each other tomorrow, right?"

"Yes. Where?"

"Here. Under the guava tree." He looked amusedly at the guava tree like he had just noticed it. It was the first time I saw him smile. Then he looked at the guava in my hand. "You like guavas?"

"Yes. You want one?"

"No thank you. That one is for you."

"No. We can share."

"Next time maybe."

I gave up. Njideka and Oreva had now seen the guava and I was sure they would beg me. I only wanted to share it with Tunde.

He merely glared at my two friends. He didn't say a word or wave. He didn't look back either as he sauntered away. We would meet during break the next day, under the guava tree.

"Vera has a husband, Vera has a husband!" Njideka chanted in a singsong voice. Oreva was chortling and stretching her out hand to the guava. I shifted it to my other hand and hid it at my back.

"Vera, so you're soon going to marry, *enh*?" Oreva asked while trying to reach behind me.

"I will do your invitation card," Njideka said.

"You people should stop now. If not, I will not give you guava! Oh!"

I waggled the fruit at them. They calmed down. "After all, don't you have your own husbands in class?" I muttered under my breath.

We ambled towards the tap and they promptly forgot about Tunde.

I did not forget though. That night I thought about him as our family had prayers. I wondered about my mother and what her reaction would be if I told her I had a friend who worshipped Ogun. I was sure she would send me for deliverance in the church where I would shout and turn and roll on the floor until the devil came out of me.

Yet for some reason I didn't care. I was going to be Tunde's friend. I wanted to be his friend. I wanted to share his sadness. I wanted to know this boy who sang so well, yet sang sad songs.

The next day Tunde came. And the next. And like that for a whole week. Every day he would sing one new dirge; sometimes for his mother, other times for the school, and then once he sang for the guava tree. He sang most of the songs his mother taught him, only a few had he formed himself, and they were in Yoruba. He would explain it in English afterwards. Many times he sang with that

faraway look in his eyes, like he was detached from reality. Every day we met there, one guava would fall from the tree. Then we would share it. Without washing. He said he usually ate them that way. After two days of eating unwashed guavas and suffering diarrhea, I regularly brought a can of water with me.

We soon formed a routine. It became something to look forward to. I didn't get to know so much about him, nonetheless. He didn't say much. He was mostly evasive, in an artless way. He just sang and told me about his father, how he would drink while coming from church, and beat his mother in the name of the Lord. He wasn't rueful when he said it. He said it like he was reading his times table. With each passing day, I thought Tunde was getting stranger. Once, I told him he was weird. He said his mother told him he was a special child.

Our routine went on that way for two weeks until one day when I didn't find him at our usual spot. I waited till the bell went. He didn't show up. The next day, I returned but he wasn't there. For a week he did not come. The guavas kept falling, but I did not feel like eating them.

I knew he was in primary one, still I didn't know which of the six arms he was. So I asked God one night before going to bed to cause him to come the next day. I don't think God listened because the next day he still didn't come. Perhaps it was God's way of telling me to obey my parents. To stay away from a non-Christian.

But he also goes to church, I defended myself before the other voice in my mind. The voice that was supposed to be my conscience, or God.

Only sometimes, the voice replied.

It kept occurring till I shut it out permanently. I was tired of the altercations.

I stopped coming to the tree. For a whole week I did not go. I was tired of looking. I assumed he didn't want me as his friend anymore. One hot day, I felt a longing for guavas, so I took a stroll to the tree, silently praying one of the other children hadn't already picked them all. As I approached, I heard his voice from a distance. He was singing in Yoruba again. I scampered towards the tree, forgetting about the guavas. He stopped singing.

"Where have you been? I have looked for you for more than three weeks now," I quizzed. Then I saw his face. A huge plaster was on the left side. It was like a knoll of sand or chippings placed on smooth road. It had altered his face.

"What happened?" I stroked the side of my face, indicating.

He smiled a half smile. "My father, he hit me," then added quickly, "He didn't want to."

"So why did he?" I touched the plaster. He winced.

"I was preventing him from beating my mother. He wanted to use his beer bottle on her."

"Jesus! With the bottle?"

He nodded.

"What did your mother do?"

"She can't fight back. It's against our belief. You don't fight a man as a woman."

"What if the man wants to kill you?"

He was quiet. The way he was when he wanted to change the line of conversation.

"Do you want to hear my new dirge? It's in Yoruba and English."

"What is it about?"

"Everything."

"Everything?"

"Life and Death. You and me, all of us."

"Did you form it yourself?"

"Yes. While I was at the hospital. But I borrowed most of it from my mother's dirges. And the tune, too."

"Why did you stop your father from beating your mother?" I

didn't know the question was still lurking in my mind.

"He would have killed her."

"Why does he hate her so much?"

"He doesn't. He cannot control himself when he is drunk. My mother says when he is not drunk, he is very kind and good."

"Is he?"

"I don't know." He opened his palms to me. "I haven't seen him when he is not drunk." There was an awkward shift of his feet. "The title of the song is 'Bits and Pieces.' My mother gave me the title."

"Why did you title this one?"

"I just wanted to. It's long, and it took me two weeks to form it."

He started singing. The tune sounded familiar, like one of those church hymns. He sang first in Yoruba, then switched to English. The song was about life and death. How we live our lives in bits and pieces, like a puzzle. How different people and different things form part of the puzzle, and how we finally die before we want to, without knowing that we had already died in bits and pieces while we were alive; like a puzzle being taken apart, little by little. How the day we die is not really the day we die, but the day our final piece is pulled apart and our final string is broken, when the bits in our mouths eventually snap. He sang that we should not care about tomorrow but to live bit by bit as life came, piecemeal.

I was crying by the time he finished the song. I cried for almost all his dirges. I now knew why he liked crying. It really was like cleansing. There was something about this particular dirge, though. After crying, I was still distressed. Like I hadn't cried it all out.

He stopped crying. I stopped crying too.

"My mother always tells me that Life is about today, not yesterday, not tomorrow, because we never know how much of us has died, and when the last part of our puzzle will give way. She said if we didn't know, then we should live every bit and piece of our life fully as if it was our last, as if it was a dirge."

"Your mother tells you a lot."

"Yes. We are very close."

I peered into his eyes. They were not sad. They were not happy. They were just empty, like no one was home.

"Tunde!" I called.

"Yes?"

"I hope you are alright."

"Yes."

"Will your wound heal?"

"Yes." He tapped it.

My stomach growled. I looked up at the tree. "There is no guava today?"

"There is." He retrieved two guavas from his bag. "I saved them for you."

"Two?"

"Yes. The two of them fell while I was here."

"Two for the first time. It's always one."

"Yes." He kept one and gave me the other as the bell went.

We started walking to our classes. I remembered something.

"Which arm are you?"

"C," he said.

"Okay. Maybe I'll come to your class tomorrow. What is your full name?"

"Tunde Ladipo. Take the dirge." He folded a piece of paper into my hand.

"Which one?"

"This one I just sang now. 'Bits and Pieces.'"

"Okay."

As we were about to part ways I asked if I would see him tomorrow. He was already walking away. He hadn't heard me.

The next day, he wasn't at the tree. I remembered I knew his class and his full name so I decided to go there. I asked after him. They said he didn't come to school. That night during family prayers I tried to hum the tunes of "Bits and Pieces". My mother caught me and smacked me, saying I had dozed off during prayer and was mumbling nonsense. I couldn't sleep later that night so I searched for the paper he gave me when we last met, the one with the dirge. I finally found it in one corner of my room. I read the words till I fell asleep.

I didn't see him for the next four days. Then one morning as I got into school, I saw him. He was on the wall of the admin block on a poster, rather his face was. The poster read *Obituary*. I read it twice but did not cry. I only felt like I had a heated iron run over me. My head began to ache. I felt cold and hot all at once. He was dead. Tunde was dead.

I was walking back quietly to my class and only stopped by the staff room when I heard raised voices.

"That boy was always being abused; I said it."

"He was a strange child. He would never talk. That's the problem."

"You saw the wound he had now. Big one!"

"Where?"

"On his face! You saw it!"

"It was his father. Fighting with his mother."

"The man has finally killed him now. Hope he is happy."

"He is the one who killed him?"

"Yes, now. He wanted to beat the woman again and the boy tried to prevent him, and he flung the boy. Just like that. Gbam! His head hit the wall. They're even ashamed to bury him."

"*Heu*! My God!"

"Is it not the same man that they say raped his daughter and the girl ran away?"

"*Ezi okwu*? Is that so?"

"The daughter will come back now, definitely. Now they have killed her brother."

I was imprisoned by inertia, drinking it all in.

As I continued to my classroom, I tried to envisage Tunde's head smashed. That head with the pretty face and rabbit ears. That was when I began to cry.

Alan D. Harris
Wayne State University
"Undivided Attention"

Monday
December 5

I wasn't trying very hard to study for Wednesday's American
history quiz — almost begging for a distraction. That's when Grandpa
said to me as I sat at his dining room table, "Listen up, Soldier. I need
your undivided attention."

"Yes, sir."

"Do you know what happened on December 7, 1941?"

I've learned that you have to be careful around Grandpa's house
with questions that require a yes or no answer. There's history
according to the rest of the world and then there's eyewitness history
which Grandpa prefers to recite to whomever will listen. Every once
in a while the two historical accounts pretty much match. Still I tried
to play it safe and replied, "Huh?"

Grandpa lives just down the street. His house is quieter than
mine, usually. I emptied my backpack out in front of me. Class notes,
broken pencils and Kit Kat wrappers scattered across the dining room
table. Faces of young sailors in old picture frames seemed impressed
at how much junk a kid nowadays can carry around in a school
backpack. One or two old photographs propped up on the table and
a couple more hung on the walls seemed to snicker at me.

I guess *Huh?* wasn't a good enough answer. Grandpa limped back
to his bedroom. He had Grandma's old record player on. She never
threw anything away, especially music. Now that she's gone, Grandpa
plays her favorite song over and over again, just like today. I once
asked him who the singer is. He shook his head and barked that it
was some guy named Sinatra — like I would know. I can tell you that
Grandpa plays that musty old song every time he looks through his

memory box. That's what he calls his collection of yellowed black and white snapshots. His memory box reminds him that he was once more alive than he is now. It reminds him that he once had two good eyes. It reminds him of all the people he's met in this world and hopes to meet again.

I couldn't concentrate. I couldn't sit down and study the stuff I was supposed to — like history notes. I studied everything else instead. I studied the sounds in Grandpa's house, the music, the rustling of pictures in a cardboard box and the packing of a suitcase. Then it came to me. I got up and looked at the calendar on the side of the refrigerator — December 5. Grandpa walked out of his bedroom with a suitcase and a paper bag.

"You seen my cap?"

"You're going to Chicago, aren't you," I asked.

"I had it a minute ago."

"When you leaving?"

"Tomorrow. Then the boys and I will meet up Wednesday morning for breakfast."

He handed me the paper bag. "You need me to go over anything?"

"Nobody will ask," I answered as I reached for the bag of old photographs.

He looked disappointed as he muttered, "Too bad." I admit that I'm not the best student at school. But I'm a great student away from school. Truth is, I study all the time. I study everything but what my teachers want me to. I study my grandfather as much as I can. I don't care that I won't be ready for that American history quiz. I know Grandpa wants to tell me his story again, and that's good enough for me. It's a story about why he always goes to Chicago for breakfast with his old Navy pals. He's been going every December for as long as I can remember. But I know Grandpa hopes that someone — anyone — is willing to listen to his story, if and when I get a chance to retell it. It's important to him and a guy named Bob.

214

Bob was from Chicago.

Grandpa hopes that the paper bag full of pictures will help tell
the story, just in case some kid in class ever wants to understand
what really went on that December day. I don't want to make him
any sadder than he already is this time of year, or I'd tell Grandpa
that I don't really think anybody in my class cares what happened on
December 7, 1941.

So after he told me the story again, Grandpa said, "Make damn
sure I get my pictures back."

"I promise. I'll bring your old pictures back, just like I did last
year, and the year before that."

What'll I do with just a photograph

to tell my troubles to?

When I'm alone

with only dreams of you

that won't come true

What'll I do?

Wednesday
December 7

I walked into class carrying both Grandpa's story and a paper
bag full of memories. The bag was stuffed in my backpack. I figured
that's where they'd stay. I sat down at my desk behind Martin. I was
not looking forward to another history quiz I was ill-prepared for. But
before he handed out the quiz, Mr. Bennett, announced something:

Today is a day that will live in infamy.

That kind of scared me. Scared the whole class. We thought for a moment that this was going to be one really hard quiz. Nobody was really sure what Mr. Bennett meant. So of course, Martin raised his hand and asked, "What do you mean?"

"Have you ever heard of Ford Island?" answered Mr. Bennett. I guess adults were taught to answer questions with questions. Grandpa's not the only one.

"Is that where Ford Mustangs run around the countryside in large herds?" Martin asked. There was a silence. Most of the class didn't think Martin was kidding.

Martin's blank expression convinced me to join the rest of the class. As his best friend in middle school, I had given him the benefit of the doubt for as long as I could.

I saw this as not only my chance to get Martin—but also to finally tell Grandpa's story. I raised my hand and said, "My grandpa was stationed on Ford Island on December 7, 1941. It's an island within an island. It's in the middle of Oahu, one of the Hawaiian Islands."

"Very good, Mr. Kogut!" Mr. Bennett said with a satisfied smile. "Ford Island is actually surrounded by a small inlet from the Pacific Ocean. It's not exactly in the middle of Oahu, but close enough."

"Yeah, like I said. It's an island within an island—just like what I'm about to tell you is a story within a story." That's what Grandpa says. "One of many stories that needs to be told about December 7, 1941."

Martin looked over at me. I whispered, "Grandpa never said anything about Mustangs."

"I wish I had known your grandfather had been there," said Mr. Bennett. "I would have liked him to be our guest speaker so he could share his account of what happened."

"Oh, I can share that," I said. "He tells me the story every year. It doesn't change much. If you like, I can give it a shot."

Mr. Bennett smiled. "Please do!" he said as he set aside today's quiz. "Come on up to the front of the class."

Normally I would hate having to speak in front of class. But I knew this story. It's easy to talk about stuff you know—as long as nobody asks any questions. Matt Boles, my personal bully, raised his hand with a question.

"Yes, Mr. Boles," asked Mr. Bennett.

"If Mr. Kotex tells a good long story, will we still have to take a quiz?" The class giggled, mostly the girls.

Mr. Bennett thought about the attempt to put off academic accountability. He then nodded his head agreed there would be no quiz if my good long story received everyone's undivided attention.

People, especially teachers, are always talking about this thing, *undivided attention*. I just hoped that I would get enough of it, because I didn't want to take the quiz either. I stood up and looked around the room. As my dry throat dried up and my legs wobbled, I began to understand what undivided attention was. For the first time in my life, everybody in the room seemed to look straight at me, eager to hear what I had to say, wishing, hoping, and praying that I had enough to say to avoid today's quiz. Even Matt Boles looked my way, as though counting on me to avoid another red-penciled foreshadowing of future failure. I started the way Grandpa always starts. I think it concerned Mr. Bennett, but the class glued itself to my every word as soon as I said it.

"Four out of five people benefit from going to church."

Mr. Bennett stopped me. "This is a story about Pearl Harbor, right?"

"That's where the story takes place," I answered. "Should I go on?" Mr. Bennett nodded with uneasiness and curiosity.

"My grandpa was in the Navy," I said, "probably along with a lot of your relatives. He joined up when he was only 19 years old."

"What year was that?" asked Mr. Bennett.

When you're told a story so many times, dates are the first thing you memorize. "1936," I answered. "Grandpa was supposed to come home in February of 1942. That's when his six years were up."

"Did he come home like he wanted?" asked Elizabeth Harger, who was seated next to Martin in the front row.

"Nope," I answered.

"Why not?" asked Bobby from the back row.

"Pearl Harbor happened on December 7, 1941," I replied. "All enlisted men had their discharge orders changed. No one could come home until the war, which started at 7:55 in the morning on December 7, 1941, was over."

"My Grandma from Texas taught me about Pearl Harbor," said the usually quiet Robert Burrell. "Lots of people died that day."

"That's so sad," said Elizabeth.

"Do you know what ship your grandfather was assigned to?" Mr. Bennett asked me. I could tell that the teacher wanted to keep this old story on track. So I told the class about the ships.

"They named a lot of ships back then after birds and fish and people and cities and states. Grandpa was on a ship named after a state, Arizona. There were over 1500 sailors who lived and worked on his ship."

"Fish?" asked Bobby.

Mr. Bennett chipped in, "Submarines were often named after fish."

"Cool," Martin said. "We had submarines."

"So did the Japanese," I added.

"Was The Arizona the only ship named after a state?" Martin asked.

"Nope," I said. "There was also The California, The Utah, The West Virginia, The Nevada, The Tennessee, and The Oklahoma, for sure."

Mr. Bennett smiled because I was back on track. The fear left his face but he looked as curious as ever. He was giving me his undivided attention. So I went on.

"Grandpa was one of five men who loved the game of hockey and were stationed at Ford Island. Grandpa was the only hockey player that worked on the Arizona. But his best friend and these three other guys worked on a much smaller boat called the Vestal. The Vestal was a repair ship that was assigned to The Arizona."

"Your grandpa had a best friend?" asked Bobby.

"Yeah, he sure did have a best friend," I replied looking over at Martin. "The way Grandpa tells it, he was a pretty funny guy."

Martin smiled, jumped up and asked, "What kind of boat was The Arizona?"

"Most of the ships named after states were battleships," I answered. "The Arizona was battleship."

"Cool," said Martin.

Matt Boles raised his hand. I looked over at Mr. Bennett and he just nodded at me like I was in charge. So I pointed a nervous finger at my personal bully. Matt stood up and asked, "Could you tell us more about the hockey players?"

I couldn't tell if I was getting off track again—but I still had everybody's undivided attention.

"Even though this was in the winter time," I said, "there were no ice rinks on Ford Island. I don't think there was a single ice rink to be found anywhere in Hawaii. Since Grandpa and his four buddies missed playing their favorite sport, they had hockey sticks sent to them from their hometowns while the other sailors were getting cookies and magazines and love letters." Again the girls in the front row giggled. "And every chance they got, the five friends played street hockey on the base, right there at Ford Island."

"What did they use for pucks?" Martin asked.

"They would either steal golf balls from the officers' golf bags or use potatoes," I explained.

"Potatoes?" shouted Matt Boles.

"Grandpa and his buddies played street hockey every Sunday morning. Sunday was supposed to be a time of rest, except for the crazy Marines. Grandpa called them crazy because they were the only ones flying maneuvers on Sunday mornings, target shooting, and dropping fake bombs just for practice."

"That sounds pretty crazy, even to me," replied Martin.

I slowly pulled the bag of pictures out of my backpack and continued with the story. "Every Sunday, before street hockey, Grandpa invited his buddies from the Vestal over to The Arizona for breakfast, then they'd go play. Sunday breakfast on board a battleship was always special. Lots of good grub."

"What's grub?" Martin asked.

"Food, dummy," answered Matt Boles, who was still giving me his undivided attention.

"What was the funny dude's name?" asked Martin.

"The dip-stick's name is Fartin' Martin," answered Matt Boles.

Mr. Bennett didn't look too pleased with his choice of words, despite the uncontrollable giggling throughout the entire front row. But I did everybody a favor. I took a deep breath and corrected my personal bully.

"Grandpa said Bob's name was Bob. That morning Bob talked the other four guys, including Grandpa, into going off Ford Island to attend church services at Pearl Harbor."

For the first time, Bobby spoke up in support of a story he had never heard. "Eight o'clock mass," he said. Elizabeth and several of the girls in the front row stopped giggling in order to nod their heads in agreement. I had all kinds of undivided attention now.

"Like always, the five friends carried their hockey sticks with them whenever they left Ford Island, passing pucks between them. They did so on their way to church that morning. They had often told other sailors that the sticks were for protection since they were not allowed to carry live ammunition in their side arms. After all, they were not in a war zone — yet."

Martin raised his hand. Matt Boles shouted out, "No more dumb questions." I looked at Martin and asked softly, "Is this a dumb question?"

"No way," he said. "I promise."

So I pointed at Martin and he stood up and asked what sounded like a dumb question to everyone but me. "On that day, December 7, 1941, did they use a golf ball puck or a potato puck?"

"Great question," I replied. I could see Mr. Bennett had started getting out the quiz. "Potato puck!" I said. "Potatoes were every-where. The United States Armed Services stored small mountains of potatoes all over the base and around the shipyards."

"Potatoes?" asked Mr. Bennett.

"Potatoes were everywhere," I repeated.

Mr. Bennett smiled and set the quiz back down. "I didn't know that," he said. "Go on with the story."

"Five minutes before church started, they heard an explosion. The five friends looked up. Airplanes filled the skies. Grandpa said to the others, 'What in the H…E…Double hockey sticks are those crazy Marines up to now?'"

"Bob from Chicago pointed to a red sun painted on one of the wings and shouted, *Those ain't Marines, Sailor! Run for the church! Yesiree Bob*, the other four shouted as they all ran for shelter at the church up ahead. The five of them ran shoulder to shoulder all in a row, all keeping up with each other. A Japanese pilot saw them. He brought his small fighter plane close to land and strafed the road where the five friends ran for their lives. The pilot strafed right down the middle of the road."

"What does strafe mean?" asked Matt Boles.

Mr. Bennett decided to answer Matt's question. "A machine gun mounted on the nose of the Japanese fighter plane, probably a Zero, shot at those men as the nose pointed towards the ground." I didn't know Mr. Bennett knew about such things.

"That's called strafing," the teacher said as he bit into his lip and turned to me.

"Bob fell down," I told the class. "Bob from Chicago, who wanted to go to church, who ran in the middle surrounded by his hockey buddies, fell to the ground. He took five bullets from the machine gun. One bullet hit his leg. Another one went into his lower back. That bullet came out of his belly button. Two lodged in his chest, but they missed his heart, and the last one took his right ear lobe clean off." I touched each place on my body to show everyone where Bob from Chicago was shot.

"Were the other guys shot?" Martin asked.

"That's just what Bob wanted to know. He asked my grandpa if anyone else was hit. As planes buzzed all around them, as the bombs exploded and smoke filled the skies, four friends huddled around their dying pal. *Nosiree, Bob*, they answered. In the front row, I noticed that Elizabeth Harger's eyes had grown wider than I'd ever seen them.

"Bob from Chicago smiled as he bled," I said as I watched what might have been a tear roll down Elizabeth Harger's red cheek. "He smiled, knowing he had taken a bullet for each of them. Now Grandpa knew about such things as wounds. Some bullet wounds are worse than others. Bob was bleeding from his chest and his stomach. Grandpa always said gut wounds are the worst."

"Is that it?" Martin asked. "Is that all they said to a dying man?"

"Nosireebob," I answered. "They all said thank you to Bob from Chicago. They thanked him for talking everyone into going to church that morning instead of having breakfast on The Arizona."

"Why?" asked Martin. "What was for breakfast?"

"Grandpa never said," I said. "But while the five pals walked to church, the Arizona was torpedoed by Japanese submarines below the water and attacked by Japanese bombers from above."

"What did Bob from Chicago say when they thanked him," Martin asked.

"Nothing, dummy," said Matt Boles. "He was dead."

"Not true, not yet," I corrected my personal bully. "The four sailors huddled around Bob from Chicago in the middle of the road, in the middle of the battle, too sad or too frightened to run. Grandpa remembers how he cried as he stuck his finger into Bob's belly button in order to stop the bleeding."

"Eww," Martin said.

I ignored him and continued to tell the story the way Grandpa always tells it. There he was, finger in the belly button of Bob from Chicago. Bob looked at his gut wound and laughed. Bob thought it was pretty funny — a funny way to die. He then said to Grandpa that it could have been worse; "You mighta had to stick your finger up my…"

Mr. Bennett's well-placed cough meant for me to keep the story moving.

"According to Grandpa, Bob smiled at each of them, saying, 'I pray you boys remember all the wonderful things in your life.'"

"Then what?" asked Matt Boles.

"Black smoke and explosions filled the air as Grandpa screamed, *MEDIC* as his friend kept talking. 'It sure helps me pass over,' said Bob from Chicago, with his eyes wide open, 'to the light on the other side…'"

"What light?" asked Martin.

It's dark here, Bob said as Grandpa's finger covered over with blood. *But I ain't afraid. No sir, I ain't afraid cuz I remember everything. I remember who I am. I remember my family, my loved ones, my friends — everything.*

Although her voice was shaking, Elizabeth Harger was able to ask, "What did that mean?"

"Bob from Chicago was pretty sure that it was better to die with your memories than without. That's what I'm guessing. I wasn't there, but that's just what I think. It's like sometimes you have to pretend you were there to understand what they went through."

"What about the other ships?" Martin asked as he changed the subject. "Were any other sailors on The Arizona hurt?"

Mr. Bennett looked over at me. I looked back at him and said, "I got this." I opened the bag to find a picture of The Arizona. But I found something else instead.

"What's in the bag," asked Martin.

I reached in and pulled out Grandpa's old cap with the letters USN on it. Mr. Bennett and I looked at each other. Without saying a word he let me know that the rest of the story should be told by someone wearing the cap. So I put it on, turned to Martin and answered, "Out of the 1500 men who lived on The Arizona, over 1100 didn't live anymore."

"Wow," said Martin.

"Twenty-two American ships were shot, torpedoed, sunk, or destroyed," I added.

"Wow," said Martin.

"Two-thousand, four hundred and three Americans died that day."

"Wow," said Martin.

Robert Burrell raised his hand. I looked at Mr. Bennett and again he nodded to me. So I pointed to the usually quiet Robert Burrell. He stood up and asked, "Did your grandfather tell you the story about Doris Miller?"

"No," I answered. Then I realized that there must be many stories within the story of Pearl Harbor. "Was she your grandmother?" I asked.

"No," the usually quiet Robert Burrell said with a sneer. "Doris was a man, my grandmother's brother. The white folks called him *Dorrie*."

"Did you want to tell the class a Pearl Harbor story about your relations?" Mr. Bennett asked Robert.

"No," said Robert as he sat down. "Just wanted to know if anybody tells his story but us."

"Who is us?" asked Martin.

"I said no more stupid questions," shouted Matt Boles, my personal bully. "So Kogut—what exactly did your brave grandpa do? Did he run away?"

I adjusted my cap and looked right past Martin and Bobby and Robert. I looked past Elizabeth, who had tears on both cheeks, and I looked straight into the eyes of Matt Boles.

"For your information," I said to my personal bully, "my grandpa stood up and threw potatoes."

I don't know why, but Elizabeth Harger stopped crying. She started to smile as I continued to hold her undivided attention.

"You mean hockey pucks?" asked Martin.

"I mean potatoes. Big ugly potatoes with scary eyes all over," I said. "The Japanese pilots were only 25, 30 feet off the ground as they tried to kill as many Americans as they could. But the potatoes looked like hand grenades. Grandpa and his pals stood in front of dead Bob from Chicago and hurled potatoes. Thanks to those potatoes, and the bravery of four ordinary guys who had simply decided one day to go to church, plane after plane after plane changed course and flew away."

"Cool," said Martin.

"I think your grandpa's wrong," said Bobby, "Or you're telling the story wrong."

I wasn't sure how I could be wrong about retelling a story I had heard a hundred times. And I didn't like anybody telling me Grandpa was wrong.

"Explain to the class why you think so," ordered Mr. Bennett to Bobby. I held onto the envelope of pictures and waited for Bobby's answer.

"Didn't your grandpa say that only four out of five people benefit from going to church?"

"He sure did," I answered.

"Well, I think five out of five people benefited from going to church that day. Four men lived to tell the story about how one man got to be their guardian angel," explained Bobby.

"What's a guardian angel?" asked Martin.

"We all have one," said Bobby. "And one day we all might be one — just like Mr. Bob from Chicago."

"Not me," shouted Matt Boles. "I'm no one's guardian angel."

That's for sure, I thought to myself. But Bobby turned to my personal bully and replied, "Even a guy like you could be a guardian angel." Challenging Matt Boles was never a good idea. So before Bobby needed his own angel to protect him from my personal bully, I decided to pass out the photographs of burning ships named after states. There were pictures of the skies full of enemy planes and even pictures taken from those same planes as they dropped their bombs.

Some might think they were just pictures, but I feel they're more like tiny slices of Grandpa's memory, like post cards that say *WISH YOU WEREN'T HERE*. Like whispers that echo *Remember Everything*. The class turned their undivided attention over to Grandpa's photographs as those old black and white pictures told the story better than I ever could.

Angel Berry
Oakland Community College
"The Humble"

"Therefore to him that knoweth to do good, and doeth it not, to him it is sin."
James 4:17

My name is Hattie Mae Cline and I am eighty-three years old. I'se
born in the year 1893 on a cotton plantation in Mississippi. My pa was
a sharecropper on Mr. Joe Michaels' land. My ma and pa had nine
chillun', three girls and six boys. I'se the eldest chile.

Well, my ma was a woman what had religion. She made sho' all
us chillun' known 'bout the savior, bless His heart.

I was a chile who was wild, honey. I was young and beautiful,
slender and big-breasted, the color of warm honey with big, brown
eyes and long legs. I like to go out to the juke joints and dance and
holla, listen to jazz and drink that moonshine wit' a little reefer. I'd
hang 'round wit' a different fella almost every night – white or black --
and they put in my hand whateva I asked for. So that's the way I went
on for a while there.

I ain't forget none what my ma had told me. Always when I laid
down at night the Lord would say to me, Hattie, what are you doing?
I would always mean to do better but I was having fun, honey, and that
likker had me.

Slowly but surely, He wore me down tho'. One time I remembers
I went and got me some money from a man, right, and I tell you soon
as I get home and lay on my bed to rest didn't the spirit jump right on
me! I knows what it was cause I got this hard buzzing all through my
body. Ain't another feeling like it. Did I do right after that? Nope. So the
Lord got more rigorous. *What's your name*, He would say to me at night.
Hattie, I'd tell 'em. Did He forget me? He was forgetting who I was! *I'm
Hattie Mae Cline, Lord*! I lay there and fell asleep worried, honey.

Once I was there in the darkest dark I had known and the Lord said, Hattie, do you want to die? I guess, I told Him. Well, I started to fall fast into the abyss – what's the word? Plummet. I began to plummet into the abyss so fast that my heart dropped. No, no, I screamed – and just like that I awoke and, chile, I knew where I had been on my way to. I hear a suffering voice say, Oh, Hattie, I can't take this for eternity. Hattie, I wish you could feel one drop. One drop of damnation! Lord, Lord! And it ain't no God in hell. No more talking to my Jesus? I can't live like that, I say. And so I began to follow the path as it's written here a little, there a little. It whatn't none easy neither. The Lord was mad at me, but he chastened me wit' love tho', chile.

Now I'm gone leave some stuff out what's only 'tween me and the Lord, but He supported me and helped me put one foot in front of the otha'. And then I had to forgive myself as well. Ain't no excuse for living like a heathen on purpose.

Well, He lived wit' me after while and He neva left. We goes on like that still, me stumbling, and the Lord grabbing me afore I fall. Same been true throughout history. When folks get to pointing they fingers I say, oh no, King David was a righteous man, but he killed a man for his wife and God forgive him; Paul murdered followers of Christ 'til the Good Lord showed him the way, but folks be just a pointin' and got filth in they closets piled up high.

Now let's talk about the flip side. Just like there's God, there's also a devil and he is mean for sin, chile. My ma used to say he eat feces. Lucifer will attack anything God loves just to hurt Him.

I remembers this one time I'se dozing in my bed and a demon jumped on me. This was 'round the time I'se just starting to try and get myself together. I opened my eyes 'cause sumthin' was on me heavy, and I was a fightin' and a scratchin'. I throws it off me and I was a hissin' like a she-cat and that thing fled. I surprised myself how I fought.

Another time I dreamt I'se in a room and there that devil was molesting a woman against the wall. Poor thing, I'll neva forget her. I'se scared to death. I looks to my right and I sees one them dolls what look like a raggedy ann – big tho', tall as me sitting in a rocking chair. It had big, black buttons for eyes and its mouth was stitched on and it was beckoning to me. My Lord! I hopped on His lap and we rocked there together and He says to me that if I eva' see the devil just look over and He gone be right there. Well, my word! I sho' appreciate it, Lord.

Well, I continued on the path. The Lord would say, Hattie, follow me. I'se obedient to the Lord 'cause He tells you the right way to go and who to deal wit'. It's your own choice if you don't listen. He tell you straight up, too. Ain't no pussyfootin' around – ain't His way.

I prayed and prayed and I talked to the Lord all day everyday – when I was going here and going there, and doing this and doing that. I seek his counsel in everything, chile, and I swears He got the best advisin'.

Anyway, I had darn near stop screwin'. Jesus was working his magic and I ain't won't nobody touchin' me. I was still sippin' on that shine tho' 'cause I knew soon He was gone chase that off, too. Sho' nuff, He says, Hattie, you gone stop that drinking for three months. Three months? Who was gone do that? Humph!

He got them three months out me tho' and didn't that devil try and tempt me in the last days and God send a believer to strengthen me? She said, naw, sista, we gone drink apple juice. Thank you, Lord. After them three months I was just fine, honey. But now I got to be rid of my tobacco. Cut me a break, Lord! Can't do nuthin' 'round here, I stumps off. Do that, go here, talk to this person, don't talk to that person – and He ain't gone leave me alone about my tobacco? What's next, I thought? Stop gossipin', Hattie, He comes back. My word!

Well, like always when you loves the Lord, here come the devil. So I'se laying on the couch one night. It was cold outside and I'se all wrapped up warm to the neck in a blanket. I'se dozin' and I remembers feeling real cozy. All of a sudden I gets a hard yank on the foot! I hurry up and looks down and I don't see nuthin so I gets comfortable again. Suddenly I feels two strong hands wrap theyselves 'round my ankles and damn near drag me off the couch. I grabs the back of the couch wit' my hands and gets myself into a sittin' position and me and that devil fought like that wit' him trying to drag me down into water. Yes, yes. My feet was in water and he was trying to pull me down in it. I got to 'renched a leg loose and got to kickin' him all in the head hard as I could. I was furious! Then all of a sudden I'm in midair right there in the living room.

The only time I had been threw in the air in my sleep was when the Lord came in my dreams and toss me around sometimes. He would throw me and toss me and I'd just relax 'cause wasn't much I could do about it. He wanted me to trust Him that He wouldn't let my head hit the wall. This thing here wasn't the Lord. This was a huge serpent that was wrapped around my body and he was squeezing me. He was trying to bind me. The rage I felt! I got to kickin' and cussin' and then I heard one word – PRAY. Just that simple. So I started, Our Father, who art in heaven, hallowed be thine name…And that wicked dog dropped me. I got up and dusted myself off and then woke up sitting right there on the couch. My word!

I'll say one thing, I don't know why the Lord called me. I'm stubborn as all hell; will do anything to pick a fight with a bully; I cusses like a sailor; and I only love followers of our Lord. God wants us to spread His word but I agrees wit' Jonah. Humph! If we don't put forth an effort to have a relationship wit' our God, it's not His loss.

Woman gone tell me one time wit' spite that it ain't no God. See, this was one of them unbelievers that's used to a Christian that wants to convince them about the glory of the Lord. Not me. I told that woman I don't care what you believe. You betta get your wicked ass away from me.

Lord says to turn the otha' cheek cause vengeance belong to Him. I'ma turn my cheek awright, and that whole side of my body wit' it so when I swing that momentum from the turn gives my fist the right amount of power to knock they teeth out.

Many are called but few are chosen, and the connection ain't for everybody. That's what I tells the Lord. I tells Him, Lord, folks wanna do what they wanna do and they don't want no holy structure 'cause then they gots to mend they ways. Some folks is wicked to they

heart. Lord, concentrate on the ones that love you. That's how I sees
it. People ain't been right to Him since the beginning. He don't ask
for much. It burns Him up to see folks chasing after otha' gods and it
burns me up that He care 'bout'em. Jesus bled his precious blood for
us and we still gotta chase them suckas? Pssh. I can't chase somebody
what done heard the same stories I have. If you want to deny your
Maker, fine wit' me. I ain't no recruiter. To each his own is what I say.
I know the Lord don't like that, but I ain't perfect.

Jess Barnes
Cape Naturaliste College (Australia)
"Smile"

Lightning cracks its whip of intense light as I stumble along the uneven ground. I can smell the blood, my blood. Three deep gashes run along my raw back. They are coming for me. They know I escaped. It only took three years, but I did it.

Adrenaline floods my broken body. A loud boom of thunder rocks me to my core. Then, a shrieking noise pierces my ears. The hounds. Damn, thought I had made more ground.

My feet pound the sharp rocks but the pain doesn't register immediately. Fear smothers me. I see the outline of trees just as I hear another godforsaken howl. I swear quietly, and look up into the sky and see the moon smiling at me.

Just keep running. If I just keep running, I know I will make it.

Once I enter the sleeping forest, rain pelts the pine needles above. Good. The backbiting rain should mute my footsteps and drown my scent. Just as the ground shifts into a steep slope, all hell breaks loose.

I see the silhouette of the first creature charging straight form my left side. I swivel just in time and my heel connects with its throat. I hear the distinctive crack just as the second and third hounds emerge from an ancient pine tree.

My heart pounds in my ears as their eyes glisten with the hunt. Sharp and yellow teeth reflect the moonlight and drool dribbles down their wicked snouts, waiting for me to make the first move. Begging me, like predator and prey, for the bloodthirsty kill. Bearing my own teeth, a vicious smile spreads across my face.

I am Cordelia Dust, not their common prey.

A cold and calm feeling seeps through me. I study each filthy dog. One is the color of many browns, and around its neck, the dirt-covered fur has been chaffed away. I assume it's from the thick but tight leather and metal barbed collar it wears to keep it in line. The other hound looks like pure ferocity. A flash of lightning reveals cunning crimson eyes. I realize it's using the animal as a mask for the being inside. This was not what I was expecting. Its body is all jarred and ready for the fight. It wants to kill me. It wants revenge.

I tilt my head just an inch and they charge, mouths ready to tear my flesh from my bones. Glad for the silver blade I pulled from my captor's corpse, I fling it straight into the front right leg of the brown mutt, stopping it in its tracks. Revelation floods the hound's clever eyes.

As I run to fetch my weapon with deadly grace, the ferocious hound turns and places itself in front of the other injured animal. I curse loudly and fling my elbow into the side of the dog's head. I leap over the unconscious hound and am amazed to find the injured one still standing, even with a dagger in its main leg joint. I then plant my knee into the injured hound's jaw with a crunch.

Clasping the hilt of the dagger, I wrench it from the now-dead brown dog's leg. With one swift movement of my wrist, I slice the unconscious one's exposed throat. Blood now covers my hand.

I turn and run.

The rain is still seeping through my dirty rags for clothes, soaking my black hair till icy water is dripping down my spine. Tears blur my eyes. The creatures deserved to die, but a part of me still hates killing.

As I make my way through the relentless and howling wind, another crack of lightning splits the sky in two. The terrain begins to even out. I'm going to make it. I can see my freedom just on the horizon.

A man covers my view and grabs me by the throat. No, no, no. This cannot be happening. How did he find me? He throws me towards the open tree-line and I roll. I stop just near the edge of the disappearing ground. I pull myself up and stand. I will not be afraid.

"Now, now, where can you go?" The man yells with a mighty voice. A wicked smile splits his face.

"Not with you!" I scream back at him.

Only one choice left. I want to taste that freedom I had three years ago. I will not be a prisoner anymore. I turn and face that smiling moon and smile back as I plunge over the cliff.

Yozue A. Davila
Quinsigamond College
"Reflections"

The sky, such a beautiful playground for the clouds and stars to play on, its oceans of colors crashing into the Sun, its blankets warming the chilly Moon. Why could I not be born in the sky, why did I have to be born a star of the ground? I've heard stories of the sky as why the Sun sets red, it being a romantic secret between the Sun and its betrothed Moon. But a story that has always inspired me is that of shooting stars, my Pappous always told me this story for bed, he would say that we came from the sky and that we then landed on Earth as babies from shooting stars and our only true mission was finding a way back to the heavens above.

****

"Hey Proteus look at the water!" Samir yelled excitedly, as his hands encircled a reflected cloud in the Ocean.

"Don't you wish you could touch it in real life? What would it feel like?" Proteus replied with that joy of boyish wonderment that never seems to tire of imagining something new.

"I would say it's like a lump of cotton candy! Man I would love to eat it."

And with that, Samir proceeded to demonstrated his love of cotton candy by inserting his head into the water face first his with mouth eagerly open as if to really taste what he saw, where the cloud's image had been painted upon the water only seconds before. What a silly Indian boy!

"Don't be silly Samir, clouds have no taste they're made of gas and water! What taste does water have? None, right Proteus?" Dimitrios, the Russian boy, laughed, while attempting to build a sand castle. "Plus, if it would be anything it would be a house for the stars, I mean, they work all night so they have to rest at day, don't they?"

"Nonsense. Aren't they like ice cream?" Samir interrupted. "I mean doesn't it make sense? It melts under the Sun and that's why it rains and it's cold. How else could you explain the snow!? I think people gather the snow and add flavor to it that is all."

Proteus stood up, with a grin, to watch his two friends engulfed in his own boyish wonderment of how silly his friends could sometimes be, especially Samir. He could not keep himself from laughing at such good friends who wished to believe that clouds are food or houses.

"Well, what about the stars?"

"Don't start! You have told us the story Proteus- 'we used to be stars, blah, blah, blah.'"

"Don't be so harsh, Dimitrios. So how do we do it, Proteus?"

With a laugh, I threw my arms around my two friends Samir and Dimitrios, and pulled them with me to the sand. "I have an idea."

My eyebrows jump up and down with excitement.

"We have to use the water." I pull them in closer. "Think about it- you guys talk about clouds all the time but you're missing something: water! How else does the water reach the sky and come back down to Earth?"

"And what of Gas?" Samir asks.

"Or Gravity?" Dimitrios implores.

"No, no, see- water is much different. How do you think water reaches the clouds? When it rains, where does it come from?"

Dimitrios and Samir stay quiet for a second and then they start laughing.

"That is a good one, my friend!" Dimitrios starts laughing nervously.

"Yeah, you really got us this time." Samir signals to Dimitrios. "See you tomorrow!"

My friends left me with a laugh in heading for their homes; the

Sun, too, eventually laughed its way below the horizon. I lay on my hammock, just outside of my shack, under the palm trees, where I could easily peek at the sky beyond my feet. I lay there, quietly rearranging the stars to my desire, as a small cloud began gathering itself overhead to pour its tears to Earth as rain. After an afternoon in the sweltering summer Sun, the rain felt refreshing, invigorating.

Enjoying the coolness of the gentle evening shower, I reached down from my hammock to grab a pebble and send it skipping into the Ocean. With no reason other than it was something to do, I kept tossing as many as I could reach until finally I grew bored, having run out of pebbles.

My hammock grew full of water while lying comfortably in it, with one pebble left in my hand. The ocean had become calm and still once more with the light of the stars reflecting upon the gentleness of the whispering waves; the Moon had just begun rising.

It was then that the mischievous boy within me chose to make himself known. A particular star dancing upon the ocean waters had caught my attention. Of all the stars dancing that night, only it appeared to be a bright blue. In its solitude, it appeared in need of company. Instinctively, I hurled the remaining pebble at that beautifully bright blue star on the waters, taking careful aim so as not to miss.

I climbed out of my hammock to empty the rainwater upon the ground and began gathering more pebbles to toss at that lonely blue star. But it seemed that no matter how carefully I aimed, I missed it every single time. I was about ready to give this foolishness up when an idea struck me. I took one last pebble, and this time, I threw it at the star directly above in the darkened ocean of the sky. I was certain that I had hit the star. Then, to my amazement, my pebble tossed skyward began to plummet in an arc back towards the Earth, pulled by gravity to strike the ocean's waters perfectly within the bright blue star's dancing reflection.

Tink! I heard a sound, as though the pebble had struck something in the ocean. For a moment, I thought it must have hit the other pebbles I had tossed previously. But then, how could that possibly be?

Curiously, I got closer to the ocean in gazing upon the bright blue star's reflection. In shock, I began to see it move through the water, its dance becoming more like a stagger. Looking up from its reflection to the star in the sky, I saw it had begun to move, but not steadfast through the sky — no. It was falling.

In that moment, I felt, inexplicably, like jumping into the Ocean in an attempt to follow its direction. It fell out of swimming reach and I got out of the water discouraged and confused. Heading back towards my shack, my eyes spotted another pebble. Scooping it up to toss it skyward with all of my might, frustrated anger fueling the energy driving my arm, I couldn't believe my eyes.

I saw a blue glow moving in the ocean; it was getting closer to the shore right in between the ongoing battle of the waves and sand. I was afraid and held the pebble behind, redirecting its original path towards the strangeness I imagined. A boy emerged from the waters, the pebble leaped back into the ground. I thought I was seeing things because of the rainy night. The strange figure crept closer; I remembered the stories my Pappous told of the ties between the ocean and sky, the stars, the clouds, sun and moon. I now believed them.

"Are you from the sky?" I shouted in fear.

The boy silently approached me and I fell to the ground in panic until a friendly hand broke the grip of fear choking the air. I looked up and saw a familiar smile on the boy's face. I took his hand, and when I stood up, I found someone I had known for years in that boy's eyes: I was seeing myself. The rain stopped.

"Surprised?" the mysterious boy smiled.

"Don't hurt me!" I shouted, trembling in a fearful confusion.

"Don't be a fool. I will explain."

I looked up at the cheerful boy, in terror.

"My name is Caelesits, nice to meet you."

His hand stretched out and gave my hand a shake I thought

only my friends and I had come up with. He picked me up, telling me to follow.

The boy jumped into the water and pointed at a grey cloud, saying, "Grab it."

"That's impossible! It's only a reflection, my mouth mumbled.

I dipped my hand into the reflection and felt something squishy and wet between my fingers. I grasped it and pulled it out, a piece of cloud. I couldn't believe my eyes.

"Come on! Taste it!"

I looked, baffled, towards the demanding boy, investigating the piece of cloud. I stuck it into my mouth and closed my eyes to amplify its taste. It was incomparable- a chocolate taste I had never experienced before. I put the piece back into the reflection and watched the sky as it assumed its normal shape. I pulled my hand out, and as soon as I looked back, the boy was gone.

I went into my shack and awaited the daylight and to tell my friends all about it.

****

As I woke in the morning of that school-free day, I ran over to find my friends outside, waiting for me.

"Are you sure it wasn't a dream, Proteus?"

"How do you expect Dimitrios and me to believe this?"

I reached for a pebble, saying, "I threw it up to the star and, when it landed in the ocean, on its own reflection, it shot down! I ate a cloud and it wasn't cotton candy or ice cream, it was chocolate! You guys have to believe me! If only Caelestis were here."

Dimitrios grabbed me and shook his head, saying, "You have to prove it to us, pal."

My friends left, but and I stayed outside, contemplating the ocean and sky in front of me when, suddenly, a rush of wind knocked me over. As I lifted my head, I jumped back. How scared was I to see Caelestis standing in front of me.

"You have to stop scaring me like that."

"I'm sorry- here, put this on. I'm going to teach you something today."

He tossed a necklace with a stone of yellow and orange. He had one around his neck, too, but his was white and blue.

"What is this?" I put it on, admiring its colors.

"It's a sun stone. I have the Moon stone. We need to wear these when we are together.Now, come. Let's stop wasting time."

 He gets near the water and carefully watches in the ocean's reflection, a bird flying in the sky. He submerged his hand and pulled the bird out from the ocean, no longer in the sky.

"With me pulling out this bird, do you doubt its reality? Was the bird flying in the sky or swimming in the Ocean?" He let the bird go and watched it fly back up in the air.

"If you say he was flying you are correct. On the other hand, if you say he was swimming, you are also correct."

I was completely confused at what had just happened. I looked at my hands in complete amazement.

"It's all about perception, Proteus. Technically, birds swim in the waters of the sky; they don't fly, they don't soar, they swim- because, water connects them. Follow me!"   Caelestis dives into the Ocean, and I search for him in the waters until I heard his voice from above. "Don't be scared Proteus, just dive!"

He was sitting on a cloud asking me to join. Instantly, I was submerged in the waters with my eyes closed, and when I opened them I saw the ocean far below me. I was swimming in the sky. I reached to Caelestis and laughed.

"I can't believe this! How is it possible?"

The magical boy explained it all: We were all stars- a reflection of everyone ever created – and while some are meant to live on Earth, others are meant for the sky. I understood. He was my reflection; the person who stared back from the mirrors of the ocean. And just like my Pappous used to tell me, he said stars on Earth all return to the sky to become one person. But, he said, only those who believe will find out the truth. Others would only know in the end.

We talked and walked on clouds, bathing in the rainbow, drinking it in. It was a magical place indeed.

"It's time to go, Proteus." Dust from cloud particles stuck to his clothing.

"Will we see each other again?" I asked.

"We will, but for now our time is up. Next time, show me things of your world."

"As for your friends, let them find the truth on their own," he said with a wink.

The sun slowly faded away and a beautiful moon began to peek out from the sky.

The ocean spat me out on the sandy beach. I looked up and couldn't believe that I, Proteus, the imaginary boy was among the stars.

My friends arrived at that exact moment.

"Well, Proteus, we are here!" Samir shouted, kicking sand.

"Come on, don't keep us waiting!" Dimitrios said, pushing Samir to the side.

My head was still swimming, remaining high above in the sky. Dimitrios shoved me, and I got up with a smile, pebbles in hand, and gave them to my friends, walking back to my shack.

"Hey! Where are you going?" the Russian boy said, confused. The Indian boy looked plainly at the pebbles.

"Just start throwing pebbles," I chuckled, closing my shack's door.

I watched the sky through my roofless shack and thought of Caelestis. It was true, all true. Two shooting stars blinked in the sky as my friends pounded at my door. I laughed.

Word spread fast and every one visited my once lonely waters.

Meteor showers- that's what scientists called them, but I was the only one to know the truth: the truth of Reflection.

"Sometimes the Sky can be a little too high to reach, but if you wait for its reflection in the wide Ocean, you will never miss it when tossing pebbles at the Moon; there lay your Dreams."

Daniel Grier
Massachusetts Institute of Technology
"Hello, Mr. Morrison"

Clark Morrison awoke to find his bedside empty. This was not unusual. His wife Anne was already at work, hoping to show her supervisors there was good reason to give her the raise she now needed. Clark winced with renewed guilt as he thought of Anne at her desk, her head bowed and her eyes dry as she poured over yet another sales ledger.

Clark had recently been a writer at the Tuesday Times, a tawdry newspaper masquerading with faux-legitimacy whose success had nevertheless put it to press even on the days for which it was not eponymously named. Two weeks ago, the Times had told Clark to leave. He had weathered four years of editorial complaints, but it was finally determined that his writing was truly unappealing and that the Times just couldn't afford to keep him on staff.

So Clark was still in bed at 9A.M. when the sun, shining through haphazardly-drawn curtains, finally woke him. Rubbing his eyes, Clark threw his legs over the side of the bed, his exposed feet startled by the cold reality of the world beyond the bedsheets.

As always, he stared blankly at his bedside table, clarity coming back to him as he organized in his mind a comforting mosaic of objects he had placed there—pictures of his wedding, a once-beautiful leather notebook that had been given to him by his father and now contained the hurried scribbles of his dreams, a dirty penny that he had found almost twenty years ago when he was still a child, lying on tails, but which had not prevented him from having a surprisingly lucky day after all, the candlestick piece from the game Clue, which Anne had brought to him one night as a joke after their power had gone out.

Clark touched the penny as he stepped out of bed, folding the comforter back over his pillow as he did. The continuation of his morning would require coffee, so Clark slumped into the kitchen in search of the dark grounds that might bring the lucidity he desired. When he entered, Clark saw on the refrigerator a note with his wife's handwriting: 12:30 - Dental appointmnt.

It was an old joke of theirs, making pointless abbreviations to save precious millimeters of space, and Clark smiled, thinking about the note. A dawning sense of anticipation descended upon him. It wasn't that he didn't appreciate his wife's joke, but it was not what filled him with a quickening joy. Instead, it was the task, however simple, that had been set out for him- conferring to him the meaningless responsibility of traveling to this annual place of ritual mouth-cleansing.

Ever since he had been fired, Clark spent most of his day inside, cursing the capitalist, money-eyed trustees who sealed his fate at the Times, even as he told himself that it was a terrible job at an even worse newspaper. At times his thoughts would circle back, and he'd admit that he'd found a routine there, a pleasant rhythm which carried him from day to day as he convinced himself that he was a beacon of reason and eloquence in a sea of immature squawking. He hated what the Times had done to him, and yet, he bought each new issue to see what kind of word-stuffed excrement they were now putting to print. In the moments between his ready-made meals and his half-hearted pep talks, an insidious lethargy had taken over. Even when Anne returned from work, he could find no energy to greet her, no capacity for conversation.

It was the note, however, that stirred in Clark the purpose imparted by a pending deadline, a mysterious impetus he did not wish to question lest he allow his idleness to return. So, with a sense of tenuous optimism, Clark set about preparing for the day to come.

He remembered Anne many nights ago presenting to him a torn page from a cooking magazine. *Healthy portions of fruits and vegetables make for a healthy mind!* it read, helpfully. Later that week, Clark had framed it and put it up in the kitchen, displaying the newly minted piece of artwork. You can never trust art, Clark had then said to Anne, and yet, now, hoping to believe it, Clark prepared a harvest festival of a breakfast. He made, as his mother had always done, an omelet bursting with tomato, red onion, spinach, mushroom, and cheddar. He then fumbled around with an orange before deciding to cut it straight in half with a knife, and then again, and then again, and soon he was eating the orange like a child, the sweet, juicy pulp dribbling down his chin and into the sink as he bit each slice.

When he was finished, he showered, dressed, brushed his teethed, flossed, brushed again, and was out the door, stepping into a rather cold October morning. Clark lived a half-mile away from the nearest bus stop, and so, with his chin tucked into the inside of his jacket's collar, he struck out along the cracked sidewalk, determined to let the momentum of his good mood carry him out into the bleak morning.

As he walked on, Clark could not prevent his mind from wandering to weeks prior. The gruff voice of his manager, wearied by years of dealing with perceived ineptitude, echoed anew in his mind. *Hello, Mr. Morrison*, it said. *Terrible weather we're having.* It wasn't like his boss to talk to him at all, let alone about something as mundane as a meteorologically anomalous day in September. Clark knew then that for whatever reason the senior branch manager of the Times called him to his office, good news was not forthcoming. *Please, take a seat…*

He pictured now an alternative ending to that day. Instead of taking that seat, he announced his intention to resign, and instead of moping around his desk for next the two days, he devoted his energies to a new article — *The Hidden Cuticle Appeal: An Insider's Astonishing Investigation of the Nation's Most Dazzling Displays of Epidermal Nail-Coverings.* Clark couldn't help but chuckle to himself as the boss of his imagination gave approval for a front page story. His laugh was short but audible, and Clark noticed that his sidewalk co-inhabitants were allowing him a wider berth than they might have otherwise, and he bit his tongue in response to a wry sense of satisfaction at the absurdity of the scene.

His amusement subsided with perfect timing when he spotted his elderly next-door neighbor approaching from the other direction. Mrs. Thatcher was perpetually in a sour mood, and nothing set her off quite like seeing another person in a good one. She was a survivor, though. Widowed at 36. Mother of six. She hadn't once asked for a favor in her life. Clark almost couldn't blame her for being the advice-mongering, self-righteous, curmudgeon of a crone that she was.

Mrs. Thatcher seemed in quite a hurry, the click-clack of her steel-tipped cane resounding with a surprising frequency. Clark supposed the impatience with which she hobbled back to her house was due to the fact that she had to water her prize-winning geraniums, or feed her precious, smarter-than-you cat, or really any task that could probably stand to wait thirty minutes.

"Hello, Mrs. Thatcher," Clark said when she was near enough, slowing down and turning to greet her. His mother had always told him to take time to talk to the elderly, and Mrs. Thatcher was no exception.

"Hello, Mr. Morrison," said Mrs. Thatcher tersely, refusing to slow down.

Before Clark could manage a response, he was facing not Mrs. Thatcher, but the faded back of her purple flower-spotted overcoat. He was surprised to feel slighted by the encounter, given that he'd rather have not seen her at all. An obstacle in her path, that's what he was. An impotent obstacle.

Clark imagined running into the dentist's office, insurance card in one hand, pen in the other, daring somebody to turn him away. He'd sign in on their waiting list in bold capital letters, like he was bleeding from the teeth. One baptismal fluoride treatment, please, he'd say as the dentist ushered him through the folding doors leading into his operating chambers.

Clark felt oddly comforted by his deranged future-self as the bus finally pulled into the empty space in front of Maxwell's Silver Hammer, a hardware store on the east side of Bakersfield owned by a guy name Samuel.

"Please, take a seat," said the bus driver, gesturing through a small crowd standing in the front of the bus to some empty seats in the back.

"Thanks," said Clark, depositing 90 cents in coins into a bucket by the driver's side.

Clark found a seat in the back corner, where it seemed like the city was stockpiling its supply of dirt and rust. Beside him, an old man leaned back with a newspaper, looking, as far as Clark could tell, like he was actually at home in his favorite arm chair. Clark noted with some relief that he was not reading an issue of the Tuesday Times. He almost wanted to reach out and thank the man.

"Terrible weather we're having," said the man, cutting short Clark's thoughts on the matter.

"Sure is," said Clark, looking through the murky almost-window to his other side. The man turned back to his reading.

Clark thought back to his first article at the Times. His supervisors had sent him to "The Stadium," a local baseball field which had managed to co-opt the completely generic noun. He was told to write whatever came to mind there, to get his feet wet and enjoy the sunshine as a token of acceptance into the staff of the Tuesday Times. Not a bad perk, thought Clark. The team playing there went by the name of the Bakersfield Batters.

Clark had been so busy with his work, he hadn't given the outing much thought in the past four years. He hadn't returned since, but he could still remember the alternating light and dark grass, cut in perfectly parallel lines, the dirty-beige uniforms of the Bakersfield Batters as they ran off the field at the end of an inning, the feeling of status and importance as he sat there transcribing the commotion around him into his notebook.

Had it really been four years? Clark thought to himself as he reached up to signal to the driver that this was his stop. Clark shuffled by the old man, being careful not to disturb his admirable state of bliss, and out onto the street. The bus pulled away as a cold gust of wind rushed to greet him.

Two more blocks and he was at the front door of the dentist's office, still trying to ascertain that it had been four years. Yes it had, he concluded, as he opened the door. How had he forgotten?

"Hello, Mr. Morrison," said the receptionist as he entered the warmth of the office. He'd lived his whole life in Bakersfield, and not once had he gone to a different dentist. "Terrible weather we're having."

"Sure is," said Clark, scrawling his name quickly on the waiting list.

"Please, take a seat," said the receptionist, pointing to the waiting room where other patients gathered in collective boredom.

Clark's thoughts turned back to the baseball stadium before he could even sit down. Three days before the game, the Times had run an article urging its readers to attend the Home Runs for the Homeless event. For each home run, the organization would donate a hundred dollars to the Bakersfield Homeless Shelter. Clark had decided that this would be the subject of his article. He'd portray each glorious at-bat as another chance to save the world.

It was only later when he called the shelter to get more details on their involvement that Clark realized that the shelter had withdrawn its support from the event. Apparently, the stadium's owners were siding with a police officer who had injured a ticketless Batter's fan when he attempted to enter the stadium midway through the game. Unfortunately for the stadium and its promoters, that man had been a regular at the shelter.

The story had been a gift from journalistic heaven, and Clark had been determined to extract from it each tantalizing detail. Clark remembered submitting his draft for approval a day later, proud and naïve.

Clark shifted in his waiting-room seat, the events of his past flooding back to him, breaking the invisible levee that had held them there.

Clark's supervisors had returned his article to him, but it was bleeding with their edits. As he read them over, his curiosity turned into a resentful confusion.

But it's more complicated than that! Clark had complained. The editors had taken out the part which mentioned that the actions of the police officer were under criminal review. The article now read as if the homeless shelter was completely uncompromising and unrealistic in its accusations.

The editors replied that there was too much detail for a newspaper article. What's more, the The Stadium gave the Times free advertising space. It would be foolish to damage their relationship so prematurely.

Clark scrapped the whole piece.

"Hello, Mr. Morrison," said a sudden voice on the outside of Clark's consciousness.

Clark turned around in his seat to face the voice, seeing that his dentist, Dr. Landauer, was standing at folding doors, ready to serve as his escort. Dr. Landauer was already looking back down at his clipboard by the time Clark had gotten up and reached him.

"Terrible weather we're having," said Dr. Landauer as they walked together through the sterile hallway.

"Sure is," said Clark, looking out the window of the room they'd arrived at. On the counter was a placard introducing which hygienist would get to put sharp metal objects in his mouth today; Ms. Nancy, it read. In the center of the room, a big robotic chair loomed.

"Please, take a seat," said Dr. Landauer as he left, insinuating that the hygienist would be in shortly.

Clark climbed into the giant recliner. As he continued to remember details from his failed article, anger built inside him. The day after the editors had basically rejected his whole piece, his supervisors had given him a new task, a playful piece on the results of the county's annual pumpkin festival, which Rumpelpumpskins had won in a landslide. He'd been duped.

Clark wasn't rekindling an old ire. This was new. He'd been annoyed then, but not mad, and now, after years of living in the intoxicating fog of the Tuesday Times he had found himself in a clearing, and he was outraged—outraged at the Times for their self-serving dishonesty, outraged at the market for rewarding such obvious underhandedness, but mostly, outraged at himself for letting his complacence ruin his life.

"Hello, Mr. Morrison," said the too-sprightly voice of a person Clark could only assume was Ms. Nancy. Clark worked on unclenching his jaw, while she went about setting out the tools she'd need to make his teeth sparkle. She pulled up behind him, adjusting his chair so that his face was directly beneath hers, looking up into her eyes.

"Terrible weather we're having," she said.

Clark wanted to respond in the affirmative, but it was too late. She'd already stuck a shiny metal hook and mirror in his mouth, and there was no way for him to tell her how he felt.

ESSAYS

Savanna DeWeese
The University of Tulsa
"Death and Cigarettes and You"
– Winner of the 2016 Scythe Prize for Essay

I watch the haze pull through the city like smoke through lungs, like the final slow drag of what you swore was your last cigarette, thick and taunting.

I come in every day and draw the curtains back. I sit by you, typically asleep, and turn towards the window. I lean my head against the top of the chair, my hair presses against the back of my neck, and I squeeze your hand. Your eyelids flutter open, and you say, "There's my girl," through chapped lips and a twinge of heartache; I smile slightly, probably more aware of the weight of the situation than you are.

I watch you inhale sharply, drag your shaky hands across the hospital's starchy, pale blue blanket; you open your hands to gesture towards me and begin our routine.

You talk about taking me to Muncie for the first, and what was the only time. You talk about how we always talked about going back and how much fun we had. You talk about watching my pure white hair whip around in the wind because I liked the top-down freedom feeling, and you liked that I liked it. You don't talk about getting pulled over for driving 80 miles an hour down some back road or me crying for 40 minutes after the cop left.

You talk in golden moments only.

Each time you tell a story it's a little different than the last—a little brighter. You leave out sad endings and arguments; you leave out nights spent at your best friend Jim's house because mom was "tired of your bullshit" again, whatever that means. You don't talk about the days you spent pretending to be at work in hole-in-the-wall coffee shops around downtown or nights on the living room couch. You don't talk about any of that.

You remember sticking our fingers into the cold lake you grew up on. The clear water jutted fast past rocks and fish and everything. I remember feeling so at home in my little body standing next to you with cold water passing between our toes. My nails painted cherry blossom pink to match my new dress and yours a paled yellow from years of construction boots.

You took my hand to help me across some slick rocks, and said I was so much like my mother in a way that felt like an insult just as much as a compliment, and somehow I understood that was okay.

You talk about running down to the tennis courts, still barefoot from the river; we played pretend tennis for hours before I finally hit the ball to the moon and lost it. We lay down to watch it fly out of earth and into space. You say you could've lain there for days.

You talk about Shanghai. You say it's the first city that made you feel alive. You say people really know how to live there. The youth, the freedom, the rush of feet against the pavement at every hour of the day, the little westernized noodle shops. You tell me that I've got to go someday, you tell me the first night I make it to Shanghai, find a taxi and tell the driver to take me to *Miàntiáo hǎo*. You say they are the best goddamn noodles I'll ever have for no more than just a buck twenty-five.

Oh, and the owner, oh god the owner just loves foreigners; he'll keep you there an hour past closing talking about how nice it is to see globalization, and I mean really *see* it and then he'll insist you take at least three extra bowls home, no charge.

He's an old guy too, you tell me; the type of old that just baffles you, like lost his right thumb fighting for the Nationalists in '42 old, like still hates the Japanese old, like probably mentored Confucius. Seriously, get this guy's noodles.

 I told you we can go together someday; you let out something like a scoff, and I turn away. You continue on, there's a little pearl shop at the end of the pier on Zhongshan Road. You ran down at dawn in the rain because they get a new shipment in every Monday and you wanted to make sure you got a perfect purple pearl just for me. It was pouring rain, and you were running, and you should've felt lost in that huge city where you couldn't even speak the language, but you'd never felt that whole. You got the purple pearl and gave it to me for my eighteenth birthday. I've worn it ever since.

I remember most of the things you talk about, but I remember them in different ways. You remember me, thirteen years old, at our favorite mini golf course, with blue bows in my pig tails and a really bad swing.

I remember you, shoulders squared, perfect aim at the bubble gum pink ball you let me pick out. I remember knowing, no matter how bad my score turned out, you would subtract at least seventy points for seventy different things I did right.

You ask me if I remember the hot dogs they had at the mini golf course, or was at the baseball stadium? And if I remember spilling ketchup all across my shirt and crying until you squeezed a packet out onto yourself too. We spent the rest of our lunch dipping hot dogs into pools of ketchup on our clothes and making fun of the people who made funny faces at us.

You told me most people forget how to have fun when they grow up, and just because you've got a mortgage doesn't mean you can't eat ketchup off your pants. I wasn't sure what you meant at the time, but I remember wondering what mom will think when she sees our clothes blotched and stained a light pink.

You talk about Harley, the Davidson, and the name of the best dog we ever had. You talk about our first motorcycle ride every spring, and how mom worried so much every time you took me for a spin, but how worth it the feeling was. Riverside was the best place for spring motorcycle rides, and right before dusk was the best time to do it. We'd stop halfway to downtown at the small park with the purple curly slide, and you would let me play in the retiring sunlight.

Our favorite game to play was trains; I was always the conductor, and you were always my customer. I would bake mud pies and serve you on your ride, and you would tip in hugs and kisses and always say the dessert was abso-fably-lutely-tutley delicious, and I would chant it back like a tongue twister. We would ride home, and mom would criticize the dirt on my dress, say something under her breath about how late we were, but I didn't care. Not then, not at ten years old.

You keep talking about the games we played at that park, but I am only partially listening now. I am remembering so many times coming home, holding your hand, walking through the back door you'd say, with your voice low, something like "Don't tell your mother." or "This'll be our little secret, right?" and I would, of course, say yes and skip along to play with my dolls upstairs.

Only minutes later mom would come up asking about the blood on my knees or the hole in my dress or what all that racket was about and I would, of course, confess. We *were* at that park again after dark or on the bank of the river by the rocks with the cotton mouths or at Jim's house. She would smile, kiss my cheek and thank me for always telling the truth. But I knew that just meant they would fight about how "It isn't safe for her to be playing by those rocks" or "What kind of example is Jim supposed to set anyway? Do you really want your daughter to end up like that?" and the argument would slowly drift from me to money or how we never visit mom's parents anymore or those damn Lucky Strike butts and empty Scotch bottles. When my parents fought about me, they were never really fighting about me. I know that.

You talk about taking me for a ride on your childhood penny skateboard. It was electric blue and impressively sturdy for all those years you spent escaping with it. I was something like six years old, so
you held my hands and guided me through the path in our front
yard garden.

It wasn't long before we lost grip and let go; I didn't make it far enough alone to be loose in the street, but I crashed against the pavement hard enough to bleed. I cut my head, my hands and knees. I cried until you carried me in tickling my feet.

You don't talk about how mad mom was, how she couldn't believe you could be so careless and how, of course, you didn't mean it. You left and didn't come home for three days. But you don't mention that part, and I understand why.

I hear myself say things too. I croak out "Critical condition," "Six days," "Life support won't last forever." I respond to your calls and Facebook posts; I thank them for their consideration a little too coldly. If they cared, they would come. Sometimes you get flowers. Yesterday you received a bouquet of daisies. You smirked and asked if someone was dying.

I threw up.

I remember my first heartbreak. I was 19 years old when I found out what it feels like to watch someone unlove you. I came home crying and screaming illicit things at nothing in particular. Mom took me out for ice cream. Three bites into my mint chocolate chip double scoop and forty-five minutes into utter silence, mom started telling me about a fight she had with you once. She told me about the way the sunlight hit your eyes in the early evening, about how you two had been fighting about cigarettes and dirty dishes and money, always money, and then you were standing by the sink waving a dirty plate, and the sun crept in across your face in pink and golden shadows, and suddenly nothing felt like it mattered to her.

She tells me about how the yelling felt like an interruption, and she couldn't remember why she was so mad anyways, and her knees lifted from the release of the weight, and nothing felt heavy. She took your hand and hushed the world. Then she said she didn't know it, but in ten years she would be signing the divorce papers thinking about how the pink and golden shadows couldn't save you two from yourselves and thinking about how many, many times people have written about light dancing across the human body and how still no one can fully capture that pink, fading, easy, weightless feeling that she lost.

I remember her saying sometimes the world will give you a thousand reasons not to love someone, but it only takes one reason to stay. I figured I was mom's reason for staying with you as long as she did. I've always wondered what yours was for staying with her.

I don't remember why mom said these things. I don't know if she said them more for herself or for me. But I remember feeling easy on the car ride home. Like somehow I was okay because mom was okay. This was the first time she talked about you since the divorce and the last time she talked about you at all. There was a sweet sort of sadness in her voice, a calm, reposed sort of nostalgia. I know everything was a lot more compli-cated than it seemed to me at thirteen years old when you two broke. I know there is a lot between mom and you I will never know, and I know there was a time when you both really did love each other. It was hard not to blame myself sometimes.

I ask you why you stayed for so long. You ask what I mean, and I ask it again, I ask why you stayed with mom for so long when all you did was fight about everything. You are quiet for a while, and I sort of feel bad for bringing it up. You say you are sorry and that you don't really know, and then you tilt your head back and shut your eyes tight, and then I am the quiet one.

Suddenly, you are crying and mumbling about how you wish you could've been better; you are squeezing my hand and apologizing and saying you never wanted to be a fucking disappointment of a father. You are crying and saying I shouldn't look up to you; you are saying I deserve better, and I am quiet because I know it's true.

I take your hands and squeeze them back. I kiss your forehead, and we both cry harder.

The only other time I saw you cry you were stumbling drunk out on the porch. Usually when you got like that mom would take me upstairs to play with dolls or Lincoln logs, but I was sixteen years too old for those things, and mom wasn't home this time. So I went outside. You were ranting about something to do with work and how no one shows you any goddamn respect these days, and when I walked out, you lost it. I tried to take the bottle from you, but you grabbed my wrist, twisted and cocked your other fist back. We both knew you would never hurt me like that, but in the moment I was scared. You realized what you were doing, dropped your fist and the bottle, sat down, cradled your head and cried. We never talked about that night. You left and came back two days later, and we pretended everything was fine, and I wondered if you even remembered.

You talk about being eighteen and falling in love with mom. You say the first time you saw her, she was reading Dickens in her car with the window down, and you have no idea why, but you walked by and asked her out. You say she smiled this weird sort of half smile, knowing smirk and said yes. You say she smiled that same smile before you kissed her on your wedding day, and when you took her dancing at the Blue Lagoon

for your tenth anniversary, and when you learned to play "Heartbeat" by
Wham on piano for her. That was her signature, golden moment smile.
You say I have the same one, but it's a little quirkier – a little crooked, a
little more unruly. You say it's because I've got a lot of you in me, and I
know that's true.

You talk about pushing your little brother around in a wheel barrow
outside the house you both grew up in. You stop and ask me where he is
now, and I don't know, so I say he is racing cars in Indiana still. You make
a face that somewhat resembles a frown and say it isn't fair how quickly
time moves, and I understand.

You ask if he's ever going to get out of that small town and see something
real for once. I tell you he has tickets for Paris in September— the whole
family is going. You shut your eyes and whisper, "Finally," more to
yourself than me.

I almost feel bad for lying about this one.

It takes a while, but you end up talking about the first time you came
home, carrying mom across the threshold. You talk about accidentally
tearing her dress on the door frame, the sound of satin stretching and
giving, the sound of small pearl shaped beads scattering across the freshly
waxed, dark wood into piles of rose petals.

The sound of held breath and bursting laughter— you say that was
the best goddamn thing about her. I can see you two, your beautiful,
untouched bodies making dizzy, crooked paths to the bedroom.

You are young and without care. You are doing what you are supposed to
do. You put on an Elvis record and she will dance, and the night will fade
to day in a pale parade of laughter and love and youth, and it will be the
first time everything felt so free and the last time she looked this beautiful.

The nurses look in every twenty minutes or so with worry, raised
eyebrows. I wave them away with steady hands. "We are okay," I say, and
I mostly mean it. Some days I mean it more than others.

Today is one of those days I mean it less.

I am watching your hands rise and fall slowly in time with the rhythm

of your stories. I can see almost every vein in your arms stretched across
your skin like tree branches, like your whole body is in constant bloom.
Your skin seems stretched, too, across sharp bones on the precipice of
breaking out. I don't remember what you are talking about; your voice
is cracking; your words are strained. I am still; I take your weary hands in
mine; you look up and close your eyes. We do not move, and no one talks
for thirty-five minutes.

You talk about getting out of here and returning to the dirt or whatever. I
do not listen when you talk about that.

You say, "Take a road trip to Muncie for Chrissake. Sprinkle me across
every lake you pass on the way and anywhere else beautiful: the roadside
McDonald's we stopped at for ice cream, the old tennis courts you grew
up playing on, the hill behind your brother's lake house with a thousand
daffodils."

"Sprinkle me there," you say.

You ask me where mom is and if she'll be coming here later. You ask it like
you've seen her in the past seven years; you ask it like you never left.

I tell you that she can't today; she's busy staging a play in New York
City right now, and you say you understand. You say she was always the
ambitious one, and you say you're so proud of her, and you ask me what
the play is about.

I say it has something to do with orphans in Calcutta, and you say something about her heart.

I know you loved her. I know you didn't want to leave.

You ask me if I remember our surprise picnic in the park. You picked
me up from school in the middle of the day and surprised mom on the
way. We went out to the park by 41st Street and sat on our favorite quilt. I
remember you pulling out blueberries and turkey sandwiches and cheese
and grape soda and chocolate covered strawberries and sweet rolls. We ate
and laughed and joked and sang and my tummy was bursting with food
and aching from happiness, but I didn't mind. You were kissing mom on
the cheek, and I was covering my eyes and holding her hand, and we were

doing what families are supposed to do.

I didn't tell her you were in the hospital, we don't talk about you, and she wouldn't have come. I know what she would think, "Not so lucky anymore is it?" or something about how "Bad habits have a worse way of catching up eventually." I figured I'd spare the awkward phone call filled with "Oh um, I'm sorry, but I'm so packed this week, and your uncle is in town," trailing off into halfhearted condolences and "Let me know if you need something..."

She hasn't mentioned your name for seven years.

I need a break so I go to the nearest ice cream shop and get one double scoop chocolate chip cookie dough and one mint chocolate chip in a cup, your favorite. I bring it back and you have a few bites and set the cup aside. I watch your mint chocolate chip melt slowly. I think about the last time I had that flavor.

Mom had picked me up from school like she always did, in line by 2:20, never a minute later. I hopped into the front seat and shoved my backpack in the back. Where the usual "How was your day, sweetie?" would've come in, I turned to see her on the phone with one finger suspended in the air to say "Sorry, one minute." She hung up, took a slow breath, and said "Okay, how about some ice cream?"

The last time mom offered me ice cream in the middle of the day Grand Pop had died, and the time before that Scout had gotten out of that stupid hole in the fence again but hadn't come home, and I could guess from the heightened frequency of fighting to mom sleeping in the guest room to your drunken stupors, what this ice cream was for.

Everything over that next year fell rapidly. Your stuff ended up on the front porch in black trash bags, you ended up in rehab for a variety of problems, I ended up in counseling session after counseling session after counseling session, and mom ended up with full custody.

Over time I was allowed to see you more and more. We started seeing each other for 30 minutes then an hour then two until we were allotted afternoons together. Besides Jim, I was pretty much the only contact you had. I guess your conservative suburban Methodist family didn't want

much to do with an alcoholic, drug-head bum, and I understand why.
I spent my teenage years convincing myself it was not your fault and
remembering the good days. Most of the time it was nice to see you; we'd
watch movies in your apartment or make vegetarian lasagna or plan trips
to Indiana we both knew we could never take. It was different, but it was
okay.

I snap back from my thoughts and realize you've fallen asleep. I take your
melted ice cream to the garbage and wake you up.

You don't even miss a moment; you start talking about Chili Billy's, home
of the Chili Billy Chili Chomper.

You talk about me singing their slogan for twenty minutes before our
meal arrived.

You said I hated Chili and never finished my food, but you loved to take
me there because we laughed the whole dinner through.

I don't tell you Chili Billy's went out of business years ago, or that we
only ate there once because something about rotten tomatoes and food
poisoning. I do not remind you how bad the service was. I say,

"WELCOME TO CHILI BILLY'S HOOOOME OF THE CHILI BILLY CHILI
CHOMPER." I say, "How much chili could a Chili Billy chomp if a Chili
Billy could chomp chili?" I say, "Let's go there for dinner tonight," and
you sigh and say you aren't hungry quite yet, and
I understand.

You break the conversation with another coughing fit and incidentally
stain the bed sheets with blood. I close my eyes tight and call in the nurse.
She comes in to check on you.

She moves slowly and intently; I watch her the whole time. You don't
seem to notice. You start up again, talking in your golden moments.

I watched her tuck her hair behind her left ear and take notes. Her face
didn't change, but she moved her gaze up towards mine and locked eyes.
I tried to make a face that asked, "How bad is it?" Her face shifted slightly,

only for a moment, to a tender, worrisome wince, but I look away because you are talking about Muncie again. Wondering out loud where your brother is. I say, "He's on his way to Paris, remember?" You turn your head towards me and say, "About time he got outta that goddamn town."

Every year I got a little pink card in the mail from Miss Shelly's dance studio that read "Miss Shelly's Annual Father Daughter Dance," and every year I begged you to take me. Every year you promised you would. We never went, but I somehow still got excited for the promise.

You ask me if I remember those dances; you ask me like it was a tradition for us to go. I wonder if you remember we never went, but I say yes and talk about the dress I want to buy for this year's dance.

You tell me that I always look best in baby blue, and I know that was the truth.

It almost feels real.

Your hands are so frail. You can't even get out of bed to sneak a smoke anymore. You don't care. You ask me about the summer and what I am going to do, and I tell you I have an internship with the school. You say, "That's so fantastic, sweetheart," and you look at me like I'm holding the moon. Then you ask me the same thing twenty minutes later, and I tell you I'm going to Italy this time, and you say you wish you could come, and I tell you that you can and squeeze your hand.

You feel okay and I feel like shit ,but I smile and squeeze your hand tighter.

You talk in slow sporadic moments. You let memories linger faded by your soft, raspy voice. I listen closely, but I do not catch them all.

Something about catfish whiskers and orange soda in June.

Something about pinecones.

Something about Christmas Eve two years ago.

Something about mom and something about something you miss.

You talk carefully, but your voice moves in and out.

You do not repeat yourself.

I etch every thing you say straight into my brain because I'm afraid it'll be the last.

The hard part is you do not seem to mind.

I talk rapidly in quick short breaths and awkward bursts. I say, "Remember Indiana, remember 80 miles on the freeway and that Elvis song about a hound dog, remember blue snow cones and even bluer tongues, remember Harley, remember the boat, remember driving the boat, remember pulling me on the tube behind the boat?"

Voice cracking and throat straining I push memories and memories and memories out of my mouth; I feel my own vocal chords straining and ripping and breaking.

I feel them breaking.

I cram memory after memory into the thin air between us.

Your hands are cold and heavy.

I don't cry, I say remember Martha's wedding and my flower girl dress you picked out?

Remember watching movies in your new apartment and my first car and motorcycle rides and the little park by 41st? Remember dancing to Springsteen by the pool the first summer we had it? Remember my piano lessons? Remember how much I hated my piano lessons and making fun of my instructor Mrs. Robertson? Remember Harley? Remember the father daughter dance? "Can we go? Can we go this year please, Dad? Let's go."

I feel foolish. I squeeze your hand.

Your hands are so cold, and I'm still yelling good days at you. The nurses are trying to calm me, and I squeeze your cold, heavy hands, and I do not let go. I say, "Remember Indiana, remember 80 miles down the freeway, remember Elvis, remember showing me your records, remember buying me a record, remember?

Austin D. Kirkham
The College of Idaho
"Who I Haven't Been: The Dangers of Method Acting"

Constantin Stanislavski invented a style of character comprehension that thespians warn against but almost always draw from. Deep psychological association with fictional characters per dialogue and direction offered by a script is plainly dangerous. Heath Ledger drove himself mad from it, not because of *The Method* but because of The Joker. There are characters that players feel comfortable slipping into the mind of, but it's all the same.

During my freshman year at Mountain View High School, my drugged out, purple eye-bagged drama instructor referred to a book which articulated Sanford Meisner's technique of method acting. The tools helped me make people cry, but I wanted more.

So we made a mistake together -- he let me borrow the damn thing.

It led me to many minds that were not my own.

This is our story.

Reverend Chasuble, Oscar Wilde's *The Importance of Being Earnest*

A devout man with some Irish in his vernacular; he taught me about mixing virtue with vice. The character has a muted love of his counterpart, the also entirely faux professional Miss Prism, which breaks loose at the end. *Oh, Latitia!* I remember chirping in sacred garb, behind fake glasses and caked foundation. This is, however, where Meisner's suggestions came into the fray.

Instead of memorizing a script, instead of just saying words, the point is to *become* Reverend Chasuble on stage before the spectators. I did not sell it to myself. I was still myself on the stage. There were changes though- scratches on the coffee table of my mind. No myelin lacquer would hide the dents. People noticed, but no one knew where it came from.

Those dents started an addiction. The performance was met with much applause and, to be frank, no one had clapped for me before save acts of delinquent or youthful idiocy.

A thespian was born.

The Ghost of Christmas Present, Charles Dickens' *A Christmas Carol*

The show ran almost immediately after Earnest, otherwise I would have been Scrooge per the director. Thank Hell that did not happen. Small roles are nice. They do not invade the head space quite as much. The costume was pretty ridiculous: a storm cloud wig paired with a vanilla beard, all lined with tinsel above the flowing, ornamental emerald-crimson gown. *Damn it if I didn't have fun spinning the tinsel*. It was a shit show, which meant I did not have to care as much.

There were also distractions. Second girlfriend of my existence. First kiss (on opening night to boot because thespians are *dramatic)*. Surprise surprise. For much of the show I focused on my next audition's monologue, the opening soliloquy to Shakespeare's *Richard the III*. In that, I'd be dark and brooding and edgy and over-the-top.

Peter, Edward Albee's *Zoo Story*

This is the role I do not want to talk about. *Peter*. This was the script that did the most damage. It started the anxiety, it ended the peace of mind. Peter is an average fellow who lives a milquetoast life with a wife, two daughters, and cats he never wanted. Peter takes a seat at a bench and is approached by Jerry.

Jerry has some issues but his actor had deeper issues. We competed to out-method each other.

He won.

See, the play ends with Jerry deconstructing Peter's entire routine life and demonstrating that all of his framework is pointless and the reason for his inner misery. Peter snaps a bit, but Jerry snaps first. He takes out a knife; the two struggle; Peter holds it in a defensive position and then Jerry lunges at it. He dies.

There was a day where I could have made the choice to stop using the method, but I didn't. It was the day that Jerry's actor let me into the headspace that was being built.

He described his research on serial killers: a man that turned women's nipples into a belt, cannibals that feasted upon victims from dogs to children. The examples continued for about twenty minutes uninterrupted while the director, that same drama instructor which started it all, was outside and away. Then he told me he had my death planned, though it *would never actually happen; it isn't in the script.*

For two weeks longer I continued building Peter's mentality. He was repressed and anxious, afraid of the world and afraid to live. He was muted. He died, but the method lived on. Jerry's actor went on to become a resident student at Utah State University's program, and I dropped out of the play.

Even then, there were more shows to audition for. The warning had not been received.

Friar Lawrence, Shakespeare's *Romeo and Juliet*

My first-kiss girlfriend was Juliet. Romeo was played by a piece of garbage that claimed to have performed the play before in *Italian,* in *Greece.* At age thirteen. I was in charge of delivering his poison vial and, on closing night, hocked a fat phlegm nugget in it. He didn't notice. The cast called me a hero. I regret it.

That play itself is another regret. Remember Meisner and Stanislavski? They came back. I was wearing fake, rounded glasses and crafted Friar Lawrence as this type of proper gentleman with a little bit of pizzazz in his manner. By the end, he felt less like a man of the church and more like a butler. That is the role of the actor, however, to serve and serve.

I was so accustomed to speaking in iambic pentameter that my sentences turned to Elizabethan sonnets. This is not hyperbolic. I struggle with it still today, but *then* was when it hurt more. People were worried about my manner having changed. I was more formal, more concerned about *God* and *morality*. The fun-loving rascal faded away because my job was to be a Friar. The addictive part was the applause, the laughter.

One night Romeo managed to miss his cue by some entire thirty-seconds, which is plainly ludicrous in the world of theatre. Worse, it was a scene in *my office*. The lights came up, he was missing. I had to act quickly. There was foliage nearby, and I immediately started fondling it with a researcher's eye, in the character of this strange fellow. It persisted for the pause- the whole pause. It must have looked ridiculous.

But the audience loved it.

They loved it so much that two photographs in the yearbook showed me gazing at the lovely plastic ferns. The photographs seem a bit much, but it makes perfect sense.

Largely because I had to do the exact same thing the following night.

Dr. Victor Frankenstein, Mary Shelley's *Frankenstein*

It was my first lead role. Victor is still there in my mind. I hear his thoughts; I was the one that started them.

In the first two weeks, I had the entire script, including the parts of others, fully memorized. This was useful, but not altogether healthy. All I wanted to do was make the audience feel this character's tragedy by making it my own.

It was the empathy, one for a fictional character, which allowed for *the change*. Where other characters were decidedly more put together, Victor was charged with a kind of inconsistent emotion that was visible in the words he was saying, when he was saying them, and how I knew he would say them.

The words on the pages melted into my neurons. On stage I looked actors in the eye for *I was Victor Frankenstein.* I wanted them to know that. On stage I screamed in anger, broke things, and stunned the audience because I was Victor Frankenstein. When my wife died, when my best friend died, I wept and cried out per the exact words of the script.

And then there was The Monster.

A nervous home-schooled kid that had somehow managed to grab a part in the production played the role. A bit taller than I, with short sheep hair, modern black-frame glasses shaped into rectangles, some unfortunate weight at his chest; he had all the makings of a gentle soul.

He did not know how to pretend.

When I say that, I mean that when he was stage-pushing me, he actually used force. It conditioned me to true terror for the bruised kneecaps, the shredded cheek skin (*Thank you, make-up*), and the incident on closing night.

Henry had just died, chucked into the main power source for the laboratory. Thunder cracked, booming throughout my ancestral home. Elizabeth was buried as well and the beast before me proceeded to throw my father out the tower and to his doom. Tears ran down my cheeks; I shouted for peace, but there was none to come -- only vengeance for my mistakes. The biggest one, right there before me, threw me at the table from which his own life had originated and with such force that the back wall began to collapse.

I'm going to die.

Hands on the chains, they surged with electricity that sent me howling to a crisp. The lights dimmed. The play was over.

Shaking, I got off the table and the wall behind me came crashing down.

It was my last role in high school and earned me my International Honor Thespian award. At the ceremony I was stiff and unsure. There was not going to be another play here, all of that was done and over as a result of time and age. It was time to move forward, past the plays of old and into adulthood.

It was stiffness from terror, for I knew I had to walk into the world outside without a real identity. Just an award, some scripts, and lines from unreal people reverberating in my mind.

Carrie Loughry
Towson University
"I Am"

I am eleven years old. I have just begun puberty and my body resembles a stitched up rag doll. I am awkward. I am short. I have legs and arms too long for my body. My naked face still has the roundness of childhood and my skin is clear. My legs have begun to grow thick, dark hair, and after some girls comment on it I stop wearing shorts.

I am in middle school. I don't have any friends. No one teases me, but no one talks to me either. I am invisible. I am the only child in my class whose parents are still married. My parents may still be together but they argue too much. The days of peace are few and far between, and silence becomes the norm. My mom and I go to church while my dad stays home. My Sunday school class speaks about divorce. Secretly, I wish my parents would divorce, so everyone would pray for me.

I am twelve. My mom and dad sit me down and explain that they are seeking a divorce. I remember my wish and wonder if it's my fault. They assure me that it's not. I think it is. My parents say that they will remain friends; however, I don't believe that for a second. I spend most of my time now crying in my bedroom. When I tell the girls in my gym class about my parents, we make a pact to never divorce our husbands. Several of those girls have not kept that pact.

My parents sell my house. It's a beautiful log cabin on the side of a mountain in West Virginia. It's the house with all my childhood memories. I have purple carpet in my bedroom, Pocahontas sheets on my bed, and more toys than one child needs. We have a beautiful black lab named Lexi. She and I spend many hours running and playing in my backyard. My life in that house is everything I have ever known, and it's crashing down around me.

Now I am two months shy of thirteen. My mom and I move into a tiny townhome in rural West Virginia. It's just us. The house has white walls and white carpet. It's impersonal and distant. She and I try to make it a home. We hang pictures, light candles, and set out knick knacks. Slowly but surely it becomes our home.

My mom is my only friend. I look forward to leaving school every day, just because I'll get to see her and have someone to talk with. We watch television together every day after class. Every so often, we have a yes day. A yes day is when the answer to the question, "can I get this?" is "yes!" During the summer we have fun Fridays, since my mom has every Friday off. On these days I choose what we do. Sometimes we go swimming, sometimes shopping; once in a while we just stay home and have an indoor picnic and watch Disney movies. I always have fun, no matter what we do.

I turn fourteen. I have a fear of nobody showing up to my birthday party. I decide to just avoid the inevitable and skip a party altogether. My mom and I pretend that we are just excluding everyone from my celebration. She just makes me a special dinner and bakes me cupcakes. I'm grateful for my low-key birthday. Our Christmas is the same way. I wake up early to find presents under our tree, my mom baking cinnamon rolls in the kitchen, and Shania Twain's music playing throughout our house. As I open my gifts, my mom apologizes for not having more presents, but that's all she could afford. I fight back tears as I tell her that it's perfect, and I appreciate everything she's done for me.

I am also fourteen when I think about killing myself. It's a thought that has never crossed my mind before, but the depression has its grip on me. Weeks and weeks go by, and I am sad every day. I manage to keep my grades up, but find it a challenge to wake up. I go to bed every night thinking it would be okay; it would be okay if I didn't wake up the next day. I don't want to hurt my mom, so I keep my feelings to myself.

I am fifteen when I cut my wrist for the first time. Shane, my first boyfriend, had broken up with me. I think it's the end of the world, as most fifteen year olds do. My emotions overwhelm me, and I find comfort in the crimson line on my wrist. I do not feel any pain. I only feel relief for those few seconds as those droplets of blood roll down my arm. For those few seconds, I am calm. I don't feel the grip my depression has on me. I hide my wrists from my mom. I use makeup and long sleeves to hide the evidence.

I am sixteen when she finds out. Tears roll down her face and she hugs me close. I try to explain that I didn't really want to die; I just needed relief from my emotions for a minute. She is devastated and I am too. She gets me help, but I have no interest in it. I know she loves me, but she doesn't know what to do. Neither do I.

I am eighteen when I am formally diagnosed with bipolar disorder. At first, it feels great to finally have a name to my ailment. I learn that the times I felt amazing weren't just breaks from the depression. It's a cycle. Hypomania/depression over and over again. Soon a feeling of shame sets in; I feel ashamed to be different from everyone else. I feel like a freak. All I have ever wanted was a normal life. I want a job I love, a loving husband, and two kids. I want the white picket fence and a dog. My mom tells me I can still have all of that. I feel too broken to have a normal life. I drop out of treatment and go into denial.

I am twenty-one when I ruin my first real relationship. Bryan loved me and I loved him, but depression loves no one. He tries to make it work, but my constant depressive episodes and constant suicide talk leave him exhausted. He tells me that he loves me, but he has to love himself too. He hopes that this will give me a push to get the help I desperately need. My mom makes me tea and listens to me cry. When I want to give up, she gives me tough love. I can't keep living my life this way. I need to put Bryan out of my mind for a while and focus on getting myself healthy. She tells me that if it's meant to be, he will come back.

At age twenty-two, I celebrate my first full year of being in remission. I have found successful treatment, brought up my college GPA from 1.3 to 3.0, and wake up in the morning finally happy with myself. I wait for Bryan to come back.

He doesn't.

I'm twenty-three and I have a setback. A boy I love doesn't love me back. I start to cut my ankle, but it doesn't feel right. I have come too far to throw it all away. I put the blade down and just go to sleep. The next morning I hug my mom, and thank her for everything.

I'm now twenty-four and wish I had all the answers. I have ups and downs, but my mom is always there. She's there through losing my job, graduating from CCBC, ending one relationship and starting another. I am finally building a life that makes me proud.

I'm almost twenty-five and I think I am going to be okay.

Jasmine Respess
New College of Florida
"Braids"

Sadly, I never really learned to braid. I can do a simple three strand braid, but nothing more. This is one of the lessons I missed out on as a mixed kid living in a predominantly white town.

Growing up, I spent most of my time outside. By the swamp, in the woods, or in swimming pools. Having braids would have saved me grief brought on by tangles, frizz, and likely even head lice.

"You're going to have to stop playing with white kids," My mom would say after applying mayonnaise and lice poison to my thick curly hair. "You cannot keep coming home with bugs," she would add as she picked at the weird, translucent bodies with the small green handled pick. Not that choosing not to play with white kids was a real option in my Central Florida town. They were everywhere. Also, they had fun stuff like trampolines, dirt bikes, and video games. I was surrounded by towheads and pigtails. It was not easy to convince me to wear braids.

"Come sit," my mom would say. On the rare occasion I would comply with being groomed. All the tools would be laid out.

"Spray bottle?" mom would ask.

"Check," I'd answer.

"Comb?"

"Check."

"Ties?"

"Check."

The last thing my mother would ask about would be the Softee Herbal Grease, which I referred to as green goop. If not for this product, I might not have minded having braids all that much. But since I could not imagine any of the white neighborhood girls ever using the stuff on their corn silk hair, I resented it.

"Grease?"

"Yes," I replied barely hiding a grimace.

I'd sit between her legs, and my mom would begin the long process of combing out my mid back length hair. Now, I would never even dream of combing out my hair dry, but this is how mom did it.

"Your hair used to do whatever I wanted," mom reminisced when she took breaks to rest her hands. "With just my finger, I'd put it in a ring and it would stay."

I frowned.

Those days were long gone. As I approached puberty, my hair had turned into a mass of different curls. Each follicle produced a different texture.

When my mother sectioned and combed through my curls, enough hair would come out for at least one other head of hair.

"Ooooww," I'd whine. My mother would offer a rushed sorry.

I do think she was remorseful, but she had to complete the task at hand.

For me, these braid times came before relaxers, hair straighteners and long before buzz cuts and hair dye.

"Your hair is your crown." my mother would say, loosely quoting the Bible. A relic of her Pentecostal upbringing she had not left completely behind.

Unlike many stories I have heard from other women of color, I had not suggested the relaxer. I do not think I had a concept of something like that even being possible. It wasn't that I hadn't dreamed of having glossy satin hair, I just did not believe that curls so encompassing could be wrangled straight.

In the fourth grade, as picture day was fast approaching, my mother took me to a beauty shop at the back of a JCPenney's. All of the hair dressers were black. Each woman had some sort of creative hairstyle. The hairdos included extremely long brightly colored weave or intricate patterns shaved into one or both sides of the head. I worried they would want to do something like that to me. Something that would make me stick out even more.

"Wow, she has got a head of hair on her," the woman who would be doing my hair said. "When someone comes in with their hair up, I make sure I clear my whole night, and it looks like you, my dear, have enough hair for two or even three ponytails."

The rest of the women, armed with hair sprays and hot combs, nodded in agreement.

Except for the times my mother's family got together in the summer, this was the largest gathering of all black people I had seen in my life.

I was not totally sure what would come of this appointment. The women's eccentric looks did not make me feel very confident. I thought that if it was so easy to get perfectly straight hair, I would have already known about that. I did hope that the hair dresser would at least make it possible for me to run my fingers through my hair, wear my hair completely down without anxiety, and make it so I could easily put my hair up without a mirror or a brush. I hoped that she would make it so I did not have to wear braids ever again.

I sat in the salon chair until my legs were totally asleep. Two hours had passed, but we were not even halfway through. The dresser had shampooed and conditioned my hair, nothing out of the ordinary. In fact, that was quite pleasant, but what came next was decidedly not.

The hair dresser applied this putrid smelling, chemical cream to my roots. She then worked the terrible cement like product all over my hair.

I waited and waited. Totally positive that this crap was going to burn off all my hair, when two white people walked in the salon.

It caught me off guard.

"We want to get her hair straightened," the older woman said.

She was around thirty-five, with a long blonde ponytail and a slightly over grown bottom half.

"We thought this would be the best place to come," she said. "All the normal salons said it wasn't possible."

Normal! Did they not realize this was our private space?

The girl was completely silent. I looked her over. Her hair was dirty blonde -- curly, but not kinky. She was freckled, but had very pale skin. I glanced at her hair again. It was big and frizzy, but still unmistakably white in texture. In no way did this girl look anything but white. She looked even whiter than the kids I hung out with. At least when they went outside they would burn then tan. This girl looked like she had never got a bit of sun a day in her life, regardless of apparently living in the sunshine state.

"Let's see," the salon woman said.

I wanted the salon lady to say no. I wanted her to say this place is not a last resort.

"Well I am sure we can work something out," the stylist added with a friendly smile. "No Problem."

I sat and fumed.

Why does her mom want to change her?

Why isn't she saying anything?

Is curly hair that horrible?

I became so hot, I forgot about the very real heat the product was causing on my head.

The hair dresser looked away from the woman when she heard me whimper in pain. She took me to the sink and spent at least 20 minutes washing the white hot cream off my scalp and hair.

With the water whooshing in my ears, I could not hear all that was said between the salon women and the white lady, but I caught that she had made an appointment for her daughter to get her hair relaxed next week.

I would never see what would become of the white girl's hair after her turn at the black salon, but after four and a half hours, I saw what became of mine.

I was washed, dried, brushed, burned, and styled, only to be left with a mass of too straight hair that smelled strongly like the Softee grease I had grown to loathe. All the white girls would be in disbelief, but they would quickly discredit me, noting that my straight hair did not move as freely as theirs. That it did not smell light like cream and strawberries. That it was just a bit too oily to the touch. The worst part was my hair would curl back up just as ferocious as ever the second it got wet.

"You're so lucky to have such long hair," the hair dresser kept repeating during the process.

I did not feel lucky.

I still do not know how to braid.

Katherine Ann McMorris
Hope College
"Trichy Business: The Analysis of a Trichster,
Alphabetically Arranged"

Accident

You remember your reflection, your tweezers, your blood, your frustration.

On that morning in eighth grade, it began as an accident. You didn't plan on changing your daily behavior for the rest of your life as you examined yourself in the mirror. You want to believe your brain had already rewired itself before you pulled out your hair for the first time. Because that doesn't happen by accident.

Body Image

It's not a body-image issue. It's a reverse body-image issue. When you try to fix how you look, it becomes worse. It's a parasitic relationship. You wonder if you'll ever look "right" again. You focus so much on your outward appearance that you forget about the bigger picture: no one will notice if one hair is out of place. No one knows that one hair on the back of your arm feels thicker than the other ones. You're fixing your body, but it's not a body-image problem; it's a mental problem.

Cancer

"Why don't you have eyelashes?" In the middle of a ballet class during an Achilles tendon stretching exercise, a fellow classmate brought up your condition. "Maybe you have cancer," she contemplated. To a thirteen-year-old unfamiliar with medical practices, hair loss equaled cancer.

You didn't know what to say in response.

Diagnosis

"Do you remember the first time you pulled out your hair?" you sat across from your psychiatrist in her office filled with books the size of shoe boxes.

"It started when I noticed my top and bottom eyelashes were touching each other. So I thought I could use nail clippers to trim them. At first it started with just a few, but then I decided it looked even worse. So I grabbed tweezers and pulled them all out. Then when I didn't have any eyelashes left, I went to my eyebrows, then my scalp. I started pulling everywhere and I couldn't stop." Even as you said those words you sat on your hands.

"How do you feel when you pull out your hair?" the psychiatrist asked, scribbling notes into her clipboard. You noticed the clock was running four minutes slow.

"It feels like I *have* to do it or I won't feel right. If the hair looks weird I have to pull it. If it feels different I have to pull it. If it draws any sort of attention to itself, I have to pull it," you responded.

"Have you ever heard of trichotillomania?"

"Is that what I have?" Finally. Answers.

"Yes. It's probably part of OCD. Those go together sometimes."

"So what do I do?"

"You keep coming back so we can work on it."

Eyelashes

You relish in pulling out your eyelashes, not because of some masochistic desire to force yourself to cry but because it gives you a high. It's liberating. With each pluck the brain releases a series of chemicals, producing an effect similar to the Prozac or Zoloft you take to help stop the urge to pull. One by one, your fingers glide up and down your eyelid until they rip the hair from the flesh in one fluent action. The contrast is shocking: first you meticulously hunt, and within seconds the damage is done. Only after you blink and recognize the absence of eyelashes do you stop. Temporarily. A line of blood decorates your hairline.

In approximately six days, your eyelashes will start to grow back. Until then, you focus on the rest of your body, moving around until you can find more hairs from which you can release tension.

Fingers

After studying for two hours, you look up only to find a pile of tiny brown hairs by your feet and an exposed patch of skin on your scalp. You pick up each individual hair, caressing the end and bending and holding it up to the light for a better view. You remove the skin from the tip of the follicle and flick the hair into the growing pile beneath you. If you do not find the hair appealing, you toss it away sooner than others. And if it accidentally slips between your fingers before you can fully examine every aspect, panic instills and you begin the frantic search for the single hair that fell into the nondescript beige carpet. Your hands graze the floor, and receive a shock of joy when you find the hair you dropped so suddenly. Hands scoop up the damage and flush it down the toilet – hiding the evidence of another binge and purge. Then you do it again.

Gimmicks

Trichotillomania affects approximately 4% of the population, and to this day, no one has found a solution that works every time. As a result, your daily routine is full of gimmicks your cognitive-behavioral therapist suggested to help you resist the urge to pull. Driving between school and work, your hands sport warm gloves in the winter and thin, cotton gloves in the summer. Because pulling while driving is as dangerous as drinking and driving: you can't concentrate. Your parents bought you a guitar and how-to books because they hoped your fingers would form callouses and inhibit you from pulling. It works, sometimes. You treat your tiny, silver, spinner ring with an importance equated to an engagement ring, and you keep pictures of eyes around your room to remind you what "normal" eyes look like. But nothing solves all the problems.

Hats

The hat you wear to the movie theater becomes more important than the blue raspberry slushy you just spent seven dollars on. You know that every dull moment equals an opportunity to pull, so you invest in hats to distract you. They distract the people around you, too, from noticing any new bald patches.

Inspection

You basically give yourself an entire military medical examination prior to every shower. You start at the toes: there are four hairs on your left big toe (there were five yesterday), and they all look the same, with the same blonde shading and length, so they stay. That doesn't mean you don't spend a few minutes stroking them, though, just to ensure they don't cause you unnecessary frustration. You pause at your ankle because you find three darker hairs your razor missed during the last time you performed your sacred ritual. Your fingers slowly rub back and forth, feeling the thickness in comparison to the other hairs nearby. These are different; the darkness and coarseness means they have to be removed. Your fingernails squeeze together and within seconds three crimson pinpricks of blood surrounded by red skin replace the three hairs. But you hardly feel the pain anymore. You don't pull for the pain; you pull for the relief. The inspection of every hair on your body continues until you have "fixed" the dark and thick hairs on the back of your left arm and the single hair that is longer than all the rest on your elbow. After a methodical twenty minutes, even the one hair on the back of your thigh, which is only accessible via extreme contortion and flexibility, is removed.

Jokes

"You could be the 'before-model' for a hair-growth product!"

"You probably save a lot of money because you don't wear mascara!"

"So do you believe in aliens since you look like one?"

Kisses

You opened your eyes for a brief second and that's when you noticed it: his out-of-place eyelash. As you drew away, he gave you a look. You explained your dilemma and asked if you could pull out his eyelash because it was bothering you. He smiled and you thought that meant "yes." His face contorted as you yanked it out. Later, he told you he wasn't interested in you because you weren't his "type." Apparently his "type" is a girl who doesn't pull out other people's eyelashes.

Lies

"Why don't you have any eyelashes?"

"Well, ever since I was little my eyelashes have randomly fallen out. My parents think it might be genetic."

You never realized how well you could lie until you wanted to hide your secret. You hate having to tell people about an unpronounceable condition whenever something looks wrong, so instead you fabricate your own stories. They become more and more elaborate, because you don't just have to explain your appearance, but you have to explain your lifestyle as well. The brace you sometimes wear around your elbow is *not* to prevent your arm from inching up toward your scalp. It's because your eight-page essay resulted in tennis elbow the day before. And the Band-Aids you wear on your fingers? No, you did not burn yourself on the milk steamer at your coffeehouse job. Nor are you afraid of swimming. You are afraid of your makeup washing off, exposing a freakish girl with no eyebrows. And does anyone actually believe you have an unnaturally low body temperature, which is why you sometimes wear socks over your hands? Who knows? But regardless, the lies continue because the hair pulling continues.

Mirrors

When you were little, you questioned how a movie could show a person looking in the mirror but not show the cameraman in the background. Your mom explained that the crew always stands at an angle, so you can see the person perfectly in the mirror, but you can't see the crew. It's like magic.

You wish trichotillomania were the same. You wish you could look at yourself without seeing everything that comes with the broken life of a trichster in the background. Every morning, you stare at yourself and see the tiny imperfections: the scars on your stomach and breasts and arms from digging into the skin, the patches of eyelashes, and the smear on your arm where the makeup rubbed away from your eyebrow as you were sleeping. Mocking your struggle, the mirror reminds you that you will never look "normal."

Normal

What is "normal," anyways?

Outlier

The DSM-V-TR classifies trichotillomania as an "impulse-control disorder not classified elsewhere." Basically, it's an outlier and psychiatrists don't know where to put it. So you float in limbo, because five years ago they believed it was similar to obsessive-compulsive disorder, but now they believe it's closer to Tourette's syndrome. How would you feel if you were classified simply by being "not classified elsewhere?"

Peace

You never feel completely "at peace." You know there will always be another hair, another urge, another pull, another scar. And you cannot pull everything. You notice that the girl next to you in psychology class has one hair on her eyebrow that juts out differently than all the rest. The cashier who swiped your credit card at Starbucks has a line of hair on his neck that he must've missed earlier that morning. You can't pull out their hairs. You try to calm yourself. You have to calm yourself. *There's more to life than an out-of-place hair, Katie.*

There's more to life than an out-of-place hair?

There's more to life than an out-of-place hair.

Quit

"Can't you just stop?" your dad asks in the evening when he comes home from work and notices you sitting on the couch playing with your hair.

"Don't you think if I wanted to stop, I would?" you find yourself yelling back.

"Just put your hands down."

"I can't."

"Fine. Then go in the other room where I can't see you."

Your mom enters the scene.

"Honey, she can't just stop!" your mom snaps.

"Yes, she can! She will!" your dad barks back.

"It's not that simple! You don't get it!"

"Fine!"

"Fine!"

You can't just stop and you can't make them stop.

Revlon

You never leave your house without your Revlon tweezers. In fact, you own four pairs. You know you should try to go a day without them, but the one time you lost them you spent over two hours tearing apart your room just to find them. They're the only way you can stay focused temporarily.

Self-Harm

You tell people you're not depressed. Trichotillomania does not equal cutting. Trichotillomania is about pulling for relief. Sure, it hurts, but that's not the point. The point is that pain is a by-product that comes when you try to "fix" everything.

Time

"What took you so long?"

"I was just getting ready."

"For over an hour? What were you doing?"

"Oh…just, fixing things."

Understanding

You drag your father to informational conferences and send your friends video clips in the hopes that they comprehend your condition.

Can you sympathize with that which you do not understand?

Visibility

Sometimes you notice hairs underneath the skin and have yet to disconnect from the rest of the body. But if they are dark enough to be visible through a few thin layers of white flesh, they are dark enough to pull. Your body has become a feeding ground, characterized by the pricking and jabbing of safety pins, nail clippers, and tweezers, only to leave a trail of blood and scars.

Why?

"Why do you pull out your hair?"

"It feels good."

"Do you feel stressed?"

"I don't know."

"Why can't you stop?"

"I don't know."

Xanthous

Xanthous [zan-thuh s]: Pertaining to people with yellowish, red, auburn, or brown hair.

You add your own word:

Trichotilloxanthous: 1) pertaining to a person who pulls out her yellowish, red, auburn, or brown hair, or 2) pertaining to a person who dyes her hair red to keep others from noticing her bald spots, or 3) pertaining to a person with yellowish, red, auburn, or brown hair who does not know how to stop pulling it out.

Yes

Yes, one day I will have eyelashes.

Yes, one day the urges will subside.

Yes, I can stop this.

Yes, I will stop this.

Yes.

Zillions

Zillions of hairs cover the human body. You know you can never fix all of them, but you try anyway. At the same time, you always try something else; you try to stop. Just because there's no known cure doesn't mean you should accept futility. So until a day comes when you have found the perfect solution, you just start over. Everyone has to start somewhere, and for you it might be as simple as saying "head up hands down" and once again preparing for battle.

Kosette Isakson
George Fox University
"My Mother the Naturalist"

My childhood ran on a system of points. The points never added up
to anything, but there was always a way to earn more points or to lose
the ones you had. My mom was the keeper of the points.

"Oh, extra points for you!" she said if I emptied the dishwasher or
one of my sisters gave her a compliment.

She bribed us with points, too.

"What do I get if I help you cook dinner tonight?" I might ask.

"Lots of points," she would answer. The points never had a specific
amount, simply "a lot" or "extra." They could also be "big points" or
"major points," if we did something particularly special.

"Extra points to whoever can find the most treasures," she announced
at the start of a hike to Skilak Lake. "Treasures" could be many
things—bird feathers, wild flowers, animal tracks, pieces of trash (to
be thrown away), or the ever-exciting animal scat on the trail. Inexplicably questing after these meaningless points, we always managed to
find treasures. In this small way, my mom taught me to view all parts
of nature as precious and exciting.

In her poem "Messenger," Mary Oliver addresses this idea that there
is always something to be found, noticed, and appreciated. She writes,

> …Let me
>
> keep my mind on what matters,
>
> which is my work,
>
> which is mostly standing still and learning to be astonished.
>
> The phoebe, the delphinium.
> The sheep in the pasture, and the pasture.

Like Mary Oliver, my work is loving the world. I learned this from my parents, especially my mom, beginning with spending time outdoors and finding those treasures of nature.

I was lucky. My childhood was steeped in nature. My dad worked hard each year to give us countless summer adventures. My mom also gave me a gift, one that took me eighteen years to fully appreciate. My mom taught me to see.

She opened my eyes to the world of nature I live in. She taught me to watch chickadees and nuthatches as they eat birdseed from the feeders and raise families. She taught me to marvel at the red headed woodpeckers. She showed me the geese and mallards as they migrated each year. She taught me about the garden by letting me plant, water, weed, and harvest everything from carrots to flowers to raspberries for making jam. All this she taught me in our yard. But my childhood wasn't confined to the yard.

My childhood was wild.

 I grew up in Hidden Lake Campground, the Kenai Canoe Lakes, Resurrection Pass, the Yukon Territory, the San Juan Islands. My bedroom was a tent, my nightlight was the moon, my lullaby was the eerie call of the loon. My mom taught me to eat the new, soft needles of spruce trees for vitamin C and to fry fiddlehead ferns in butter in the spring and pick wild blueberries in the fall. It has taken me a while, but I now realize what a treasure it was to have a naturalist as a mom.

Resiliency

Nothing ever fazes her. Nothing slows her down. Whether it is forgotten pieces of gear, blisters on her feet, or unexpected rainstorms, she handles the situation. In fact, she takes it on like an exciting challenge. For my mom, the glass is always half full, and she can make it all the way full by cutting off the empty part.

She does not allow the cold or the rain to ruin a trip. I learned quickly as a child that when it rains we just put up our tarp or grab our raincoats and keep going. If the rain continued without ceasing as it did one stormy afternoon on the day I turned eight, my mom simply said, "Get in your tent and wait until morning. Happy birthday."

Down vests and hot chocolate can always cure the chills and a crackling fire can make the rain seem minor. There is nothing my mom likes better than the challenge of creating comfort and order in the midst of nature's extremes. This is the clash between Mother Nature and Mother Isakson—the former can oftentimes be harsh and unforgiving, but the latter has taught me to rejoice in the little things and accept the hardships of nature along with the fun.

There are no showers or toilets on a trip to the wilderness. Taking this challenge, my mom makes personal hygiene the afternoon entertainment as she washes her hair with river water off the side of the raft or uses the leftover warm dish water to shave her legs. In the middle of a hot, sweaty afternoon of hiking mile after mile, she makes everyone stop and offers extra points to anyone who walks out into the freezing stream and sticks their head under the water.

Occasionally there is a slip in the careful planning and packing process, and when my mom gets ready to make oatmeal for breakfast, she discovers we forgot the oatmeal. Unconcerned, she simply uses a handful of nuts, some butter, leftover packets of instant oatmeal or cream of wheat and maybe some syrup—she stirs it all together and tops it with wild huckleberries growing nearby.

The simple relief of a warm, dry tent at the end of the day always manages to bring my mother joy and keeps her looking forward. She can't wait to get up in the morning and start the fire and boil water. She can't wait to load the canoes and push off on the day's journey. She can't wait to find a camp and make it a home. She can't wait to climb into her tent after the fire has died down and the stars peek out from the clouds. She lives in perpetual anticipation for what comes next, and this is how I strive to live my life now.

The Birds

At first it was just the little ones who came to eat from our feeder and nest in our birdhouses—chickadees and nuthatches, mostly.

I learned their names and listened to their singing. My mom always pointed out the beautiful red-headed woodpeckers, and I would rush to the window and press my face against the glass, as though the woodpecker was about to set off fireworks.

We watched birds from the back porch or from our big front window. Sometimes there would be a loud thump, and we knew a bird had flown straight into the glass. I ran to the window to look down and see it. We kept the cats inside, and I went out to check on it, the tiny body lying in the snow, stunned. Usually they recovered and flew away. But not always. Once I buried a bird I found on our neighbor's front path. It was a stunningly beautiful Bohemian waxwing; its brown feathers still smooth with the perfect red and yellow markings and a drop of blood on its beak. I buried it in our garden and marked the spot with a rock.

My mom knew the birds by their calls. When we were out hiking in Alaska or in Washington, she could identify the sparrows and warblers by their songs, and she would tell us what they were singing.

"That one is saying, 'I'm a little pretty bird!'" she said in an exaggerated copy of its tune.

When the birds were talking to each other, mom knew what they were saying. This opened up a whole new world for me. I learned to look at birds, and all of nature, as a living, relational community.

My mom knew the sea birds, the songbirds, the big birds, the ground nesters and migrants. She fed the little ones peanut butter all through the winter to keep them warm and full. She volunteered to be a "baby bird mom" for birds who fell out of nests, feeding them until they were strong enough to fly away.

Once during my sophomore year of college, while driving with my roommate and her brother from Oregon to Washington, I commented on all the geese, hawks, and ravens I had seen on the drive.

My roommate turned to me and said, "Why do you always notice birds?"

I paused, unsure of how to answer the question. Didn't her mom ever teach her to notice the birds?

The Garden

My mom begins gardening before spring arrives. She starts the seeds in small trays and puts them under heat lamps in the house before moving them to the greenhouse and finally to the yard. In the summer when I answer the phone and the call is for her, I can find her somewhere in the yard, kneeling in a circle of smoking mosquito coils, her hands in the dirt, preparing the ground for columbines, lilies, or foxgloves.

When I look around our yard I can see a small paradise, the results of her work—blooms of all colors and shapes, hanging baskets, railroad tie boxes of vegetables, two swings, a pond with a small fountain, all backed by a greenbelt of Sitka spruce and birch trees with various bird houses hidden in the branches.

Like many things, the garden started out as a chore for me. I liked to plant the carrots because it only took one afternoon, and I liked to eat them when they grew by the end of the summer, but I didn't like to turn over the dirt in the spring or weed the flower beds or transfer sprouts from their trays into the garden. As I got older, I began to enjoy the garden more, though I still like it best when mid-summer hits, and the work mostly includes pulling off dead blooms and harvesting raspberries or fresh lettuce.

My mom's lifelong devotion to her garden and continuous hard work to bring it to life each year has taught me to appreciate nature at home, not just in the wilderness. She has made our yard into a welcoming place for the birds and the butterflies and even bigger animals. I often look out onto the yard to see a mother moose and her calf sleeping in the afternoon sunshine leaving imprints in the grass.

Although I didn't know it as a child, this act of gardening was an even more important part of being a naturalist than any of our camping trips could be. My mom helped me interact with my place at home, every day, taking an active role in the nature just outside our door.

While this didn't seem nearly as exciting to me then, I have since
learned how much can be gained by keeping a garden. John Muir may
have walked off into the mountains to be at one with the Sierras, but
Gilbert White's life work, *A Natural History of Selbourne*, was written
in and about the place where he spent his entire life observing. Like
Gilbert White, my mom is familiar with the soil, the insects, the native
and nonnative plant species, and the animals of the place where she
lives—all because of her garden.

The Stories

In my sophomore year of college I took a creative nonfiction writing
class and discovered a little more about the kind of writer I want to
be. I realized the beauty of the genre and knew that if I was ever going
to write something it would need to be about my own experiences.
Something about nature. Something about my life.

I should have known much earlier that creative nonfiction was right
for me—after all, my mom had read hundreds of true story accounts
of people's adventures. Mountain climbers, kayakers, canoeists,
hikers, sailors—if anyone had written the story of their adventure, my
mom had read it. She read nearly every book about the Pacific Crest
Trail, which might explain something about my obsession with it.
Her love of true adventures inspires me to write down my own. She
doesn't care much whether the author writes well or not, is creative or
fact-driven, or has ever written before. She likes them all because of
their honesty and because of their stories.

I am thankful for the opportunities my parents gave me to have experiences worth writing down. Aldo Leopold once wrote, "We grieve only
for what we know." My mom has taught me to know the natural world,
and while this has indeed brought me grief as I watch its threats and
struggles, it has also brought me unspeakable joy and peace. By having
a naturalist as a mom, I became a noticer like Mary Oliver.

Oliver declares her work is "mostly rejoicing, since all the ingredients are
here." Even as I prepare to graduate from college and eventually move

on from my life with my parents, I know I will always be finding
treasures, earning points, and embracing this work of rejoicing because
all the ingredients are here, and I now have the eyes to see them. No
matter where I go or what I do, I can notice the birds, the soil, the trees.
Learning to be a naturalist has enhanced my experience of life every
day by allowing me to see what goes on around me in a deeper way.

As I embrace my role and follow in my mother's footsteps, I begin to
understand her joy and her resiliency. When I pay attention to nature,
I can't help but rejoice and be thankful, even as I grieve. I go forward
now with a purpose and a vocation that will follow me wherever I go.
This is my ultimate treasure.

Megan Franzen
University of Minnesota Crookston
"The Game"

At first it's like a game of hide-and-go-seek. It's fun. It's simple. You follow it through an amiable maze, lost in a sense of pure contentment as you encompass one another in a shroud of mutual enhancement.

The trial of this maze, however, starts out as a one-time thing; it *always* starts out as a one-time thing. Nobody ever thinks they'll do it forever. Nobody ever believes that this game of hide-and-go-seek could take a deadly turn for the worse, disappearing behind a corner and switching places with the deadly gamble of Russian roulette.

No, it's simply *fun*. It's not a need. It's not a craving. It's not an unavoidable necessity that would drive you to do unthinkable acts of horror.

It's *fun*.

The first step of the game starts off with a snort or a puff; it's nothing intimidating, nothing to be afraid of. You're offered it cordially like it's an honor. So, you take it like one.

The veterans around you inject needles in their arms, inhaling sharply as they plunge the taunting liquid through their veins. You are invited to join them in their quest, but you decline. Needles are for the people who *need* it. Needles are for the people who have let it manifest into a dark chasm of deadly craving. Needles are for the people who have let the fun get out of control.

But you won't let it escape your grasp. It's a game of hide-and-go-seek, and this is *your* game. You'll always be one step ahead of it, watching with a knowing eye and ready to stop at any moment if the game isn't fun anymore.

You're better than those other screw ups; you're special.

Special as you may be, though, you still find yourself reluctantly scared;

this is the stuff your mother warned you about. This is the stuff the schools hid from you. This is the stuff that could get you in a *lot* of trouble.

But along with the fear comes the invigorating sensation of rebellion, and before you know it you've already done it, and there's no going back. You are ripped from the driver's seat of your life and forced to watch as the game takes the steering wheel.

Then, out of the nowhere, the initial fear you had is gone. Suddenly you're encapsulated in the warming blanket of peace. Entirely encompassed by pure serenity, you disown the warnings of your mother, and you forget the cautions of your school. This isn't like the other drugs; this one is simply pleasant.

It doesn't hurt you. It doesn't knock you out. It doesn't make you psychotic.

It simply makes you content.

Everything is pleasantly beautiful. You can't even describe the feeling; it's nothing like you thought it'd be. The sun is bright, lighting the dark room you're confined in with its tantalizing rays of affection. The feeling surrounding you is blissful, rushing through your veins, prickling across your skin, tingling throughout your brain, flooding into your eyes, ringing through your ears, fuming at your fingertips, steaming in your nose, and filling your soul with a calming sense of peace and ease.

How could something this good ever be thought to be bad?

The people you sit there with, however silent they may be, are suddenly your friends. You can't help the potent feelings of affection overtaking you as you are catapulted into a land of ecstasy, and you simply lay your head back, smiling slightly as sensations of happiness sweep over your skin.

This wave of bliss washing over you is tantalizing, so you decide to follow it. You chase the feeling of ecstasy in a delighted pursuit, begging the warming sensation of serenity to continue its course through your veins, allowing yourself to stay anchored in the dream you have been immersed in.

This game you have decided to play doesn't even feel like a game to you. It feels like being reunited with the innocence of childhood, eradicating any worry, fear, or doubt you may have had and replacing it with a euphoric splendor that charges through your being in an empowering surge.

For hours you sit there playing the game. For hours you are encapsulated in its warm embrace. For hours you let it drive your life, watching as it finds a way to ease your mind and stimulate your senses. For hours you allow the salvation to overcome you, reveling in the intense feeling of tranquility you had never before seen, and encouraging the essence of the game with welcoming arms.

The next morning you awaken to the sweet afterglow of the night before, a faint sense of peace drifting over your mind as you get ready and leave, wondering how this game could be considered deadly when it left you feeling so good.

There was no aftereffect. There was no hangover. There was no feeling of regret, nausea, illness or defeat. You simply felt empowered.

So, you decided to play the game again.

Pretty soon the game became a weekly diversion. The land of your dreams was sitting right beside you every second you resided in reality, reminding you of the glory of the high, and begging you to play just one more time.

Before you know it, someone is offering you a needle, and you look at it tentatively, remembering the time when you had vowed never to inject. You remember claiming that the people who inject are in need; they don't play the game, they are *owned* by the game. As you begin to shake your head, however, they tell you that it's no big deal.

It's the same as snorting it; it just makes it happen faster.

How could you argue with that logic?

The first time you do it you puke. Cradling the toilet like it's the only solid thing in your life anymore, you find yourself wondering why you ever did it in the first place. This game of hide-and-go-seek has taken its first turn for the worse, and you decide it's not fun anymore.

But it's not that easy.

You try again a day later in hopes of making it to the serenity again. They tell you it'll work this time. It'll feel good this time. You won't get sick this time.

And you don't.

Your veins throb with the elixir as it rushes throughout your body, and it hits you like a wall, eradicating any worries, fears, or doubts that you may have had and replacing them with the blissful sensation of absolute tranquility.

You revisit that state of warm relaxation that you have become so fond of, lapsing into a dream where nothing accompanies you but the mellow essence of felicity. The high has become a comfort blanket, and before too long you find yourself unwilling to let go.

It doesn't take long before the visits become a regular thing, and the game turns more into a chore. You're no longer amiably playing peek-a-boo with a feeling of ecstasy, but rather playing tag with a feeling of dread.

The high isn't a high anymore; it's become a state of normalcy. The throbbing through your veins now comes as a relieving salvation rather than a glorifying transcendence. You start to hate it. You hate the game, you hate the high, you hate the nightmare that has become reality, and you begin to hate yourself.

It becomes monotonous. It becomes a schedule. Stab. Live. Exist. Pain... Stab. Live. Exist.

A miserable agony reverberates through every part of your being. The skin that used to prickle with excitement now squirms with discomfort. The eyes that used to be flooded with euphoric colors of contentment were now flooded with the painstakingly horrifying images of reality. The soul that the used to fly free to the land of dreams was now imprisoned in the land of consequences, staring longingly through the bars at the normalcy you had taken for granted.

The drug has become a necessity. What was once the recreational essence of relief has morphed into the very elixir of life.

It is an obligation that cannot be overlooked.

The needle is your punishment, and every time you force it into your vein and are brought back into the state of normality, you are overcome with a feeling of relief and guilt, filling you with a concoction of confusion that brings back the anxiety that you so long to be rid of.

Reality has transformed into a nightmare, and what you had once called a dream is now an unsatisfying state of normalcy. The simple life you had once lived before partaking in the game seems so far behind you that you can't even remember what it was like. Existence now revolves around a needle, and everything you do is haunted by the terrifying whispers of death in your ear, reminding you that you can't avoid the game for too much longer.

Hide-and-go-seek is for children, and you're not a child anymore. You have seen the other side, and you'll never be able to just play hide-and-go-seek ever again.

The game has morphed itself into the dangerous gamble of Russian roulette. Every time you stab that needle in your arm, you are sitting there with a gun to your head, your body shaking and your head spinning as you force that grueling liquid to course through your resenting veins, waiting for the pounding of your heart to signal its arrival at your core. So far, the barrel has seemed entirely empty, but it won't take long for you to arrive at the bullet.

The bullet is small, black, daunting, and fearsome. It sits there waiting for you, and at first you are terrified of it.

You fear the time that the trigger is pulled and isn't accompanied by the hollow sound of an empty barrel. You are terrified for the booming sound of death to come shooting through your head, ripping you from the only life you have ever known and catapulting you into the cascading spiral of the unknown.

But pretty soon death seems better than the agonizing revolving spiral that you are trapped in. Soon enough that bullet becomes a desired token, symbolizing a release into salvation that only death seemed capable of delivering.

What was once your biggest fear becomes your greatest desire.

Pretty soon you can't take it anymore. The hatred you feel for the game and everything it consists of is so deep that it's tearing you apart from inside. Your tolerance has grown too high. The price has become too steep. The game is pulling ahead, and you are cowering in the background, watching as it swiftly overtakes your life and drives away with it, threatening to crash it and leave it to burn.

You have seen the other side. You have seen a side of the universe that you were never meant to experience.

The game has become your punishment.

Before too long you have people telling you that you need help. You have a problem. You're sick. You look like hell.

What do they know? They don't understand. It's not a choice anymore. The game has won. The game owns you. You'd do anything to get a pinch. All you need is a pinch.

Now you use it just to survive. You inject just to exist. You let it destroy your body in one last futile attempt to reach that high. Watching your life float by as though you're watching a movie, your conscious thoughts revolve solely around the game, and, even though it's not fun anymore, you can't walk away.

It's too late for that.

You become desperate. You no longer have the money to afford the normalcy. The demands of the high have become too steep, and it sits complacently on the tip of a mountain that your increasingly weak body can no longer climb.

Your parents realize the extremity of your condition when you come groveling to them for money. Unconcerned about your appearance and blinded to your issue by your tormenting needs, you lurk around town like nothing more than a ghost, striking fear in the hearts of those that loved you and pity in those that didn't.

Finally, they put you away.

You know what they're doing, but you don't care. They don't understand. None of them understand. You can't help it; you *need* it.

The rooms are small, the people are cold, and the air is frigid. Everything hurts. It all hurts. Nothing can make you comfortable. Nothing can help you but the high. You *need* the high.

Lost in a world of darkness and encompassed in a shroud of torture, you find yourself wandering helplessly through a hallway of agony and misery that seems to have no exit. Your body begins crumbling minute by minute, and for the first time you begin feeling the cold fingers of death start clawing at your skin.

You puke. You shiver. You convulse. You scream. You shout. You wail. You claw. You rip. You tear. You pound. You punch. You kick. You squirm. You writhe. You swear. You curse. You struggle.

You cry.

You cry like you have never cried before, and between your sobs you beg the Devil to come and claim you as his own. A pathetic junkie like you doesn't deserve to go to heaven. Surrounded by your sins and filled with your wrongdoings, you come to the realization that God doesn't care about you anymore. And why should he? He tried to warn you. He sent you signs. He made it obvious that the game was one only played by losers.

You didn't listen.

You were special.

You were going to beat the game.

A torturous cold encompasses your body as you cradle the toilet, puking up whatever your body had left to emit. Trapped in that icy room with nothing to warm your frozen soul, you scream into the emptiness, trying to conjure some sort of company to ease your pain.

The barrel isn't empty anymore. You can see the bullet. It's staring you right in the eye. Death smiles as his finger brushes the trigger, and in his gaze you can see the faint glint of satisfaction as he watches you squirm in terror.

Months later you will thank them for helping you eradicate the façade of a nightmare that the drug had draped over reality. You will thank them for putting up with your harsh words as you slashed at them and pounded on the walls. You will thank them for grabbing the gun from Death, throwing it in the trash and wrapping you up in a blanket to warm your icy body.

You will thank them for ending the game.

Your reality that had been, however, will never again be the reality that *is*. The game will always be there, watching you from a distance, trying to entice you with its dangerous possibilities. The faint disappointment in your parents' eyes will never truly fade, no matter how much they deny it. You had hurt them in a way that they will never truly be able to forgive, and every action you perform will be carefully watched, their gazes filled with a distant worry that will forever plague the back of their minds.

There are nights you refuse to succumb to the refuge of sleep. There are nights you do nothing more than cry, running your fingers gingerly over your scarred arms as your salty tears soak them with your regret.

You cry because you lost the game.

You cry because your reality is no longer normal *or* a dream. You reality has become tainted, filled with pitiful stares and weary glances. Society looks at you differently, unable to eradicate the image of a pitiful addict, cowering in the corner, trying in vain to beat the game that has never once seen a winner.

Hide-and-go-seek is meant to be fun, Russian roulette is meant to be exhilarating, and games are meant to ease the mind.

What is heroin meant to do?

Senel Wanniarachchi
University of Colombo (Sri Lanka)
"Becoming Me"

Bhoomi (then Kumudu) and I studied together at our all-boys college in Colombo. We weren't friends, really- he was one year senior to me, but I knew of him (everyone did). While we practiced for the Shakespeare Drama Competition at the college main hall, Kumudu and his friends practiced for their Sinhala dramas for the national level competitions. Kumudu would almost always play the female lead. For us- teenage school boys, this was quite a spectacle, and Kumudu and his friends would often be made fun of. They called him the 'p-word' (a Sinhala expletive) and all other kinds of names. While in my first encounters of Kumudu, he seemed taken aback and clearly distressed by the unending bullying. As time passed by, it seemed like Kumudu was unaffected by the endless name-calling and bullying; he even fought back a couple of times almost as if the bullying made him stronger and more resilient.

Once Kumudu completed his A-Levels, I never heard from him.

A couple of months back, an email invitation I received from the International Planned Parenthood Federation through the Family Planning Association of Sri Lanka said that I've been selected for a youth consultation on sexual and reproductive health and rights. The two other young people who were selected from Sri Lanka were Chamathya from the Girl Guides movement and someone by the name of Ms. Bhoomi Harendran.

At our first preparatory meeting at the FPA, I met Chamathya first. Then Bhoomi walked into the room--this tall girl dressed in a sari. There was something really familiar about Bhoomi, and it didn't take me long to realize that this was, in fact, Kumudu. 6 feet tall, with long straight hair, Bhoomi looked like any other girl you'd meet at the movies or at the crosswalks.

The conference in Bangkok made me understand the importance of sexual and reproductive health and rights and the need to ensure that all people are aware of and exercise these rights they are entitled to by virtue of birth. That one week we spent in Bangkok together also allowed Chamathya and me to actually get to know Bhoomi and listen to her story. This also allowed us to witness, first-hand, the stigma and prejudice that she experiences on a daily basis.

Chaz Bono once said that gender is between the ears and not between the legs. Kumudu always felt like a girl trapped in a boy's body. She grew up watching Madhuri Dixit, she wanted to be like her, to dance like her. She was her idol. As she grew up, she started nosing around her mom's closet. She had no examples of people experiencing what she was; this only reinforced the shame she felt. Playing female roles in college productions allowed Kumudu to be herself. It was probably her inability to blend in that made her audition for drama. That opportunity to feel like being true to herself, even for just a moment, was worth all the bullying, the hate crimes and the name calling. Ironically, even though stages are actually built to act, for Kumudu, it was as if she was acting everywhere else, trying to please the world, and she really felt like herself only onstage.

But drama couldn't drown the loneliness and the confusion. She was scared and felt like there was something wrong with her.

After she left school, Bhoomi started to grow her hair and nails and wear makeup. The changes "Made me feel more like myself," she said. She decided to undergo treatments and take hormones. Soon her parents and relatives excluded her from family gatherings, and finally she was asked to move out of the house. But no one offered her a place to live.

The look on the immigration officer's face when he saw Bhoomi's passport, the judgmental stares and flirtatious whistles of passers-by in the streets of Colombo (and Bangkok) mirrored how people are just used to a binary of black-and-white.

Looking back, I am ashamed I made jokes about Kumudu in school behind his back and I'm ashamed I couldn't stand up for him when other kids bullied him and called names and for not making an effort to get to know this brave young person. We were all products of an education system that doesn't even acknowledge the existence of, let alone the rights of people with non-binary gender identities.

Today Bhoomi has come a long way. She is a sexual and reproductive health and rights advocate trying to change societal attitudes about those issues. More than anything though, she is being true to herself and doesn't have to feel like she is living a lie. Her passion is to be a model and an actress. (This is on the verge of coming true!) One day she will have a sex confirmation surgery. She wants to fall in love, get married and be a mother, and she wants to be happy. (If that's not too much to ask for).

Srishti Chaudhary
University of Delhi (India)
Today I Cannot Write: The Legacy of our Colonizers

Writing about not being able to write is a common theme in literatures across the world. In modern terms, it is the writer's block, "the condition of being unable to think of what to write or how to proceed with writing." I attempt to relate the Indian experience of writing in English, and how subtly, yet profoundly, it is affected by the legacy given to us by our former colonizers, in the form of the 'universal' language, brilliantly beautiful yet irreparably hurtful.

On a trip to China two months back, I was chatting with a few associates, and they complimented me, telling me how good my English was, that it sounded just like standard English, that it had very little accent. I looked at them quizzically- but obviously- we studied in English medium schools, I studied English literature, we talk in English more than half the time. If a language is in use so much, why wouldn't we be good or fluent in it? We never went around complimenting each other in India on our English. And so they asked, do you also speak English at home with your family? No, I said, not so much- a little bit, but not so much as outside home. Aah, they said, so it is your social language. You use it, they explained, in your social circles and at your workplace.

Another time, another place. As school children, we went for an exchange to France, and again they had conceded, "Your English is very good. No, we French, we are the best in everything, you know. We are the best country in the world; America comes second, yes, but France is number one. But you guys, oh you guys definitely speak better English. Do you also speak it at home?" "No," I had said, "not at home no, not English- our social language."

 It can be stated safely, I am presuming, without reference to facts and stats, that for most Indians across the country, and by most I do mean more than ninety percent at the minimum, English is not their mother tongue; it is not their first language. Sure, we might have been conditioned to learn words like cat and bat, recite Johnny-Johnny to twenty smiling relatives, to say goodnight after dinner, but English was not our conversational language, at the beginning it was not. When I got hurt, I never went to my mother saying, "Look mommy, I got a boo-boo." No, I went to her saying, "*Mamma ek balti khoon nikla hai.*" I lost one bucket of blood- obviously an exaggeration there, but boo-boo, never came to my mind. English is not a language that our families gave us- it was a special gift by a special government for its dutiful citizens, a passcode into the world. Our families gave us Bengali, Hindi, Kannada, Assamese, Marathi, but English, our country gave us English.

English seeped into our lives like a language does. It came in the guise of how it became cooler to listen to English music when we were thirteen, how our teachers would say we'll be punished if we talk in Hindi at school, how claiming you understood every line in an English movie without subtitles gained you impressed looks, how we were given the choice to drop Hindi after class eight and take up any other foreign language. It seeped into our lives, disguising itself as our compulsory subject. You could pick math or physics or history; you could choose to study economics or psychology or accounts, but English, everybody had to study. It was the compulsory subject, whether you chose science or commerce or arts.

And so, how could it not seep into our writings? I was thirteen and it was the first time I attempted to write a fictional story on such a grand scale. The story was quite thrilling, honestly, and some days I still wish I had made something of it. *A terrorist group took over a school, deploying a terrorist in every classroom, as the children fought back using their pencils and compasses, chalk dust and water bottles, stationery stuff of a school life.* But I struggled, I struggled, and I struggled, not because I did not know the story or wasn't able to write it; I struggled because I could not name my characters. The Indian names all around me, the names of my friends and teachers, my own name indeed, did not sound real enough for an English story. It just did not seem authentic.

Matt, I named a character, because Matt sounded English; Matt seemed like he belonged in an English story. And my terrorist group called themselves The Jungle, yes, and their head was called The Lion. And when I was faced with the eventuality of choosing Indian names, because an average classroom in India is not filled with Matts and Lizzies and Ashleys, I tried to pick Indian names that could sound as un-Indian as possible. It wasn't due to any personal aversion that I harboured for Indian names; it was simply the sound of such names, sounds which never fit in English books. In all the stories that I had been made to read in school, all the books I had bought from the bookstore, all the TV shows that I watched, Lizzie McGuire and Hannah Montana- these stories never had an Akshita or a Shreya, an Aditya or an Anuj, names which were very popular at that time, names which were all around us in person, but never in the books we read.

Then there is the question of writing in English itself. Any story in the world, to make itself legible and publishable, dictates that it is narrated in a single language, barring its interspersion with foreign words or phrases, it is essential that the narration must be in one language. And then again it happened: my story had a grandfather, and how do I justify that he spoke such perfect English? I had never seen any grandfather to be so fluent in English. My story involved a squabble with the domestic help. How many women who swept your house every day, did the dishes and cooked the food, raked the leaves and collected the garbage, how many of them spoke in English? It was a conundrum that I just could not, and still cannot, sometimes, resolve. If everybody in the story spoke in English, the story did not sound real; it did not hold true; my characters lost grit.

"Fiction must stick to the facts," Virginia Woolf once said, "and the truer the facts, the better the fiction." So how do we deal with it? Something about it doesn't sound real. A lot of Indian characters speaking in English, and a lot of names, did not sound real, did not sound genuine. Yet we have to deal with that fact. I try to think of what language do I think in, maybe that will give a clue, but as soon as I try to determine my thinking language, I immediately forget what I'm thinking. My thoughts escape me, forever elusive. I start counting in Hindi, and then stop after a point, realizing that I do not know the counting beyond a certain number.

With the advent of internet technology, however, and the increasing realization of our globalized times, and the past few years when Indian fiction has erupted, it is easier to make peace with these facts. It is easier to relate the Indian experience in English because the experiences are made more common, more popular, normalized to a huge extent in the books we read and the articles we keep scrolling through our social media websites.

And yet there is a split, a split which all writers writing in English must face, whose mother tongue is not English. The split is in the self- personally, for me, the split in my Hindi self and my English self, in my home life and my public life, in my personal language and my social language. This split in myself- in two languages is my hindrance. It is because of this split that today I cannot write.

A lot of Indian writers have dealt with this split in incredibly creative ways. Anuja Chauhan frequently uses Hinglish words for an urban novel, which I feel is the strength of her style. Her style doesn't pose, as terms like yaar, arre, bhai, and toh among others become as commonplace in her stories as they are in real life. Amitav Ghosh uses unique narrative styles to find his way around relating this Indian experience in English. Arundhati Roy placed *The God of Small Things* in small town Kerala, where English is definitely more prevalent than the rest of the country, and even she uses Malyalam phrases and words frequently in her novel. Chitra Banerjee Divakaruni's *Palace of Illusions* narrates the *Mahabharata* from Drauapadi's perspective, a retelling of the epic. The theme of the story is so poignant and powerful that it automatically posits itself as outside normalcy, and we never need to connect it to contemporary reality. As for Tagore, I will never be able to understand how he does it. He places his stories and themes of suffering in such beauty that even his translations never seem to have undergone it.

However, the fact arises that one way or the other; we must deal with it, whether it may be by alienating our subjects or adapting contemporary usage of English as a language in a way that is relatable. The only other language that I know, Hindi, I am ashamed to admit I am not so good at anymore. I can speak it well, but I read it much slower in comparison to English. As for writing, I've been out of practice for years. It is my fault and the fault of so many others around me, the fault in our system, and hilariously so, the fault in our stars. And it is a beautiful language lost to me.

A lot of post-colonial writers talk about this as well. Kenyan writer Ngugi wa Thiong'o renounced his usage of English as colonialist and began to write in his native Gikuyu and Swahili. Nigerian writer Chinua Achebe talked about writing in English, but in a way that made it his own, away from the classical, traditional English. That is what we have happening in recent times; new words are added every day, curated and abbreviated by their context, especially with information technology. All countries which underwent colonialism go through the same experience.

On the other hand, think of countries like England, America and Australia. English, there, is the mother tongue for the majority; people of all classes speak it. The dialects and the slangs vary, but primarily, it is easier to represent that community in writing, because the split is not present. Then there are scholars who argue against homogeneity and for multilingualism. Aijaz Ahmad makes a case for multilingualism, that we are all capable of learning multiple languages fluently and using them in our day to day lives. It is only the system, which teaches us that we need to have a primary language.

But today, I cannot write, not because I don't know the story, or I am unable to write, but because I face a split in myself. I am unable to understand how to represent this uniquely Indian experience in a language that seems inadequate for it. With the ghost of a language that refuses to go away, and another language that is always inside me, but never truly feels mine, I must struggle to reconcile with this split, finding new ways every day to sound acceptable, in both worlds.

Wendy Rhodes
Florida Atlantic University
Oz

There are moments in life that forever change us — choices that shape the entire course of our futures. Decisions that are so monumental there is no turning back, and we never experience the world nor see ourselves the same way again. Today is one of those days.

Today, I escaped from prison.

I remember the day I was sentenced — a hot spring afternoon a lifetime ago. The sun sizzled like fire in the sky, and the ocean waves gently lapped the shore not far from where I stood. Adorned in white and surrounded by friends and family, I accepted the life sentence imposed by seven simple words:

"I now pronounce you husband and wife."

I had married my angel. The one who vowed to take care of me and love me as we grew old together. The one who shared my hopes and dreams. The one who would lay down his life to keep me safe and protect me from the world outside our walls.

Our walls. The four walls that became my cell throughout the painful years that refused to end. The four walls that separated me from everything and everyone I loved. The four walls that hid the secrets of the hell I shared with my angel.

Like Dorothy, what began as a dream devolved into a nightmare from which I could not awaken. I believed I was following the yellow brick road to Oz, but instead found myself crushed by a falling house.

My angel could not keep a job. He devoted his days to drinking, laced with heavy drug usage. I was a cheerleading nursemaid. I nurtured him, encouraged him with patience and compassion. I played the role of supportive wife better than Meryl Streep.

He joined Alcoholics Anonymous. Repeatedly. But with each relapse his desire to control and manipulate me increased. His anger intensified. The scope of his abuses widened. The only thing that didn't change was my willingness to believe his lies.

"This time will be different. I love you. You are the best thing that has ever happened to me. I need you."

And then he would relapse again.

During those times, my angel told me I was worthless. He spewed forth venom like a deviant serpent from the fiery underworld. He exploited my deepest fears and used them to try to destroy me. He told me that my life would be over without him.

In a futile attempt to convince myself, I assured everyone that my life was good. I became an Academy Award winning actress. I was happily married to my angel. We were trying to have a baby. And as I performed scene after scene of my carefully scripted deception, I secretly thanked a God I did not believe in that my prison was not made of glass.

Because, unlike me, glass cannot pretend to be something it is not. Glass is transparent, and I did not want anyone to see what I had become. I did not want anyone to see the fear, the shame, and the humiliation of having allowed my life to become so desperate.

"Marriage is forever. You must stand by your husband. It is not his fault. He doesn't mean to hurt you. If you love him enough, he will change."

I was glad no eyes could penetrate the walls of my prison. They would have witnessed the rage, the aggression, the abuse in every imaginable form. They would have seen my cries and the anxiety caused by my escalating fear of my own husband. They would have found me married to a man I loathed, gazing into a mirror that reflected the image of a person I no longer knew.

My world had become not unlike Dorothy's — a land where trees threw rotten apples at me and flying monkeys threatened me at every turn.

I had nothing. My angel had stolen everything of value and sold it for drugs. He had destroyed much of the evidence of my life before him. He had taken my ruby slippers. I had nothing left but my angel and the four walls of my prison.

And then one day it happened. I remembered Glinda the Good Witch telling Dorothy that she had the power to go home all along, and that she needn't look any further than her own back yard.

So I searched my own backyard. And there I found it. Buried beneath my child-bearing years, my self-esteem, my little-girl dreams, and the evil mirror in which I could no longer bear to look, I found it.

My courage.

And this morning, after my angel left to meet his mistress, I dug it up. I walked to my car, not pausing for a moment to look back, to ponder what could have been or to wonder what I might have done differently. And I drove away.

I imagine him watching me drive. My angel. Except now I see that my angel has horns. And a pitchfork.

Today I escaped from prison — paroled by the courage that was buried in my own backyard the entire time.

What will become of me? Will I find Oz or will another house drop on me?

Suddenly, as a promising breeze blows through my hair and tears of relief stream from my eyes, I see it. I see it gleaming gloriously on the horizon!

The Emerald City.

Ryan Skayrd
University of Central Florida
Smaller Moments

I cradled the small box in my right hand, keeping the label faced downward. The man in front of me wore a windbreaker with a pixelated, camouflage print, and the woman behind the counter smiled at him—a crescent moon, ear-to-ear kind of smile that revealed paralleled dimples on her cheeks. The cigarette boxes behind the register framed her in multicolored rectangles hidden with golden words of health warnings. The line behind me grew like a game of Centipede; every time I looked behind me there seemed to be another person and now the line started to wrap around the closest aisle. I could feel sweat under my hoodie.

"Hello. Are you in our rewards program?" the woman asked me once I stepped forward.

"No."

"Is this all today?"

"Yes."

She scanned my item. "Would you like a bag?"

"Yes, please."

I slid my debit card and began answering more questions: *Is this amount correct? Cash back? Would you like to donate to St. Jude's today?*

Yes. No. Not today.

I took the bag from her and tried to smile. "No receipt, thanks," I said, already walking toward the glass doors.

***

"So how many do you take in a day?" she asked me.

"Depends."

"On average, then."

My arms remained crossed. This was our third session together.
"Maybe three or four."

"Three or four per day?"

I nodded. She wrote something down on her yellow notepad.

Everything in her office was beige, the color of coffee with just enough
cream—the walls, the rug, her hair. Reruns of "The Office" circulated
in the waiting room, but inside, it stayed just as bland as I remembered from my visits weeks prior.

"And you sleep more than normal now," she said. "So you don't
exercise a lot?"

"Sometimes." The light sliced through the curtains, creating a white
line against the bookshelf behind her.

"What kind of exercise do you do?"

"Sometimes I run."

***

It felt like the lights were getting brighter somehow. I returned to
my dorm shaking with sweat, damp against my hoodie. Today was
a good day—three miles in 27 minutes. I made sure to drink enough
water to flush out any sodium leftover in my body that might have
been bloating me. I had been trying to drink a gallon per day.

Shakiness was normal after a run, but today, I felt different. I couldn't
focus. My tiny dorm seemed to be smaller somehow, closing in
slowly, trapping me in this place I call my body like a cage without
bars. Words became deceptive puzzle pieces that I could not quite
fit together, and my thoughts were somehow external rather than
coming from within, floating around me like cigarette smoke before it
gets lost in the air. My heart rate increased, pumping like music with a
steady bass, blurring my vision. I paced. I had to keep moving.

"I think there's something wrong," I told my mom over the phone. Five minutes in, my throat felt like it was closing, my trachea moving in on itself like a fist.

"Just breathe," she said. "You're having a panic attack."

"No, something's wrong, mom," I said. I convinced myself I was dying. She didn't know I hadn't eaten that day, or anything since lunch the day before—a carefully calculated garden salad (220 calories) with three tablespoons of balsamic vinaigrette (120 calories). I told myself that after the run, I deserved something bigger to eat.

"Ryan, you're stressing yourself out," she said. She told me that this time in my life is hard because of the transition and something about prioritizing what I wanted.

She stayed on the phone with me until my breathing became steady again. Before we hung up, she added, "Maybe you should talk to someone."

I didn't want to talk to anyone, but I promised her I would. I didn't want help. I wanted to be skinny. I wanted to be thin like I used to be. But in my fogginess, after the panic episode, all I wanted was food.

***

I walked into the gas station with the same goal as usual. I had to make sure I got enough food to fill me up without making it obvious it was just for me. The more food and the more diverse the snacks were, the more it looked like I was buying food for other people. I preferred salty, but often would buy a couple candy bars filled with dripping caramel and cloudy chocolate to round out the cravings.

The best parking spots were on the sides of the building away from the glass fronts. I put my car in park and took a chug of my Coke Zero. With the nutritional facts facing away, I opened the bag of Flaming Hot Cheetos, an appetizer that left red, fingertip scars as a savory, lingering reminder of the taste. I slowly scraped each fingertip with my teeth, biting and digging under each fingernail for every last taste. The Fig Newtons were easy to get down quickly, followed

by the peanut M&Ms. When I opened the bag and poured a handful
of the colorful beads in my hand, he was already at my window. He
nodded, as if to say hello. His beard was the same color gray as the
hair that stuck out under his wide-brimmed hat that shadowed most
of his face. Appreciate

"Excuse me," he said with the window between us. I rolled it down
just enough to hear him.

"Hello," I said as I cupped the M&Ms in my hand. The heat had
already made the pieces dot rainbow colors on my palm—green
glazed against my life line.

"Spare change?" he asked. "Anything? Just trying to eat."

"I'm sorry, I really don't have anything."

"Then what's that?" At first I thought he meant the M&Ms, but I saw
him pointing at cup holder filled with coins. Silently, I reached with
my free hand and grabbed a fistful.

"It's not much, man," I said. I rolled the window down more with my
elbow, just to fit my hand through.

"It's something," he said. "'Preciate it."

Before he could ask for more, I rolled up my window and told him
to have a nice day. I drove away, looking into my rearview mirror,
watching him walk around the corner into the gas station, wondering
what his lunch would be. I drove back to my dorm, eating the candies
one by one.

***

"Let me ask you something," she said during one of our sessions.
"Are you controlling the food? Or is the food controlling you?"

***

I smoked cigarettes on the fifth floor of the parking garage near my
dorm. It was usually empty there. I sat on the edge of the concrete
wall and flicked my cigarette, watching the ashes burn out into the

night. I created constellations from embers the size of dust. The star systems I studied told me I was smaller than I thought, while the drifting ashes reminded me I was bigger.

I felt better when I left because I allowed my body to feel something other than hunger. My neck was sore from staring into the sky, my lungs tired, and I walked back to my dorm passing signs that warned of alligators.

***

"Stand here." Her hands felt light on my shoulders like the straps of an empty backpack. She flipped her yellow-paged notepad to an empty page and handed it to me with a pencil. I gazed into the full length mirror on the other side of the room. She stood behind me and spoke softly. "Draw yourself," she said. "I'm going to step out of the way so you just see yourself. I want you to draw what you see."

I looked at myself. My eyes were greener than usual that day, and my striped sweater hid any imperfections I found on my body; it hung limp around my torso. My beard was getting longer than usual. I hoped I could hide my cheeks that way.

"Whenever you're ready," she said.

The more I looked at myself, the more I didn't want to recreate my body on paper, the more I didn't want to eat.

But I did. I always did. That's why the pills were necessary.

***

I sat in Modern European History during the spring of my freshman year, and I couldn't feel them through my jeans. Usually, before I left I would make sure to hide at least one in my pocket, two if I knew I'd be gone a while.

I searched my pockets while the professor discussed World War II. "Now, from our reading, who can list some of the Axis powers?"

I took out my wallet and opened it in my lap, pushing old receipts and the backup condom hoping to find any hint of blue underneath. I thought it could have fallen in somehow.

"Germany, Italy, and Japan," I heard someone say.

I know I have one. I placed my keys, wallet, and phone on my desk while my peers around started to watch me. I sat up enough to search my back pockets.

"How 'bout the Allies?" the professor asked.

It was obvious that I was searching for something now as I moved in my confined space; the desk that was too small, and the plastic chair too hard below. I turned my front pockets inside out. The pill, about the size of a pinky nail, fell to the ground. I picked it up, already knowing the people around me saw. They probably wondered what I was on or what the pill was, if that was the reason I acted so frantic. Maybe they were right.

"And what year did the US enter the war?"

I looked downward for the rest of the class, pretending to take notes though not knowing what I was writing.

***

The word lingered between us. It sounded heavy. The bulbous, round *B* fell like balloons without helium, the long *e*'s screeched like rubbing Styrofoam. I protested.

"That's not it," I said. I told her I was trying to look better, that I was health conscious. I worded it that way, too. Health conscious.

"Bulimia isn't about throwing up all the time," she told me. "Your system is becoming dependent on the laxatives." She said something about taking probiotics and drinking kombucha to help my system get back into a normal rhythm. I tried kombucha once before. It tasted like feet.

I still didn't understand. I was a guy. I was trying to lose a little weight I gained. That's all.

"It's not always about throwing up," she said. "Using laxatives is a bulimic tendency, Ryan. It's the same thing, just from two different ends."

***

Eventually, I promised her that I would throw out my laxatives. And I did. "You should try something small in the morning, too," she told me. "Like a banana or yogurt."

I'll admit it helped sometimes. Starting the day with something healthy made me promise myself to continue this way. The 500 calorie days became fewer, but on those days, when I was left with my brain screaming at me in hunger, my organs churned and begged for something other than water. One night, I returned to the same spot in the McDonalds parking lot, and I parked my Toyota 4Runner under the yellowing hue that glowed onto my dashboard from the light above. I could almost see where the ketchup dripped from my hamburger onto my center console. One burger down. One large fry. Another burger. A kid's meal. Three chocolate chip cookies for a dollar.

I returned to my dorm and needed a laxative. I searched my medicine cabinet for a forgotten box only to find sample packets of face wash and travel sized hand creams taken from hotels. I could feel this food inside of me, the grease and fat mixing into my system. I could feel the fat spread like a virus. I looked into my reflection, at the sink, at my toothbrush resting in its gray holder. I flicked the bathroom fan on. The white noise hum filled the room.

It's the same thing, just from two different ends. I heard clearly.

The grout in between the floor tiles dug into my knees, creating lines like X and Y intersections in my skin. I held the toilet with my left hand and looked into the water shaped by a broken ring of mold. I gripped my toothbrush in my right hand, the bristles digging into my palm.

I started slowly, seeing how far I could go before I gagged. The end of my toothbrush tasted like leftover peppermint candies as I guided it slowly into my mouth, onto my tongue, grazing over my taste buds, jamming it into the back of my throat.

My eyes became glossy and I released a broken howl from within.
A roaring croak. My back arched, my spine curved, my nose filled
with the same hot liquid that I tasted in my mouth. It looked like an
exorcism. Looking down, I saw it hit the water, landing and sinking
under the water's surface like a feather in midair until it touched the
porcelain bottom. The taste lingered for a while until I used the same
toothbrush to clean my mouth.

I looked down into the toilet with my eyes still pink and wet. The pile
of thick, gristled fluids rested against the white like a child's smeared
finger painting. Below me sat everything I was scared of, but yet
somehow, I felt relieved. I felt accomplished. I stood there for a while
mesmerized, my throat gritty and dank, until finally I flushed. The
water invaded in a rushing spiral, breaking apart the settled pieces
from their resting places and taking the hot liquid and broken parts
down into the toilet, to a place I could not quite see.

Lindsey Campbell
Southern New Hampshire University
"The Square Root of Infinity"

With a smooth movement, he has lifted the solid metal object from the box and placed it gently on the desk. It's cylindrical, steel gray, about 16 inches in diameter, and around 30 pounds. He blows off dust and rakes aside layers of brown spider webs. He investigates the prototype, scrutinizing the contraption rapturously, and then goes to work with a Q-tip in the crevasses, working his long fingertips around the lip of the hand-machined rotor. His eyes forceful, his brow fixed, he pauses, strokes his long beard with a thick hand, and stares for a long time.

The first bolt proves more difficult to remove than he had thought, and he has to hold the metal and grip hard. The dark shadows drifting through the open window curve along the sinew of his back; his long auburn hair falls forward over his shoulder brushing his wrists; rain patters in black puddles and pours off the tin gutters and the forest with crackles and pings. Slowly the bolt loosens and then releases. It is a testament to the age of the drive, which had been sitting in a mossy cabin in Oregon for an undistinguished amount of time before it made its way to California, to our bedroom.

He sets aside the socket wrench, placing it carefully on the tottering table, and reaches to me. The backs of his fingers are smooth on my cheek. As I've learned to do when a man reaches for my face, I brace myself against his power and refuse to flinch; I'm surprised, again, when he comes to me with grace and tenderness. My anger has nowhere to go and dissipates around me like a vapor, and I could swear I become lighter.

He is shirtless, standing over me where I curl on the bed spread, the desk lamp behind him dazzling his tawny skin, a silky and hard man with hair glistening from his cheek bones to his neck and across his chest, down the cleft of his abs to the top of his jeans. Straight rust-blonde hair to his belt, flaxen and flickering over his forehead; bearded and rippled and divine. He will not walk by me without acknowledging me: a wink, a gaze, a smile of affirmation. I marvel at him, the miracle of his presence. I can't believe it. He is carved of gold.

Our living space is condensed and tiny, the way we are most comfortable, and the cream walls look a ruddy yellow in the darkness. In it is contained a double bed, a fold-up table or desk with a flowered red table cloth, an antique steamer trunk for storage, eight square feet of speakers from which currently a deep cello pulses; an ozone machine, a coffee maker, a bedside table he crafted from wood and a milk crate, two mismatched wooden chairs, a small strip of floor, and him. He is a tall rugged mountain man who reads with glasses and braids his hair, who listens to opera and to hip-hop, who cooks and cleans and builds houses. He honors my few special objects and expects the same of me; the force of his charge prickles the hair on my arms.

The rain releases in a loud electric down-pour that rocks the trees outside the window, the trunks moaning and cracking, the needles whipping and churning. He reaches again to the desk behind him, where he works by night, neat and squarely piled dress-right-dress with his scraps of notes and equations, a laptop, a pipe and lighter, a neat mug of pencils, the twisted sprout of a cedar bonsai, tea with honey, and an electric pencil eraser; then he presents a dusty old manuscript, water-stained with who-knows-what, corners chewed and sagging, clearly an object of both intense love and hate. Someone's murdered infant. Some man's aborted love child. An intriguing man who has died a quiet lonely death surrounded by greasy soldering irons and Tesla coils and silvery titanium rods and an old cracked yellow typewriter.

"This is the detailed description of the motor. As I take it apart, I can see each component individually, and then I can figure out why it's not working. And fix it," he adds with a wink. He leafs through a few yellow pages and points to some shapes and numbers. I'm aware of the heat of his shoulder, the lamplight refracting off the whiskers of his neck, the curve of his bare spine disappearing beneath his jeans.

"I have no idea what that is," I say. "But if you read it with your pants off I bet I'll understand it better."

He chuckles because he knows I am capable. He will explain it to me over again as long as I ask. I'm not a burden to him.

My husband had almost made me forget what a strong man looks like. In my childhood, I learned that women are the strong ones, not men at all. Like most weak men, my husband looked outside himself for his own definition; when I would not provide, he lashed out, coiled and struck, angry at my security. He could not stand the idea that my happiness should exist outside of him; like a starving person whose stomach rejects nourishment, he pushed me out, bit off my self-agency and then found it indigestible. He pushed and pulled against the weight of my armor until he tired himself out. And I left. Our marriage certificate is lost in an abandoned junk drawer somewhere in a forgotten past life.

The night rain outside the open window momentarily lulls to a steady shower and percolates through the pines, blackening the bark and sending a cool wind swirling through the room. He points to the diagram and delicately explains the equations. He's articulate and he smells like split wood.

The prototype is an electric motor made of two spinning titanium discs, magnetized rotors that when rotating in different directions ionize the particles to produce an electromagnetic field. More electricity than is actually used, so this is a generator and an alternator and an electric motor in one. Hand-made and designed in a mossy old cabin in Oregon by a dead man we've never met. I never would have known what the thing was. He knew what it was immediately.

I sift with curiosity through the documents, titled in calligraphy with a curling blue letterhead, and come across a bundle of decaying envelopes containing letters from the Department of Defense, the Canadian Defense Counsel, the Tesla Convention of Inventors of America. We have considered your design, we have reviewed your work, thank you for your contribution. Filed by date, 1980 through 1984. There are patents with elaborate drawings, carefully drawn graphs displaying test results and analysis, pages and pages of exhausting mathematical equations. There are also letters from a woman. One by one as the bolts are painstakingly loosened and removed, he places each one neatly on the table and cautiously gives the top rotor a wiggle. A cold gale blows rain into the room and the light briefly flickers dim. He lifts the rotor and sets it aside revealing the rusted steel discs beneath, and grows quiet and contemplative.

The pages of the manuscript are soft and droop between my fingers. I discover that it's an autobiography. I read quietly, with the intensity of a husband reading his cheating wife's diary:

The Wall of Light: Part 1.

The Life of Tesla.

Large-Print written, so you can understand it. (By Nikola Tesla).

Written 1919, Published 1971,

HEALTH RESEARCH.

Books are our sordid slow painful foreplay; intellectual probing has become the prelude to hard fast sex. Our only sense of the passing of time is evidenced by the growing collection of books on the shelf. It has a blend of Hawking and Dawkins, Nostradamus and Harris, R.R. Martin and Twain; our topics ranging from pseudoscience to anthropology to faith to musical theater and lots between. But dark secrets come in dusty boxes, and we cannot conceal our intrigue. It was all headed to the dump, but someone realized better and intervened. "I'll take all that to the dump for you," he'd offered. Now the boxes occupy our bedroom, and we occupy our time with a stranger's unfinished story.

My husband never understood the meaning of completion. In all honesty, I never did, either. Poor guy, so small and soft, so ineffectual; The Couch Potato who thought it was a Man. The man towering over me is everything that he would have feared: Norse, blue eyed and tough, confident. With a thunder bolt, he would be Zeus. With a hammer, he would be Thor. When he could crush, he is gentle; where he could conquer, he builds. I want him to rape and pillage me.

"Do I treat you like a piece of meat?" I once asked.

"Yeah, but it's fun sometimes."

I open the old manuscript, inhale a draft of soil and lichen, and begin to read.

Page 1. The progressive development of man is vitally dependent on invention.

Beneath the top rotor lies an eight-pointed plate made of layers of rusted steel." This is badass, he says twice. Look, he says. I have to clean this rust, but when this is running, it will spin and produce enough energy to power itself plus run the whole house." I drift into oblivion staring at his curved lips and a neatly groomed red-blonde mustache and a beard past his whiskered throat.

I want you to fuck me, I say.

He's getting used to my mouth. I do not hide behind propriety. I have always been too honest.

I once told my second husband that my life could best be described as a series of small projects. "Life is constitutive, and you're here because I made a spot for you," I said. He didn't understand, took my boundaries as a threat, but I shrugged it off the way I'm known to do and continued constructing my life, one board and nail at a time, sometimes loving what I had produced and sometimes loathing it and tearing it back down. I didn't seriously consider the role of a husband in the constitution of what I was planning; like glue under a nail, or caulking under a screw, the men I had brought into my world had served superficial roles, simply there to weatherize my ship in case of a storm. I had tried hard to love them, but I had become so hardened to devotion, so desensitized to attachment, that each divorce was more and more like picking off a tick and less like sinking a ship.

The light of our window casts a shimmering yellow square across
the wall of rain falling outside. It's looking and smelling a bit like
snow, frosty and metallic in the air. I move to the foot of the bed and
switch on the space heater before I nestle into my pillow and work my
way through Tesla's writing. Within two minutes, the bedroom is a
comfortable blend of hot and cold air.

*Page 2. The moment one constructs a device to carry into practice a
crude idea, he finds himself unavoidably engrossed with the details of the apparatus. As he goes on improving and reconstructing, his force of concentration
diminishes and he loses sight of the great underlying principle.*

In my adult life I have never believed in magic, or god, or romance, and
decided early on that I would have to build my marriage out of what
I could salvage from the burn pile. If there is no love, at least I might
have a fighting chance at arranging a functional partnership. But I was
too focused on the apparatus and lost sight of the principle.

When he glances at me over the desk, a face that seems to have materialized out of my past, my stomach loses its sense of grounding and
I free-fall in terror and feel an unusual sense of redemption. I have
known him before. I loved him in my youth. I would see him after
school, so tall and mature and intelligent, and I finally resolved to get
him home somehow. He remembers every detail of that night... I had
made a bed in the tall grass beside the house, and he remembers what
I said to him, how I kissed him, what I was wearing. He remembers
that I wanted him to be my first, I held his arms and rode him, and
he says that back then I was intimidatingly confident, despite my
fear when I took him into my hands that first time; he described me
as popping in and out of existence, and says that I was perplexing to
a man with a scientific mind, and the harder he tried to observe me,
the faster I blinked out of being. And he remembers the flashlight in
our faces, and my brother threatening to kill him if he ever came back
around. He was told to stay away.

"I didn't want to stay away."

"It was my fault, I'm sorry you got blamed." The boys always
get blamed.

When he's lost in thought, he removes himself to another place, the laugh lines around his eyes softening, his focus crystallizing over into a distant tender blue. He spins the rotor on the desk, inspecting it from different angles. "I see what he did wrong," he says. "Look, it caught on fire right here." He thumbs away a smudge of black soot.

(Sometimes, when he speaks, I cannot differentiate between my own thoughts and his voice. Sometimes, when we converse, I cannot tell if I spoke or thought, and how, or whether, he has responded.

"Did you know, at the moment of death, the body loses seven ounces?"

"Are you trying to say I have a soul? I don't believe in that stuff, I retort. It can't be measured or tested."

"I didn't say soul. Can you hand me that screwdriver please? Thank you." I said that at the moment of death, the very second that the body's electric charge loses ground, the body loses seven ounces of something.)

My brother didn't kill him, and life continued. I saw him again a few years after that and he had a wife. Soon after that, I had my first husband too.

Page 3. Our first endeavors are purely instinctive promptings of an imagination vivid and undisciplined. As we grow older reason asserts itself and we become more and more systematic and designing. But those early impulses, tho not immediately productive, are of the greatest moment and may shape our very destinies.

The removal of the steel disc reveals twists and coils of copper wire, a network of curling nodes in a circle. He lifts the coil out of the motor and hangs it on a nail on the wall. As he tinkers with the cam shaft, I read and wonder silently what Nikola Tesla would have said had he known about quantum physics. How truly sad, if one chooses to see it that way, that he was not here to study it.

The law of Quantum Entanglement says that once two particles become connected, they will affect each other from any place within the universe.

Measure the one, the other will be acting exactly counter to the first. Once entangled, they become a system and cannot be measured independently ever again. It's a mystery how these particles become involved in each other's activities; what equation there is to predict which will become entangled and which will simply ride by undisturbed is one of the many great mysteries of physics.

And entanglement is irreversible.

It turns out his wife had tried to run him over and hit him with her car. She went to prison, and he went to the hospital. She didn't kill him, and meanwhile, I had managed a four year enlistment in the army and escaped twelve months of combat somewhat intact. During Hurricane Katrina, I was in Iraq. I remember standing over *Life* magazine in a circle with my squad, the hot dust whipping in coils around us, and crying for them. How did we end up here when we were needed there?

("Where were you during Katrina? I went to New Orleans after my wife tried to kill me, he says. I figured if my life should end it should do so while serving a purpose.")

He pulls his hair back into a ponytail and ties it, tugs at his beard, shifts his glasses down his nose. His body is a solid flexible mass of sinew; he bears the scars of many incredible journeys and close calls. He could be made of rebar and granite. I want him. I want *him* the way I always have wanted him and always will. I'm so sorry I cheated on you with all those husbands, I say wordlessly. I can see by his eyes that he's forgiven me. Because we both know, instinctively or with a deeper perception refined by the sharp blade of hurt, that without the tools accumulated through the breaking of hearts we wouldn't have been equipped to love each other as fully as we each deserved. Once you have really hurt somebody, you learn to see love on an entirely new level, one of action and intention; I was deeply affected by the knowledge of my own power.

Alternating current changes; it has waves. These principles are testable and predictable. They fit within a scientific model and follow a pattern of natural law. The circuit must be complete for the circuit to function. It's all a big circle, pretty easy, really. If they don't connect, the electricity does not flow, and the wire remains flaccid and lifeless.

He says he will finish the drive. He'll fix it and do it right.

Page 8. But instinct is something which transcends knowledge. We have, undoubtedly, certain finer fibers that enable us to perceive truths when logical deduction, or any other willful effort of the brain, is futile.

Before my discharge from the service, I had melted into an alcoholic coma and drifted across Europe for two years with a husband I hardly remember now. I searched for indelible meaning in vain. When California called me back, I unplugged that husband and left him standing at the airport, his arms raised in question, the answer to which was already obsolete, if it ever existed. I don't know how I did it, just disconnected and drove away without looking back; he clung to me like a charged magnet until I snapped one day, and my poles flipped. That's the only way I can explain it.

I hope he found love. All I can ever hope for is someone to step into my shoes and complete the circle I began in life. It's incomplete until it arrives back at the beginning. And if I can do it myself, before my death, how victorious would I be? Life is circular, not linear. And oh, so very short.

I had made my way back to the States and continued my pursuit of fulfillment, an endeavor that was driven by a weak and flimsy understanding of myself and a dangerous cocktail of late 20's hormones. Abstinence is a fully charged ion spinning recklessly in a vacuum. I considered the thought that maybe I was gay. I had some girlfriends. They were sexy and fun, and I loved them, but they were soft. He was hard.

When I saw him again I was playing guitar in a café, and he was with a woman. His hair was past his elbows then, and I felt it in my hands as I pressed the strings. She knew who I was and hurried him out the door before I could say anything to him. Probably better that way, back then. I didn't watch them leave, didn't look to see her grip his arm protectively as they snuck away. I didn't acknowledge the empty space within me, nor did I recognize it as longing. I will not long for something I know I have no access to. I took my tips to town that night and got raging drunk at the bar. I eventually tried filling the void with another husband. I don't give up very easy, especially when the formula appears so simple on the outside. I pursued completion and fulfillment in the sanctified union of man and woman, had another beautiful wedding, painted my heart pretty colors, filled out another packet of lies and empty promises. I structured it the way I had seen it done, but I could not be content. I knew this but signed my name anyway. My second husband had a magnetic field around his heart, and I arced off it dispassionately and violently again and again.

During this time, my not-yet-lover had split up with that girl and was pursuing his own self-actualization, sailing to Chile and Panama and the Gulf of Mexico, leaning out over the water and letting dolphins nose his hands, eating avocados on tropical beaches, lounging listlessly in the moist shades of green gardens. His boat is solid and long and heavy. I was on a cruise ship in the Bahamas when the earthquake in Haiti destroyed the island. It rocked the ship and terrified the passengers. He had just left the Gulf mere weeks before, headed back to California.

("Where were you during the earthquake?" I asked.

"I was holed up in a cabin in the mountains in Mendo. It was a lonely time, I spent a few years just being alone," he said.

What happens when a man spends time alone? I wondered.

He comes up with all sorts of brilliant plans and becomes restless to invent.)

When we had both returned to the Sierras, our home, he was with a new woman. I was a grocery clerk at a health food store, and I saw him paying for fruit and quinoa at another cash register. I studied him and searched for happiness in the blue of his gaze and saw a sort of fulfillment that captivated and frightened me. When our eyes locked something passed between us with the intensity of a million volts. I could tear my eyes away but not my sight. His image would be burned on my retina for many more years before I saw him again.

("It's kinda crazy," he said once, "but when you were in Germany, I was in Europe too. I passed by your work on the train every weekend. How is that possible? What if we had bumped into each other?"

Why hadn't we bumped into each other?)

Outside the bedroom snow has begun to fall. It quivers in the lamp-light just outside the window, as if asking to come inside. The puddles suck in the flakes the instant they touch them. The chill that flutters up my arms and twitches the pages is a still, cold cloak.

Page 17. Most persons are so absorbed in the contemplation of the outside world that they are wholly oblivious to what is passing on within themselves.

He sees me gazing absently at the coil of copper on the wall. "Still reading?" he asks.

I realize that I've been spacing out and sit up to stretch. He points and explains his progress on his project. I revel in the soft rumble of his voice.

A Kromrey coil functions like an electromagnetic magnifier; each coil intensifies the electrical charge coming through it, and it only allows the particles to move one way. The "left hand rule," he calls it.

For all his height, he moves weightlessly the few feet from the desk to the bed and back. He is busily scratching a pencil across paper when I catch his peripheral eye. He winks at me.

There was a time when I believed that I was beyond repair, that the chance of genuine romantic desire was lost to me. I once had an apartment with a couch and a dishwasher and a boyfriend and all the other conveniences of day to day life. One day I stood up, looked out the window, something passed within me, and then I got into my truck and drove away and never came back. I left everything except a few changes of clothes and my pictures. I didn't tell anyone, I just left the key on the counter and didn't look back. Never said a word. I could never be a pillar of salt.

I retreated to my mountain home in the Sierras and lived in a room in a house and later on in a tent for some time; I never missed a single object in that apartment and never sought to replace any of it. I gave up on the semblance of normalcy. I thought myself too flawed and emotionally deformed for love. But when *he* came to me and was happy to love me, and love me in the way that worked for me, suddenly all of it made sense. The divorces, the wandering, the instability, the aversion to houses, the large dramatic hasty sweeping life changes. Every move I had made up until that point, no matter how insane I had felt doing it, suddenly had a meaning. Like a circuit board with no purpose or design that somehow lights a bulb and sends warm tendrils into every darkened corner, my broken parts were given function. Every single one of them.

You're just my kind of kooky wonderful, he says.

He had recently left a woman, and I, a third husband. It was effortless; their faces dissolved like sugar in water. He comes into me fully and touches parts of me that had lain dormant, waiting for me to allow entrance. He tells me he's a lucky guy. I don't believe in luck.

("I found the equation for love," he says.

"No way," I answer dismissively. "Too many variables, too many derivatives." "Everything in the universe can be explained mathematically, " he argues. "Impossible," I answer. "If it existed, I'd have found it by now.")

A timeline of his life and mine would not be a line at all, but a series of copper loops strung over twelve ceramic nodes and soldered at 2 o'clock. Lucky for us, time-space-gravity doesn't exist in linear form, but can be folded, melded, and stretched. We don't pick up where we left off, but rather, we circle back around. I look up from the manuscript and peer at him; the lamplight has cast a writhing shadow on the dingy yellow wall behind him. The drive has been disassembled, and the pieces displayed in a row on the desk where he inspects them individually, frankly, each helplessly exposed to a singular and thoughtful examination by the one man in my life capable of seeing things in their broken-down components; each part played a role within the whole. No single element represents an entire entity, but rather, the system operates cooperatively on the same principles. The inventor's job is to design a model that will run on minimal materials, and discard any parts that don't support the fundamental task.

Nikola Tesla believed he came to earth from Venus in a space ship. He was also the first man to harness wireless signal transmission, and he was brilliant, if not batshit crazy, although he missed out on the development of quantum theory. I turn the last page, sorry that his story is ending. It is getting hot on one side of the room, but the window stays open always. The wind has stopped, and the air is completely motionless.

The crusty boxes recovered from the abandoned cabin in Oregon reveal a strange and brilliant man full of interesting theories and unique inventions. His picture slides out of a folder and onto the floor. He is not Tesla. He is Ron.

Ron died before completing a project he spent the final years of his life on.

I watch a beautiful man articulate another man's passion in the space of less than a page, for no reward. He is entirely selfless.

(At the moment of death, the body loses seven ounces of something. I don't get it. Let's have sex.

Electricity is fluid. Like language, and death, and marrying men you don't love. Love is much more fun when it's reciprocated, isn't it? It's, like, exponential.

I know the equation of love. I figured it out when I saw you again after all those years. When you said hi, it just clicked.

Love is not measurable. You can't test it or predict it. You can't quantify something intangible, I insist.

He writes it down for me.

Quantify love? Love, represented by L and self by S, would look like this: L equals L times L divided by S squared, times the square root of infinity. And that, he says, raking his course fingers through his auburn-blonde hair, is my Nobel prize.)

The kiss he renders hits my soul with the force of a million lightning bolts.